THE WAR ETERNAL

FROM COLD ASHES RISEN

ROB J. HAYES

FOR EVERYONE WHO HAS GIVEN UP

PROLOGUE

THERE IS AN INHERENT NEGATIVITY TO LIFE and growth, perhaps as a sort of morbid way to balance some grand scales. I don't mean literal scales, of course, but instead I speak of the opposite forces within our world that balance each other out. The Rand and the Djinn are perhaps the best example of this. They cannot exist without each other. The rules of our world bind them together inextricably. When a Rand dies, so too does a Djinn, and the same is true the other way around. They exist in tandem, equal forces, and balanced. It is a fact that made their eternal war even more idiotic. Both peoples knew the only outcome could ever be mutual destruction, yet they fought anyway. They ripped holes in Ovaeris, shattered an entire continent, and even tore open a portal to another world, and they did it all over a slight neither side could see the truth of. The Djinn created the Other World, Sevoari, and asked the Rand to fill it with life. They probably expected luminous beings full of glorious purpose. The Rand gave them nightmares. Literal nightmares plucked from the dreams of the people of Ovaeris. I don't think it was ever meant as a slight, but more likely a consequence of the Rand having very little in the way of imagination. They made up for their lack by searching the minds of us *lesser* peoples. So much of our world, shaped by a misunderstanding that our *gods* refused to reconcile. Let me assure you, regardless of whether you give your war a fancy name like *The War Eternal*, it is still a war; and the people who will suffer most from it are those caught in the middle.

I have been drawn off my original topic. I often find my mind wanders when I consider the impact the Rand and Djinn have had on our lives. On my life. I believe it is anger that does such a thing. I can never forgive them for the things they have taken from me. I refuse to try.

Back to the negativity of life and growth. It is perhaps somewhat fitting that we learn more from our defeats than we do our victories, as though the world is somehow set up to give the losers a better chance next time. We grow more from failure than we do success. I am a prime example, I admit it. My successes have only ever led to stagnation, whereas my failures have always driven me to greater effort. It is no surprise that I have failed so much more than I have succeeded. And we are forged less so by our fortunes than we are by our tragedies.

I had just lost. I had been beaten. I had failed. And I had just committed the second worst tragedy I have ever experienced. Silva was dead, killed by my own hand. She put me in that position, gave me no choice. One way or the other she had committed herself to dying, and all that remained was for me to choose how. How could she do that? How could she claim to love me as I loved her, and yet force me to be the instrument of her death? Perhaps the greater tragedy was that neither of us realised that there was another way. A way that would not only have kept Silva alive, but also set her free. I have mentioned that I hate the Rand, and Mezula most of all. Well, this is why. She asked Silva to do it, to die for her, to die in her place. Mezula knew full well what she was doing by sending me to Do'shan, and the fucking bitch did it anyway.

Despite my losses and failures, or perhaps because of them, I had grown powerful. Ssserakis, the ancient horror that possessed my body and soul, had learned to lend me its strength and even manifest itself within my shadow. It fed on fear and leaked that power into me, and I had used it to form shields and blades, and even wings of shadow. I had absorbed the fury and raw power of an Arcstorm. It flashed in my eyes like lightning, and I could release its power even without the aid of an Arcmancy Source. I had attained four Sources, almost as many as I could sit in my stomach at one time. Pyromancy, Arcmancy, Portamancy, and Kinemancy. It's true, I had also just learned that they were the bodies of dead Rand and Djinn, crystallised magic only Sourcerers, those of us who are the descendants of gods, could use. I cared little where my ability to wield magic, or the magic itself had come from, but instead only what I could do with it. Only what I could achieve with whatever power I could muster. I have always been ambitious, perhaps a little too much so. I still don't know whether it was that ambition, or my grief, that made me test myself against a god. Whichever it was, I came up short.

After venting my full rage and power against the

Djinn, Aerolis, all I managed was to stagger the creature and elicit a threat of destruction should I continue. Then came the Iron Legion, the man I had admired for years. A hero in my eyes. Never meet your heroes. Mine turned out to be the architect of my demise. As powerful as I had gotten, or at least as powerful as I believed myself to be, I realised then that I was out of my league. Loran Orran, the Iron Legion, was perhaps the one Sourcerer who had ever lived who could make a god shut up and listen. And he did. In his presence, even Aerolis was cowed.

CHAPTER
ONE

Prophecy is a foreign word, the meaning lost in
translation.

- Belmorose

"THE AUGURIES ARE NOT SIGNS THE CHOSEN
one has come. They're instructions on how to create one."
The Iron Legion's secret. The fruits of a lifetime of research,
and he dropped the revelation between us so easily. I
struggled to understand at first. My mind was still reeling.

"You experimented on us at the academy." I was still
so exhausted my voice lacked the condemnation it should
have held. The Iron Legion had taken children into his care,
children who trusted him, and he had experimented on
us. Altering our bodies with crystallised magic to suit the
purpose of a millennia old prophecy uttered by a mad god.

The Iron Legion nodded, his smile gone and face

grave. "Yes. I tried it with animals first, even monsters from Sevoari, but none were compatible with Sources. Still, the research was not wasted, I did discover the exact value of a life in terms of the energy it contains."

I saw Aerolis rumble closer, the rocks that made up the Djinn's body grating as they shifted against each other. "How did you force creatures to absorb my brothers?"

"Ahh, that was my first challenge. No terran Sourcerers could answer the question, and even the great library of the tahren had no useful suggestions. I had to get inventive. Simply swallowing a Source wouldn't work, obviously, that's how all Sourcerers use magic and it's only a matter of time before rejection makes our limitations so apparent. And that's where the hammer comes in." The Iron Legion waved towards the hammer discarded in the centre of the amphitheatre. "Not for nothing is it called Shatter. Truly such a remarkable item. It is capable of breaking anything. Even a Source. What couldn't be achieved by conventional means, was made easy. I injected Source dust directly into the blood. I admit, it took some trial and error. A few subjects were lost."

The implication of those words certainly made an impact. How many of my classmates had died at this madman's hands? This man who we trusted to protect us, to teach us. This man I had idealised as a hero. "Who?"

"Ah, names. Not my strongest talent. There was a young boy, a Vibromancer and Photomancer both. Quite rare. I've never actually met anyone able to control quite so well the stresses that pairing of attunements put upon the body and mind. I will admit I was a little overzealous and I overtaxed him by using the same pairing of Sources to alter him. I can assure you it was the last time I tried it with two

Sources at once."

An image flashed into my mind, something I had long ago forgotten, or perhaps something I had been forced to forget. Barrow Laney, a classmate at the academy and a friend I had spent countless hours with, locked inside a cage. His face was a ruin of gouged flesh and wrecked eyes, his ears long since ripped away. I shook my head to rid myself of the memory, but I couldn't help but see it now. I knew it wasn't my imagination. I remembered it.

"You bastard!" I spat the accusation with as much force as I could muster. "You moon-damned fucking arsehole!" Fresh tears welled up in my eyes and rolled down my cheeks as I struggled against the magic that held me. I'd known Barrow had been driven mad by his attunements, we all had. The tutors announced it to us after he went missing. But I had always assumed they had found some way to comfort him, or at the very least ease his suffering. Now I remembered the truth that had been hidden from me for so long. It wasn't Barrow's attunements that had driven him mad, he'd always been so careful to manage them, it was the Iron Legion's bloody experiments. And even after the madness had taken him, the fucker had kept poor Barrow locked in a cage to study him. All my rage, grief, and struggling came to nought. The Iron Legion's magic held me tight and I sagged against it, watering the ground with my tears. "Bastard."

The Iron Legion cleared his throat. "Yes. Well, advancement is built on the back of failure. That young man's sacrifice paved the way for others to flourish. Most notably, yourself and Yenhelm. What I discovered was really quite fascinating. The absorption process is incredibly painful for the subject, and rejection occurs quite quickly, but if the subject accepts the Source dust within themselves…"

"How many?" I asked through gritted teeth. "How many of us did you torture?"

I glanced up just in time to see the Iron Legion shrug. "All of you, I suppose. Though torture really isn't a correct term for it. In many ways it was no different to testing you for attunements. Yes, there was pain, but the lasting benefits more than made up for any discomfort you felt."

"What lasting benefits did Barrow receive?" How could he not see it? How could he not see the pain he had caused? How could he not understand he was a fucking monster? "You didn't even put him out of his misery."

"Must we focus on the failures?" The Iron Legion asked, then sat up straight and glanced over his shoulder to where Ishtar approached, sword drawn. "That's far enough. Tamura, would you mind joining us?" Another stool grew out of the dirt.

Tamura sauntered over with a smile, glanced at the stool, and then sank down onto the floor, gathering his legs up beneath him. "Only a fool fears knowledge," the crazy old Aspect said. "But the knowledgeable often fear wisdom, for it is sometimes hidden behind the guise of foolishness."

The Iron Legion smiled. "It's good to see you, old friend." His gaze shifted to me. "I'm glad you found a suitable teacher, Helsene."

"Eskara?" Ishtar asked as she braved another step forward. I shook my head at her, unable to find the energy for words.

"Tell us about the Auguries, if you will, Tamura," the Iron Legion continued.

Tamura turned sad eyes my way. "All my fault. I didn't see the madness. Hard to see the ocean when you're drowning in it."

"It is not madness I suffer from, Tamura," the Iron Legion said. "It is purpose and an unshakable will to see that purpose brought about. No matter the cost."

Tamura ignored the Iron Legion and kept his eyes on me, an unfathomable sadness there. "I gave him the Auguries. I didn't see. All my fault. I'm sorry."

"Life and death, together." The Iron Legion shook his head at Tamura. "At first, I thought I would have to inject one subject with both Necromancy and Biomancy, but after my experiment with that young Photomancer…"

"Barrow!" I spat.

The Iron Legion shook his head. "Names really aren't important at this point, Helsene. I realised that forcing a body to absorb two Sources was simply beyond their physical limitations. We may be the descendants of Aspects, but we are also, for the most part, terran. But that's where you and Yenhelm came in. You shared a bond that went deeper than almost any I've ever seen. I admit, at this point I was relying a little bit on conjecture. No real scientific proof, only hope. I injected a Biomancy Source into Yenhelm, and a Necromancy Source into you. You might have noticed that you feel a connection to the dead even without a Source, and with a Necromancy Source inside your powers are amplified. As I said, benefits."

I sniffed, tears still dripping from my chin. With my hands locked by my side I couldn't even wipe my face. "If we were your prize subjects, why did you let us go? Why not keep us in cages like Barrow?"

"I couldn't. I simply saw no way to generate the conditions needed for you to fulfil the second and third Auguries while locked in a cage. And, of course, my

brother's war made things difficult. He insisted that all
our Sourcerers were put towards victory rather than my
research. But don't think I didn't keep track of you. I kept
an eye on all of my potentials. Except for Alderson, she
truly has disappeared. I suppose it doesn't matter anymore.
Young Yenhelm has fulfilled both remaining Auguries."

"You kept an eye on us?" I hissed the words. "We
were sent to the Pit!"

"I know. I put you there."

What is there to say to that? I suppose I could have
accused the Iron Legion of ruining my life even further, but
honestly, he wouldn't have cared. Atrocities of even the most
abhorrent kind were nothing to him, not while in pursuit of
his research. I have never struggled to find enough hate to
go around. Prig, Deko, the Overseer, the Emperor, Mezula,
Prena. Silva. The list goes on and on, and I often find myself
at the top of it. I think I struggled to hate the Iron Legion at
the time. I struggled to comprehend the impact he had on
my life. And still, I barely even knew the tip of it.

"Renewal," Tamura said, his eyes locked on me.

"Yes." The Iron Legion nodded. "Or rebirth. But those
are only two words. The full Augury, Tamura. As you once
told me."

"Confided in you. Secrets whispered from one lost
soul to another. Terran kindness repaid and then betrayed."

"The Augury, Tamura." Judging by the sharpness in
his voice, even the Iron Legion had limits to his patience.

"A resurrection. On the verge of despair, when
all hope and love are lost, when betrayal and pain have
stripped the soul clean. The flesh and soul are reborn
together."

"Josef died down in the Pit," the Iron Legion said.

"I have it by his own account, written by his hand. And yet the Biomancy I put inside of him reknit his flesh. Remade him. Dead and yet alive once more, renewed. Life and death together." He laughed. "Almost two of the Auguries in one. But of course, there is a third. The unity of purpose."

"Two forces, each separate, each mired in irreconcilable differences. Acting together, cooperating towards an uncommon goal." Tamura nodded sagely, a sly grin on his lips.

The Iron Legion spread his hands wide. "Your original escape from First Blade Neralis gave me the prime opportunity to create the circumstances needed for Yenhelm to fulfil the final Augury. I placed him with the Knights of Ten and gave them a purpose. You. Together, Yenhelm and First Blade Neralis hunted you across Ovaeris. And when finally they found you... the uncommon goal. One to cause death, the other to preserve life. I did not, however, expect Yenhelm to absorb a second Source, and in such an uncharacteristic method." The Iron Legion looked toward Aerolis.

"This was your experiment, Loran, not mine," the Djinn rumbled. "Just what are you hoping to achieve?"

I felt hopelessly out of place. A pawn being pushed about by players in a game I didn't even understand. The exhaustion wasn't helping. It's fairly difficult to compose a solid thought when it's taking every bit of willpower you possess just to keep from passing out. And I couldn't keep my attention from wandering, my eyes from slipping to look at the body. I could see her. Silva. She didn't look dead from a distance, just peaceful, as though she were sleeping. But no. She was dead, and I had killed her. Right then I didn't care about the Iron Legion or what he had done. I wanted to break free of his hold, to run to my lover's side, and weep over her body. I wanted to hold her, to kiss her, to love her one last time. I wanted her to wake up and tell me everything would be alright. Even though I knew it would be a lie.

"I am trying to correct your mistakes, Djinn. My research will fix the world."

"And I suppose you gain nothing from it?"

The Iron Legion stood, facing up to Aerolis. "Well of course I do. You know what I want, Djinn. You tricked that out of me last time we met."

I felt Ssserakis stir inside me. The horror was as exhausted as I, but there was fear all around us. Within us. I could feel its strength returning bit by bit. And I noticed my shadow extending along the ground, thin tendrils snaking their way towards where the Iron Legion had his back turned.

I will kill him for both of us.

I shook my head and whispered. "He doesn't know. You're the one thing he doesn't know about. My only advantage." I couldn't say the rest. I couldn't admit that after everything I had already lost, I couldn't take losing Ssserakis as well. What if we failed? What if the Iron Legion knew some way to rip the horror from inside of me? I could not, would not risk it. I could not face being alone.

The Iron Legion and Aerolis were still arguing and I was forgotten for the moment, though I could still feel the magical pressure pushing down on me, locking in place. Even if I weren't held tight, I doubt I would have made it close enough to the Iron Legion to strike. Even Ishtar, as stealthy as she was, couldn't move without the man glancing her way.

All the more reason to use me. I can end this madness.

Tamura was watching my shadow move, following the snaking path. He looked up at me and shook his head, sadness in his eyes. I'm still not sure what that meant. Was he agreeing with me, warning us not to strike? Or was he just now realising what I harboured inside of me? I had never spoken to him of my possession. I had never spoken to anyone about it, not even Silva.

"What if you fail?" I whispered.

"I won't fail," the Iron Legion said. As he turned back towards me, Ssserakis drew back, my shadow pooling beneath me once more. "I've planned this for longer than you have been alive."

That was our chance!

"There'll be other chances," I said.

The Iron Legion narrowed his eyes and stepped closer. "Who are you talking to?"

Tamura came to our rescue. And he paid a high price. We all did.

CHAPTER TWO

THEY SAY IT'S ALWAYS THE ONE YOU DON'T SEE coming that gets you. That's not always true. Sometimes the one you don't see coming, just pisses you off.

"My chance is now!" Tamura shouted. He launched himself upwards and caught the Iron Legion square in the face with a punch that I have seen fell much larger men. Loran staggered back a step. A single step. That's all we could manage, even with the element of surprise on our side and Tamura giving it his all. He tried to follow it up. The old Aspect stepped into the punch and made to grab at the Iron Legion. Tamura always excelled at the close quarters fighting. But the Iron Legion's defences were up by then and Tamura just rebounded from an invisible barrier.

The Iron Legion turned pitiless eyes on Tamura, a dark stare that promised pain. "That was a mistake, old friend." He reached out with a single hand and closed it into a fist. Tamura was crushed between forces no one could see. It was the only time I ever saw my friend scream. The only time I ever saw him in any real physical pain. The pressure pushed in on him from both sides and Tamura was lifted from the ground. I saw his arm snap. All for me. All to protect me.

Guilt is an odd thing. It is almost always overshadowed by other emotions. When I saw Tamura in so much pain, knowing that it was all because of me, I felt an anger so red hot the world receded around me. A tunnel vision with Tamura's agony at the centre of it. But anger fades. Long after the red-hot rage dissipated, the guilt of it remains. Refuses to leave me. He may have volunteered himself as sacrifice, to distract the Iron Legion, but it was my fault. I did that to him.

Even crushing Tamura, the Iron Legion kept his hold on me as well. I struggled against the magic keeping me captive, but all I did was exhaust what little energy I had mustered. Fresh tears tracked down the weary lines of my face and I screamed. No words. I had no words. Only pain.

Ishtar was the first to act and the closest to us. She launched into a sprint, sword already moving for a strike, and then stopped, pitching forwards with a crack as her ankle snapped. The earth had risen around her left foot, encasing it in stone and her own momentum broke the bone. Her head struck the ground of the arena and she didn't rise.

Horralain screamed and I felt his fear. Horralain's fear. I didn't think the man could feel it. I glanced up to see the big man had closed some of the distance between us, but was on his knees, screaming at something none of us could see. I'm sure I've mentioned before just how much I detest Empamancy. There is a good reason for it. The Iron

Legion felled Horralain, one of the most brutal thugs I have
ever known, with nothing but a glance, instilling within
him some primal fear I don't think Horralain ever managed
to remove. The legacy the Iron Legion left on all of us runs
deep.

Hardt was slow to move, his grief weighing him
down more surely than any physical load ever could. No
sooner had he reached his feet, then a sand golem dragged
itself from the ground in front of him. Some golems are
far more dangerous than others. Rock and metal are often
considered at the top of the list, but the truth is, while they
are hardy and resilient, they lack the flexibility that many of
the more subtle forms can take. Hardt did not understand
this. He swung a single punch at the golem, a strike that
would have shattered bone, and his fist sank deep into the
body of the construct. The golem then lurched forwards,
engulfing Hardt almost entirely before solidifying, trapping
him inside its body.

With Tamura still trapped in the Iron Legion's
crushing grip, and I still held down by a kinetic force I could
not resist, only Imiko remained to save us all. I do not blame
her for her actions. I cannot. She did perhaps the one thing
I would never have considered. Imiko collapsed onto her
knees, just a few paces from the Iron Legion, and screamed
at him. "Stop hurting my friends!"

The Iron Legion turned his dark stare on Imiko and in
my mind all I could see was the broken body he had left of
Barrow. "Don't touch her!" I hissed.

"I have no wish to harm any of you," the Iron Legion
said, turning away from Imiko and striding back to me.
"You attacked me." With a flick of his hand, he sent Tamura
careening away. The crazy old Aspect did not get up.

We were done. All of us beaten with so little effort the Iron Legion didn't even look ruffled. Even the single surprise punch Tamura had landed on the man wouldn't bruise, his Biomancy would make certain of that.

You should have let me try. Even Ssserakis lacked the conviction of its words. We all knew just how soundly we were beaten.

"The only reason I am still here at all is as a courtesy to you," the Iron Legion said. He waved his hand and I found myself plucked from the earthen stool by a kinetic grasp, dangled upright before the man. Throughout it all, the Djinn waited nearby, silent and patient, simply waiting to see the outcome of our conflict. "I admit," the Iron Legion continued, "I have put you through some hardship. It was necessary. I needed to put you within a suitable environment, you see. There needed to be catalyst, which would trigger the changes I made and allow you to fulfil the Auguries. I understand that this was not pleasant for you."

"Pleasant?" The word burst from me along with an incredulous laugh.

"Quiet, child!" the Iron Legion hissed, and I found my jaw clenching of its own accord, locking up tight.

There is a horror in helplessness. One far worthier of fear than anything Ssserakis ever showed me. It is that same helplessness the ancient horror instilled within me the first time we met, down in the deepest dark. It is the same helplessness that Prig forced upon me down in the Pit. I detest feeling helpless. Even if I know I can't win, I will revel in the fight because there will always be a chance. But the Iron Legion crushed me with his invisible grip, held me so tight I couldn't speak, couldn't move, couldn't breathe. And I knew with a sobering certainty, there was nothing I could do should he choose to end it. There was nothing any of us could do. We were fucking beaten! Even Aerolis, a Djinn, a god, seemed powerless when measured against Loran Orran.

"I am not without mercy," the Iron Legion said. "But my patience has its limits. I am trying to fix the mistakes wrought upon this world by others. Of course, I understand it would always be a thankless goal. Most won't see the necessity for bringing them back…"

I will admit, I stopped listening. It was not out of disinterest, but out of fear and panic. I could not move my head, but my eyes slid sideways to where Hardt was held, encased in a golem of hardened sand. He couldn't pull himself free from that, and neither could he see or breathe. There is only so long a person can survive without air, and terrans are renowned for being the very worst of Ovaeris' peoples for holding their breath. Still, I couldn't help him. I couldn't help anyone. I couldn't save them. I couldn't do anything. I slid my gaze to where Aerolis waited, pleading. I hate pleading, begging for help where I cannot help myself. Even worse when that pleading falls on deaf ears… or I suppose eyes, in this case.

"Are you even listening, Helsene? I'm trying to explain why your hardship was necessary, so you'll understand the sacrifices I have had to make."

The iron grip on my jaw loosened and I drew in a deep breath. "Just go!" I shouted at the man who had once been my hero. We ignore so much as children, or perhaps we just see things so differently. I once saw the Iron Legion as strong and regal, radiating with power, and handsome in way I didn't even understand at the time. Through my younger self's eyes, he was a hero, everything I aspired to be. If only I had seen him then as I do now, through the eyes of an adult. I know I couldn't have changed anything, couldn't have stopped him. But the Iron Legion didn't deserve my adoration, and if I could turn back time and take it away, I would. A petty victory, maybe, but then that is certainly one of my traits.

From the corner of my eye, I saw Hardt's one free hand drop and hang limp by his side, his struggling ceased.

"I don't care why you did it." The lie came easily to my lips. They always have, where Hardt is involved. "You've won. Just leave us alone. Fuck off!"

The Iron Legion snorted and shook his head. "A wasted opportunity. I hoped you would come with me. Willingly. You may not be the *chosen one*, but I could still use you. Yenhelm will…"

"Go away!" I screamed. Anything to stop him talking. Anything to release his grip.

Another shake of his head. "I hope for your sake we never have cause to meet again, Helsene. So much wasted potential." A portal snapped open behind the Iron Legion and I saw a dark room with a couple of lit candles illuminating a desk and a nearby bookshelf. Josef stood near the desk, a panicked look on his face like child caught with a sweet pastry before dinner. "I'll be back for the hammer, Aerolis. When you realise the truth and beg me to help you." With that, the Iron Legion stepped through the portal, and it snapped shut behind him. The crushing grip that held me vanished and the golem engulfing Hardt crumbled around him. His body hit the floor and didn't move.

CHAPTER THREE

PANIC! THE DJINN SAID SOMETHING ONCE THE Iron Legion was gone, but I ignored the rumbling of the arena and lurched to my feet, stumbling towards Hardt's body. Imiko rushed to my aid and I pushed her away. I shouldn't have done that, but I was determined to move under my own power, and she had more important things to do.

"Check on Tamura," I hissed and kept limping on. Tamura lay nearby, a crumpled form. He looked so small, frail. Broken. We were all broken in one way or another, and I couldn't check on everyone at once. Imiko rushed away with a nod, perhaps the only one of us not hurt. No, that's not right. Imiko was certainly hurt, just not physically. I should never have let her come to Do'shan. My little sister was never quite the same afterwards.

Ishtar lay still, unmoving. Her foot was still encased

in stone and blood leaked into her fur from a gash on her forehead. I shouted at her as I passed, and she groaned. I took that for a good sign and promised I would come back once I had seen to Hardt. The big man still hadn't moved, and I refused to accept what I already knew was truth.

Horralain was sitting in the sand, his head in his hands and was rocking back and forth. Whatever nightmare the Iron Legion had locked his mind into would not be easy to escape, and I couldn't risk what he might do to anyone who tried to bring him round. People in that state have a habit of lashing out, not seeing anything around them, only the terror that infects their mind. I could feel that fear flowing from him in pulsing waves. The pleasure of it made my head spin and I very nearly stopped. The desire to pull closer to Horralain and soak in his dread was overwhelming. And also not mine. At the time, I found it beyond difficult to separate myself from Ssserakis. The longer we spent together, the more the lines between us blurred. My own fear over Hardt was all that dragged me away, I think.

"He's alive," Imiko shouted, crouched over Tamura. "But not in a good way. His arm is broken and he's making less sense than usual."

Tamura was alive. I took solace in that, if nothing else. Guilt threatened to undo me. All this had happened because of me. Tamura had attacked to distract the Iron Legion and the others had reacted. So many hurt, maybe even worse, just to protect me and the horror I carried inside.

When finally, I reached Hardt, I collapsed down next to him, my left leg screaming in pain. I think perhaps I had twisted it when the Iron Legion dropped me. The big man was face down in a small mountain of loose sand. I had to lift his arm and put my back against it, bracing myself and pushing with every bit of strength I could muster, just to roll him onto his back. He wasn't breathing.

"Your bodies are so fragile," the Djinn said close by. I hadn't even noticed him drifting closer.

"Can you help?" Hope is a horrible thing. It only ever leads to even greater despair.

"Biomancy is the realm of the Rand," the Djinn said. "You could always raise him as another of your ghosts."

I turned furious eyes on the Djinn. "If you won't help, then GO THE FUCK AWAY!" Shouting rarely helps anyone, but it sure does feel good to vent some rage from time to time.

Silva would have known what to do. Her body lay nearby, bloody from the wound I had given her. Lifeless. Gone. I refused to look. Too much grief, too quickly. Too many of the people I loved, dead. I choked back a sob. "What do I do?" The words came out as a whisper of pain. "WHAT DO I DO?" Then a scream of agony.

My ghosts crowded around me, so close I felt stifled. They were a swarm these days, all of them appearing at once, risen and drawn forth by a power I didn't know how to control. Necromancy was a part of me, infused into my blood. A gift and a curse, the product of the Iron Legion's torture. Isen was foremost among my ghastly retinue. His face was still a wreckage, the result of Josef's anger and jealousy. Still, he somehow managed to look sad as he looked down on his elder brother.

"I'm sorry." I've never been good at uttering those words to the living, yet they've always come so easily to the dead.

Isen's ghost leaned over his brother's body and put two hands on the big man's chest. When he pushed down, his hands went through the body.

I sobbed. I had done this. My fault. And both brothers had paid the price for my stupidity. For my powerlessness. "I killed both of you."

Isen's ghost mimed pushing down on Hardt's chest a few more times, then bent his ruined face over Hardt's and puffed out what was left of his cheeks. Then he went back to pushing his ethereal hands through Hardt's chest.

"Intriguing," said the Djinn. "Does the ghost realise it has no physical form? They do tend to be pale afterthoughts of who they once were, fading over time until nothing but the image of them remains."

"He knows." Realisation hit as the words escaped my lips. I shuffled around Hardt's body until I was occupying the same space as Isen's ghost. It felt… strange. Familiar and alien all at once. Not cold, I always felt cold inside ever since Ssserakis had possessed me. It felt as though I could almost feel all of Isen's memories, everything that had once made him *him*, but they were just out of reach, and the more I reached for them, the more they slipped away.

I copied Isen's position as best I could and mimicked his movements, pressing down on Hardt's chest. Then I moved with the ghost, opened Hardt's mouth, drew in a deep breath and blew it out. It was hope that drove me to it. Such an odd sight I must have made. But I had to believe that Isen's ghost knew something I didn't. That perhaps it remembered some of what his brother had once taught him. Because I knew, out of all of us, only Hardt would know how to bring himself back.

I don't know how many times I copied the actions of Isen's ghost. Enough that my arms felt wobbly from the effort and my head was spinning. Long enough that I didn't realise it had worked until Hardt's hands closed around my own to stop me. He was coughing, eyes unfocused, and sand on his lips. You're probably thinking we shared a heartfelt reunion then, full of hugs and joy. You'd be wrong. Hardt pushed me away, rolled onto his side and vomited. And my joy was short lived. Hardt was alive, but I could see Silva's body, and I knew there was no bringing her back.

"What happened?" Hardt said eventually, after throwing up clumps of wet sand.

"We lost." I couldn't seem to drag my gaze away from where Silva lay. "He beat us all in moments."

"Argh. Big Terrelan monster," Ishtar's voice was laced with pain. "Stop watering the sand with your tears and help free me. I don't know which hurts more, my foot or my head. No. No, it's my foot. Definitely my foot."

Imiko helped Tamura to his feet and the old Aspect staggered, almost pulling them both back to the ground, but Imiko has always been stronger than she looks. Together they made their way to where Ishtar lay on the ground. With her foot trapped the way it was, there was no way my sword tutor could free herself, and the pain was considerable as she was happily telling us all.

"Can you free her?" I asked the Djinn. Aerolis nodded but didn't help. "Will you?"

"I see no reason to," the Djinn rumbled.

"You're just going to wait here and watch us gather ourselves?"

"I'm curious. It's been quite some time since I've had a chance to observe your kind. And I have nothing else to do."

I struggled to standing. My left leg felt stiff, wooden and painful, and hurt whenever I put weight on it. Still,

I limped closer and stared up at the Djinn. "Free her." I pointed at Ishtar.

The floating stone I took for the Djinn's head turned to the side a little. "Why?"

"Call it returning the favour. We freed you."

A rumble of laughter echoed around the amphitheatre. "You did nothing of the sort. The sphere around this place was my doing, not the Rand's. And you had nothing to do with breaking it. I am still trapped here, and Do'shan is still secured by unbreakable anchors. All you did was kill the Aspect for a greater power than the Rand offered you."

I ground my teeth together. Imiko lowered Tamura to the ground and looked at the earth that had risen to lock Ishtar's foot in place. I caught her shaking her head.

"Free her," I said to Aerolis. "And I will free Do'shan."

"Done." No sooner had the words rumbled out from wherever they came from, the earthen lock around Ishtar's foot crumbled back to sand. My sword tutor pulled her foot close and rolled over, already fumbling for her pahht shoes to inspect the injury. I turned away from Aerolis, but the Djinn spoke again. "It is no small task you agree to. So, I will grant you three days to accomplish it."

"Fuck you!" I sent the Djinn a withering stare then turned back to Hardt.

The big man had finished throwing up and looked at me with an odd stare. "What happened, Eska? I felt... encased. I couldn't breathe. Then everything just faded away."

"You weren't breathing by the time I got you free of the golem. I had to, um, breathe for you, I think."

Hardt narrowed his eyes. "How did you know how to do that? I've only ever seen one person do that before, my old ship's doctor."

I weighed up the options and decided I simply didn't have the energy to lie to him about it. "Isen showed me. His ghost has been following me since the Pit. I didn't want to tell you because… It's my fault. My power. My guilt, I guess, dragging your brother's ghost along behind us. I didn't do it on purpose. I promise, I didn't mean to…" I ran out of words. There was no excusing the pale existence I had trapped Isen in.

Hardt took a moment. I think he was mulling it over in his head, deciding whether or not he could excuse one more of my atrocities. "Is he here now? I don't see him."

"No one does, only me. And I think he's gone." I looked around for Isen's ghost. The rest of my ethereal baggage was still there, lingering close by, watching me, but Isen was gone. He never came back. Whether that was because he felt his time on Ovaeris was finally over, or because I felt I could finally let him go, I don't think I'll ever really know. But I hope he finally found peace, released of the servitude I had unwittingly forced upon him.

Ishtar growled out a string of curses that would have had me grinning any other day, but I didn't have it in me to smile. Hardt shook the metal knuckles, slick with blood, from his hands and reached out. I helped him up. I say that, but there was little I could do to help him. Sometimes it's the intent that counts far more than the effort. He made his way over to Ishtar. Hardt was our berserker and healer rolled into one and he could wound or mend as easily as each other, but he always preferred to help people where he could, rather than harm. I let him go and went a different way.

Silva's body, dressed in her white robes under leather armour, lay where I left her. I approached slowly, dragging my left foot and bracing myself for the pain of seeing her face one last time. Cold closed around me in a way I hadn't felt for a long time; a cloying, freezing thing that tasted of despair. I don't think Ssserakis did it on purpose, I think the horror was trying to pull away from me, either to give me space or maybe just hide from my grief.

My shadowy blade had caused a wide wound in her chest and her robes were stained red. Her skin was pale, no real colour left to it. Even Silva's hair seemed less vibrant than it had just minutes ago. It felt like so much had happened since I killed her, but in truth it was no time at all. I knelt over the body of the woman I loved, and tears dripped from my chin onto her face. She was gone. Every bit of her. The way her eyes lit up when negotiating a deal. The frown that always crinkled her brow whenever I found the right spot as we made love. Her love of favours. Her love of her family. The kindness she showed to everyone, even those who didn't deserve it. All of her, gone.

I remember a story, a romantic fable I read once back as a child. I was devouring fantasies in the library when I should have been studying. The story was about a prince, handsome as they always are, as well as ferocious and charming. He fought his way across a battlefield to find the woman he loved. The prince challenged her captor, a Sourcerer with designs on his kingdom, and somehow overcame all odds and won the fight. But the Sourcerer was a petty man, and in his final moments he struck a killing blow on the prince. Hero and villain died together. The princess ran to her would be saviour, amidst all the carnage and cried for her lost love. The stories always have the prince and princess in love, *true love*, despite never having met before. The princess's tears fell on the prince, and miraculously he came back to life, all mention of the fatal wound forgotten. They lived happily ever after, as people often do in stories.

Those stories are nothing but lies. True love takes time, not serendipity. No amount of will and skill and luck can defeat a Sourcerer without magic of your own. And all the tears in the world can't bring the dead back to life. Even knowing this, I still wept for her. My true love.

"I'm sorry, Silva." The words tasted like lies.

Are you? She was a weakness in you. You cut that weakness free in return for a promise of power. Real power.

I shook my head, weary from exhaustion and grief. "Not now, Ssserakis." I couldn't take the horror's accusation, but I couldn't help but consider the possibility. Silva was dead, killed by my own hands, and in return, the Djinn had promised me Sources, and the knowledge of how to truly use the power they contained. I'd be lying if I said the promise of power didn't feed a hunger inside of me, but these days I wish I hadn't paid the price. It was too damned high.

CHAPTER FOUR

COLLECTING OURSELVES AND TREATING OUR
injuries took some time. We were, all of us, wounded. The
Djinn grew bored with *observing* us, and vanished, the
rocks that had formed its body falling to the floor of the
amphitheatre and a gust of wind blowing past us all.

Hardt laboured at binding our injuries. I think the
work took his mind off other things, but I could tell by the
glances he kept sending my way that we had a conversation
coming. There were so many things for us to talk about,
so many of my secrets to air, I wasn't sure which one was
eating away at him. He snapped the haft of a discarded
spear and used it to form a crutch for Ishtar but warned her
the ankle was broken and it would take time to heal, if it
ever truly did. A Biomancer would have been able to help,
but I doubted we'd be seeing either Josef or the Iron Legion
again any time soon, and I knew no other Biomancers.

Tamura's arm was reset, the bone making a sickening crunch as it snapped back into place. The old Aspect hissed in pain but didn't scream. I think I would have screamed. Hardt bound the arm in a makeshift sling formed by tearing a dead soldier's tunic.

Horralain was another matter entirely. The giant thug had some cuts and scrapes, but no serious physical injuries despite the beating we'd all taken. But the Iron Legion had trapped him in some sort of nightmarish prison, a use of Empamancy I had never heard of before. It certainly wasn't one they taught at the academy or I'm sure the bitch-whore, Lesray Alderson, would have tested its effects on me. His fear was a cloying miasma around him that I longed to devour. Ssserakis drank it in from a distance, and begged me to move closer, but I wouldn't. The temptation convinced me I might lose myself in the intoxication. When I asked if Ssserakis knew how to snap Horralain from his fear induced stupor, the horror only laughed and asked me why we would do that, when the big man was such a hearty meal.

Imiko moped, and I had not the will to draw her out from her melancholy. I could barely keep my own head above the waves of grief that threatened to drown me. Only the thought of the power I would attain, and the idea that Josef was still alive, kept me from succumbing. Only her little ringlet, Kazh, seemed to brighten her mood as the little beast wound its way between her legs and perched on her shoulder, feeding itself something it found within the sand. Even Ishtar, normally so irrepressible, seemed beaten, depressed. She didn't even bother to insult me. It's not surprising really, she had just lost her entire company, so many of her friends were dead. Career soldiers and mercenaries expect to lose their comrades, but I think the mark of a true leader is when they still feel the pain of it, no matter how many losses have passed by.

We made a camp of sorts, right there in the amphitheatre. Once Tamura's wits had returned to him, the old man set about pulling together a shelter made of cloth and spear hafts. How he managed it with a broken arm, I don't know, but I'd already long since stopped wondering at Tamura's many talents and odd abilities. I tried to help him as best I could, but I feel I only got in the way, especially when he said: *The rain is wonderful when you are thirsty, but a nuisance when you wish to cook dinner.* I didn't let him push me away. Much like Hardt's ministrations were keeping him busy, keeping him distracted, I needed the same. Anything to keep me from slinking back to the corpse of my lover. There were buildings nearby we could have moved to, some were ruins and others were dilapidated at best, but any of them would have provided some shelter from the wind and blistering cold. However, we couldn't leave Horralain, nor attempt to move him, and I wouldn't leave Silva's body. I wasn't ready to say goodbye.

Snow started to drift in, small flakes at first, but they settled all the same. The sphere had sheltered the arena from the weather, but now that it was gone, I knew the cold would soon turn even that place into a frigid ruin. I collected my Sources and placed them back in my snuff pouch, all except the Pyromancy Source. I turned it over and over in my hands, rubbing my thumb across every surface time and time again. It was a small Source, the size of grape, and smooth on all sides except one; that side was rough to the touch like unvarnished wood. I rubbed it again and again until I knew it's every curve and contour. I gripped it in my hand so tightly my bones protested and my palm bruised. I

pressed it against my chest, and even picked open one of my
wounds and pressed the Source against it until it was sticky
with my blood. However, Josef had absorbed the Source
from Neverthere, the ability seemed beyond me. Perhaps
he really was the chosen one, fulfilling the Auguries. And I
was once more just the deviant child holding him back from
greatness. Eventually, I popped the Source in my mouth and
forced it down. It was too soon, really. Only hours since I
suffered from late stage Source rejection, and I had neither
rested nor recovered, but I needed the warmth. I needed the
fire inside to chase away all the icy pain.

Imiko had vanished, as the little thief was wont to do.
I shouldn't call her little, by then she was already taller than
I, but I always have. Hardt gathered as many spear hafts
and axe handles as he could find and snapped them to make
kindling. Then I set them ablaze. I could tell by the feeling in
my gut, I only had a few hours, at most, before I rejected the
Source again, and I had one more thing to do with my fire
before I allowed that to happen.

Leaving the shelter and the little fire I had started,
I crossed the amphitheatre and once more made my way
to Silva's body. The cold turned her flesh a pale blue that
matched her lifeless eyes. I settled down next to her on
the ground, my left leg splayed out before me, and waited
for my courage to show up. After a while, Hardt sat down
across from me. He had a new coat, larger than before, and
pulled it tight around him, his breath misting as he puffed it
out.

"Aren't you cold?" he asked as he handed me a small
stoppered bottle.

"Pyromancy keeps me warm." It was mostly true.
I wore the same cured leather armour I had been wearing

for days. If you have never worn the same clothing for an
extended period of time, let me assure you, it becomes a part
of you, like a second skin stuck in place by spilt blood and
sweat. Underneath the armour, I wore serviceable trousers
and a blouse that was stained with blood in dozens of places.
I should have been freezing, but I was used to the cold.
Ssserakis was darkness and fear and ice, and my body was a
frigid place even at the best of times. The Pyromancy Source
was a little fire inside, and I used it to warm my skin, but
the cold from the horror possessing me would never melt.
"What's this?"

"Rum," Hardt said with a smile. He had his own
little bottle as well. "You'd be amazed what you can find on
a soldier's body." The amphitheatre was littered with the
dead. They were all there because of me, and yet the only
corpse I made there was Silva's.

We both sipped at the rum in silence for a while.
It was sweet, spiced, and fiery all at once, with an odd
fruitiness to it. I liked it and the feeling it put inside, but I
would have preferred wine. It was foolish really; I knew I
had an hour at most before I would be throwing it right back
up.

"Josef is alive," Hardt said eventually.

It was probably the one thing that was keeping me
going. Well, that and the promise of power. "How do you
feel about that?" I asked.

Hardt sipped at his bottle again. His eyes were on
Silva, but his gaze went through her. I wish mine could have
done that, but she was all I could see. "I'm not sure. He
killed Isen. He tried to kill me, and you. We befriended him,
cared for him, and he betrayed us."

"I betrayed him first." A hard thing to admit. Just a

few years earlier I wouldn't have been able to. The truth, of course, is far more complex. We had been betraying each other for years, back and forth. I was just the first to not forgive.

"You didn't try to kill him," Hardt said.

"I did kill him."

"That wasn't you, Eska. That was Yorin. And Josef didn't die."

I shook my head, the rum turning bitter in my mouth. "He did die. And I killed him. It was my fault he was there, my choice not to bring him along. If I had tried harder to convince him... If I hadn't pushed him away... I killed Josef. I killed Isen." I paused, hating myself, the words festering inside like an open wound. I forced them out and my voice broke with them. "I killed Silva."

"Eska." A big hand gripped hold of my shoulder and Hardt turned me a little to face him. "You're not responsible for the actions of others. You didn't kill them."

"Silva..."

Hardt let out a sigh and drew his hand back. "You didn't kill the others. And she didn't give you a choice."

Some arguments are destined to go nowhere. Hardt would always excuse my actions, and I would never give up my guilt. It was mine. I had earned it, and I'd be damned before I let anyone take it from me. Even him.

"Do you want to kill Josef?" The question needed asking, but I feared the answer.

Hardt didn't reply right away. He had to think about it. That added weight to his answer, made it more certain. An answer in a moment is fuelled by passion and is likely to change as emotion wanes. But an answer given after a pause so long it becomes awkward... well, you know that answer has been considered. You know there is thought behind it, consideration. That's an answer that has been reached with both head and heart.

"I don't want to kill anyone, Eska. That doesn't mean I forgive him. I don't think I'll ever be able to forgive him, even if you can." Hardt drew in a deep breath and shook his head, his eyes distant. "But I don't want to kill him, nor even see him dead. I'm not sure what form justice for murder should take. Maybe he deserved to be down in the Pit, but then maybe so did I." It dawned on me then, perhaps I was not the only one drowning in melancholy. We both fell into a comfortable silence, each sipping our rum.

"It's not a secret I didn't like her," Hardt said eventually. "I didn't trust her. But I saw how she made you smile. I guess it confused me a little… or… maybe it felt like a betrayal of my brother?" I didn't bother to point out that I never loved Isen. "She made you happy. And that's something worth mourning, I suppose."

I sniffed and wiped tears away. When I opened my mouth to speak, I almost choked on my sadness. No words came out.

"I blamed her for Kento," Hardt continued. "I know that isn't fair. I know it was your choice, but I blamed her all the same. Perhaps if I had been able to look past that, I'd have seen a bit of what you saw in Silva."

When Hardt looked at me, I broke. "I tried to find her, Hardt," I squeezed the words past my closing throat and the tears running down my cheeks. "I tried to get Kento back. I demanded it. She's gone. Mezula said…"

"Stop," Hardt snapped. He shook his head. "I don't want to know, Eska. I can't hear it."

He was right. It was my shame, my torment. I had no

right to burden him with the knowledge that my daughter was dead. It was a weight I had to shoulder alone.

You're not alone. Ssserakis' words were a comfort, though they probably shouldn't have been. No doubt the horror meant to frighten me, but I found strength in the assurance of its company.

"The longer you leave it, the harder it'll be," Hardt said, his voice soft and comforting like a distant rumble of thunder.

I nodded and Hardt stood, offering his hand. I ignored it and instead crawled closer to Silva, bending down over her face and whispering my final words to her. I won't share them with you, nor anyone. Those words, my heart and soul poured out through a whisper, are private. Suffice it to say I choked on them, my final goodbye to the woman who opened my eyes to love. Even Ssserakis withdrew, allowing me a moment of true privacy. I placed a final kiss on Silva's lips, and with it I breathed out fire.

When I drew back, Hardt helped me to my feet. His indomitable support was something I have come to rely upon, and I needed it then more than ever. Together, we watched the fire I breathed into Silva consume her. A localised inferno burning my love to ash. Something hardened inside of me as I watched her burn. I can't truly explain it. I can say only this, a part of myself burned along with her.

"What do we do now?" Hardt asked me as we watched the funeral.

Send me home. I ignored the horror.

"What do you mean?"

"We're all here because of you, Eska. Not blaming you, just stating a fact. We're stranded here on Do'shan. We can't go back. The Rand will be after us now, she'll know what happened here, and Coby… Well, she never really liked any of us." Least of all me. Coby had been looking for a reason to kill me from the first day we met, and her resentment only grew as did my relationship with Silva.

Hardt continued. "That old Sourcerer might have claimed the Terrelan Emperor is done with us, but Prena Neralis doesn't seem the sort to let it go. And I don't think the Emperor will be willing to let an Orran Sourcerer go about his kingdom. So, where do we go? What do we do now?"

Home!

"I'm not looking for answer right now, Eska." Hardt clamped a big hand on my shoulder. "But it's something worth considering. In the meantime, let's get some rest. I think we could all use it."

I let him turn me away from Silva's ashes. A good thing about Pyromancy, you can set a fire so hot even bone will be reduced to ash. Hardt steered me towards our makeshift shelter where Tamura and Ishtar huddled around the fire, both injured and morose, sharing their own bottle. Imiko was nowhere to be seen, and her little ringlet sat on Tamura's lap, huddled in a woollen cloak, nervously twitching its head around as it looked for its mistress. Someone had draped a couple of cloaks over Horralain's shivering form, but the big man still hadn't emerged from his nightmare. I alone had not robbed the dead for warmer clothing, but I knew it wouldn't be long before my Pyromancy Source killed me, boiling my insides. I would need to retch it up once more before that happened.

"Not yet," I said, shrugging free from Hardt's gentle hand.

"Eska, you need to rest as well as the rest of us."

"Not yet," I spat. "Not while one of us is still in danger."

CHAPTER
FIVE

EACH STEP CLOSER TO HORRALAIN WAS LIKE
wading through a miasma. Each limping lurch made the
world recede around me a little further. Every inch closer
I crept brought on a new, heady rush of pleasure. His fear
was like nothing I had ever felt before. A city, any city, is full
of fear. It flows through the streets and alleys like the wind.
It cares not for the boundaries of house or home. Fear rises
from the inhabitants, one and all. Little fears, blinding terror,
niggling anxieties. It is a constant meal for a horror such as
Ssserakis, and just as that monster drank it in, growing fat
and strong on the power of it, I benefited too. The Pit was
like a city in that regard. Fear was everywhere, all the time,
making me strong and lending me power. Ro'shan was
no different, nor the Polasian capital. Even Do'shan was
veined with streaks of fear waiting to be mined, although
much of that was fear of me thanks to my murder of so

many of the feral pahht. Horralain was different. This was
no inexhaustible supply of dread slowing suffusing the
world, he had become a furnace of fear, burning hotter than
any person has cause to. It couldn't last. I knew it. Ssserakis
knew it. Sooner or later, the terror would become too much,
the stress and strain on his body too great. Sooner, rather
than later, Horralain would fall, killed by a prison of fear he
did not know how to escape from.

The world around me blurred as I struggled closer,
feeling as though I was pushing my way towards an inferno,
pushed back by a cyclone. Somewhere close by, I heard
Hardt say my name, but I waved a lazy hand in his direction,
hoping he took the hint. By the time I was standing just
a few paces from Horralain, I could barely breathe. The
pleasure of it was so intense I felt myself growing hot and
tingling all over. The giant thug rocked back and forth on his
knees, oblivious of both the cold, and me.

"What can we do?" I asked. I probably looked strange
to the others around me, braced as though struggling against
a powerful wind, and talking to myself.

*Do? Bask in it. Revel in the feeling and the strength. Drink
in as much as we are able. I used to inspire this sort of fear in
my minions every day. The strength it gave me... Even Norvet
Meruun didn't dare challenge me.*

"What?"

*Norvet Meruun is one of the lords of Sevoari. You would
call it an Abomination, a pulsing mass of flesh, tentacle, and bile,
throbbing beneath the surface of my home.*

"How does that help me free Horralain?"

Ssserakis laughed in my head. *It doesn't.*

"Help me, Ssserakis, or I will make you hurt."

For a few moments there was nothing inside. Then I

felt the horror grow curious. *How?*

"I'll open up another portal. And another. And another. I'll keep opening them up until that thing on the other side takes notice again, and I will step through. And this time I won't let you hide inside of me." Something strange happened then. I felt a new fear. Not Horralain's. Not my own. I felt Ssserakis' fear. Whatever lay on the other side of the portals had taken an interest in the horror, and only our link, and my desperate searching, had allowed Ssserakis to return to me.

Your minion is trapped inside a construct. Form a link, and I will carry us both across the bond.

"What?"

Reach out and touch the fool.

The world lurched around me. The frozen amphitheatre was gone. My friends were gone. The ashen remains of Silva were gone. I found myself in a luscious great hall, decorated in golds and reds so deep they looked bloody. Pillars surrounded me, extending into a thick darkness like tar high above. The hall extended into forever in every direction, so many pillars it seemed impossible. Hundreds of people clustered in front of me, each one wearing fanciful clothing that I had only heard the likes of in stories. They wore all the colours I could imagine, from dainty yellows, to rich browns, to white so bright it hurt to look at. And each one of the people was talking, voices raised in a cacophony of sound that echoed about the hall to repeat upon itself, layering noise over more noise.

"What is this place?" I could barely hear my own voice over the shouting of the men and women in front of me.

A construct. You would call it a dream. I was born in one, pulled together from a thousand different experiences. You've been in one before, when we first met.

"Down in the Pit. You trapped me in a darkness and cut me."

My shadow laughed at me. There was light in the great hall, but no source, yet my shadow extended out to my left and up onto one of the pillars. As I watched, my shadow detached from the pillar and stepped closer to me, free of any surface. It was blacker than deep night and held my shape too consistently. Ssserakis watched me from the shining pits of green light that were my shadow's eyes.

"You have form here?"

The rules here are different. I can take any form I wish.

I glanced down. "As long as we're still connected? You can't separate from me."

My shadow laughed, green light spilling out around the jagged edges of its mouth. *Of course not. You know so little of possession. I cannot leave you, Eskara. We are stuck together until you die.*

"What? That seems like something you should have told me before I agreed to carry you." The horror was right, I knew little about possession. Almost nothing, actually. It never once occurred to me that I had no idea how to remove Ssserakis. Worse still, I realised that to fulfil my promise and send the ancient horror home to the Other World, I would have to die. Of course, I still had no idea how to go about such a thing anyway.

You didn't ask. You offered yourself up as a vessel before you knew all the facts. That is hardly my fault.

"What about in the portal? That thing separated us."

No, it didn't. We were still connected. That is how I found my way back once you opened a portal.

It was a lot to consider. Too much, given I was there to rescue Horralain, not debate with the horror inside of me as to the definition of separation, and the eventual terminus of our relationship. I turned away from Ssserakis and started towards the throng of people. They were packed in tight. Some were waving arms, others making rude gestures, and all were shouting.

"I don't have enough workers to tend my fields."

"Taxes are higher in my village than his."

"Thieves took three sheep from one of my farmer's flock."

I tried my best to ignore the inane chatter and pushed into the crowd. Memories of the Pit came flooding back to me, of standing in line near the Trough, pushing my way around the other scabs to get a slop of gruel. Frustration blossomed inside, and with it came anger. I was not that girl anymore, powerless and weak. I would no longer suffer being lost in a crushing crowd. With a shout, I drew on my Pyromancy Source and set my hands on fire... Well, I tried. Nothing happened inside the construct.

Ssserakis' mocking laugh reached me despite the noise surrounding me. *The rules are different here, Eskara. You have no magic. You are simply one of the actors in this play, and the rules apply to you as much as any of these images.*

"But they don't apply to you?" I shouted at the horror.

The rules never apply to the puppet master. Only those with strings to pull.

"Does that mean you're in control here?" I asked as I pushed my way between another group of shouting people.

No. Your Iron Legion created this construct, but he learned how from me.

One of the crowd jostled me and I will admit I lost

all composure. I have never been one for great patience and I was exhausted. Odd, that my exhaustion crossed over to the construct, yet my injuries did not. I lashed out, striking the nearest of the crowd in the face with a punch that would have made Hardt proud. I pushed at the woman on the other side of me and elbowed the man behind me in the face. For a few brief moments space opened around me and I could breathe. Then the crowd closed on me once more, even more tightly than before. Those I had struck paid me no mind and bore no injuries; they only went back to shouting at something in front of us all. A curse of being quite short, is that I have never been able to see over a crowd. I sometimes envy those blessed with height, until I see them smack their heads on low roofs and doorways.

By the time I reached the front of the crowd, I was clutching my chest and panting in exhaustion. Ssserakis stepped beside me, my shadow passing through the throng as though it was not there. I longed to turn about and lay into the crowd. They might not feel my attacks, nor even be inconvenienced by them, but throwing some punches would make me feel better.

Before the crowd, I found Horralain. The giant thug huddled on a grand, golden throne that would have looked overly ostentatious had I found a god sitting upon it. Tears rolled down his cheeks and dripped from his beard, and he wore a large crown on his head. Horralain's gaze passed over the crowd standing before him, his eyes roving from face to face. He passed me by and there was no recognition there, only blind panic and tears.

I rushed forward and grabbed Horralain by the shoulder. A part of me hoped that would be it, once I had found him, we would both be dragged out of the dream. Of

course, things are rarely so simple. The big man didn't even
seem to notice my hand on his shoulder.

"Horralain, come on. We have to go." I tugged at him,
but he remained rooted to his throne, and moving a man that
size is never an easy task.

I stepped in front of Horralain then and slapped him
hard in the face. His eyes continued their endless, terrified
circuit of the shouting faces.

"Horralain," I shouted his name over the noise of the
crowd. "Snap out of it. Help me fight through them. We'll
find a way out."

The big man's eyes washed over me, not even
realizing I was there.

My shadow moved in front of me, peering down at
Horralain. *Impressive. I'd be proud if I wasn't too busy hating
him for dragging me from my home.* Ssserakis turned to look
at me through gleaming green holes in the face of my own
shadow. *The construct is built. The rules are set. You have neither
the power, nor the knowledge to break them, Eskara. So how do you
win when you can't cheat?*

I thought back to my time in the Pit once more.
To my time at the gaming tables, hours upon hours of
gambling what meagre possessions I could scrounge up. The
snuff pouch at my belt, the one I hid my Sources in was a
memento from those days, one of the very first things I ever
won. You couldn't cheat at the gaming tables, there were too
many eyes watching. Too much of a crowd. You had to play
within the rules if you wanted to win, but that didn't mean
you had to play fairly.

"Why is this Horralain's greatest fear?" The truth was
already coming to me. "What is there to fear here?"

Not all fears are monsters and pain. Yours aren't. Your

greatest fear is...

"Shut up! We're not fucking talking about me. What is there here to fear? People. Wide open spaces."

You're thinking too literal, Eskara. Fears are not things. They are thoughts. You do not fear the knife, so much as what it might do.

"Decisions!" It all seemed so obvious once I had the answer. Every person in the gathered crowd wasn't just shouting, they were asking questions, requesting aid, demanding a decision. Horralain wasn't scared of the crowd, he feared the responsibility of being in charge.

I stepped in front of Horralain, blocking his hulking form as best I could, and turned to face the gathered crowd. I had to raise my voice to a shout to be heard. "My name is Eskara Helsene." A thought occurred to me; I had to play within the rules of the game. "Chancellor Eskara Helsene. I'm here to make decisions on behalf of..." I glanced back to the big thug cowering on his throne. "King Horralain?"

The crowd kept up their shouting, pointing and waving for attention. I singled one of them out, a tall man with a forked beard and a yellow silken robe. "What's your issue?"

"Two of my ships were lost at sea during a storm. I need money to rebuild or I'm done for."

Why that would be an affair of the crown, I had no idea, but I could only guess these issues were of Horralain's own imagining. "The treasury will provide you coin to rebuild one ship; a loan you repay once you have earned enough to build a second."

The man bowed his head. "Thank you, wise king." And then he faded away.

I pointed at another member of the crowd, an ancient

woman with more wrinkles than hair. "What do you have to bring before the king?" I could not keep the derision from my voice, but Horralain's demons didn't seem to notice.

"My husband is dead and left behind only daughters, and the daughters of daughters. The magistrate says my home should go to my husband's brother."

I scoffed at that. "The home is yours. It belongs to you and whoever you leave it to."

"Thank you. Thank you." The ancient woman sketched an awkward curtsy and faded away, just as the man before her had.

Have you ever wondered just how long it takes for a compassionate ruler to mete out decisions upon their subjects? Horralain's fear conjured less than two hundred of these clamouring demons, and I dealt with every single one. I was beyond bored and struggling to stand by the end of the first ten. By the time the last of the crowd faded away, I felt like leaving Horralain there to rot. Still, I think I acquitted myself quite well. Despite the imaginary kingdom he had constructed, I made the decisions based upon what I thought was fair, and what I thought was believable enough to be accepted. If only my own rule had been so well received. Or maybe if only I had kept a level head more often in such discussions.

Once the last of the beggars had faded away, I turned to Horralain. His head was in his hands, tears squeezing out between fingers. "They're gone, Horralain," I said. "Listen? Do you hear the silence?"

Fingers shifted and Horralain peered out between his hands with a single eye that darted this way and that. Then he lowered his hands and raised his head. "They're gone," he said in that slow voice of his, as though he needed to consider each word carefully before it left his lips.

I nodded. "All of them. I dealt with all of them." I took a step towards the pretend king and my back twanged in pain. When had pain started to seep into the construct? "Can we go now? There's nothing left to fear here."

"Thank you." Horralain's voice cracked on those words.

"You're welcome. Now stand up and let's go. Ssserakis, how do we get out."

Simple. Just make that first step of progress.

I let out a groan. "Horralain. Stand up and step away from the throne."

The big man levered himself to his feet, took one step forward, and faded away. I remained.

"Ssserakis? Why am I still here?"

I could actually feel the horror's confusion. *You appear to have made his construct your own. Do you really desire torture so?*

I glanced at my shadow to find green light spilling around its grinning mouth. It's an unnerving thing seeing your shadow move independently of you, even when you know how it is happening.

"Progress, huh?" I took two steps forward, turned, and lowered myself onto the throne.

And then I was back in the frozen amphitheatre. My friends gathered around me. Hardt had draped a cloak over my shoulders and Tamura was laughing and drawing something in the sand with a stick. Worst of all though, was the awestruck eyes of Horralain, staring at me.

CHAPTER SIX

I HAVE LONG SINCE DISCOVERED THAT I HAVE a strange ability, something unique and both wondrous and mortifying. I think it is a facet of my innate Necromancy, that magic the Iron Legion forced upon me. I can absorb the memories of the dead. Not all of them, only fragments, rarely enough to form anything but a brief glimpse into another's life. But sometimes a brief glimpse is all you need.

These are not my memories. They are Josef's.

Josef skids to a halt on the floor, but it's too late. Already too late. The portal snaps shut, and with it goes the light. He lays there in the dark, heart pounding, breath coming in short sharp gasps. He wants to move, tries to move. Can't. The darkness is everywhere, everything. It blankets him, smothers him, reduces the world to nothing

but monsters stalking through the black. Stalking. Stalking
him. He hates the dark. He's always hated the dark. Down
in the Pit, there was never anything but darkness. He would
have done anything to get out. He did do everything to get
out. He did the one thing he had never wanted to do.

He curls up into a ball. Makes himself small, quiet.
Hiding from the creatures in the dark. Hiding from fear.
Hiding from his own thoughts. It doesn't work. It can't. His
heartbeat is thunder in his ears. His thoughts echo in his
mind. So loud. So unwelcome.

How was he still alive? Again. How was he still alive?
Eska! She knew. She'd seen him. She knew! The Iron Legion,
Loran Orran. What had he done? It was him. It was all him.
It was always him.

Tap tap, tap tap, tap tap. A new noise. Not one of his.
One of the monsters come to get him. He curls tighter, blind
in the dark, heartbeat booming inside, outside, everywhere.

A mumble of words, something sharp sounding like
a curse. He doesn't recognise the language, but words have
a weight to them, a sound that is unmistakably language.
There is no magic to them, but words possess a magic all
of their own. The right words can cast a spell, manipulate
emotions as surely as any Empamancy. And words can break
spells. His fear recedes. There is no monster in this darkness,
but there is something. Someone.

"Hello?" His voice is croaky. The words scratch his
throat. How long has it been since he used his voice? How
long has it been since Yorin slid the knife across his skin,
blade biting into flesh, cutting through his life, leaving him
to bleed out in the dark that he fears so much.

More mumbled words. The tapping draws closer. A
grunt, so close Josef can feel the air move against his skin.

"And they call me blind." The voice is harsh, chewing on words rather than speaking them.

A sudden snapping noise and flames sprang to life nearby. Josef startles. Scampers back as the flames reveal a small, furry, eyeless face with a manic grin and sharp, serrated teeth. A tahren! He's never seen one before, but it could be nothing else. The little creature is grey with age and some of its fur has worn thin. It wears a belt covering its loins, trinkets hanging from leather loops. A bandoleer crosses above and below each arm, festooned with little pockets.

The creature scratches at its bulbous belly with clawed hands and points at the lantern. "You take it," it says in that thick voice. "I don't need it."

Josef stands and reaches out slowly. The little creature looks harmless, but the most dangerous things often do. He snatches the lantern and backs away quickly. Shining the light around him. He's in some sort of laboratory. There's a large desk, full of books and ruffled papers, a huge Source being used as a paperweight. Along the nearest wall are lines of bookshelves, each one packed with tomes.

"I'm guessing you're the chosen one?" the tahren says as it waddles away.

Josef shakes his head. "No! I don't think so. I'm just... My name is Josef Yenhelm."

"Inran of Rock Helm," the tahren says. "And if his mastership has brought you here without escort, you must be someone more special than *just*."

"Where is here?" Josef asks.

"His mastership's personal study. Where were you before?"

"Do'shan."

Inran lets out a whistling breath. "Half the world away. He's pushing his Portamancy to the limits."

The tahren walks over to a nearby table and shoos away a rat that was nibbling at the leftovers on a plate. He scoops up the plate and a nearby mug, sniffs at the contents, and shakes his head. "That's gone off. Do you see a bottle around anywhere? I'll need to replace it before his mastership tries to drink from it."

Josef crouches and scoops up a mostly empty bottle from the floor. It smells of vinegar and reminds him of home. His first home. His father always smelled of vinegar; used it to clean the saddles and tacks. Vinegar and old leather. Such comforting smells. "Your master is Prince Loran?"

Inran shakes his head and laughs. "His mastership isn't a prince. Can't be a prince without a kingdom... or princedom."

Josef follows the tahren as he continues moving about the room, picking up discarded plates and pushing papers into orderly piles. He keeps his distance. He doesn't trust the little creature. "But he is Loran Orran?"

Inran snorts. "Of course. Where do you think you are?"

"I don't know," Josef says. His throat closes and he coughs, coughs, coughs. He can't stop coughing. He feels so weak and weary, his limbs leaden, weighing him down. Is that what innate Sourcery does to a person? Without a Source to draw the magic from, the power must come from the person. Of course! The magic is his. It is him. The healing, it must have drained him. Josef pats at his chest where the sword had pierced him, run him through. No trace of a wound, not even a scar.

The tahren plucks the bottle from Josef's hands.

"Maybe you should sit down. Your heart is racing, and you smell stressed. This way." Inran leads Josef back to the table and pulls out one of the chairs. Josef is too tired to be scared anymore, too tired to mistrust the simple act of kindness. He collapses into the chair. "I'll bring you some food and something to drink," says the tahren. "Would you like that, boy?"

"I'm not a boy."

"Of course, you aren't," Inran says. He pats Josef on the arm and waddles away, his claws clicking on the stone floor with every step. Josef places the lantern on the table and stares into the flame, watching dance a futile little jig on the wick.

"Oh," Inran's voice floats out of the darkness. "I'm sure his mastership mentioned before he sent you on ahead. Don't touch the cages."

Josef remembers cages from another time, full of animals and monsters, cowering in fear, clawing to get out. He also remembers his friend, Barrow, trapped in such a cage. What if he's done it again? What if there are more children here, locked in cages? Experimented on. Tortured.

There's a sound like paper ripping and a new portal opens. For just a moment, Josef sees Eska, held suspended in an invisible grip. He wants to go to her, to hold her, to be held by her. He wants it more than anything, that reunion. They've been apart too long. They were never meant to be apart. Loran Orran steps through, and the portal snaps shut behind him. She's gone. Taken from him once again. Half a world separating them. Frustration and exhaustion war within him and Josef sobs.

Loran Orran flaps his robes, depositing dust and sand on the floor, and glances towards Josef. "I hope you're not as ungrateful as your friend, Yenhelm."

"Is she alright?" He asks, begs. He needs to know she's alive, can't fathom a world without Eska in it.

Loran Orran waves away the question. "Inran? Inran, why aren't the torches lit?"

The tahren mumbles words, so quiet they were nothing but a whisper.

"Well that's all fine for you. Some of us can't navigate in the dark." Loran moves off into the darkness, grumbling something Josef can't hear. A thump and a curse later, and a torch on one of the far walls sputters to life, orange flames eagerly licking at the wall. Loran Orran rubs furiously at his left knee through his robes. Behind the prince, set out along the wall, are dozens of cages, metal bars shining in the torch light. Some are empty, but not all. They are not for animals and beasts. These cages hold people! Terran, pahht, tahren. Prisoners, ragged and malnourished. The dead eyes of those who have accepted their fate and have no fight left in them.

Josef lurches upright and backwards, pushing away from the table, his chair tips and clatters to the stone floor. "I've seen this before," he says, his voice weak and rasping.

Loran Orran turns to Josef, his eyes bright in the torchlight. "You remember? You and Helsene both, odd that the memory block has degraded on you. Perhaps the others, too, are beginning to remember. Interesting."

"What did you do to us?" Josef asks. But he already knows. Deep down, he already knows.

"What does it matter? The past is past. That's actually the first rule of Chronomancy. The past is always behind us, the present moves ever forward at a varying pace, and the future is always looming, always changing."

Josef staggers back, his legs entangling in the chair.

The world tips and he hits the floor in a painful sprawl. "You put magic in us. Are you doing the same to them?" He points toward the cages.

Loran Orran stops by the table and plucks the lantern, holding it forward. He looks like a kind old man in the gloom, his wrinkled face a picture of sympathy. It's all lies. "It really doesn't matter what I did to you, Yenhelm. What matters now, is what we are going to do together."

"What?"

A gnarled hand reaches out, hanging in the air in front of Josef. An offer of help, of partnership maybe. An offer veiled in secrets. "You are the chosen one, Yenhelm. I made certain of it. I made you the chosen one, and together, we're going to bring the Rand back. All of them."

CHAPTER SEVEN

I SLEPT FOR A FULL DAY. ACTUALLY, IT WAS more like a day and a half. After pulling Horralain from his nightmare, my exhaustion finally caught up with me. We moved away from the amphitheatre, though I do not remember doing so. Back down the path leading up to it and out into the city of Do'shan once more. Hardt found us a building, one that wasn't occupied by the feral pahht, and we claimed it for our own. Apparently the ferals fled at the mere sight of me, even stumbling and barely conscious. They feared me as feverishly as they worshipped Aerolis. I suppose that was something I had earned. They were not the last people I taught to fear me.

As soon as we were inside, I collapsed against a crumbling wall and knew no more. Hardt draped half a dozen cloaks over me as I shivered my way into sleep, and I'm told Horralain stood guard for hours until a similar exhaustion took him. The big Terrelan thug became a second shadow after that day. He devoted his life to protecting mine, perhaps as payment for a debt he felt he owed, or perhaps just to show gratitude. Maybe it was because he needed someone else to make the decisions for him, and I had stepped into that role and proved more than capable. It's a shame his dream problems were so much easier to resolve than my real ones.

When finally I woke, I was ravenous. I have been hungry a great many times in my life. Down in the Pit we never had enough to eat, and all Sourcerers develop a hunger that is beyond the need for food, but after days of sleep, the hunger was something else. We had a decent store of salted meat, taken from the packs and pouches of dead soldiers, but it would last only a few days at most. I wondered if our small flyer was still nearby. There was a town below Do'shan, we had passed it on the way, and there would be food aplenty down there.

Our group was subdued. Not just in attitude, but there was something else as well. A cloud of ill feeling hanging over us all. Horralain followed me about like a lovesick fool, dogging my heels. Hardt watched the city outside, standing guard near an empty door frame. Ishtar paced, refusing to admit she would be better served by resting her ankle. And Tamura sat nursing an old kettle he found, boiling the water within and occasionally adding things to the mix. Worse than all of them, though, was Imiko. The little thief sat in a corner of our building, staring at nothing. Not even her little ringlet could cheer her solemn mood. She barely even noticed my approach. I kicked her foot to get her attention, and Imiko startled, fear bleeding from her eyes. It shamed me that I caused that fear. With a sigh, I lowered myself down next to her.

"Does he have to loom so close?" Imiko asked sullenly, nodding at Horralain. The big man was standing over us both.

"Go away." At my order, Horralain took two steps backward and waited there. "Apparently looming is what he does now."

Imiko snorted and went back to her thorough contemplation of the floor.

"You couldn't have stopped him." I guessed at her feelings. During the Iron Legion's assault, the little thief hadn't fought like everyone else. She hadn't even tried, just collapsed and screamed at him to stop hurting her friends. It was more than I managed. "Even Hardt and Horralain couldn't get close, you had no chance. I guess, sometimes a passionate plea is worth more than a knife in the back."

Imiko sobbed and drew her knees close, hugging them against her chest. I reached up and put an arm across her shoulders, pulling her into a hug. It felt awkward, and not just because the girl was taller than I, but because it wasn't the sort of thing I did. That was how Silva comforted people, with compassion and contact and love. I comforted people by drinking with them and burying the pain.

"We'll get him," I promised her. "I'll get him. I'll repay him in kind for all the pain he caused us. The Iron Legion will die for everything he has done, all the atrocities. For what he did to me. For what he's doing to Josef even now." Imiko let out a whine, but I wasn't listening anymore. My anger was a boiling thing inside of me, bolstered by Ssserakis' confirmation that the Iron Legion would pay. "I just have to find him first. Learn some new tricks. We need more power."

"It's not that," Imiko said between sobs. I realised I was gripping her tight, and she pushed away from me, tears rolling down her cheeks. "I know I couldn't stop him. I don't care. I killed someone, Eska. More than one." She reached down beside her and pulled up a small knife, the blade stained reddy brown with drying blood. "People are dead because of me. Because I…" Imiko held the knife before her, gripping the hilt hard between white knuckles. It shook in her grasp, as though she wanted nothing more than to let go but couldn't unwind her fingers. So, I did it for her. I took her hand and peeled back her rigid fingers, then plucked the knife away.

I don't know how to console people, I never have. Comforting and easing people's pain is simply not one of my skills. It's a lack in me, and I'm aware of it. It is not because I do not understand, and not because I do not feel for them, but simply that I know no words that can help. Silva was good with such moments, always knowing just what to say and when to say it, or sometimes when to say nothing at all. All I know how to do, is shoulder the burdens myself. After all, what's one more death, or even a hundred more, laid at my feet?

"It's not your fault, Imiko. It's mine." Truer words, I have rarely spoken. "You just held the knife. I gave it to you. I directed it. Without me, there would have been no need, and no target. It's not your fault. It's all because of me."

I looked about our little group. Homeless and wounded. Beaten and sullen. Even down in the Pit, despair had not crouched above our heads so closely. It wasn't just comfort or consoling they needed, and those who did would be better looking towards Hardt and his giant shoulders. They needed something else from me. They needed direction and purpose, and I had that to spare.

Pushing back to my feet was difficult. Sleeping in the chill had stiffened my limbs, and my ankle still hurt from being twisted. Between my various cuts and the cracked rib, the simple act of living was painful, but I've endured worse. At least my injuries would leave no memorable scars, not like some I have suffered. My hand found my left cheek and rubbed along the proud line Prig had left there, a reminder that even the pettiest of actions can leave a mark upon the world. All eyes turned to me as I stood there, as though my friends could all sense the weight of what I was about to do. Even Ssserakis stirred within me, its curiosity distracting it from the fear that surrounded us.

"Horralain, come with me." Terrans and pahht share a few common traits, and among them is strange attraction to mystery. Everyone could sense I had made a decision, and the implications hung in the air between us. When I stormed out of our little building, Horralain on my heels like a loyal dog, the others followed behind, driven on by curiosity.

I marched towards the amphitheatre as well as my leg would allow. It was more of a limping lurch, but I put my all into the act. Hardt asked a question behind me. Tamura answered him by saying *A fire does not see the ash is leaves behind. It has already moved on to burn something new.* I wondered if I was supposed to be the fire he spoke of. I'm not certain a metaphor has ever been more apt for my life. Everything in my way burns and all I leave behind is ashes.

Feral pahht watched us from shadows, their fear making them stand out to me as clear as the day was gloomy. Ssserakis was still weak, but the horror had fed well during my day and a half asleep, and my shadow shifted with every step as my passenger tested its new limits. Perhaps it was a result of our bond growing stronger, or perhaps the horror simply better understood its own capabilities within my confines. It claimed Ovaeris was different from Sevoari, the rules were different, yet I think neither of us truly knew what that meant. We were both discovering what the other was capable of, even as we discovered what we ourselves could do. For all our differences, Ssserakis and I made a good team.

I pointedly ignored the blackened sand where I had burned Silva's body. I needed no reminder of the consequences of my actions, especially when I had another act in mind that I knew might bode even worse for us all. Dozens of frozen bodies littered the arena floor, most of them already stripped of anything useful or worthwhile. Corpses do not rot and fester as they should in the cold, they stay preserved for a long time. Imiko let out a strangled sob and I heard Hardt rumble a few words. She would fare better in his care than mine. Discarded weapons, many of them bloodied, lay forgotten amidst the sand. Close to the centre, next to a giant body with a crushed chest, lay the great hammer; one of the ten weapons that fell when the moons collided. Its head lay half buried in the sand, its haft sticking upward.

Blood spotted the sand near the centre of the arena. Some of it was Josef's from where Prena had run him through, and some of it was mine from the injuries I had sustained. Already it seemed so long ago, but in truth it was less than two days gone. I stopped near the two small pillars that had been grown from the floor, the evidence of my meeting with the Iron Legion. When I turned around, I found the others nearby, watching me and waiting as though I were about to do something wondrous. I suppose they weren't far wrong. I was about to change the world.

"Aerolis!" I shouted the name to no answer. None of us had seen nor heard the Djinn since it fled the amphitheatre two days earlier. I think the others were happy about that. I should have been, too.

What are you doing, Eskara?

"I made a deal." I was answering Ssserakis, though I suppose the others thought I was talking to them. "Actually, I made two deals. It's time we both made good on our promises."

"Aerolis, the Changing!" I raised my voice even louder than before.

A wind rushed into the arena, stirring coats and hair as it came. Imiko clung tighter to Hardt's side and the big man sent a worried glance my way. Ishtar let out a groan and hobbled closer on her crutch, mumbling as she settled down on one of the earthen stools the Iron Legion had grown from the sand.

"I hope you know what you are doing, terrible student. This creature is not a thing to be trifled with."

"I made a deal to free you, Ishtar," I said. "I suppose we could have just chopped your leg off instead."

My sword tutor let out a chuckle. "I did not say I am not grateful. Only that I hope you are not stupid."

The wind grew to a howl and blew in from all over the arena, coalescing into a swirling maelstrom of madness just a few steps away. I squinted against the sand thrown into the air.

"I am not some servant to be summoned." The Djinn's voice was no longer a grating rumble of stone on stone, but more like a whistling howl of a cyclone.

"And yet…" I said with a savage grin.

The swirling vortex grew more violent and the Djinn drew closer. Wild winds tugged at my coat and looted cloak. "In your arrogance, you are mistaking my patience for generosity, terran."

I didn't back down, instead raising my chin in defiance. I could feel the Arcstorm inside of me and knew my eyes were flashing with the lightning I kept bottled up. "And you mistake arrogance for competence, Djinn."

Ishtar groaned beside me. "If you had told me you were going to start another fight with this god, I would not have sat so close, terrible student."

The winds of the Djinn seemed to calm a little at her words. "At least your pahht knows how to properly pander to its betters." There is a truth hidden in that statement, one I have spent many years ruminating over. In my many dealings with those creatures that we mistakenly call gods, I have discovered that the Rand truly desire our worship. They changed us. In many ways, they really did create the terrans, the pahht, and the tahren. They took what we once were, and warped us to be more to their design, and they did so because they wanted to be gods. And they wanted us to elevate them to that status through belief. The Djinn, on the other hand, do not care what we believe, they just want us to bow and scrape and flatter. Unfortunately, I've never been very good at any of those things, so I chose to stand there defiant instead.

"What is it you want, terran?"

"We made a deal, Djinn," I spat the words into the centre of the vortex. "Ishtar's freedom for yours."

A hissing laughter whistled around the arena, stirring up sand and whipping it in every direction. "Be careful of your choice of words. You would tie yourself into an impossible task."

The Djinn are not to be trusted, but take that warning to heart, Eskara. Make no further deals with this creature. Get what we are owed and leave it to rot here on this island.

"What happened to wanting to kill it?" I asked.

The churning winds drew back a little, the Djinn pulling back into itself slightly. "Who is it you talk to, terran?"

It was your grief, not mine, that led to your rage. I just directed it where it belonged. Now we both know this creature is beyond us. For now. It offered you power. Take it. Learn from it. Then, let it fade away to obscurity up here on its floating prison. Become the deity it wishes to be.

"I agreed to free Do'shan," I said, trying to ignore Ssserakis. The horror could get quite passionate when it talked about rule and the worship of others. It longed to be back in its world, where it was one of the rulers. "To let you travel the skies once more."

"You did. And you are running out of time."

"That is a hefty price you paid," Ishtar said. "Just to free little me."

I turned to her and shrugged. "I'd pay it again. In an instant."

Ishtar chuckled. "Such a terrible student, but a better friend. Thank you, Eskara." Ishtar rarely used my name, only when the weight of the situation called for it.

"I gave you three days, terran," the Djinn continued.

I let out a snort and smiled. "I don't need them. Tell me about the chains. What are they made from? Why do you need me to set you free?"

Tamura chuckled. "The chains are Iron, not made from, but of."

"But the Djinn are the masters of earthen magic, no?"
I asked. "Surely you can break the chains yourself."

A chill breeze gusted through the amphitheatre. "The
crazy Aspect confuses the matter. I suspect, deliberately.
The chains are alive. Grown from one of Mezula's children,
one she named Iron. He rests at the heart of my city like
a parasite. His limbs worm their way through the rock,
an infestation of unbreakable metal, locking my prison in
place."

"He is the chains?"

The Djinn paused a moment before answering. "The
chains are Iron. Surrounding him, enveloping him. A great
web buried inside the rock, a fat spider cocooned at the
centre."

It should not have surprised me as much as it did. A
similar monster lives in the centre of Ro'shan, a giant whose
bones grow upwards to form the very city. One of Mezula's
many children. I have never learned the name of the creature
that lives in her mountain, providing shelter to all Ro'shan's
citizens. As far as I am aware, there is no way down to meet
the living heart of the city. It slumbers there, responding to
the will and whim of the mother. Iron was not so different
in scope, though with a far-removed purpose. An Aspect
created for the sole reason of keeping Do'shan anchored to
the earth. A creature of metal limbs that fed on the nutrients
of the earth, sucking up what it needed through the ground
so far below. I wonder if it was aware of us, of anything that
happened around it. How much intelligence had Mezula
granted her child of iron?

"Why can't you destroy him?" I asked. "You're a
Djinn, aren't you? Powerful beyond measure, worshipped as
a god. Has Mezula truly bested you so easily?"

I perhaps should not have taunted Aerolis so. There was a saying back in Keshin, one I remember for some reason despite the passage of years. *Don't poke the fire. It cares not whether you burn.* The wind picked up once more, the calm breeze turning to a howling gale. Sand was sucked into the air and whirling tornadoes formed around us. I shoved my hands into the pockets of my coat and pulled it close around me, but my cloak whipped about me in a mad flurry of activity.

"Eska?" Hardt's voice raised to a shout over the wind. I glanced over to see him crouching low, braced against the fury of Aerolis' gale. Imiko clung to Hardt's arm, white knuckles standing out even in the frigid winds.

What are you doing?

"So much bluster!" I had to scream into the wind just to be heard. "Give up the show, Aerolis. It doesn't fucking impress me." You might wonder how I could be so calm and confident in the face of such power. A hurricane was blowing through the amphitheatre, trying to tear us all from the ground. Localised tornadoes tore at the sand and the earth beneath. The sound was deafening. The violence of the storm, mind numbing. Yet we were all of us, unharmed.

I have a taste for gambling, a vice earned from countless hours at the gaming tables down in the Pit. The thrill of a wagered bet, the anticipation of victory or defeat, the battle against an opponent who desires to take all you have. But I learned long ago that for most games of chance, the outcome relies not upon the cards or chips or dice, but upon the players. A lesson from Josef, whispered down in the dark just moments before the oblivion of sleep, but a lesson I had taken to heart. Bet against the player, not against the game. Silva taught me a similar lesson, that negotiation is much like gambling. Sometimes it is worth giving something away, losing a round, just to see how the other person will act. Occasionally it is worth feigning value for an item that means nothing to you. Knowing when your opponent is bluffing, is nine tenths of any victory.

The storm grew yet more violent. Ishtar slumped sideways off her little pillar and clung to it. Tamura crouched down, curling into a ball and clutching at the ground. Even Horralain and Hardt, each as big as a horse, had trouble bracing against the fury that whipped through the arena. Ssserakis snaked my shadow into the earth beneath me, anchoring me against the buffeting, and I leaned into the winds. One last gasp of defiance. One last bet into the bluff.

"Enough, Djinn!" I screamed into the winds and the Arcstorm roared to life around me, lightning sparking off my skin and lighting up my eyes. It is a strange thing, the storm I carry inside; it reacts to strong emotion. Pleasure and pain, fear and exhilaration. It is sometimes awkward in that regard; I have been known to accidentally shock lovers in the throes of passion. But most often it reacts to my anger. "You're not going to harm us, so give up this pathetic fucking act and tell me what I need to know!"

The winds died so suddenly that Horralain pitched forward and sprawled upon the ground. I probably would have too if not for Ssserakis anchoring me to the earth by my shadow.

You gamble so easily with your own life, but risk all to protect those around you. A foolish trait that will lead to your death.

"What do you care?" I whispered the words as quietly as I could.

I have invested a lot of time and effort in you, Eskara. I will not permit you to die until you have sent me home.

The swirling vortex of the Djinn reformed before me; the winds reduced once more to a whistling breeze. "How can you be so sure, terran?"

I stood before the Djinn and straightened my back, refusing to show any measure of the fear I felt. "Because you need me. If you could free Do'shan yourself, you would. I can do it for you. And you know it, or you would have already killed me. That storm you just summoned was an attempt to intimidate, all show and bluster. Just like Vainfold, you posture and put on a bloody impressive show in the hope I will tell you how grand you are. Well you are. You're Aerolis, the Changing. You are rock and wind, and probably countless other things. Grand and magnificent and powerful. There, have I appeased your bloated fucking ego yet? Can we get on with things?"

Tamura snorted in laughter. The crazy old Aspect was sitting cross legged in the sand. "All of life is mirrors. Reflections of truth are often lies."

"As mad as your mother." The Djinn's words hissed around the arena.

"Why can't you destroy Iron yourself, Aerolis?" I pushed.

The vortex of wind shifted slightly. It was hard to look at the madness of the Djinn's form, difficult to focus on such a writhing mass of nothing. Impossible to tell where the creature's attention lay. "We made these mountains, my brothers and I. Five of them. Our bastions in the sky. Fortresses from which to wage the War Eternal. We made them to resist magic, our own and that of the Rand. We did not consider how insidious our sisters can be. Once again they subverted our creations."

"Once there were five. Lights in the sky. Beacons of hope and wonder," Tamura almost sang the words. "Two were torn down amidst fire and flesh, the ground ripped asunder at their ending. One was drowned, swallowed whole, a gift from Rand to mur. That left just two lights in the sky, endless circling, closer year by year, until one day." Tamura clapped suddenly, the slap of his hands echoing about the arena. He looked up from his hands with a sly grin at the Djinn. "Just like our moons."

"Quiet, Aspect!" Aerolis roared. "I may need this Sourcerer's help, but you are nothing to me."

"I have a name, Aerolis," I said, pulling the attention back to me. It seemed far safer than letting it linger on any of my friends. "And it is neither terran, nor Sourcerer. Your brother knew well enough to learn it. So should you. So will you!"

I think maybe I pushed too far, demanded too much. I admit, I have never been good at knowing when to back down. "Do you learn the names of the insects you crush underfoot?" Aerolis asked. "Or perhaps of the animals you kill to eat? No. Why learn the name of something so brief in its existence?" A gust of wind that sounded suspiciously like a snort passed through the arena. "Be content that I know your name, terran, and I will use it when you prove worthy." Oh, how I fucking hated that.

Another step towards the Djinn and I felt the wind of its form tugging at my coat once more. "You're no longer powerful enough to break the enchantments the Djinn placed on the flying mountains. With each death, your people grew weaker. Just like Vainfold no longer has the power to escape his crown, you can't affect Do'shan anymore. So how can the Rand? How is it Mezula is able to do what you are too weak to?"

The wind grew cold around me. I might have shivered, but the horror inside was colder still. "The Rand did not use magic. Iron is a living creature. His limbs are chains which tunnel their way through my home, infesting it. The mountain resists magic but pick and shovel and time could achieve what all my power cannot." The Djinn paused and a wind breezed through the arena like a sigh. "Unfortunately, the creatures that remain here are not bright. Directing them is possible, but only to a degree. Teaching them to use weapons of war to attack invaders was difficult enough, but they simply do not understand the need to dig out the chains infesting their home."

"Weeds!" Tamura shouted. "Even the smallest plant can crack stone."

I do not see how we can break something even the Djinn cannot unmake. Coddle the creature with promises and run. Let us be done with it.

I ignored Ssserakis. The horror was playing a game I didn't yet understand, and every time it counselled me, its advice changed. Instead, I focused my attention on the Djinn. "I promised to free Do'shan. And I will."

A laughter rippled through the arena. "Would you like to know the consequences if you fail?"

"Why would it matter?" I turned from the Djinn and nodded to Horralain. "Pick up the hammer."

A roar of wind stirred the amphitheatre once more. "I will kill anyone foolish enough to touch that thing." The Djinn's words were no idle threat, that much was obvious. Horralain paused, glancing between myself and the whirling vortex.

"Ignore the wind, Horralain. Pick up the hammer."

I turned back to the Djinn and took another step forward. "Stop getting in my fucking way! I don't know why you're so afraid of this weapon, but I can feel the fear on you." It was true. The taste of a Djinn's fear was a heady thing. Perhaps that was why I was feeling so bold, the intoxication of such a powerful fear. The strength that flooded my limbs washed away the exhaustion of the past few days. Ssserakis seeped its power into me, readying me for a confrontation both of us knew we could never survive. I tried to ignore the false confidence it loaned me, but my hand inched towards the snuff pouch at my belt, and my stomach growled at the thought of a Source inside.

Horralain reached the hammer and extended a hand. It hovered just before the haft. Blood still speckled the weapon, both from those it had killed, and the final moments of the last person to wield it. That same person lay dead and cold on the ground nearby, his chest collapsed inward under the force of the Djinn's magic. It served as a grisly reminder to Aerolis' promise to kill anyone who touched it.

An odd stillness settled around the amphitheatre, and I had a strange feeling the Djinn would remain trapped on Do'shan forever before it allowed anyone to touch the hammer.

You've killed him. Ssserakis' whisper felt too much like truth.

"We're not going to turn on you, Aerolis," I whispered. "I don't know why you hate the hammer so but let me use it to free you."

Horralain's hand wrapped around the hilt of Shatter.

CHAPTER EIGHT

I SOMETIMES THINK THAT ALL OF LIFE IS A series of moments, each one a balancing act upon a razor's edge, destined to fall one way or another. The outcome of those moments is irrevocable. Harsh words spoken can never be taken back, no matter how many apologies might be uttered in their wake. Time spent drinking yourself into a stupor is time spent often wasted, often squandered. As any Chronomancer will tell you, time is a finite resource. I bear the proof of that, my body and soul bearing two different ages. And life once taken cannot be given back. Again, I am somewhat of an expert on that matter. I have taken so many lives in my brief time on Ovaeris, and I would happily give most of them back if I could. Most of them. There are those I would guard jealously, even should all the lords of the Other World come to claim them from me. There are some lives I have taken who truly deserved it.

Horralain gripping the haft of Shatter was one of those moments. I could see it going either way. The outcome all came down to Aerolis. I could not say why the Djinn was so scared of the hammer, I had yet to figure out the truth of that, but there was something primal in that fear. Something that went beyond reasoning. I felt it through Ssserakis, and the horror knew it well. It was a master of fear, a creature born of it, and to it. The horror's very existence was to draw out the fear of others and feed upon it. There was no fear it did not understand intimately. Well, perhaps no fear except its own. It wasn't until possessing me that the horror came to understand that it too could feel fear.

The moment passed. Horralain survived.

"Will it work?" I asked.

For a moment the wind grew suddenly hot, like a warm breeze on a cool day, there and gone, leaving nothing but pimpled flesh in its wake. "The weapon can break anything, but Iron has absorbed much of the enchantment we worked on this mountain. His body resists magic."

"So, you don't know?" The mighty Djinn, a creature that called itself a god, and it didn't fucking know.

No answer but the whistling of the wind.

There is but one way to find out. Living metal, a monster at the heart of the city. Make it fear, Eskara. Make it fear us!

There was no easy way to go about the task. We could not kill Iron at his heart, buried deep within the mountain, instead we trekked east, towards the first of the great chains. There were four of them, giant things, each link twice as big as a house. They dwarfed the size of Ro'shan's great chain and anchor, and I suppose that was the point. The chains on Do'shan were never meant to be removed, they were to keep the flying city in place for eternity

Feral pahht watched us from windows and shadows both, so many eyes tracking me. I knew they were there even when I couldn't see them, by the fear they gave off. It was fear of me. In my rush to *save* Silva and the others, I committed slaughter. I saw many of those I killed as ghosts, and I was becoming quite adept at picking out the living from the dead. Ssserakis revelled in the fear, a joy the horror hadn't felt since being ripped away from its kingdom in Sevoari. The ferals didn't attack, I think they were too frightened to consider it, but their presence was unnerving. I swallowed down Sources as we walked and felt the rush of power in my stomach once more. The Arcstorm inside of me recharged itself from the power of the Arcmancy Source, and lightning crackled around me, intensifying the fear from the ferals.

Aerolis followed us from the sky, keeping a wary distance. The ferals looked up and bowed to the Djinn as he passed. A foolish belief in a false god. We were all guilty of it, really. I, too, once believed the Rand and Djinn to be gods, all powerful and all knowing. At least until I met a few of them. They are petty creatures of unearned power and self-gratifying delusions. They lord knowledge and wealth over those of us they deem lesser beings. They fool us into believing that we should be grateful to them, for they made the world what it is. It is all lies. The truth is, Ovaeris was here before the Rand and the Djinn, and if I ever have my way, it will be here long after they are all gone.

By the time we reached the first of the four chains tying the flying mountain the ground below, we had quite a following. Feral pahht, for the most part, curious enough to overcome their fear of me, and their awe of Aerolis. Ishtar did not accompany us. Too injured to walk, and too proud to be carried, she stayed back at our little house we were calling home. All my other friends were there, not wanting to miss out on what I was about to do. It is funny in many ways; Horralain carried the hammer and it was that giant who would also swing it, yet the act would always be attributed to me. True leaders take responsibility, not only for their own orders, and the consequences that follow, but also for unordered actions. I am responsible for more than a few atrocities committed on my behalf, despite never giving the orders. I am old enough and wise enough, these days at least, to know that I should have kept a warier eye on those under my command.

The edge was perilous and crumbling. Bits of the mountain, rocks both large and small, had long since broken away and floated there, caught in the grip of the same magic that kept the mountain afloat. Despite the erosion, there were no large satellite islands, unlike Ro'shan which had three, orbiting at varying heights and speeds. I approached the edge with caution and a will to show none of it. I have ever been good at putting on a show of bravado for an audience. Closer to the chain, I had to brush a few floating rocks and some dirt away. The first of the links erupted from the mountainside just a short way below the surface, no more than twice my own inconsiderable height. Even so, it would be impossible for Horralain to hit it from where we stood, and difficult to lower him down.

"How do we get him down?" Hardt asked, creeping close to the edge, yet keeping his weight on the back foot. "One of your portals?"

No! That thing is watching, Eskara. There is something about this place. This city. It is closer here; its attention is focused. It senses me through you, and it is curious.

I shook my head. "A portal is a bad idea. There's something watching on the other side of it."

Aerolis drew close, yet still far away from Horralain and the hammer. I felt the wind of the Djinn stirring my cloak, and others pulled their own clothes tighter. I had a Pyromancy Source inside once more, keeping me warm no matter the chill air.

"Do not engage with it, this thing on the other side," Aerolis hissed.

"Why? What do you know of it?"

"That it will tear you apart if it takes an interest." The vortex intensified. "I would suggest not attracting its eye."

The Djinn was not telling the truth, but then that didn't surprise me, and it shouldn't surprise you. I have noticed the powerful rarely tell the truth, but instead only offer up parts of it, enough to placate anyone with questions. And enough to hide true agendas behind the shadows of false truths. Secrets are a commodity. They are worth so much until they are revealed, and then they are worth nothing. I unpicked many of the Djinn's secrets before I left Do'shan. I learned the truth about them and the Rand. And I discovered why, despite all their power, the Djinn never use portals.

"Can you help us get down to the chain?" I asked Aerolis.

"No." The Djinn sounded sullen and sulky." My power is trapped here as Mezula's is trapped on Ro'shan. We are each of us prisoners in cages of the other's making."

"There must be something you can do. You are a Djinn, master of earth, metal, and stone. Your people are the wind, you are fire, you are lightning. So, stop sulking behind the walls of your cage, and help me break them."

After a few moments of blowing in my face, the Djinn's maddening turned away from me, the wind no longer pulling at my cloak. One of the nearby buildings, a squat thing of grey stone and in dire need of repair, crumbled into a thousand rocks, as though it hadn't just been worked stone. The rocks floated through the air towards us, all to the cooing purrs of the nearby ferals, then started reshaping themselves into a set of steps. The steps crashed to the ground with a thump that I felt through my feet and then slid forwards until they dropped over the edge of the mountain. I heard a clang as they hit the first link of the chain. The Djinn's whirling form turned back to me. "The rest is up to you, terran."

The steps were not wide, nor deep, and with the wind howling about us at such a height, it was treacherous footing. I went first, choosing the inelegant method of sliding down each step on my arse. Dignity is all fine and well, but the threat of a fatal drop will do wonders to cure you of such vanity. I chose the safest option to descend and Horralain copied me, Shatter held rigid in his hands.

Once my feet touched the chain, I knelt and pressed a hand to the freezing metal. I could tell no difference between that and any other metal, but then Ingomancy is not one of attunements. However, I had senses no other did, and yet I felt no fear from the chain. It seemed to me, that it was nothing but cold, lifeless iron. I stood and backed up a small step to allow Horralain past me and he grunted, his face intense with concentration I could well understand. We had, both of us, climbed the great chain at Ro'shan and neither of us wanted a reminder of such a harrowing ordeal.

I pointed at the next link in the chain. "That one. Hit it."

Horralain hefted the hammer in his hands, a look of consternation creasing his brutish features. "You don't need to be down here," he said in that slow voice of his.

I snorted and braced myself against a gust of wind that threatened to rip me free from the precarious footing. "Just get on with it, Horralain."

The big Terrelan grunted, swung Shatter up, over his head, and brought it down on the next link in the chain. He didn't swing it like a weapon at an enemy, rather like a pick at a rock. We were, all of us, forged into what we are by the Pit. It remains in us and will continue to do so long after the rest of Isha has forgotten its existence.

A large section of the link shattered into jagged shards of metal that crumbled away, falling into the void below. Do'shan trembled.

I do not idly say that the mountain shook. I do not mean a localised shudder, but more like an earthquake. Which was somewhat disconcerting given we were so high up, the ground below was a hazy image of muted colour and little else. Horralain and I both collapsed, gripping hold of the chain for our lives. I must admit, I'm quite glad the big thug had the presence of mind to keep hold of the hammer. A wave of fear washed over me, and I almost drowned in it. Ssserakis drank in as much as it could, but even the horror had limits. It was as if the mountain itself was terrified. Still the chain held. Horralain had hit it too high up and the links had not yet parted.

"Hit it again," I shouted over the roaring of both wind and mountain. Horralain turned wide eyes my way, but there must have been something in my flashing glare that convinced him not to argue. He scrambled to his feet, swung the hammer once more, and brought it down on the last of the link clinging in place.

Another section of the link shattered and fell away, and with it went the chain. I suppose I should be glad the link we were standing on was half buried in the side of the mountain. I had not the foresight to think what might happen once the tension was taken away. The mountain shook once more, fear mixed with pain turning into a scream so loud I could not tell if it were Iron's or my own. Still, I crawled to the edge of the link and watched the chain fall to the earth below. It took a long time, or perhaps it only seemed that way, and the devastation it caused look so small. But it is not. Each link as large as two houses and there were hundreds of links. Trees were crushed below the falling weight, and the earth itself was scarred. I did that. Caused it. A permanent rent in the world. Even years later, the forest is struggling to recover, to reclaim the damaged ground. Horralain and I both stood and watched until the chain came to a crashing stop. The dirt and dust thrown up into the air made for a dizzying.

Eventually I looked up to Horralain. He gripped hold of Shatter with white knuckles. I noticed then the mountain had stopped trembling, at least for now. "Three more to go," I said with a smile I didn't feel.

The following two chains went more smoothly, relatively speaking. It took a large part of the day to traverse the city to each one, and we collected more feral pahht each step of the way. They tittered and purred amongst themselves, excitement and fear in equal measure. Even they could tell something momentous was afoot. I think perhaps the trembling of the mountain scared them out from their underground dens. The weapons of war sat silent and I was thankful for it. They worshipped and obeyed the Djinn, and

Aerolis accompanying us was a vital endorsement.

The other chains were closer to the surface of the mountain and could be reached with only a careful drop over the edge. Even knowing there was a surface below, it is quite a thing to dangle one's legs over the edge of nothing and let yourself go. The incessant call of the void tugged at me, but my determination was set, and I ignored the fatalistic desire. I don't know why I felt the need to stand beside Horralain each time he swung the hammer. Perhaps it was because, even though he was swinging Shatter, it was my choice. My will. My responsibility.

I watched each chain fall to the earth so far below, and I felt the monstrous Aspect within the mountain shudder with pain and fear. Perspective is an odd thing. I saw the Aspect as a monster, a parasite of unequalled scope. A thing to fear. But Iron was not just that. The Aspect was as much a prisoner on Do'shan as the Djinn. Mezula had installed Iron and given her son purpose; to lock himself in place and the mountain with him. He could not move. Could not run. Could not hide. And the chains were as his limbs. I was shattering those chains, breaking his limbs, chopping them off. And all Iron could do was tremble. He couldn't even cry out. Iron was never a monster; he was a pawn in a game much greater than him. A victim. Mezula was the monster. And so was I.

With each broken chain, Do'shan shifted. It was not a fast shifting, but the pull of its sister city tugged at the mountain. They were designed to orbit one another, a constant whirling dance across the face of Ovaeris. By the time we came to the final chain, it was pulled taught, the city straining to be free and join in with its sister's dance.

In the light of the day, I could see something on the

horizon, a small dark blur against the blue sky, fuzzy to my sight. It was our surviving flyer; a wooden ship kept aloft by some contraption with propellers, powered by a Kinemancy Source. Our larger flyer had been shot down by the feral pahht and the weapons the Djinn made for them, but I felt some hope at seeing the smaller vessel still flying nearby even after days without contact. If we could bring it in, at least we would have a way down to the ground. It had not escaped my notice that the moment I broke the final chain, we were stranded on Do'shan.

"Your kind are everywhere these days," the Djinn said. Aerolis was floating above us, its form a grey blur of movement against the blue sky. "There is another Aspect on that ship."

"What do they look like?" I asked.

The Djinn laughed, hissing wind. "She looks angry."

Hardt groaned beside me. "Coby?"

I nodded. "She probably hid on board as the operator without us ever knowing. A spy to report back to Mezula."

"Could we shoot her down?" Imiko asked, her voice more timid than I was used to from her. "Like they did to our larger flyer."

"No." I only breathed the word, but I meant it. I'm not sure if it was mercy that made the decision, or guilt. Silva's blood was on my hands, no matter what Hardt or anyone else said. She wouldn't want me to kill her sister. Despite all the friction between them, Silva always loved Coby no matter what. "Let her go. The Rand will hear about this one way or another. I'd rather not kill any more of her children if possible."

Hardt's big hand landed on my shoulder with a firm squeeze. I didn't need to look to know he'd be smiling. He was always proud of me when I chose against violence. None of us realised what that decision would mean. How it would come back on us. A part of me wishes I had at least tried to end it there. Mercy is almost always the harder choice, with the more dire of consequences.

"Horralain." I pointed to the chain. The link was almost level with the ground, there would be no climbing needed to reach this one.

I have known people, leaders and those in positions of power, to make grand speeches to those nearby whenever an event of some importance is taking place. They spout eloquent words and phrases designed to inspire emotion, anger or pride most often, designed to take hold of a crowd and spur them on to action. Without direction and purpose, and often even with, that action leads to violence. Cities have fallen on the word of some fool with a loud voice and an audience. I am not one of those people. When I speak it is with purpose and intent rather than volume. I leave grandiose speeches to those with a better vocabulary and looser morals. Besides, any speech I gave at the breaking of Do'shan's chains would have been for my friends' ears only, and they would have known the words for as empty as the hole Silva's death had left in me.

No words uttered at the final chain. Only a grunt as Horralain hefted the hammer, the squeal of shattering metal, and then a scream so loud it shook the foundations of the mountain.

I don't know if Iron died that day. I like to think the Aspect still lives inside the core of Do'shan, but then maybe such a hope is cruelty. Perhaps it would be kinder for him to have died, rather than remain locked inside his enemy's stronghold. A prisoner with no hope of escape or rescue.

His life's purpose, to lock Do'shan in place, was taken from him. Then again, maybe if he does still live, I gave him the freedom to see the world from up high. Either way, the mountain shook, and his scream of pain was so loud the feral pahht scattered, hands clutched to their ears.

Do'shan started to move. It was a slow thing, but then both flying cities move slowly. As the broken chain fell away to wreak gravity's damage on the ground below, I felt that familiar lurch under my feet as the mountain moved free of its terrestrial shackles. The wind gave a freezing gust of joy, and then Aerolis faded away with a laugh. Where he went, I don't know, but the Djinn was still bound to Do'shan, unable to leave. Still, I had given him a measure of freedom. You might think he would be grateful, but Djinn are creatures of deals and terms, and Aerolis counted it as a debt paid for freeing Ishtar. I'm not sure the two are really comparable, but I'm still glad I paid it. Ishtar deserved that much from me and more besides.

The flyer didn't move, even as Do'shan sailed away from it. Coby watched us go. Part of me wanted to show her a rude gesture, certain she would somehow see it. A younger me probably would have. But I was older and not nearly as rash. And I had so recently murdered her sister. I decided she was welcome to her anger and hatred.

CHAPTER NINE

THE WEEKS FOLLOWING MY FREEING OF
Do'shan were not easy for any of us. I did my best to ease
Imiko's melancholy, but we quickly ran out of booze and
I had no other ideas of how to drown grief. Of course, I
didn't really understand; Imiko did not so much grieve for a
person, but for a loss of innocence. I turned the poor girl into
a murderer, and it was something she never quite managed
to reconcile, regardless of how good she is at it. Ishtar's
irrepressible cheers returned as she regained some of her
mobility. I think I helped with the cheer, at least. My sword
training continued, despite a sprained ankle and broken ribs,
and I often made her laugh by overbalancing and ending up
on my arse. She even figured out a way to join in, hobbling
along with a crutch in one hand and a sword in the other.
I learned a valuable lesson from my sword tutor in those
weeks: Ishtar will always be better than me with a blade.

Even barely able to move, she still bested me every time.
Also, being smacked across the head with a crutch hurts.

We saw Aerolis from time to time, but the Djinn
spared us little attention. He was busy rebuilding Do'shan,
turning the ruins into a more hospitable city, building new
fortifications and repositioning weapons of war. It was
easy to understand. Aerolis expected retribution. He knew
Mezula would not simply accept Do'shan's newfound
freedom. There was a new battle coming, and the Djinn
intended to be ready. I did not forget that he had agreed to
teach me the hidden secrets of Sourcery, but I gave him time.
I gave myself time, as well.

My ghosts followed me everywhere. Nobody else
could see them, not even Ssserakis, but they belonged to no
one else. Before Do'shan, they had only ever appeared to
me one at a time, but up on that city they crowded around
in their dozens. Many of them were feral pahht. I had killed
so many of them, but the woodsmen from the Forest of Ten
made an appearance, and even a few of the terran soldiers,
though I had not killed any of them with my own hands.
Isen was gone, and I admit I felt an odd loss at that. I think
I missed him, even if he was just a faded apparition of his
former self.

By day, I trained, not willing to let my body soften
from inactivity. Blade work some days, unarmed sparring
on others, and all the while I held my Sources inside, their
power ever at my call. But at night, I belonged to the Other
World, Sevoari. Ssserakis maintained it was my own power
that drew us there, perhaps an effect of the Iron Legion's
experimentation. Apparently, I had absorbed some of the
magic from an Impomancy Source. It was not enough to
bring monsters across, but it allowed us to visit Ssserakis'

home. I think the horror was grateful for that, not that it would have ever admitted to it.

As always, the Other World was dark, yet also strangely light. No sun, stars, or moons grace the sky, yet the world is lit in an odd assortment of greys and browns. Light with no source. The Djinn made a true marvel when they created that world.

It was my power that drew us to Sevoari, but Ssserakis was the guide. The horror showed me things that no Impomancer had ever known about. It is an odd school of Sourcery, quite poorly understood even in my time. Impomancers project an immaterial spirit into the Other World, able to drift about, yet not interact. But when an Impomancer touches a creature from that world, they act as a conduit, bringing it across the space between worlds, allowing it to manifest in Ovaeris. It is not a pleasant process for either Sourcerer, or the creature brought across. And some of the inhabitants resist. Ssserakis resisted when the Iron Legion brought it across. Even in its own world, the ancient horror was not strong enough to resist Loran Orran. None of us were.

I woke in the Other World, yet there was not light. Not even the soft grey luminescence. I awoke to darkness, yet I knew I was there. Sevoari feels different, almost as though there is a constant pressure trying to compact me while I am there. It feels odd, but also somehow right, like being wrapped in a tight embrace by a loved one. There is a strange comfort and security to the tightness.

"I can't see anything." I raised a hand and waved it in front of my face. When an Impomancer projects themselves into the Other World, they have no body, no real form at all, just a presence. But it was different when I appeared there in

my dreams. We were there, Ssserakis and I, able to interact
with the world and its people, but we were also not there.
In those times, I existed both in Ovaeris and Sevoari at once,
and not as a formless spirit, but as a terran. It's fair to say
I was out of place and stood out. I did not belong in that
world. I dread to think what might have happened had I not
had Ssserakis there to protect and guide me.

Stop using your eyes and use mine.

"You don't have eyes. Do you?"

No. I could feel the horror's amusement. I might
have laughed had it not been for the pitch black and the
odd scraping noise that seemed to be growing louder by the
moment.

I blinked, and when I opened my eyes again, I found I
could see through Ssserakis' unique night sight. The ancient
horror was a creature of fear and cold and darkness, so it
was no surprise that darkness held no secrets from it. The
world around me appeared in sharp detail, but without any
colour. At first, I believed that to be just another part of the
location—we were deep underground—but I know better
now. Ssserakis could not see colour. The ancient horror
viewed the worlds only in terms of light and darkness. I
think that was what hurt Ssserakis so about Ovaeris. It was
not the light or brightness as the horror claimed, but rather
it was the inability to comprehend colour that caused it so
much pain.

We were in a tunnel, like those I used to dig down
in the Pit, but much larger. It would have taken four of me
to reach the tunnel roof, and twice that many to reach from
one side to the other. All along the tunnel floor were little
grooves of moulded stone, as though tiny rivers regularly
ran through the tunnel, carving the rock into miniature

valleys. The rock walls were jagged and uneven, as though mined by dozens of different people, each with their own ideas of how wide the tunnel should be. I could see two more tunnels branching off on my left side, disappearing at an angle, at least one of them sloping downward. To my right was nothing but rock. And over it all I heard the scratching sound, still growing louder, or perhaps just more intense. There was something underneath that too, an echo that pulsed like placing your hands over your ears and listening to nothing but your own heartbeat.

"Where are we?" My voice sounded loud and foreign down there in the tunnel. A place no terran had ever seen before. I have ever been a pioneer in my studies of Sevoari. The first to bring an Abomination across. The first to actually step foot into the Other World. The first terran to raise an army there.

Close to home. On the border of Norvet Meruun's territory. She is closer than she should be.

I knew the name, Ssserakis had uttered it once before. "Norvet Meruun. One of the lords of Sevoari?"

The beating heart. The creeping doom. One of the nine, yes, but unlike any of the others. Norvet Meruun is the death of my world made manifest in putrid flesh. She worms her way through Sevoari, devouring all. Growing ever larger. I, alone, held her at bay. As much as I could.

The mother of Abominations, Norvet Meruun. I had brought an Abomination across once, many years ago, my very first time summoning a creature from the Other World. I thought it a small thing, slug-like, and no larger than a cat. I couldn't have known the truth, no other Sourcerer had ever seen one of the monsters before. It stole the Source from my stomach as I brought it across, severing the connection between us and my hold over it. If I close my eyes, I can still taste the grey, pulsing flesh of it. Like maggoty meat, writhing and unnatural. Fucking disgusting. As soon as the creature was out of me, it began to grow. Flesh expanded and tentacles grew in every direction. It flattened a building and killed six people before the tutors of the academy brought it down. The Abomination was put on the banned list after that, a warning circulated to all corners of Ovaeris, and, as far as I am aware, it is one warning that has been heeded by everyone. Even me. The Abomination I brought across was small, perhaps still young. Norvet Meruun was anything but small.

"What is that noise?" I asked my passenger. The scratching was a continuous thing, growing more and more persistent. I couldn't tell if it was close or far away with the echoing natures of the tunnel.

Even Norvet Meruun has minions, Eskara. All creatures of power draw those without the wit to take their own.

I looked around for Ssserakis. The horror usually manifested in some way when we visited Sevoari, but it remained tight inside this time. Perhaps because I had no shadow down in the dark, with no light to cast it. As I searched for the horror, I saw movement down the tunnel. A blur of grey legs and screaming mouths, frighteningly terran. Whatever the thing was, it noticed me somehow and turned my way. It was at least twice as tall as I and had a tube-like body, segmented all along its length. At the middle of each segment, long thin legs stretched up then pivoted sharply down on a joint. On each joint was a terran face, frozen in a moment of pain or fear. As the creature turned towards me and came on at a rush, I noticed it had no face itself, no real head at all. On its front-most segment there was just a mouth, an opening with huge blocky teeth jutting forwards. The monster rushed toward me, teeth gnashing, feet scratching at the stone beneath, and terran faces drooling some sort of viscous grey matter as they screamed in silence.

While in that state, somehow both in Ovaeris and Sevoari, I could not draw on the Sources I held in my stomach. I had no magic to fight this monster, and no weapons to wield against it. In the Other World, I was as helpless as a babe.

"Ssserakis?" The horror inside didn't answer, and the segmented monster continued to bear down on me. I took a step back, almost falling as I tripped on one of the ridges of stone that lined the floor. Then I planted my feet, faced the monster and shouted. "STOP!"

A well-intoned command can do a lot. Some creatures, and some people, are given to following commands regardless of the source. They respect the authority, whether real or implied, and react accordingly. I had authority in my tone, an iron will and the casual expectation that my orders would be obeyed. It was not something I gained from my time in the Orran military, I had an honorary rank, but that only extended as far as the soldiers assigned to protect me, and even then, they would ignore my orders if my life was in danger. My authority came from Hardt and Tamura and all the others who followed me, expecting me to lead. The truth is, I had become accustomed to being in charge, and that became apparent in both the way I held myself, and the tone of my voice. That being said, regardless of any inherent command in my voice, I was still quite surprised when the monster slowed to a stop a mere arm's length away from crushing me.

Up close the creature was even more hideous. It resembled a spider, or perhaps a dozen spiders stuck together. Its gnashing teeth were grinding up rock, cracking it apart, and the faces on its legs weren't just screaming, they were chewing also, mixing the rock with sticky saliva and then letting it drool over their chins in thin streams to the ground below. It towered over me, and I would be lying if I said I wasn't trembling at being so close to such a thing.

Ssserakis laughed inside. *I can feel your fear, Eskara. It tastes…*

"Just like your own!" I hissed the words through a clenched jaw, but the truth of it was plain for both of us to see. I could taste my fear as well, more of a feeling than an actual taste, really, but it carried a unique flavour. It was the same flavour of fear I felt when Ssserakis was being picked apart by the monster beyond the portal. I wondered at what that meant, that we were both so similar.

The monster in front of me kept chewing on the rocks in its mouth, grinding them up until they were nothing but dust. Then it turned its head and gouged a section out of the nearby tunnel wall. Still it stood in front of me, as though waiting for orders.

I stepped aside, pressing myself against the wall of the tunnel so I was out of its way. "Go." And the monster did. Without hesitation, it started forward, legs scraping across the ground, mouths chewing, screaming, and drooling. I watched it go, segment after segment after segment. It had close to twenty, each one with two spindly legs.

"What was that thing?" I asked once it had vanished into the gloom beyond the range of Ssserakis' night sight.

They dig, endlessly. It is their purpose, their sustenance, and their orders. Norvet Meruun is ever growing, worming her way through the tunnels and caverns of my world, but she cannot chew through solid rock. She fills the spaces her minions leave behind. I used to hunt them. It was the easiest way to stop her expansion.

I have since made a study of the digging monsters of the Other World, and my personal copy of the Encyclopaedia Otheria contains a whole chapter dedicated to the segmented creatures. I call them Geolids. They grow slowly, a single segment taking many years to form, and the legs even longer. Their only sustenance comes from the rock they consume, and it makes their carapace as hard as stone. For this reason, I have found it is best to go for the fleshy gaps in between segments when hunting the monsters. Waste rock is trailed behind their passage from the faces on each leg, it drips like sludge and quickly hardens to a substance even sturdier than the rock it once was. That is where all the ridges on the floor of those tunnels come from, rock paste drooled from a hundred passing Geolids. Perhaps the strangest thing about the creatures is that no two faces are ever the same. They are not, as you might assume, featureless masks. Each one is different and distinct. And the more you stare at those faces, the more of them you begin to recognise. Sevoari truly is a world of our nightmares made manifest.

"Why did it listen to me?" I truly doubted it was my order that stopped the Geolid. After all, there was little chance it spoke the terran language.

It didn't. It heard me in your voice. It may be one of Norvet Meruun's minions, but all creatures of Sevoari recognise my power. I am fear.

That was a lesson I learned and took to heart. The

monsters of the Other World could sense Ssserakis within
me. The imps, down in the ruined Djinn city, had recognised
the horror before I knew what I carried inside. They had
supplicated themselves to a power they understood, to a
lord they knew to serve. Command and control, without
the use of an Impomancy Source. The foundation of a plan
formed, whispers of power I could take for myself. There are
two ways to form a kingdom from within another. The first
is sedition, undermining the current regime and syphoning
their power away, all while adhering to whatever laws are
governing the general populace. The second is rebellion, a
military force operating within the boundaries of state. I was
never one for subtlety.

*That was not what I brought you here to show you, Eskara.
Follow the heartbeat.*

I was lost in my own thoughts, considering
possibilities and implications. That was why I didn't resist
or ask why, or even where Ssserakis was directing us. Part
of it was trust, I think. The ancient horror loved to cause
fear, both mine and others, but I also believed it wouldn't
harm me, or allow harm to come to me. We were, the two of
us, linked. For my part, I admitted I didn't want any harm
to befall Ssserakis. It wasn't fear for my own safety that
stopped me from opening any more portals, but fear for the
horror's.

I cannot tell you how long I wandered those tunnels.
Lost in my own thoughts, time passed quickly. My visits
to the Other World were dreamlike, even if they were not
truly dreams, time passed strangely while we were there.
Sometimes it would feel like only minutes had passed and
I would wake to find half the morning gone. Other times it
would feel like we travelled Sevoari for hours and I would

wake to find I had dozed off and barely minutes had gone
by. One thing I will say I was glad of; I no longer woke
screaming with every visit. I'm sure the others were even
more glad of that. But I wondered what it meant for me,
that the nightmares no longer scared me. In fact, I welcomed
them. I looked forward to them. Sevoari was starting to feel
like a second home to me, and I no longer had a first home.
It is hard to admit, but at times I was more comfortable there
than in my own world. Maybe that was another consequence
of my growing bond with Ssserakis, that I felt the horror's
pangs of homesickness. I think, perhaps, there is a different
explanation. I have always been drawn to the Other World.
I have always been drawn to the nightmares and the fear.
I have always felt, even just a little, that I belong there
amongst the monsters. But I don't. No terran belongs there.

It was something of a surprise when I rounded a
corner of the tunnel and came face to flesh with Norvet
Meruun. So absorbed had I been in my own thoughts,
I hadn't heard the heartbeat growing stronger, louder. I
hadn't noticed the air changing, growing more humid. The
low pulsing glow had gone unseen, until now. How best to
describe such an entity? In the darkness of the tunnel, and
with Ssserakis' colourless sight, it looked like a quivering
mass of flesh. I know now that it glows with a soft red
hue, like blood just beneath paper-thin skin. With each
heartbeat, each pulse, the flesh crept a little further along the
tunnel. Not much, and the heartbeat was slow and regular.
I estimated it moved no more than a handspan every hour,
but its progress is unrelenting, and it was growing down
more than just the tunnel I stood in.

"What?" I struggled to find the words as a wall of
writhing flesh blocked the tunnel ahead of me. Thin, rubbery

tentacles poked free of the mass, slapping against the rock walls with a sodden smack, then rubbing along the jagged ridges of it. The creature was slowly feeling its way forward.

Norvet Meruun. The beating heart. The creeping doom. The eventual, unavoidable death of Sevoari. This is my enemy, Eskara, just as you have yours.

A spreading tumour growing through the world, unseen beneath the surface. Or at least, unseen by any Sourcerers. Ssserakis saw it. The ancient horror had been at war with Norvet Meruun for as long as the Other World had existed. They were two creatures plucked from the nightmares of my world, given form by the Rand, and left to fight an eternal war against each other. There was a perverse symmetry in that.

This is why I must return to my world, Eskara. You see only the smallest part of this monster. It is everywhere, worming its way through my home. It devours everything it touches and spreads forever outward.

I remembered the Abomination I once summoned. The way it grew, absorbing things to add to its mass. It didn't care what it touched; everything was dragged into its flesh. Six people died that day, due to that monster. Absorbed by it. Into it.

"Does it have a heart you can strike at? Kill it at the source."

She is not a creature as you understand them to be. It is a mass with no beginning, middle, or end. All I could ever do was push her back with fear, carve bits of it off with shadow, freeze its progress. All I ever managed was to delay her, slow her down. Without me she moves unchecked.

"What about the other lords of Sevoari?" I took a step back as the fleshy mass pulsed and grew just slightly. I still wasn't sure if I could be hurt or killed while we visited the Other World, but it was the sort of thing I didn't really like the idea of testing.

Ssserakis laughed bitterly. *Hyrenaak can do nothing from the sky but watch as the world is devoured. Even if the serpent wanted to help, it is unable to touch the ground and Norvet Meruun grows beneath the surface. Brakunus is too scared and too stupid, as all ghouls are. Kekran is unable to help. As powerful as he is, Norvet Meruun would simply consume him. Aire and Dialos are too busy bickering amongst their many selves to see any danger beyond the other. Flowne fights back as well as she is able, but even her power can barely keep her territory safe from the constant advancement of flesh. And Lodoss doesn't care. I believe he would welcome the oblivion if it would end his torment, but he is beyond death. This is why I need to return, Eskara. It is not just the abrasive nature of your world. My home is in danger.*

I stepped back again as the heartbeat pulsed and Norvet Meruun crept forward. Fleshy tentacles waved out ahead of me, as though reaching to find me. I didn't like the idea of what might happen if they did. "I will send you back, Ssserakis. Once I am done."

You promised.

"And you said we are stuck together until I die. Well, I refuse to die until my enemies have paid their price. The Terrelan Emperor must pay. The Iron Legion must pay."

Ssserakis was silent, but I could feel the horror considering my words. *On that last we agree.*

I left something unspoken, a part of the truth that I knew Ssserakis would not understand. It was not just about making the Iron Legion pay for what he had done to us. I had to save Josef. I just couldn't leave my friend to die a second time.

CHAPTER
TEN

I WOULD NEVER ATTEMPT TO TAKE ANYTHING from Josef's ordeal. Even before we separated, before I pushed him away, down in the Pit, he had his own struggles. I refused to see it back then. I couldn't see past my own misery. When drowning in pain and hardship, it becomes easy to view it only from one point. To become so insular, that you fail to realise that others are struggling in different ways with different demons. This is especially true for the young. Down in the Pit, Josef was terrified, not just for himself but also for me. We were both brutalised, beaten by petty thugs for no reason other than to break us. We were both tortured by the Overseer, only Josef's torture was often more physical than mine. One thing I must give the Overseer, the man knew how to break Josef. And he did. I'd like to say I don't blame him for that. That it wasn't his fault, and anyone would have broken. But I didn't. Not quite.

Age has tempered my fury somewhat, and though I do still blame him, I have also forgiven him.

But as I have said, his ordeal was far from over. I cannot say if his suffering at the hands of the Iron Legion was worse than my own. The things I went through made the Pit look like an easy summer nap. But Josef was kind at heart. He could be brutal and merciless when it was needed, but he was always kind. He never wanted the deaths on his hands. Maybe that is where we are so different, he and I. He was *forced* to take lives.

This is one of Josef's memories.

"Do you know how much a life is worth?" Loran said. Josef hates the sound of the man's voice almost as much as he loves it.

Josef shrugs. He's already tried to find a way out. Tried and failed. He's stuck there. Trapped. Alone save for prisoners and the mad man who keeps them. The walls bow first outward and then in again, just like they had in the ruined city next to the Pit. He's travelled down every hallway and investigated every room, but there's no way out. The Iron Legion has used Geomancy to seal them in.

"I asked you a question, Yenhelm," Loran snaps. Josef shoots him a hateful glance. Loran is busy at his desk, grinding something in a small clay mortar. There's a sharp, tangy smell on the air, like vinegar left out for too long.

Josef looks away before Loran can see the hate in his eyes. Best not to anger him. Just like back in the Pit, it's best to keep his head down, try not to be noticed. "I didn't realise you expected an answer. You already know I don't have one."

"It is rude to ignore a person. Especially when they are trying to educate you." Josef didn't ask to be educated. He doesn't want to be educated. Loran doesn't care.

"A life is priceless," Josef says. How could anyone put a price, a value on life? He paces back and forth, stealing glances at the desk over Loran's shoulder. There's little else in the dark room except for a few sputtering torches and endless bookcases. "It is impossible to judge its worth, because it is subjective. Your life means nothing to most of the people of Ovaeris, yet you place a price beyond all others upon it. The life of an abban is worth a fortune to a farmer, even more to a starving man, but nothing to a king."

"I didn't ask you for philosophy, Yenhelm. I asked you for mathematics. I followed your progress at the academy, and I know you excelled with both letters and numbers. And your Biomantic knowledge outstrips almost any but my own. So, I ask you again. Do you know how much a life is worth?" Loran glances over his shoulder and there's a hard light to his eyes. An implied threat told with only a brief glance. Josef shivers and looks away.

He draws in a deep breath and lets it out as a sigh. "Thirteen." A flippant answer. That will just make Loran angry. He shouldn't have said it.

"The correct answer, Yenhelm, is *no*. You cannot possibly know the worth of a life as you have not done the calculations." Loran grinds the pestle angrily into the mortar.

Josef looks inside himself for the hundredth time since being taken from Do'shan. He can feel the Biomancy inside, something powerful and innate. It is a school of magic that is most often used to heal, repair the body and grant new energy to the patient. But there is a darker side to Biomancy. Just as it can be used to heal, it can also be used to harm. Flesh can be convinced to become wounded. Seeds of decay and rot can be planted. Disease can be nurtured into bloom. Loran's back is turned. Josef reaches out, his fingers just a whisper away. He tries to bring his innate Biomancy to bear, to force its power to harm, to unmake. But it slips away from him, resisting his commands. He can't control it, not like when he has a Source inside.

"As a Biomancer, committed to the science of healing, it surprises me you are not more interested in the mathematics, Yenhelm." The Iron Legion continues, heedless of Josef's attempt to end him. He hates this man. For everything he has done, and everything he is trying to do, Josef hates Loran.

A glass bottle lies nearby. And empty wine bottle long since drained. Loran drinks heavily some days, though never shares why. Josef wraps his fingers around the neck of the bottle, tests its weight. Is it heavy enough to kill? He doesn't know. He's never hit anyone before. He creeps forward, arm raised, hands trembling.

"For instance, how much is a life worth in terms of raw materials? How much is a life worth in terms of vigour or spirit? What about potential? All of these are pertinent questions that need answering for the advancement of the science. Until now, no one had the necessary combination of skill and will."

Josef hesitates. Can he really do it? Can he really kill a man like this? In brute force and blood. To save his life. To save all the lives of those trapped in cages. One strike might not be enough. What if the bottle breaks? Then he could stab Loran with it.

"But then of course there is more to it," Loran continues, still working away at his desk, standing with his back to Josef. "For instance, have you considered that the life of a terran may not be equal to the life of…"

Josef strikes.

The bottle shatters in Josef's hand as it connects against an invisible kinetic shield that Josef didn't even know was possible. He sags back, shards of glass falling to the floor and others left jutting from his hand. He stares at the glass in his hand. There's no pain. Then there is! Josef grits his teeth and clutches at his wrist, hissing at the molten agony piercing his hand.

"I'm disappointed, Yenhelm," Loran says without turning around. "But not surprised. I had hoped you would see the importance of what I am trying to do and help me willingly." The Iron Legion turns and there are hard, unyielding lines to his ancient face. "But then willing cooperation can be coerced."

With a snap of his fingers, the Iron Legion opens a portal. He thrusts a hand into the portal and pulls a man through. The portal snaps shut behind him. The man is dirty and thin as a pole, too old to work and too weak to defend himself. He snivelled in the Iron Legion's gnarled grip, shaking with fear. The Iron Legion gripped the trembling man by the shoulder, holding him before Josef.

"What are you doing?" Josef asks. His hand was agony, but he could already see some of the lacerations healing as his innate Biomancy repaired the damage. He'd never seen such powerful healing.

The Iron Legion squeezes the man's shoulder and he sags against the pain. There is an indomitable strength to Loran Orran. Josef trembles; how could he have hope to hurt this titan? "What is your name?" The Iron Legion asks.

"Shen Omeron." The withered man's voice trembles

as much as his body.

Loran squeezes a little tighter and the man whimpers at the pain in his shoulder. "Tell us about yourself, Shen."

"I have a family!" Shen blurts the words as though they might form some sort of shield around him. Nobody wants to kill a family man. Nobody wants to orphan children or widow a wife. Josef wills the Iron Legion to let the man go. To set him free to return to his family.

"What is this?" Josef asks. He can hear the panic bleeding into his own voice.

The Iron Legion holds Josef's gaze with his own bright stare. And then his hand begins to glow, a soft white light at first, turning to a blinding brilliance. Shen sags, his legs go limp and his trembling ceases. Only the iron grip of Loran Orran keeps the man upright as the last vestiges of colour drain from his dirt-stained face. When the glow subsides, the Iron Legion releases his grip. Shen's withered corpse falls to the floor. There's no life left in that body, not even flicker. Not even a ghost.

Loran Orran wipes his hand on his robe, staining the grey a little darker, then turns back to his desk and continues grinding ingredients in the mortar. "Do you know what I did there, Yenhelm?"

"That was Biomancy," Josef says. He knows it's true. Somehow he knows it. But it's like nothing he's ever seen before. It's a perversion, a horrific twisting of a power that is meant to heal, not harm. "You used it to take instead of give. How?"

The Iron Legion nods, a smile stretches his wrinkled jowls. "I have hundreds of prisoners just like Shen. You have seen only the smallest fraction of my laboratory. Below, I have dungeons that are full. They are not guilty. Not criminals. None of them deserve to die. But they will. Every time you disobey me, I will kill one of them. If you attempt to harm me again, I will kill ten. Their lives mean nothing in the grander scheme of things. The world is broken, Yenhelm, and if I must murder half of the people in it to fix it, so be it."

"You're a fucking monster!" Josef whispers. He can't say it any louder, the words barely forced past his terror. He can't take his eyes from the crumpled form of Shen. His family will never see him again, they won't even know if he's alive or dead.

"A worthless moniker. I am what the world needs." He holds the mortar out. "Drink this."

"What is it?" Josef asks, his voice small. A thick grey paste sits in the depression of the bowl and it smells like swamp water.

"Does it matter? You will drink it whether you want to or not."

Josef snatches the mortar away and raised it to his lips. He doesn't want to drink it. He's certain nothing good can come of it, but he can't be responsible for another innocent death. He won't allow the Iron Legion to murder anyone else to coerce him. The smell makes him gag and the taste is beyond vile, but he forces it down. The discomfort is worth the life he would save by obeying. When he's done, a wave of dizziness washes over him and takes something away. He's not quite sure what it is that is taken from him, but the body at his feet no longer seems to matter. He can't even recall why he ever cared.

"There." The Iron Legion smiles that grandfatherly smile of his. "That will make you more pliable. Sweet Silence is a chore to make and expensive too, but it will be worth it. My threat of violence to others might keep you from attempting to escape or do me more harm, but I feel you would resist what I need to teach you."

Josef can feel himself swaying, the world moving gently. "W-h-h-a-t?" The words come out slow, heavy. He struggles to form them, trying to remember how to speak. It doesn't matter. Why did it ever matter? So much easier to just relax into the fog.

The Iron Legion smiles again. "I need you to learn to do this." He gestures at the body. The corpse had a name once. What was it? It doesn't matter. It never mattered. "I need you to learn exactly what a life is worth."

Josef's ordeal was far from over. For even as I sought to turn myself into a monster, he was made one against his will.

CHAPTER ELEVEN

WEEKS AFTER THE FREEING OF DO'SHAN, THE city was barely recognisable from the ruined fortress we had first encountered. Aerolis had raw material to spare and a vision to see his city magnificent once more. Freedom, at least a pretence of it, did wonders to improve his attitude. Dilapidated homes rose up, correcting themselves. Those buildings too far gone to save were torn down, the stone being used to erect new structures. Great walls rose up at the edges of the city, just a short walk from the edge of the mountain, and the surviving weapons of war were relocated to those walls.

I woke one day to a great rumbling, as though the mountain were shaking once again, and for a moment I thought Iron had survived. I thought the Aspect was angry enough to shake the mountain apart. But it was Aerolis. The great amphitheatre collapsed in on itself, rock and mortar

and sand ripped apart. From the wreckage grew a tower.
I say it grew, because I have no other way to describe it.
To those of us who stopped to watch, the tower seemed to
build itself, brick by brick, level by level. Nearby buildings
were cannibalised as well, regardless of whether they had
occupants. It grew so tall, I had to tilt my head back to
watch its rise continue. It was a grand thing, there was no
mistaking that. With walls as thick as Hardt is wide, and a
circumference that took a full hour to walk around, it is a
sturdy structure. The very pinnacle of Do'shan. Once the
ground stopped shaking, we knew it was finally built. We
stood silent, in a sort of reverence, I suppose. It is hard not
to feel wonder at a structure so monolithic, built in only a
morning.

We thought Aerolis was done then. A magnificent
tower, no doubt, but just a tower all the same. A spire jutting
up in the middle of the city, a palace for a creature that
thought itself a god. The Rand and Djinn are not altogether
dissimilar. But atop the very pinnacle of that tower, four
horns grew from the rock, curving inward from the edges
of the tower and meeting at a single point. Light blossomed
at that point, brighter and brighter still. Ssserakis cowered
inside of me. The horror had become used to the daylight of
our world and found more than enough dark places within
me to hide. But the light that shone forth from the tip of
the spire was something else. So bright it hurt to look at. I
had to shield my eyes from its glare, and even then, I felt as
though that light was shining down on me and me alone,
scorching the darkness from me. And then it was gone. The
light moved. More accurately, I suppose, it turned. Like a
lighthouse, shining its brilliance around a full circular circuit,
so does the light atop Do'shan turn. Of course, that's not all

it does. Aerolis built a weapon unlike anything the world had ever seen atop that tower.

The ferals swarmed. You would think that such radical restructuring of their home would cause fear, but that was not the case. They worshipped Aerolis as a god and placed in him all the faith and belief that such a position demands. They did not fear what their god did to their city, because they trusted him. I would like to say that it was their simple minds that allowed them to believe, but even the most intelligent of us is subject to belief. I believe. Not in the Rand or Djinn, and not even in that thing that watches us all through the torn sky out in the Polasian desert. I believe in myself. Perhaps that makes me conceited. So be it. Even if the whole world arrayed itself against me, I would believe in myself and struggle on. That is not to say my mind and opinion cannot be changed, but that I will not blindly line up behind the masses. People can be wrong. The beliefs of an entire world can be wrong. Widely accepted *facts* can be wrong. Vainfold taught me that. The Djinn proved it, too. Or maybe I did. It was a widely accepted fact that the Djinn were dead. At least until I freed Do'shan. It was also a widely accepted fact that the Rand and Djinn were gods. They are bloody well not. I know what the Rand and Djinn are, what they really are. I know where they come from and why.

But I'm getting ahead of myself.

For a full week, day and night, Aerolis reshaped his city. The tower and its shining beacon were the last of it. When the Djinn was done, we stood in a city as grand as any I had ever seen. Though it did not have a grand population to go along with the aesthetics. Other than myself and my little band of friends, the only inhabitants were the ferals.

There were many of them, but they still crowded in the caverns underneath the city. For the most part, the buildings went unoccupied, the warehouses unstocked. As attractive as the Djinn had made its city, there was simply no one to live in it. It was still dead. And with no chain to climb, and no flyers to visit the land, we were unlikely to pick up any more passengers. More than that, Ro'shan was a vibrant paradise of a city with a lake and a forest. Do'shan was a cold, barren place. And we would all die up there soon if we could not secure new supplies. Food was running short. Before me, the ferals had run the chains, making frequent foraging trips to the land below. That was no longer possible. Aerolis' people were starving right along with us. Yet I had more important things on mind. Importance is a relative concept.

"Aerolis!" I was standing at the foot of the tower he had built. For all its grandeur, the tower had one glaring oversight. The Djinn had not given it a door. There seemed to be no way into the structure at all.

Ssserakis laughed, a harsh sound like glass shattering. But the horror was not mocking me. There was respect underneath its chuckle. *You never learn, Eskara. Creatures like the Djinn need impudent fools like you.*

"I can't tell if that was an insult or a compliment."

If you can't see a compliment, then it likely never existed. I grinned at that.

"You owe me, Aerolis. Show yourself." So many people counselled caution to me. Hardt, Tamura, even Ishtar said I should step carefully where the Djinn was concerned. Fuck that! Caution has its place, right at the back of the line waiting for whatever handouts it can get. The Rand and the Djinn were used to caution from us. But Ssserakis was right;

what they really needed was a bold kick in their bloody arses.

A fire burst to life nearby, small flames but growing greater and hotter by the moment. They started to twirl, forming into a spinning vortex. For a moment, more than one, actually, I thought Vainfold was free. I thought the Djinn had somehow escaped its prison inside the crown and had come for me. Its threat to remember me weighed heavily when I thought about it. My shadow rippled beneath me as Ssserakis made ready to defend us both. The horror was growing stronger by the day. More than that, since I had accepted it as a part of my shadow, it found the manipulation easier. We practised, when alone, and it no longer drained the horror of energy quite so swiftly.

"I have told you about…"

"You owe me!" I cut the Djinn off mid-tirade. I knew what it would say, admonish me for daring to summon it. Impotent threats were all Aerolis could throw at me and we both knew it. The Djinn would suffer my impudence as long as I remained useful to it, and I had already proved my use more than once. Besides, I wasn't lying. The Djinn owed me, and I wasn't about to let that debt go unpaid considering the price.

"I decide when to pay my debts, terran. Not you." The fire was hot, but I carried a Pyromancy Source in my stomach and the heat didn't reach my skin.

"No!" I hissed the word and took a step closer to the flames. It was uncomfortable, but then comfort has always been an alien concept to me. I wasn't sure where to focus my gaze, the Djinn had no face, so I just stared into the fire with my flashing icy blues. Not many people can weather the intensity of my stare, but then Aerolis is not many people. "I will not sit by and wait. You are immortal, Aerolis. My life will pass in a blink to you."

The flames swirled in front of me for a while and the Djinn said nothing. I didn't back down. I don't back down. The art of bluffing comes down to playing your hand and throwing yourself into it. You must make your opponent believe the lie you're telling, and the best way to do that is to believe it yourself. I told myself Aerolis wouldn't hurt me, that the Djinn would honour his deal. I almost believed it too. I think I would have, if not for the wordless fear Ssserakis spread in the back of my mind.

"I promised you Sources," Aerolis said eventually. "Take as many as you wish. A fortune paid in the corpses of my siblings."

"I only need two. Necromancy and Impomancy. Any more than that would be useless to me." I did not care for any monetary value of the Sources. I cared for the power they contained. A Sourcerer cannot wield two of the same type of Source. Well, that's not entirely accurate. They can, but they shouldn't. They really fucking shouldn't. Rejection speeds up, minutes instead of hours or even days, and the breakdown can be catastrophic. There is a raging inferno on the southern tip of Isha that refuses to burn out due to a Sourcerer with two Pyromancy Sources inside, and the result has been burning for over two hundred years.

"Take them," Aerolis said, holding out a flaming hand. Two crystals, each the size of a grape, fell from the top of the tower, thudding into the sandy ground nearby. "They are yours." The Djinn began to fade, the flames dying down.

"Our dealings are not done, Djinn!" I shouted the words before Aerolis could vanish entirely. I had to stand my ground and demand full payment now or I knew I would never get it. "You promised to teach me how to use them. How to use Sourcery."

"You claimed you already know." A blatant attempt to weasel out of the deal he had struck.

"And you told me I was wrong!" Another step closer and I could feel the heat licking at my skin, causing me to sweat despite the chill air. "I paid too high a price for your promise, Aerolis. There is nothing you can teach me that will be worth the life it cost." Tears in my eyes made the flames an orange blur, but I refused to wipe them away. I let the Djinn see them fall. Let it see what the deal we struck had truly cost me. "But I will be fucked before I let your debt go half paid. You will teach me!"

"Infuriating simpleton!" Aerolis said, his voice was the harsh roar of a fire with too much fuel. "You wish to learn but haven't the mind to understand. And I have not the patience to teach fools beyond their bounds." The fire drew closer to me, and I had the impression that Aerolis was staring into my eyes. "Perhaps there is another way. I see my brothers in your eyes, terran. I see Maratik and Jagran. Shards of them. Pieces of corpses. Memories. Knowledge. Power."

Something is wrong. The Djinn gathers power around it. Run!

I ignored the horror's dire warning. "What are you talking about, Aerolis."

"You wish to learn the true potential of the coffins you carry inside?" Aerolis' burning form drew back from me and lightning crackled around the flames. I should have listened to Ssserakis.

"Yes!"

"Then learn." The Djinn's lightning ripped into my

chest.

Aerolis waited on the last of his brothers. Vainfold loved to make them wait. Not a single meeting went past wherein he wasn't the last of them to arrive. All the others were there. All who were left. So few of them yet survived. Only six. Six Djinn, and six Rand. It was foolish, Aerolis knew that, but they couldn't stop. The War Eternal had consumed both his brothers and his sisters, and unless something was done, the world they had taken for their own would soon be free of them once more. A shame, then, that peace was beyond their ability.

There was nothing in the realm of the Djinn. They had constructed that way. It was a void, a place with no form or structure, like the space between the stars. A purposeful design so no brother would hold dominion over any other. They all had their attuned elements, after all. Keratoll, the Learned, felt most comfortable in the rock and stone. The deep bones of the world. After all, the rock was wise and unmoving. The rock remembered all. Geneus, the Guiding Light, was light. He did not burn like fire but shone all the same. Ever the leader, never the voice of reason. Elleral, the Raging Heart, was a torrent of wind that never ceased. Violent and volatile, and never at rest. Elleral counselled battle wherever it could be taken. The strongest voice left who lobbied for such blatant mutual destruction. He had been even worse since the death of Jagran, the Swift. Arnae, the Wheel, preferred to exist within time. There were not many Djinn who felt most comfortable in that state, and Arnae was the last of them. Invisible to all the lesser creatures, they went without worship as anything more than abstract concepts. Predictable as ever, Arnae counselled patience. Wait, wait, wait. Always wait.

A fire bloomed in the void as Vainfold, the Eternal, made his appearance. A raging vortex of fire that burned with such foolish grandeur. Vainfold loved the fire. It made him feel important and powerful. But here, in the realm of the Djinn, they were all equal. Each voice counted, no more than any other, and each opinion would be heard before any decisions were made. Of course, hearing an opinion and listening to it were ever two different things.

"Were you waiting on me, brothers?" Vainfold asked, his voice a crackling hiss of flame.

"We are always waiting on you, Vainfold," Arnae said. He kept track of such things. Each moment in time memorised. He liked to say the future and the past were the same thing, fixed points along a fluid line that was more circle than line, except for when it wasn't. No one understood the inner workings of time like Arnae, and none of those left alive cared enough to try.

"I'm here now. But why?"

Aerolis changed his form, liquid bubbling up around him even as the rock fell away. He coalesced the form into a series of spherical bubbles of water, orbiting around each other. The others were mired to their forms, locked into the elements they felt most comfortable in, but Aerolis was different. Every form he tried felt right at first but constricting after a while. Some of the others mocked him for lack of consistency, but he felt his fluid nature to be a boon. He could see all sides of the conflict, just as he could take any form he wished.

"Something has changed," Aerolis said, his voice tinkling like a forest brook.

"Nothing has changed." Elleral rarely listened to others, instead he blustered over them and buffeted them into his way of thinking.

"Aerolis is right," Geneus seared the words into existence rather than spoke them. Whenever he said something, the others listened. He gave them no choice. "I could feel it after we lost

Jagran, and then again after Ferinfal. We are losing our strength."

There followed a kind of silence that could only settle in the void of the Djinn realm. A true absence of sound. Even Vainfold's flames and Elleral's rushing winds muted.

Arnae broke the silence. "We were always so much stronger together. Linked as one, as hundreds, as one. Together we could move mountains, make them fly. Together we could will another world into existence, but each death shears us a little. With each death, power is lost."

"We've known this for a long time, brothers," Vainfold crackled. "The laws of Ovaeris link us to each other as they link us to our sisters. As we grow weaker, so do they. There has never been a better time to strike."

"Killing them kills us," Aerolis said. His argument was ever lost on the deaf ears of his more aggressive brothers.

"But they must be destroyed for their arrogance!" Elleral said. "Their mockery cannot be unpunished."

"Your punishment would destroy both our people." Arnae's voice sounded like the inevitability of time's slow advance.

"Then we imprison them," said Vainfold.

Old arguments were recycled. Failed plans brought up once more, as though their failure was from a lack of execution rather than a lack of knowledge. Too many of Aerolis' brothers were fools who couldn't see the truth in front of them. Too many could not understand that the road to victory lay not through violence, but through peace. The only way they could win was by not winning.

"A pocket realm could work," Arnae agreed though without his usual conviction. "But there is no way to convince our sisters to enter it."

"We should send them to Sevoari," Elleral said. "Let them wallow amidst the mockeries they created."

"We can no longer access Sevoari," Geneus' voice again

seared itself into the void, and all stopped to listen. "This is the change Aerolis discovered. With the death of Jagran and Ferinfal, Sevoari has moved beyond our reach."

"Madness!" Vainfold crackled and then fell silent, his form wavering only slightly. It did not take long for him to see the truth. His flames intensified in panic. The others tried as well, with identical results. The Djinn were no longer strong enough to reach Sevoari. The world they had created, the world the Rand had corrupted, was beyond their grasp.

Even in the void of their realm, the Djinn became erratic. Fire crackled, earth rumbled, wind howled. It was all just a speck of noise and sound and time amidst a sea of nothing. Their realm was crafted that way for a reason.

"What do we do?" Elleral was, as always, the most vocal of his brothers.

"Are we stuck here?" Vainfold asked.

"We could open a portal," Arnae said.

"NO!" Geneus again seared the command into the void. "We cannot open portals, brothers. It would find us and send us all back. I will not be trapped again." Geneus turned his attention to each of the Djinn in turn. Even Vainfold bowed under the pressure of such scrutiny. The void was created so all the brothers would be equal, but by sheer force of will, Geneus would never be equal. Still, he was not nearly adaptable enough to survive the change that was coming.

"I have an option." Aerolis had considered his best time to strike, and it was now. Now, when his brothers were weakest. Now, when they were lost in their panic. Now, before even Geneus could convince them of another path. All attention turned to him and almost he faltered. Almost. "We can still enter our pocket realms." The void was a realm within the world, not without. Unlike Sevoari, it did not need reaching. It ever existed, close at hand.

"And in our realms, we are safe from the laws of Ovaeris."

"I will not hide here for eternity, coward!" Elleral howled.

"We do not need to hide here, but we do need to hide. Some of us. At least until it is over."

"What are you saying, brother?" Keratoll, the Learned, would probably be the toughest to convince. It was in his nature to resist movement and change. It was in his nature to resist Aerolis.

"Here in our own realms, there are no rules but those we design," Aerolis said. "We are free of consequence. If the Rand die while we are here, we will be free from the bond that takes us with them."

"But there is no way to kill the Rand while we are here. Our power does not stretch outside these boundaries." There was greed in Vainfold's tone. Desire. Hope for a way to break the rules. He always did love to cheat.

"By proxy, there is," Aerolis said, tightening the noose. "Our sisters have given us the very tools we need. By trying to save themselves, they have created creatures who are sensitive to our power. These Sourcerers..."

"Aberrations!" Geneus' word seared into life between them all.

"Yes," Keratoll agreed in a grinding of rock. "They absorb our dead and use them to steal our power." For the Djinn who prided himself on knowledge, Keratoll knew so little.

"But they can be useful," Aerolis said. It was easier than pointing out where his brothers were wrong. "When they come in contact with one of our pocket realms, it is possible for us to usurp control of their bodies, while remaining safely inside our own worlds. Free from the consequences of Ovaeris' rules, but still able to influence it." He let the possibility sink in for a few moments before continuing. In these moments, Aerolis saw his brothers stepping willingly into the trap he and Mezula had laid. "They act

as conduits for our power."

"This will work?" Elleral howled into the void. Glory and hope mixed together to form a torrent of wind that would have torn forests away had there been anything besides nothing surrounding them. "We can destroy our sisters for good and then emerge from our realms to gloat." Of course, Elleral could think of nothing but gloating over those too dead to care.

"It is not enough." Of course, Geneus saw the flaw in the plan. "No conduit can transfer power without loss. There are some rules beyond the world. They are written in the fabric of the greater. Without our full power, we cannot hope to defeat our sisters."

Mezula had seen the argument coming, and Aerolis had provided the answer. "Then, we will turn their other tools against them. The creatures they created, the ones they call terrans and pahht and tahren. We can teach them to make weapons from our prison. Weapons that can kill the Rand. We arm them and send them against their own creators."

Elleral laughed, a booming gust of wind. "I love it. Just as they perverted our creation, so we will do to theirs."

Keratoll let out a grumble of stone. "If these weapons can kill our sisters, they can also kill us."

"Once we have killed the last of the Rand, it will be simple to take those weapons away from such lesser creatures" Aerolis said. "They are no threat to us. And we will rule Ovaeris, free of our sister's influence."

Arnae did not appear convinced. The workings of time ground within his form. Geneus, too, was uncertain. Geneus was always uncertain when the plan was not his. They needed a push. "We must put this plan into action, brothers," Aerolis said. "We lose power with every death. We are strongest together, working in concert. With only six of us remaining, we can no longer reach

Sevoari. Our own world is lost to us. How long before we cannot
even reach our pocket realms? The longer we wait, the more we
assure our own destruction."

All attention turned to Geneus. Regardless of the time
or place, he would always be the leader. No one had chosen him
as such, he had just assumed the mantle, and none were left to
challenge him. However, even the Guiding Light could be led where
Aerolis wanted, as long as he closed off enough of the other paths.
He and Mezula had planned for everything.

When I came to, I had no idea how much time had
passed. It has always been the way when I absorb memories
through Arcmancy. At times, no more than a moment
has passed, at others, entire days may have been lost to
me. I think, perhaps, it is determined by the source of the
memories, or perhaps by the way they are drawn out. It is
not a study I have ever put much thought into. But Aerolis
was gone. I sat in front of the great tower of Do'shan, its
rotating light still gazing out over the city, and I was alone
save for the horror.

"Did you see those memories as well?" I asked.

Yes. How?

"I don't know." The fact that Aerolis was gone
convinced me of one thing, though. The Djinn considered his
debt paid. He had promised to teach me how to use Sources
to their full potential, and somehow those memories were
the key.

They conspired together. Ssserakis sounded unsure,
as though the very idea of it was beyond comprehension.
I suppose it was, in many ways. For as long as anyone had
been alive, the Rand and Djinn had been at war. Only they
themselves remembered a time where there was peace. And

yet the proof was in Aerolis' own memories. He and Mezula had conspired to be the last of the Rand and Djinn. *Yet they still fight. They still try to kill each other. They still hate each other.*

"I need to know more." The words were as much for myself as for Ssserakis. It was not just the obvious, as Ssserakis had seen. There were answers hidden within the memories the Djinn had shared with me. I now knew how Aerolis and Mezula had ended up the last of the Rand and Djinn. I knew why and how the surviving Djinn had ended up trapped in their pocket realms. But the answers posed yet more questions. First and foremost on my mind was how those memories could teach me to use Sourcery more effectively? But I also longed to know where and how the Djinn had once been trapped? Why had Aerolis and Mezula conspired to kill the last of their siblings, and why did the peace between them end?

Aerolis will not willingly give you more. Do not offer him any more deals, Eskara. You have already been cheated twice.

"Maybe there's another way. There's one other person here who might know the truth."

He cannot remember his own yesterdays; we cannot trust him to remember the truth.

I stood and scooped the two Sources from the ground. Necromancy and Impomancy. I now held all the magic I was attuned to. Not since the fall of Orran had I had access to so much power. And if I could just unlock the secrets that Aerolis had shared with me, I would know the truth of how to use it as well.

Send me home, Eskara. My shadow rippled with the words in my head. Ssserakis' excitement eclipsed its desire to learn the truth with me. I could feel the tug, trying to pull us both out of my body and back to the Other World.

"No." I resisted, faintly at first, my mind still a whirl. *What?*

"I said NO!" I clamped down on the horror, trapping it inside of me. My shadow stopped rippling and settled back to the flat, natural darkness.

You promised me! We made a deal in the darkness. I stop killing your people, and you would send me home.

Truth is ever a tougher thing to swallow than lies. The horror had been with me all this time under false pretence. It was time for Ssserakis to learn the truth. "I don't know how to send you home, Ssserakis. I never did."

I expected the horror to rage inside, the equivalent of destroying a room in a fit of anger. I braced myself for it, ready to contain the anger and violence. What happened was far worse. Silence. Cold silence. Nothing. I looked inside and I felt no presence of the horror. Ssserakis was still there, but it had withdrawn, coiled itself into a tight ball around my heart. I shivered, cold spreading through me despite the flame of Pyromancy I carried inside. My breath misted, and then it didn't, which was even worse. Fear stabbed at me and my heart beat faster, but even then, the cold grew worse.

"Stop it." My hands were shaking, shivering, my teeth chattering as I forced the words out through numb lips. I had always felt the cold inside, ever since taking Ssserakis in, but this was different. This was the cold it had surrounded me with down in the Pit the day I first encountered it. "Ssserakis, stop! Please." I had to force the words out, and still the cold deepened inside.

I reached out with a trembling hand, the flesh an unhealthy pale blue, and with a gesture I opened a portal. I didn't even bother to give it a destination, and all it showed on the other side was nothing. Black and black and more black, the occasional twinkle of light, possibly a star. And then, in the farthest distance, somewhere beyond anything we recognized as distance, an eye blinked and rolled toward us. The creature from beyond the portals, the same one even the Djinn had feared, and its attention fixed on us.

For a time, we stood there, Ssserakis and I, both on the edge of oblivion. The equivalent of holding a knife to each other's throats. The horror could kill me from the inside. It could lower my body temperature to the point where I would just stop, or feed my heart so much fear it would burst. But I could kill it too. Ssserakis knew the touch of the creature from beyond the portals. It knew that thing would pick it apart to learn the truth of it. Every moment we stood together on that precipice, the monster drew closer. My fear and Ssserakis' mingled until neither of us could tell whose were whose. I suppose it no longer mattered.

Enough! Ssserakis blinked first and the cold inside lessened, I could feel the heat of the Pyromancy Source once more, spreading throughout my body, warming parts of me on the verge of failure. I snapped the portal closed, and collapsed, sprawling on the sandy ground.

For a long time, we both sat in silence. Defiance and pride and stubborn pig-headedness making both of us sulk. Neither of us wanted to be the first to talk. We'd just come so close to destroying each other and yet the truth remained. We were stuck together. I could not get rid of Ssserakis without dying, and the truth the horror was already coming to realise was that it had nowhere else to go. I was its best chance of going home, even if I didn't know how to do it. Well, maybe not its best chance, but I truly believe Ssserakis would take its chances beyond the portal rather than beg the Iron Legion for help.

Silence is a disease. It infects, grows, peels away all that is good and clean, and leaves behind putrid flesh. It can take a healthy relationship and turn it sour, and I was under no false belief, the relationship I shared with Ssserakis was not healthy, but the horror was mine. Mine. Mine alone. My constant companion. My secret no one else knew. We fought and we hurt each other, but it was not the damage or pain or fear that was truly threatening to tear us apart. It was the silence that followed in its wake. It is hard to cut diseased flesh from a body, harder still to convince the afflicted that it is necessary. Silence is the same. It's so much easier to wallow in silence, to allow the relationship to wither and die, than it is to extend a word of apology.

"I will find a way." It was not an apology I offered. In some ways, many ways, it was both better and worse. Any apology I uttered, Ssserakis would know for a lie. Instead, I offered my passenger a promise, offered in genuine honesty. "I don't know how to send you home, Ssserakis. But I will find a way. But not until my desires are met."

What desires?

"Vengeance." I wouldn't name it justice, not to Ssserakis. The others would want to hear it, but my horror would want to know the truth. "The Emperor and the Iron Legion have to pay. Once they have, I will find a way to send you home, no matter the cost."

I need more.

"I won't give up my vengeance." I'm not sure I could, in all honesty. The desire to see it wrought had lessened for a while. That was due to Silva's influence. In her arms I found a different reason for living. But I had chosen the pursuit of power over the woman I loved, and now my vengeance was all I had left.

I need a promise. Swear to me you will stop at nothing to enact your vengeance. Regardless of the cost, lives or otherwise. Stop at nothing. Kill the monster who brought me to this hateful world, and then send me home!

I nodded. "I promise."

If you take one lesson away from my story, from the mistakes I have made in my life, let it be this: Do not make promises. They hold us, bind us in a way that goes beyond the physical. They make manifest desire and purpose. To make a promise is to offer up your own hands in slavery and damn the consequences. I have made many promises in my life, and the truth is I have broken most of them. Each time, I think I broke a part of myself with it.

That day, I left the tower with answers, more questions, and most importantly, a purpose. One I knew Ssserakis would hold me to.

CHAPTER TWELVE

THE FOLLOWING WEEKS SAW ME STRUGGLING with the true message of Aerolis' memory. I replayed it in my mind over and over again, and soon discovered that Ssserakis saw things in that memory that I did not. The horror saw the emotion clearer than I and sensed the tension in the way the Djinn moved and spoke. It was far more astute in the subtleties of the body language of a race who had no true bodies, save for whatever element they took. We struggled with it together. The tension between us was not forgotten, nor the fact that we had come so close killing one another, but it was forgiven. And not just by me.

Aerolis would be no more help. The Djinn clearly considered his debt paid in full, and I had the distinct feeling that summoning him again would do little to shed any light on the matter. He gave me a riddle, and I would uncover the solution myself.

We took the time to heal. Ishtar's ankle never truly recovered, leaving a limp that afflicted her with every step, but she became quite nimble with a crutch. Our training continued, and despite improving, I felt she improved even faster. I still could not win against her. I couldn't even land a single blow. Imiko brooded. Her conscience threatened to unravel her, and the inactivity made her obnoxious. She was a true pain to be around in those days, and I found I missed my friend. I could fondly remember her levity and wit and the good humour that followed in her wake, but they were gone. I had no idea how to fix the situation, and even Hardt struggled to console her.

Hardt himself chafed. There was little to do up on Do'shan. The city was built and entirely unsustainable. We passed over land and sea, forest and desert. We couldn't stop. There was no anchor in place on Do'shan, and even if Mezula stopped Ro'shan, our flying city would just orbit around it. There were no flyers, and no chain, and no way for the people below to reach us. Supplies were running low, and starvation was becoming a real issue. Hardt found he had nothing to do. Horralain suffered a similar problem and contented himself with days of following me around, watching my back. I wonder what the big man thought when he saw me talking to my horror. Perhaps he thought me mad.

Tamura, I think, was the only one of us who found the change of pace to his liking. The crazy old Aspect happily spent so many of his days lounging around and staring at the sky, or studying the architecture Aerolis had risen around us. Immortality gives a different perspective on life. It is easier to feel like a day is wasted, when you have a limited number of them.

Eventually I went to Tamura for the answers I could not reason out myself. He has always possessed wisdom for those patient enough to decipher his ramblings. I found him sitting on the rooftop of the empty building we called home, tending a cook pot and a dying fire. Where he had found the kindling to start a fire, I had no idea, there was no wood left on Do'shan. One of the many things our lofty position in the sky denied us.

"What are you cooking?" I asked as I sat down across from him, lowering myself to sit cross legged.

The old Aspect shrugged. "Mostly rat." Even with food supplies as low as they were, rats still found something to sustain them. I didn't want to think too hard about what the little beasts might be eating.

I delayed, unsure of how to ask my questions. I find awkward conversations are best treated like swimming in the sea. It's going to be cold and unpleasant, but better to dive right in than inch forwards. "Tamura, what do you know about the Weapons of Ten?"

"Ahh, from the Forest of Ten." Tamura drew in a deep breath and smiled. "Ten fires in the night. Ten knights to rescue ten damsels…"

"No." It is best to interrupt someone at the beginning, before they become invested. "I want the truth, Tamura. Where do the weapons come from?" In his memory, Aerolis had said they could fashion weapons that could kill the Rand. It was the only reason I could think of that the Djinn was so scared of Shatter.

"Truth… Truth is like pain. A little provides clarity, focus, even inspiration. Too much of it distracting and quickly becomes tiresome. A good story is like this stew." Tamura seemed content with that as an explanation and wasn't in any hurry to share more.

This creature is mad. There is too much Rand in him. Too many lies clouding the truth.

"A stew is a mix of different ingredients in one pot." It is a point of pride that I was becoming so adept at decoding Tamura's riddles.

"The rat is tough and stringy. But with the right mix of ingredients, all becomes edible." Tamura drew in a deep breath and then looked at the pot with something like sadness. "But it can never be a rat again."

"The rat is the truth?" I asked slowly. "Everything else is the lie."

Tamura nodded and then poked a gnarled finger at his head. "All is stew." He giggled and then scratched at something underneath his matted tangle of grey locks.

I leaned forward and plucked the wooden ladle from Tamura's hands, smiling at the curious look it put on his face. I stirred the stew for a moment, swirling the ingredients about until I found what I was looking for. I scooped up a chunk of rat and tipped the ladle slightly, letting all the liquid and everything else drain away. Then I passed the ladle back to Tamura.

"It might not be scurrying about anymore, but look, a piece of rat."

Tamura giggled and nodded. He could be so childlike at times, throwing his whole self into the moment. That is something we lose as we get older. Children have a singularity of purpose and will. They aim for what they want and pursue it without a mind for anything else. The older we get the more we find other things to consider in that pursuit. Our will becomes diluted, our focus wider, encompassing more. We become scattered. It is hard to say which is truly the more useful state of mind, perhaps there is a healthy balance we can achieve somewhere between both.

"Yes. Yes," Tamura nodded again. "But *this* is not rat." He giggled and returned the ladle to the pot, stirring once again.

We will find nothing here but madness and lies, Eskara.

"Tell me about the Weapons of Ten," I said again.

He leaned forward. "They fell from the sky." He said it with such wonder in his voice, as if, even now, after so many years, it was still a marvel to him.

"As weapons?"

"No. Weapons don't fall from the sky unless dropped. As metal."

"Bars to a cage," I mused, thinking of something I had heard within Aerolis' memory. "Forged from their prison."

"Yes!" Tamura's eyes darted left and right, as though he was just realising it himself. I think perhaps he was. So many of his memories were lost to him, locked behind walls and blockages he did not know how to shift. But with the right prodding, it was possible to poke holes and let the knowledge flow out.

Aerolis said they would make weapons from their prison.

I looked up. Lokar and Lursa were visible. Our two moons ever grinding their way into one another. Spinning together in their eternal dance. I could see them clearly, close and huge. The day was dull and the sky was clear, and if I squinted, I could even see the cracks where Lokar was crushing and forcing its way into Lursa. I could see that chunks of the moons had broken away and were being held in the strange gravity up there. They looked so small, but each of those chunks was probably the size of Isha. Lursa was larger today, her bulk turned toward us, obscuring so much Lokar. One male moon, one female moon. How had it taken me so long to realise?

"The moons," I said.

"Yes, yes!" Tamura nodded eagerly. "Two moons there were, Lokar and Lursa, cavorting through the sky. Lokar pursued his sister endlessly, caught in her wake, drawn by her size. Ever dancing. Ever running. Ever drawing nearer to the final embrace. And then, one day." Tamura dropped the ladle and clapped his hands together with a slap. "Lokar caught his sister. They tumbled and turned and cracked and crushed. Two became one."

"And the metal fell from the moons when they collided?"

"Yes."

The weapons aren't of your world.

I shook my head. "No, they are not." I turned my attention back to Tamura. "The Rand and the Djinn, they were prisoners. Our moons were their gaols."

Tamura giggled and rocked back and forth. "Immortals trapped. Locked away like children shut in a room. Brawling, fighting, sniping. Always creating a mess. It doesn't like mess. Likes order."

"What does?"

"I don't know." Tamura slapped a hand to his head once, twice, and a third time, as though trying to shake something loose. "I cannot... see. Can't remember. There is... something bigger, greater. A parent? No. Not all terms fit, no matter how accurate. Creator?"

"The thing that put them in their prisons?" I asked.

"Yes. Something... unknowable. My mother feared it. All I remember is her fear of it."

"The thing beyond the portals?"

Tamura cocked his head at that. "The eye. It watches us all, but not all windows are open."

That's why it is so interested in us. It senses me. It senses that the Rand created me and cannot understand how when they have such limited imagination. It does not understand I come from you, not it.

"Except I was there with you. Surely it knows about terrans?"

Some things are beneath your notice. Small things. An ant you step on do not even notice.

Tamura watched me having a conversation with myself and said nothing about it. I will admit I was becoming quite lax with hiding my horror from the world, often talking to Ssserakis regardless of who was around.

"So, the moons collided. Their prisons were broken, and they came here, to Ovaeris." Tamura nodded at my words. "And they brought their war with them."

It was a sobering realisation. We were taught that the collision of our moons was just something that happened, a point in history that had little effect, save for campfire stories and the occasional moon shower of precious metal. The truth went far beyond that. Before the moons collided, the terrans were uncivilised beasts, the creatures I call the Damned. The pahht looked similar for the most part, but were feral creatures without much intelligence, walking on all fours and only upright when they stood still. As for the tahren, who knew what little beasts they were before the Rand. If not for the breaking our moons, we would all still be like that. The world would belong to the garn and the mur and the monsters. Some of Ovaeris' grandest cities would never have come to being, our skies would be clear of flying mountains. Sevoari and all its inhabitants simply wouldn't exist. The collision of our moons wasn't just some fixed point in history, it was the bloody beginning of history, of everything we now are. It was now clear to me, and undoubtedly true, that the Rand and the Djinn did not belong here. They were immigrants, fleeing a prison sentence imposed upon them. Yet it was also true they had certainly made their mark on our world. They had shaped it to their will, made it and us what we are today. We owed everything to them.

And yet, they had also brought a war to our world that has devastated it again and again. They played with the natural order of things and convinced us to worship them as gods. They created another world full of monsters, nightmares plucked straight from our worst dreams. They thought of us as worthless. At best we were pawns to be used in the great war they fought against each other. At worst we were nothing to them, lives not even worth considering. And on a personal level, their war cost me Silva. I may have wielded the weapon that struck the blow, but it was Mezula who directed it. It was Mezula who sent her daughter to die in her place.

It's fair to say the realisation put my head in something of a spin. Distantly, I heard Tamura muttering as he stirred the stew, and I could feel Ssserakis talking, but I was lost in my own thoughts.

"The weapons," I said eventually. "Why is Aerolis so scared of the hammer? Because it can kill him?"

Tamura glanced over towards Horralain. The big thug sat at the edge of the rooftop, apart from us and apparently uninterested in our conversation, despite the topic. "The metal was designed to contain their magic. It would be a poor prison if it did not."

How does any of this help us unlock the potential of the Sources you carry? Knowing where the Rand and Djinn come from does nothing but make you feel superior for the knowing.

The horror wasn't wrong there. Secrets make us feel powerful, and pride in power has always been one of my failings.

"I don't know." There were ways I could use what I now knew. Perhaps leverage with which to extort something else from the Djinn. Then again perhaps it wouldn't care. Aerolis had shown me that memory willingly, he must have known I would have seen the betrayal he and Mezula had planned.

"Consider the stew," Tamura said with knowing nod of his head.

"Aren't we done with the stew metaphor?"

Tamura shrugged and cracked a grin. It was good to see him smile again. For a long time even his spirits had seemed buried beneath mounds of misery. "Stew is varied. So many uses, so many possibilities. Do you know what's in the stew?"

"Rat?"

He shot me a withering look. "And?"

"I have no idea."

Tamura giggled. "You don't want to know."

There is a creature in my world who will answer any one question with the truth. But it only answers each question once, and it may not answer the question you asked.

"What?"

The creature is mad. And so is this one.

"Each ingredient has a flavour, a taste all of its own." Tamura leaned forward and drew in a deep breath through his nose, savouring the smell of the stew. Then he choked on the smell. "Hopefully it will taste better than it smells. Taste better than its parts."

It all started to make sense. *You understand this fool?*

"The tutors at the academy told us never to mix magic. They said it was dangerous."

Again, Tamura chuckled, shaking his head. "Not all rules are made to protect. Many are there to contain. But perhaps they were right. You have already broken the rules. Are you dangerous?"

He was right, of course. Tamura was almost always right. I just hadn't seen it before. The tutors told us that mixing magic from different Sources was dangerous and volatile, and in some ways, they were right, but they were also fools with little ambition. The magic of Sources, of the Rand and Djinn, was never meant to be used alone. It's in their very nature, in the rules that bind them. They are stronger together than apart. As more of them died, their power diminished. At their height, the Djinn created a world. They did not do that separately, they combined their power, all of them working as one towards a common goal.

The tutors taught us that mixing magic externally is safe enough. It is, after all, the very spirit of Augmancy, placing enchantments on items requires a secondary magical attunement to direct the enchantment. You cannot create a flaming sword with Augmancy alone, it requires Pyromancy as well, applied to the metal afterwards. However, mixing magic internally speeds rejection, and can lead to breakdowns. Both statements are true, but they left out the part where mixing magic internally increases the power exponentially.

And Tamura was right about something else, too. I had already done it; I just hadn't realised it. In my rage and

grief, I had assaulted Aerolis with everything I had. Ssserakis
and I working in perfect union. Shadow and blade and fire
and lightning. It is a fight we would have lost, had Aerolis
fought back, but in that frenzy, we staggered the Djinn.
We fucking hurt him. When I looked back, I realised how.
The Sourceblades I formed at the height of my rage were
different. Before, I had created the blades with Kinemancy,
then coated them with lightning or fire. But that one time I
had mixed the magic inside. The kinetic energy I used to fill
those blades was suffused with Arcmancy and Pyromancy.
I had not even realised it. Perhaps that is why the rejection
struck so soon afterwards. I don't know. What I do know,
is that mixing of magic is what allowed me to hurt Aerolis.
And I knew I could do it again.

CHAPTER THIRTEEN

I TOOK TO A NEW REGIME OF TRAINING, cautious at first. It was dangerous and I had to go slowly to make certain I didn't blow myself up, or something even worse than that like blowing everyone else up. Mixing magic inside, then releasing it, shaping it. With no tutor to guide me, and no real hint of direction, I fumbled along like a blind woman in a maze. My first few attempts were met with failure and the wounds to prove it. I almost lost a finger when a Sourceblade exploded in a gout of flame, but I just about managed to direct the fire outward, scorching sand so hot it turned to glass. Lightning was easier for me. It's strange, I have always felt most comfortable with Pyromancy, something about the flames drew me in and made me feel at home. Since the Arcstorm, which I had absorbed and held inside, Arcmancy came so easily. I was the fury of the storm, and it was me. Maybe that was why.

The fury. Fire isn't furious or angry, it is simply fire. It consumes, that's what it does. It is slow and methodical. Flames may not be predictable, but fire is. Its course can be directed and controlled. Lightning is different. It is anger and fury and rage. It can be directed, but not controlled. It follows along its own course and strikes faster than a flicker. I was angry. I have always been angry, but it was worse after Silva. I lashed out at times. I didn't mean to, it just happened. The anger was difficult to control. Often, I didn't realise it was there until it was out and the damage was done. Lightning and I shared a kinship, of sorts, that went deeper than the storm I carried. I am not proud of it.

I made some progress at least. Sourceblades that were stronger, lighter, imbued with a fire that could set metal burning. I copied the shield I had seen Silva erect around her, more a bubble really. Infusing that shield with both Kinemancy and Arcmancy, I made it impenetrable to both physical attack and magical. I learned to create a shockwave of energy, expanding out from me, that would be more than useful if I ever found myself surrounded. So many new possibilities opened up to me with the knowledge that magic was more powerful when it was used in concert, when using the principles that bound the Rand and the Djinn together. It was where the Iron Legion's true power came from. The knowledge to use magic in a way no one else fucking dared. He was attuned to over ten different Sources, could probably carry all of them at once. No wonder he was so strong.

The weeks wore on and the toll became all too obvious. Aerolis and his city could fly through the sky forever, an eternity apart from the rest of the world, but we could not. The ferals could not. We were all starving. Our supplies ran out, even rationed as they were. All of us lost flesh, and some days our hunger was all we could talk about. Some people get angry when the hunger takes them. I am not one of them, but Ishtar is, and she has the wit and the tongue to back up her anger with insults that sting as bad as sword cuts. She reduced Imiko to tears on one occasion and I rounded on her so sharply I thought we would come to blows. Not the type we dealt each other in sparring, but true blows meant to wound or even kill. We were friends, and more than that, she was a mentor. I respected Ishtar more than I ever told her. But anger and hardship do not mix well together, and we both said some things I wish we hadn't.

The ferals became vicious. As a whole, their fur was never as well-groomed or healthy as Ishtar's, but even I could see it was becoming dull and mangy. More than once I came across one of the creatures gnawing at its own leg, as though it were so hungry it was willing to cannibalise itself. I couldn't help but remember the Damned down in the ruined Djinn city. How they had been in some sort of hibernation until we came along, and how they were willing to fall upon each other, devouring the dead and wounded. How different were the ferals, really? Were they already devouring each other down in the depths of Do'shan? There couldn't be much else to eat. Even Tamura was struggling to find rats to catch.

Hunger is a horrible thing. A gnawing ache inside that feels as though something is twisting unnaturally. Hunger clouds judgement and makes everything sharp and fuzzy at the same time. It frays nerves down to the very edge of snapping, and makes the skin sallow and sunken, waxy. I may never have been the most vain woman in the world, but I was well aware that sunken cheeks only made my scar stand out more, and that made me look worse than a Ghoul.

Aerolis seemed either unwilling or unable to rectify the situation, so I took it upon myself. What we needed was a way down to the surface. We needed to be able to allow the ferals to hunt or trade, and gather wood for fires. We needed a flyer but had not the materials to build one. I had no doubt Aerolis could get the engine working, nor that he had Kinemancy Sources to power it, but the only thing we had plenty of was stone, and no amount of whirring gears and propellers could make stone fly. Whatever magic could do that seemed to be beyond even the Djinn now that there was only one of them left.

When I approached the edge of the mountain, I did so with the intention of puzzling out a solution. I had magic and the will to use it, which, I was certain, counted for something. Do'shan was above land, broad expanses of fields, green forests that looked small from so high up, mountain ranges that grew from nothing to reach up into the sky. And I realised that I recognised the land. We were above Isha. In the far distance I recognised the Forest of Ten, and beyond it the Atare mountain range. We were close to the Pit. A plan formed in my head. It was a plan Ssserakis counselled against. Vehemently.

"Aerolis!" I was at the foot of the tower once more, my shout echoing along its length. I was no Vibromancer, but I could pitch my scream to carry when the will took me.

Do you enjoy making a mockery of the Djinn?

"Yes," I said with a smile that was all for my horror and I. "Don't you?"

Ssserakis was silent for a long moment. *Yes.*

Horralain stood nearby, arms crossed and the hammer resting against a nearby wall. He had taken quite a liking to Shatter, and I saw no harm in him carrying a weapon that could destroy a god. As long as he remained loyal, at least, and I was certain Horralain's loyalty would never again be in question. Tamura and Hardt had followed me to the tower as well. They had spotted me in the approach and recognised the determined gait of my stride, the set of my shoulders. They knew I had in mind to do something historic. I was making something of a habit of it.

"Aerolis. Stop hiding in your little tower and face me." It was a deliberate choice of words. After the way he *fulfilled* his end of our last bargain, I was in a confrontational state of mind when it came to Djinn and their deals.

The ground shook beneath my feet. I took it as a good sign, though it was probably anything but. Making people angry before you gamble with them can be a choice tactic. Anger clouds the mind and causes many to act too swiftly which leads to mistakes. When they have the power to snuff you out with little more than a thought, it is probably wiser to prepare them with flattery than insults. I thought maybe I'd give that a go.

"Oh, great and powerful Aerolis, the Changing. Stop trying to impress me with cheap tricks and threats, and listen to my proposal." I'm not very good at flattery. "You want to impress me? Then listen to me. And agree to the deal that will save the lives of everyone on Do'shan." The ground continued to shake. "Or you can let us all starve to death and sit up here, alone, for eternity, or until Mezula comes to complete her treachery. Whichever comes sooner."

The Djinn burst up through the ground in front of me, his body already fully formed and towering over me. The rocks of its form rotated, loosely connected by barely visible swirls of translucent magic. It was a grand entrance that showered me in sand. I will admit, I was impressed and a little intimidated, but I refused to let it show as I wiped sand and dirt from my fraying jacket and looked up into the vaguely head-shaped rock at the top of the Djinn's form.

"Good to see we've done away with the pretence that you can't be summoned." It was mockery, pure and simple. I was pushing the Djinn, seeing how far I could go before he snapped. Believe it or not, it was a calculated move on my part. Aerolis needed to know what I was capable of.

"I am done with your insolence, terran." No sooner had the words rumbled around the square than rocks rose up either side of me. They pushed out from the ground, each as tall as myself, and rushed towards me. The Djinn truly was done with me, he was trying to crush me.

I drew on the Sources inside, Kinemancy and Pyromancy, and thrust my arms out, releasing a fiery shock wave that shattered the rocks and sent the Djinn in front of me staggering. He had not been prepared for that. Of course, I knew the trick would not work a second time. But I didn't need it to.

"You figured it out, I see." Aerolis' words rumbled with the sound of an avalanche in full flow.

I hope you know what you're doing, Eskara. This plan makes no more sense now than it did yesterday. The horror wasn't wrong, but in truth it was less a plan and more a gamble.

"Your cryptic lesson?" I nodded. "It was quite simple really, though I admit it has taken me some time to get to grips with controlling the extra power." I took another step forward, so close I could reach out and stab the rocks floating in front of me. "Do not try to harm me again, Aerolis. I don't want to fight you, but if I have to, it will not go down like last time."

A low laughter echoed around the square and along the length of the tower. "You can't kill me, terran."

I grinned, putting as much malice into it as possible. My eyes flashed with the Arcstorm inside, and my shadow rose around me like an aura of black flame. "Don't be so sure." Intimidation was the key here. For the most part, Aerolis knew what I was capable of. But the Djinn had never encountered someone who could absorb the magic of Sources. Before Josef and I, no one like us had ever existed. Neither did he know what my horror was capable of, and Ssserakis had grown fat and strong with all the fear surrounding Do'shan in the past few weeks.

Some would have called my actions foolish; I know Hardt did. But there was nothing foolish about them. Aerolis saw me as another worthless terran. A life to be toyed with and discarded on a whim. A nobody and a nothing. Fuck that! I needed the Djinn to see me as an equal, or at least as close as possible to it. A part of that desire was pride. Aerolis had shown deference and fear to the Iron Legion, and I would demand the same. Of course, the Iron Legion had fought with the Djinn, and I was trying my best to avoid just that. I was certain Aerolis could still swat me like a fly if he really put his mind to it.

"I figured out something else, Aerolis. Something you didn't mean to show me. I know where you come from." I looked up towards the moons. Lokar was prominent, clearly visible despite the bright day. The blue of his bulk shielding much of Lursa's red.

"And you think that knowledge matters?"

I shook my head. "No. I just wanted you to know. I'm not here to threaten or coerce you, Aerolis. I'm here to offer you a deal. Our third and final deal." And this time I hoped to get the better end of it.

CHAPTER FOURTEEN

JOSEF WAS DRUGGED PAST THE POINT TO RESIST. I cannot begin to imagine how that must feel. He found himself a prisoner as surely as he had when he was down in the Pit, but worse. Down there he had been forced to dig, beaten occasionally for little to no reason at all, and fed the most meagre of rations. With the Iron Legion there was no digging, no beatings, generous food, and a warm bed, yet it was still so much worse. With the Iron Legion, Josef was forced to kill.

Disobedience was met with punishment; the death of another. The Iron Legion had no conscience, a life was nothing to him but a resource to be spent. Perhaps he couldn't see, couldn't imagine all the little threads that connect a person to the world. A life branching out into a countless number of connections. Family, friends, enemies. He couldn't see the pain it caused, or maybe he just didn't care. Some people are like that, unable to feel anything that does not directly affect them.

These are not my memories. They are Josef's.

It was time. Time to take the drug. To give away control of
his body to the mad man. Time to kill. No! He couldn't think like
that. He wasn't killing anyone. It wasn't him. Wasn't his choice. It
wasn't him. It was all Loran. All Loran. It had to be.

Josef takes the Sweet Silence and swallows it willingly.
What other choice does he have? Last time he resisted, the Iron
Legion killed a young woman with dark skin and a scarred face.
He remembers her, the fear in her eyes as Loran sucked the
life from her. Then he forced Josef to take the drug anyway. A
meaningless death. They were all meaningless deaths.

He feels his will drain away as the drug takes hold.
Everything goes fuzzy around the edges. The niggling, scratchy
pain from his cut throat fades. And then there's nothing. No
feelings. No thoughts. Nothing but sweet silence and the
commands of a monster.

Prisoners are brought before him. Not one or two, or ten or
twenty. Hundreds of prisoners. Cages full of whimpering terrans
or pahht, many are too malnourished to even stand, others rage at
their confines, scream insults and threats, or make promises they
have no hope of keeping. Some are criminals, some farmers, some
shop owners. Some are just children. All are brothers, sisters,
husbands, wives, parents. It doesn't matter who they were. They're
nothing but fuel to burn now. A voice screams in the back of
Josef's mind and it sounds like his own, but he can't really hear it
and it doesn't matter. None of it matters.

They're in the lower laboratory with its reinforced walls,
cages to the sides, chains on the ground, a wide-open space
in the centre. Off to one side stands a single desk, an inkwell
and a book sitting upon it. All the Iron Legion's notes on the

experimentation are there. His successes, failures, formulae and calculations, numbers. All his research. Josef stands in the centre of the laboratory, waiting for instruction. Thinking nothing. Feeling nothing.

The Iron Legion picks up a small sceptre of plain grey metal. On the end of that sceptre sits a Source the size of an orange, clear and colourless. He moves closer, hands the sceptre to Josef, and goes back to his desk, flipping open his notebook and leafing through the pages. Josef waits. Again, he hears a voice screaming in the back of his mind. A wail of pain maybe? It doesn't matter. It's not his pain. He has no pain.

"Swallow your Biomancy Source now, Yenhelm." Josef obeys without question or hesitation. No thought. Only obedience. He takes the Source from a pocket in his trousers and pops it in his mouth, swallowing hard. The power sits inside his stomach. He can feel it. He can feel… No. There is no feeling. Only the cloying fog in his mind.

"Infuse the Source with their lives, one by one." The Iron Legion scribbles something in his notebook.

Josef turns away from his captor and approaches the first of the cages. It holds a woman of middling years with hair the colour of straw and skin as dark as coal. Her left arm was missing, taken above the elbow, the wound long since closed. Her eyes are full of sorrow and pleading. The voice beyond the fog in Josef's mind screams, but he can't hear it. Not really. And it doesn't matter. He reaches through the bars, grips hold of the woman's ankle, and sucks the life from her. It does not pass quickly, nor easily. She clings to what little life she has left, but in the end her resistance is futile. Josef's Biomancy is far too strong. The life, her energy passes through him and into the sceptre. The Source atop it begins to glow a little, as if lit from inside. It's faint, so much so it's barely perceptible. The screaming voice beyond the fog subsides, but Josef is certain he hears a faint sobbing in its place. It doesn't matter. It is not him. It can't be him.

How much was a life worth? A slight glow. A trickle of energy. The first of many. More prisoners are brought before Josef. He takes the life of each one, sucks them out through his Biomancy and pushes them in the sceptre. Into the Source. The sobbing behind the fog grows quieter.

Two hundred and sixteen terrans pass before him. Two hundred and sixteen lives he feeds to the Source. That's the number. The number of terran lives a single Rand is worth. That's what the Iron Legion's calculations have taught him. People with families, hopes, dreams. All gone.

Josef is crying. The sobbing no longer trapped behind the fog. He feels again. Thinks again. When had the Sweet Silence worn off? When had he gone from unable to follow Loran's commands to following without question? Why hadn't he stopped?

Two hundred and sixteen lives, now nothing but corpses littering the cages behind Josef. Why hadn't he stopped? Why hadn't he stopped? The Source is glowing with an inner blue light so strong it hurts to look at. So bright they could snuff out all the torches and still see into every corner of the laboratory. So fierce it looks like a snowstorm caught in a marble.

The Iron Legion makes another note in his book. "Now absorb it, Yenhelm. Take it in and give birth to a new Rand."

Should he fight? Resist. Loran will just kill more. Murder another and force him to do it anyway. It's easier not to struggle. Easier to push down the hate and guilt and grief. Easier to pretend he's still drugged. It's not his choice. Not really. It never was. He has no choice but to do what he's told.

On the bottom of the sceptre is a spike and Josef stabs it into his left hand, the metal piercing all the way through his palm. It's not like before, when he absorbed the Source from the sword that had run him through. That Source was dead, utterly lifeless. But this one is charged with life, primed with the energy needed for rebirth. He tries to absorb the Source, tries to open himself to it and draw it in. Something fights back. It resists him, pushes away. The Source glows brighter and brighter still. It hums with an electric energy. And then it explodes.

Josef wakes to find the Iron Legion standing over him, a gnarled hand pressed against his chest. He hurts everywhere. All trace of the Sweet Silence is gone now, and he feels everything. He doesn't want to feel it. Doesn't want to remember it. He wishes the numb fog would come back and take it all away.

"I've helped where I can, but the healing from your innate Biomancy is astounding," says Loran "It would be an interesting experiment to see just how much it takes to kill you, Yenhelm. Luckily, I have bigger plans for you."

The laboratory bears the signs of extreme violence. Cages mangled and ripped open, bodies strewn about the place, walls with deep scars in them. Josef raises his hands and finds them slick with blood. He killed them. Two hundred and sixteen people. He killed them all! Tears stream down his face. What is he? What has he become?

"Something went wrong," the Iron Legion says. "Something we're missing. We'll try again. Soon."

Josef lets out a strangled sob.

CHAPTER
FIFTEEN

MADNESS IS A STRANGE WORD. WE SO
often use it as an insult; claiming someone is mad, or
their actions are madness. It is a way of invalidating their
opinion or purpose. But madness is something else, as
well. It is desperation and necessity. Perhaps my actions
were madness, but they were born out of purpose. Not just
mine, but Aerolis'. The people of Do'shan, we were dying,
starving. I could have saved myself and my friends without
doing what I did. I could have opened a portal and carried
us all to safety, but I would have been condemning all the
ferals up in that city to death. I had a way to save them and
to give Aerolis what he needed to save them. My actions
may have been madness, the history books certainly claim
it so, but I did it to save them and us. I just didn't fully
understand the cost. We rarely do until it is time to pay our
debt, and by then it is too late.

This is madness, Eskara.

Hardt echoed Ssserakis' sentiment. "I don't claim to
know a damned thing about Sourcery, Eska, but Tamura
reckons this will kill you. I'm not about to let you die."

We were all gathered once more at the edge of
Do'shan, where I had broken the first of the chains. Below
us lay a rocky expanse. To the north the Forest of Ten, and
to the west was the Pit. By some magic I didn't know or
understand, Aerolis had slowed Do'shan as much as the
Djinn was able. The mountain barely moved in the sky, but
without a chain to anchor it to the ground, the slowed pace
was temporary. We had a limited amount of time for me
to do what needed to be done. What I had set my mind on
doing. That was the place, where my third deal with the
Djinn would go down. Payment rendered on both our parts
in one location.

In my hands I held a new Source, one not part of my
original deal with Aerolis, and a small length of rope no
longer than my arm. "This will work?" I asked the Djinn as
he hovered nearby, a whirling vortex of grey wind.

"I have created the barest framework of a realm
within it," Aerolis said. "It should serve as a conduit."

"Should?" Imiko asked. The little thief twisted her
fingers together, clearly nervous. The ringlet sitting on her
shoulder mimicked her action, though I doubt it had any
idea what was going on.

"This has never been done before," Aerolis whistled.

"That's not true." The words were bitter in my mouth
and I'm certain they came out as such. "This is how you
won the final battle against your sisters. The other Djinn hid
themselves away in the book, the lamp, and the crown. You
convinced Sourcerers like to me die in your place."

Aerolis laughed, a gusting of wind whipping at us all. "Not I."

"No. You just convinced the others to fight, all the while you bound yourself to Mezula and hid here. I'm sure it came as quite a shock when you realised she had betrayed you and your magic was locked to this mountain, just as hers is locked to Ro'shan."

"Betrayal from the treacherous should never be a shock," Tamura said. The old Aspect had finally ditched the sling, but his left arm was still clearly tender and he favoured it.

Again, Aerolis laughed. "And yet she sent you here to finish me, and you are undoing her treachery. The world has a strange way of working in circles, little terran."

"I have a name."

"We'll soon be far beyond the point of names."

He speaks of past betrayals, but still does not expect it. We can trap him, Eskara. Just as his brothers are trapped in their own prisons.

I shook my head. "No." The word was meant for my horror, but the others heard it all the same.

"This thing you are doing, terrible student, will not bring back the dead." Ishtar limped to stand next to me. "Guilt is a wonderful motivator, but a terrible excuse."

Only Horralain did not counsel against it. I'd like to say it's because the big thug agreed with me, but I think it more likely he simply didn't want his opinion to mean anything. It didn't matter either way. The deal was made.

I drew on the Portamancy Source inside and waved my hand, ripping open a portal in front of me. It was a large distance I was covering, from Do'shan to the ground, and it took quite some effort to maintain. That school of Sourcery has never been my strongest, and I was simply glad that the creature between the portals hadn't taken notice yet.

"Go!" I hissed the words through clenched teeth as I struggled to keep the portal stable.

Tamura was first through followed by Imiko and Ishtar and then Hardt. Horralain waited for a few moments, frowning towards the magic, only stepping through once he saw Ishtar waving at us from the other side.

I don't like it. The horror's fear of the portal almost held me back. Almost. But I have never been one to let fear keep me from what I want, even when the fear isn't my own.

I glanced at Aerolis to find the Djinn silent and hovering nearby. It was impossible to tell where it was looking, but I had the distinct feeling its attention was on me all the same. "Good luck." Meaningless words in the scope of things, and the Djinn only laughed at them. So, I grit my teeth and stepped through the portal.

It was the first time I had set foot on Isha since Picarr. But more than that, I was close to the Pit. I recognised the area and was certain I had seen it before, been there before. Squinting up towards the nearby rocks, I was certain I could see the dark opening where we had finally escaped from the ruined Djinn city, chased by the Damned and Josef and the Overseer's soldiers. The ground was covered in white powdery snow last time, but the landmarks were still there. The Forest of Ten sat in the distance, dark and foreboding. Two of my ghosts stood nearby, the huntsmen I had killed in that forest stared towards the tree line. When they had been alive, that forest had been their livelihood and their home. Now, somewhere on the eastern edge, it was their grave. The older ghost with the square chin turned accusing eyes on me and I had to look away.

A part of me wanted to wait. With the Pit so close, I felt a strange longing to return. There was a saying back in Keshin, I heard my parents use it often. *As welcoming as an old boot.* At the time I had no idea what it meant. These days I do. These days I have worn many boots, yet I have always found the oldest to be the most comfortable, the most welcoming. That is how I describe my return to that place that was so close to my old prison. The Pit was as welcoming as an old boot. Or maybe it was just the idea of it. Despite all the torture and the digging and the living on a razor's edge, there was a comfort to the simplicity of the Pit. It was uncomplicated. Horralain knew the feeling well, and I wondered how tempted he was to turn in that direction and go crawling back to Deko.

"It feels good to be back on the ground," Imiko said, already stripping off her winter jacket. The summer was a warm one, and the difference from up on Do'shan was shocking. Already my friend's spirits seemed somewhat lifted. Home has a way of doing that to us, and no matter where we went, Imiko still thought of Isha as home. I think we all did. Well, except for Ishtar, but then my tutor named home wherever she could find her next drink. "Can we stay away from flying cities for a while?"

"I second that notion," Hardt said. He was staring off towards the west.

"I don't know." Ishtar was grinning. "I like the feeling of movement beneath my feet. Of course, it could do with some more taverns. And maybe some of my people rather than those savage mockeries."

"The past shows us for what we are," Tamura said as though in agreement. "You cannot erase the things we have been, only hide from them."

Don't do it. Ssserakis spared no time for the banter of friends. The horror's attention was fixed on me and what I was about to do. *We are free from the Djinn. Let him pass by up there, trapped and forgotten.*

"No," I said again, heedless of the looks the others gave me. They were becoming far too used to seeing me talk to myself.

Your world does not need Aerolis. Do not give it back to him. Please, Eskara.

Ssserakis didn't understand. It couldn't. I wasn't just doing this for myself, to ease my conscience. I wasn't just doing it for Aerolis, or even for all the feral lives I would save. I was doing it for Silva. She had been trying to cooperate with the ferals. She had tried to save them… from me. If I let Do'shan float on, left Aerolis up there to rot, they would all die. This was my last tribute to the woman I loved. The best way I could think of. To save an entire city, regardless of the risk. It would have made her proud.

Again, my decisions brought me into conflict with my horror. Again, I overruled it. It was my body, my mind. I made the rules and Ssserakis was merely there for the ride. A passenger and nothing else. The decisions were mine to make. There are ways to punish someone without even realising that you are doing it.

"We have company," Hardt said. A band of ten, soldiers by the looks of them, wearing uniforms and carrying steel. They were from the Pit; I could smell it on them even from a dozen paces away. The smell of that place doesn't just get on you and your clothes, it gets inside of you. It might wear off after a while, but these were some sort of patrol, probably newly instated after our escape, and the smell of the Pit followed them around. They approached us cautiously, but with no weapons drawn. I'd say that was probably quite wise of them.

We made for an odd-looking group. Six of us and barely armed, only Horralain with Shatter and Ishtar with her swords. Of course, the rest of us didn't really need weapons. Tamura and Hardt were masters of unarmed combat and I had magic to back me up, not to mention a horror.

"You're trespassing on royal territory," said one of the soldiers, a tall man with a wire thin moustache that gave his appearance a sneer-like quality.

I wondered if they recognised me. If any of them would look at me and see the young girl I used to be. Perhaps a few of them dragged me in front of the Overseer, or maybe they were there the day I was stripped, dressed in prison rags, and thrown into the Pit. But no, of course they wouldn't recognise me. That girl was gone. I was a woman grown now with muscle on my bones, scars on my skin, and lightning in my eyes. Even my hair was a shade lighter than it had been, dark instead of black, and well-kept instead of the unruly mess it was before. They would not recognise me. I barely recognised myself. There was nothing left of the girl who had fought and lost at the Fall of Orran. They were more likely to recognise Hardt or Horralain. Big men usually leave a lasting impression, though it is often the smallest of us that one should truly be paying attention to.

"Are you ready?" I asked. Another question for my horror. All eyes turned to me.

Yes. There was bitterness in Ssserakis' reply. The horror was not a willing participant, but it would help me, and I needed that help. I needed Ssserakis to help keep Aerolis under control.

"What do you need us to do?" Hardt asked.

"Don't get in the way." I grinned at him, but there was little humour in it.

"What are you doing here?" The soldier with the moustache asked. "This area is under the direct control of the Terrelan Royal Command."

"What about them?" Hardt asked, thumbing toward the soldiers. I could see the real question in his eyes and his hesitation. He was asking if they needed dealing with and hoping against it. Hoping against any more violence.

I focused my flashing eyes on the soldiers and Ssserakis flared my shadow into a burning aura of black flame once more. It was an impressive sight, but it was only meant to impress. "Let them watch," I said loudly. "I like an audience."

The rope was rough in my hands as I started wrapping it around my left wrist and up to my elbow. I stepped away from the others, a few more paces towards the Forest of Ten, my attention focused on it. I trusted Hardt not to let any of the soldiers get too close while I was distracted.

Last chance to back out. This will probably kill you.

I snorted a laugh. "You're just scared I'll take you with me."

I finished wrapping the rope around my arm and tied it off, and in that moment Aerolis was there. Not beside me. Not apart from me. But inside me.

How to explain the presence of another creature inhabiting your body? Aerolis' presence was different to the others. Ssserakis existed with me; a second voice in my mind, a coldness wrapped around my heart. The horror's presence had been uncomfortable at first, even disturbing, but not anymore. I found my horror comforting and reassuring. I liked the company. When Vainfold had taken my body, it had not been to exist with me; the Djinn had pushed me out of myself, taking my place and filling it with fire. There are few things quite as unpleasant as having control of your own body usurped. Aerolis was unlike either of those experiences, though. I could feel the Djinn in my mind, aware and watching through my eyes, and I could feel his power in my chest and limbs and hands. So much fucking power. It was almost overwhelming. It *was* overwhelming. I think I would have been carried away on the rising tide of that power filling me, if not for Ssserakis. My horror acted as an anchor, keeping me grounded and stopping Aerolis from assuming control. Of course, Ssserakis couldn't do that without Aerolis knowing about it.

They argued. It is a strange thing having two creatures, both ancient beyond years, shout at each other inside you. It was noise without sound, anger without release. Two conflicting powers battering at each other with no hope of conclusion. And I stood in the centre of it, between them, holding both back. In some ways it was like putting myself between two children at odds in the height of a tantrum, only the children were larger than I, and arrogant beyond all reason. Children are rarely arrogant, that is more of an adult trait, they are usually naive, though the symptoms are often the same.

"ENOUGH!" I screamed the word so loudly that the ground cracked beneath my feet. It was not Vibromancy, though I have seen that magic shatter rock before. It was Aerolis' power channelled through me. Containing it was beyond my ability, beyond any terran ability. The Djinn simply possess too much power for a terran body. The Arcstorm, my Arcstorm, flared to life stronger than ever

before, surrounding me in an aura of crackling energy.
Lightning ripped from my skin to strike at the ground
around me. Dirt and dust and small stones rose up into the
air, floating nearby. When they got too close to another piece
of floating debris, lightning arced between them and both
would fall to the ground, only to rise again a few moments
later. The air around me shimmered with a haze. I have
never felt as strong as I did in that moment. I felt like I could
crack the earth open, rip the sky asunder. I felt like I could
have rained fire on the entire world!

My friends backed away, wary. Even Tamura looked
worried, and I couldn't blame him. The soldiers from the Pit
had their weapons out, but none dared venture too close.
Only Hardt remained close to me. Too close.

"Eska, what's happening?" His deep voice was edged
with panic.

I turned to look at Hardt then, moving with tiny
jerking motions, like a bird fighting against restraints. It
took every bit of will power I had to contain the magic of the
Djinn. My eyes flashed, my hair floated about my head like a
black shroud. My skin was glowed with the power.

"Stay back." The words hissed with power I couldn't
hope to control. Only, I had to. I had no other choice. Either
I controlled Aerolis' power, or it destroyed me and everyone
else along with me. So, I bloody well controlled it.

This creature is trying to tear me from you. There was
strain and panic both in Ssserakis' voice.

You are a mockery. Aerolis roared. *We should have
crushed your kind the moment the Rand created you.*

Do it fast, Eskara!

The voices in my head merged into a cacophony of
noise I couldn't understand. Aerolis was attempting to take

control, to wrench it from me. Ssserakis was there to stop the Djinn with shadow and cold and walls of resistance. But Aerolis was too much. His power too great. Everywhere Ssserakis tried to stop him, the Djinn shone a light so bright my horror couldn't help but wither away. Even with all my power, even with Ssserakis and our strength combined, Aerolis was still too much.

A part of me wondered if this had been the Djinn's plan all along. This was what I had learned from his memories, that Sourcerers could act as a home for the Djinn. They had done just that in the final battle of the War Eternal. This was how the last of the Rand had been slaughtered, with Sourcerers under the control of the Djinn, and weapons forged from the only prison that could hold them. We had made a deal, Aerolis and I, but now he was here he wanted control. I realised then, he was no different than Vainfold. He may have colluded with Mezula, a plan they forged to be the very last of their kind, but he had not forgiven nor forgotten. He wanted vengeance, even knowing it would kill him as well.

The Djinn are mad. The Rand are mad. It is a madness woven into their very core, their very essence. Conflict is in their nature. They are connected in a way we cannot understand. Linked so intrinsically that they cannot exist without the other. Yet they cannot stop fighting. The war between them is as eternal as they are, and even knowing that the outcome can only ever be mutual destruction, they will still pursue it with a determination even I cannot match.

We often use the word madness to invalidate another's opinion. In the case of the Rand and the Djinn, it is acceptable. They are madness. And so is their fucking war. I didn't know it at the time, but the Iron Legion sought to

bring them back to the world. To fix it by repopulating the
Rand. It was an act that could only rekindle the War Eternal,
and just like before, it would be those of us caught in the
middle who would pay the heaviest price.

I could not contain Aerolis' power. But I could control
it. First, though, I needed to amplify it even further. The
Source I held in my left hand was not large, the size of a
cherry, though ridged in some places and sharp in others. It
would not go down easily, and it would be worse coming
back up. It would also kill me in mere minutes. Time is never
on our side. For us mere mortals time is disease, slowly
eating away at us. It cannot be stopped, nor bargained with,
nor even slowed. When I popped the Source in my mouth
and swallowed it down, tensing at the pain and gagging on
the blood as it scratched my throat, I felt time take notice.
It was not Chronomancy that put me on the clock, not this
time. It was Geomancy.

Attunement does not dictate what type of magic
a Sourcerer can use, but rather their resistance to the
destructive effect of holding a Source inside. I am not a
Geomancer, but I can use that school of magic. It's just
that it will kill me much faster than the ones I am attuned
to. Rather than days before rejection starts, I had minutes.
Little time, and so much to achieve. Aerolis' attempts to
subjugate weren't making things any easier. But the Djinn
would be the architect of its own destruction if it continued,
and I would carry it out. After all, its power was at my
command now, and along with the Geomancy Source, and
the knowledge of combining magic to strengthen it, I was in
no mood to suffer Aerolis' tantrum.

Reaching up with my left hand, I grabbed hold of a
piece of Do'shan. Not a physical action, but rather something

magical. I was combining Kinemancy and Geomancy
and amplifying the result through Aerolis' own magic. I
shouldn't have been able to move a hair at that range, yet I
could feel the rock of Do'shan. I could sense the tiny fissures
and faults. And with a sharp tug, I pulled a section of the
mountain free. It was not a large chunk of rock I sent falling
to the earth below, at least not in perspective. There was an
entire mountain floating above me and I ripped free a chunk
no larger than a few houses. Of course, it didn't need to
be that large. I was proving a point. The spectacle worked.
Everyone took notice, even Aerolis. We all watched the rock
fall, the impact felt through our feet as it struck the ground
and sent up a cloud of dust and dirt.

What are you doing? The force of Aerolis' rage
staggered me and I nearly collapsed to my knees from the
assault. I must have looked so strange staggering about
like a drunken fool, the conflict was all inside, invisible to
the others. I could feel the strain the Djinn was putting on
Ssserakis, and how close my horror was to being overcome.

"Stop fighting me, Aerolis!" I hissed the words
through clenched teeth as I reached my hand up once more
and clutched at another section of Do'shan. "We made
a deal. Either you honour it now and we all walk away
happy, or I will tear your city from the sky before trapping
you inside my own stone coffin!" To emphasise my point, I
tore away another section of the mountain, letting rocks as
large as manor houses fall to the ground. It was an emphatic
display of power, and it cost me more than I was willing to
admit. I couldn't let the Djinn realise that I would succumb
to rejection long before I ripped even a tenth of the mountain
out.

You carry an abomination inside of you!

I snorted. "It's a horror. My horror. And Ssserakis is welcome here. You are not! So, overcome your prejudice and stop fighting me. Help me save your people, Aerolis."

The soldiers from the Pit looked caught between awe and the need to bolt and run. I could feel the fear on them, and Ssserakis was feeding on it to help in its struggle against the Djinn. My own friends looked as close to running as the soldiers, and I will admit that hurt a little. Even Hardt was tensed as though ready to launch into a sprint at a moment's notice.

I felt the struggle cease as Aerolis pulled back from Ssserakis. There was hatred there, enmity built upon anger and disgust. They could hate each other all they wanted, just as long as they put it aside to obey me.

You should hurry, terran. Aerolis' voice was smug inside my head. *You don't have long.* He wasn't wrong about that. I could feel something hot and wet dripping from my left ear, and my stomach was starting to cramp. Still so much to do, and so much time wasted on petty, useless conflict.

Turning back towards the Forest of Ten, I stretched out a hand again. I could feel the Geomancy, the connection to the earth around me. I could feel fissures beneath my feet, and lines of power snaking through the dirt. I gripped hold of a chunk of earth beneath a section of the forest and lifted. Caked dirt rumbled and shifted, ripping free from its surroundings. Roots tore as the trees were pulled free from their deep connections. Then it all started to shake. Earth crumbled away, crushed in my magical grip. Trees toppled, falling back down to the ground. It all just fell apart in my hands.

"I need your help," I said between deep breaths. Strange that I was so out of breath despite the exertion being magical rather than physical. Whatever the type of strain, it still takes a toll on the body. "I can channel the power, but I don't have the experience, Aerolis. I need your guidance." I wasn't a Geomancer. I had never been trained to use that school of magic. I had no idea what I was doing.

For a moment there was nothing but silence. *Try again.*

I did. I reached out and felt the magic travel along the ground between me and the forest. Then Aerolis was there with me, his presence in the magical energy flowing through me. He did not take control but guided me. Through the Djinn I could feel the ground more acutely than before. I could sense where the earth was toughest, oldest. How deep the roots dug through the dirt. And I could feel the ruined Djinn city beneath me. Together we tore a chunk of forest free from its surroundings. Dozens of paces wide, and almost as deep. Twenty trees in all, each one old and tall and strong. Together we raised that chunk of earth, holding it together even as we bore it upwards towards Do'shan.

Each minute is a small eternity when you're dying from Source rejection. The Geomancy was killing me. I could feel blood leaking from my ears and nose, and even a trickle escaping from eyes. The cramps were blinding agony, spreading out from my stomach and reaching towards my limbs. I tried my best to ignore it all, but I could feel Ssserakis' panic. The horror's job was to keep Aerolis at bay, and to keep me together. The only way it could do the latter, was to take a portion of that pain into itself. To mitigate the damage being caused to me, by absorbing it. We both suffered that day, my horror and I. We both suffered, but Ssserakis sacrificed. After all, it hated the Djinn, and Aerolis would destroy Ssserakis if possible, and yet the horror still helped us.

It takes a long time to raise tons of dirt and tree up
through the sky, and Do'shan sat high up. Time passed,
minutes maybe passed, far too long, considering. Still we
raised up the section of forest until I could barely see it. I
had to rely almost entirely upon Aerolis to guide it onto the
top of the mountain, and when it was done, I felt drained.
The pain was excruciating. It felt as though something had
broken inside of me. Still, I wasn't ready to quit.

It's too much. Ssserakis' voice was laboured.

"Can you hold out?" The question might have been
directed at my horror, but I was asking it of myself also.
There was no answer. I took it as a positive sign.

"Are you ready, Aerolis?"

I felt curiosity from the Djinn. We had done what
we had come to do. But *I* wasn't done. The power of a god
inside made me arrogant. Arrogant enough to do something
stupid beyond reason. Arrogant enough to think I could get
away with it.

I turned towards the rocks and towards the Pit.
My friends and the soldiers were all staring at me in
something like awe, or possibly terror. The two are quite
often indistinguishable, which probably says a lot about the
heroes we worship. Any enmity between the two groups
was forgotten in the wake of what I had just done. They
were about to see a far greater spectacle. They were about to
witness the true power I could wield.

I felt Aerolis in my limbs once more as I knelt and dug
my fingers into the earth at me feet. My awareness spread
out to encompass everything around me. We were closer
to the Pit than I had thought, much closer. I could feel it
beneath us; the caverns and tunnels, heat and activity. Like
a hive of ants, the terrans below us swarmed in their daily

lives. Digging, digging, digging. I turned my attention away
from it, there would be time to deal with the Pit and the
enemies I left down there later. To the east I felt what I was
looking for, the ruined Djinn city. Through Aerolis I could
feel it all, and it was far larger than I had once thought.
The city almost as large as Ro'shan or Do'shan. Its tunnels
sat dark and abandoned for the most part, but I could feel
how they wove their way through the rock. Faults and
seems. Weak walls and supporting pillars. It was too much
for me to comprehend. My mind was not large enough to
encompass it all, to see how it all connected. I was not built
for such a thing. And I didn't need to be.

"I am the conduit." A warping of my old mantra.
But I suppose in some way they were also a submission. I
let Aerolis take control, trusting Ssserakis to keep me me. I
should quit while I was ahead.

That was when I realised exactly what the Djinn was
capable of. When I realised I had been fooling myself when
I threatened the creature. Its power was beyond me, beyond
anything I could hope to achieve. Even together and at our
strongest, Ssserakis and I were no match for Aerolis. I think
it said as much about the Iron Legion also, and the gulf of
power that lay between us.

The ground shook. That is an understatement. The
tremors were so strong that some of the soldiers were
knocked off their feet, and all crouched low to the ground,
ready to run with nowhere to run to. Rocks broke free from
nearby outcroppings, tumbling downhill. Nearby birds took
to flight, and wildlife scattered in panic. Worms wriggled
their way up to the surface and thrashed about in the dirt,
unable to escape what was coming. The noise was deafening,
yet I could still just about hear Hardt shouting. Luckily for

us both, he didn't try to interfere.

Then the ground cracked open. Rock shattered and deep holes opened up. The tremors grew even stronger. Two of the soldiers tried to flee but keeping their feet beneath them proved too difficult and they ended up sprawling and clutching at the grass as though it could keep them safe. One soldier began crawling towards me, sword drawn and ready. Horralain intercepted the man and punched him unconscious with vicious competency.

My vision was dimming. The cramps seemed distant things, which was probably far worse than when they weren't. Blood ran from my ears and nose and eyes, and I could feel it dripping from my chin. My left arm felt — odd. Hard. Stiff. I could no longer feel my fingers. It was a bad sign, but I ignored it as Aerolis continued to wreak his power upon the world. He knew what I wanted, what I had decided to do, and was happy to sacrifice me to do it. It was a power no one had seen in years, possibly in generations. This display of Geomancy had been missing since last of the Rand and Djinn were killed or trapped. I was channelling the power of a god, and it was taking its toll.

New rocks burst from the earth, ripping their way free into the open air. Earth shook free, revealing the city that lay beneath. A ruined city, rising from the soil into the light of day. More and more and more of it broke free from its confines. I could feel the strain such a display was putting upon the Djinn. He struggled to do it, but also revelled in the act. Aerolis was enjoying making his mark upon the world once more. If only he had realised it was not his mark, but mine.

We could not raise the entire city, of course. Only a portion of it. A large portion, but far from its full extent.

Even so, a hundred rooms all interconnected, two great cavernous halls. All encased in rock. It did not look like a city. It looked like a small mountain hollowed out. It would do. It would serve as the beginnings of my empire. My seat of power. The eventual resting place of the Corpse Throne.

Beneath our feet I felt the panic. The prisoners of the Pit were terrified. Understandable. The earth shaking is one thing for those on the surface, something entirely different for those trapped underground.

Eskara! Ssserakis was quiet, its voice almost lost in the noise, The strain on the horror too great. I could feel it starting to unravel, and that was something I could not allow. Something I couldn't bear.

"Enough, Aerolis!" My own voice was strained also, breaking on the words. It, too, was lost in the noise. But it didn't need to reach far. The Djinn heard me, and he ignored me, continuing to exert his power on the earth, dragging more and more of the city up into the light. I could barely see from the blood in my eyes. The rejection was killing me. Killing us.

I pulled my right hand from the earth and ignited it. Aerolis ignored me still, confident I could do nothing to stop him. So, I slapped my right hand down onto my left and ignited the rope tied around it. The skin felt strange, hard and rough, like the rock we were pulling from the ground. It took only a moment for the rope around my arm to incinerate. Suddenly Aerolis was being dragged away. The anchor to me gone, he could no longer stay. I helped him along with a push, finally kicking the Djinn out of my body. He fled with mocking laughter, certain the damage had already been done. Certain I was beyond repair. He might have been right about that.

With Aerolis gone, I suddenly realised the Djinn had been delaying my Source rejection somehow. My left arm was numb, but the rest of me was wracked with spasming cramps. Blind from the blood in my eyes I reached for my snuff pouch. I couldn't feel it. I couldn't feel anything with my left hand.

"Eska, what have you done?" Hardt's voice, oddly muted and full of sorrow. I didn't have time to ask him what he meant.

I found the snuff pouch with my right hand and all but tore it open, pulling out a large clump of Spiceweed and shoving it in my mouth, chewing and swallowing as quickly as I could. We Sourcerers may be powerful, often afforded positions of high privilege for the magic we lend to those in charge, but we pay a hefty price and dignity is often amongst the cost. I have lost count of the number of times in my life where I have lay in a pool of my own vomit, retching up the Sources that afford me such power. This was one of them. I could barely move. Exhaustion and pain overcame me. Luckily, the spectacle I had just performed was more awe-inspiring than my debilitated state was embarrassing. Still, Horralain stood over me, Shatter in hand in case anyone came too close. Imiko rushed forward and pulled my hair away from the vomit. Tamura snatched up the Sources and secreted them away, while Hardt fussed over my left arm. I had just performed a miracle, a display of power no other in living memory had witnessed. I had just pulled a city from the earth. And yet, there I was, curled into a ball, wracked with pain, and unable to shift myself out of my own spreading bile, being tended to by friends with soothing words. I wish I could promise you it was the last time I have been in such a state, but I assure you, it is far from it. Overtaxing my body past the point of breaking is something of a bad habit of mine, one I seem entirely unable to break.

"Eska, your arm." I had to wipe blood from my eyes to see what Hardt was talking about. I didn't really want to see. Something was wrong, horribly wrong, I could tell by the way I couldn't feel anything. Hardt ran his hands over my arm, poking it, prodding it, and I felt nothing.

I couldn't hold it back any longer. Ssserakis was as weary as I had ever heard it, its voice small and quiet.

Finally, I braced myself and summoned what little courage I had remaining. Bloody tears ran down my face, and I had earned every one of them. Geomancy rejection, late stage. My left arm had turned to stone.

CHAPTER
SIXTEEN

IT DIDN'T TAKE LONG FOR MY NEW GHOSTS to appear. They crept from the shadows, rose up through the rock, or even ran at me screaming silently. I recognised some of them, faces barely remembered from my time in the Pit, but most were lost in the gathering crowd. Ghosts are odd things, like memories slowly fading from the world. They start out as distinct figures who look just like they did at the time of their death, but if they are kept in the world, then they begin to lose definition. Eventually all ghosts fade and become blurs, like those we encountered in the ruins of Picarr. Wait a little longer and they become no more than whispers on the wind, not of sound, but of thought or feeling. Longer still, and they become nothing, frayed away until there isn't even a thought remaining. These ghosts were fresh, distinct, angry. I would have given much to see Prig among them, the foreman who had tortured me for so long.

The fucking bastard who had scarred my face so severely. To see him dead, dragged along in my wake, would have been a balm to my soul. But I saw no Prig, no Overseer. Only fellow scabs, Deko and his closest cronies. It was all the proof I needed. I had just murdered the Pit.

Displacement, or so I am told. You cannot move a thing, without something taking its place. I pulled a city from the earth and in the void I left behind, rock and earth and water rushed in. Some great underground cavern was broken, and the water trapped within found new paths to flow into. A flood of cold, dark water drowned the Pit, filling every level and tunnel and cavern. Prisoners and soldiers alike were trapped there, died with water in their lungs, struggling to breathe. Others found they had no way out, the water blocked off their escape and they suffocated as the air ran out or starved with nothing left to eat. Or perhaps they turned on each other down in the deep, dark hole. Take away the light and the food and the hope, and it is surprising how quickly we terrans start to resemble our roots.

Speaking of the Damned, they too suffered from my spectacle. Trapped in a city that was rising and crumbling in equal measure, they fell upon each other. Fear and confusion made stupid creatures lash out at each other. Whole caverns were lost, collapsed, and it would be impossible to count such a death toll. Strange, no ghosts of the Damned, nor of the imps from the city plagued me. Only the terrans from the Pit. I will admit, I have often wondered why that is. Perhaps they were simply too primitive to rise as ghosts. Some questions do not have answers, at least not ones we can fathom.

I did not mean to drown the Pit. I did not intend to

kill everyone in it. There is no doubt I would have killed Prig
and Deko and the Overseer, had I the chance. I fantasised
about it enough times. But I did not want to murder them
all. None of them were innocent. The innocent don't get sent
to the Pit. That didn't mean they deserved to die down in the
dark. I would have set the scabs free had I thought about it.
Liberated them. But then I would have been loosing violent
criminals on the world, along with those who just committed
the wrong crime at the wrong time. I have no answers for
what I should have done, nor excuses for what I did do. All
I have is grief, shame, and ghosts to follow me around. To
make certain I never forget.

We made the short trek towards the city I had pulled
from the earth. Well, the others did. I was carried by Hardt.
A few of the soldiers followed us, at a distance, and others
ran back towards the Pit, probably to fetch reinforcements.
I, of course, already knew what they would find there, but
I hadn't the heart to tell Hardt just yet. He knew many of
the scabs, considered them friends. It is not easy telling a
person you have just killed dozens of their friends. Waves of
exhaustion washed over me. I felt off balance, lopsided. My
left side weighed heavier than my right. Geomancy rejection,
the body turns to stone. Both Aerolis and Ssserakis held it at
bay for a while, but I held the Source inside for too long, and
drew on it too strongly. From the tips of my fingers all the
way up my forearm was cold grey stone, ending just below
my elbow. I looked like an arm had been fashioned from
countless small rocks. I could feel nothing from it. I could
not move my hand or fingers, and it weighed me down.
My arm was dead, all but lost. The horror of that realisation
had yet to fully hit me. I was ignoring it, as I was ignoring
Hardt's attempts to fuss over it. There was nothing he could

do, nothing anyone could do. No healer or Biomancer could help me now. Flesh can be turned to stone, but the reverse is not true. Not even the Rand could bring my arm back.

Do'shan moved on. Whatever method the Djinn had been using to slow its progress through the sky was ended. The shadow of that mountain loomed over us as it passed. I imagined Aerolis up there, laughing at me, at the price I had paid for the deals we struck, but in truth that was unlikely. The Rand and Djinn both considered us unimportant, our lives too brief to matter. Chances were, I was already all but forgotten. I never again stepped foot on Do'shan. I do not count that a loss. It never felt like home, as Ro'shan had. No, I never considered Do'shan home. It is a flying grave, a monument to the woman I loved.

The Djinn's part in the spectacle was soon forgotten. Actually, it was never really known, but in the re-tellings of the story, Do'shan was edited out. Soldiers are ever ones to gossip. People like to say that fishwives gossip, that rumour and idle speculation are the realm of women at menial tasks. What a load of shit. Everyone gossips, but soldiers are by far the worst. I have it first-hand from a bard I once knew. He would enter a tavern and look for groups of soldiers, they are usually easy to spot, and either sit close by or insinuate himself into the group with a few rounds of watered ale. That's where he would get most of his stories, from the lips of idle soldiers. Of course, he admitted to embellishing them somewhat. I know for a certainty he embellished my own tales. The soldiers who witnessed my raising of the city soon forgot that Do'shan was there at all. All they spoke of was a woman, a Sourcerer with an arm of stone, pulling a city from the earth. I quickly became legend, a tale spreading throughout Terrelan and beyond, and all it cost me was the use of a perfectly good arm.

Hardt refused to enter the ruined city at first. I couldn't blame him for that, last time we had been there, he lost a brother. I caught him staring towards the closest entrance with a solemn look on his face. So, we made camp outside the city on our first day back in Terrelan, staking a claim but not exploring. I comforted Hardt as best I could, but we had little food and no alcohol, and my words seemed unequal to the task.

More and more of my ghosts began to appear. Some wandered aimlessly, fading in and out of existence, and I barely even noticed them. Others were more volatile. Deko's ghost spent a while trying to attack me before settling for scathing glares. He did not fade away. Along with the ghosts came the refugees. Men and women, soldiers and prisoners, all from the Pit. I had drowned the prison, but there were survivors. Most of the soldiers were stationed on the higher levels where the water took longest to get to, they made it just fine. A couple of hundred people in their uniforms, a little bedraggled, some quite damp. It turned out the soldiers were not as heartless as I had believed as a scab, many of them had stayed amidst rising water levels, attempting to save as many of the prisoners as they could. I do not know the full population of the Pit at the time of my return, only that fewer than fifty of them made it out. Hundreds died. Maybe thousands. Not since the war had I been responsible for so many deaths. The guilt of that weighed more heavily than I realised.

At first the soldiers threatened, postured. They outnumbered us, but none dared get too close to Horralain and his hammer. There were threats of arrest and detainment, royal judgement for the destruction of the empire's largest prison, but threats are nothing without the will to back them. Word was already spreading through the soldiers and prisoners; those who saw what I had done were talking, and there I was at the centre of it. Cloaked in subtly shifting shadow, an arm made of stone, eyes that flashed with the fury of a storm.

There is a power to appearance. You can claim to be a king, but if you do not look the part no one will take you at your word. I sat at the foot of a city that had risen from the dirt. Two of the largest Terrelans I have ever seen stood ready to defend me yet deferring to me as their leader. I was wreathed in power, even without Sources in my stomach it crackled around me. I made no claim to rule, said nothing in the face of those soldiers and their threats, yet my appearance made certain claims for me.

A couple of the prisoners, scabs I might have once known, broke free from the collecting soldiers. They ran towards me, pulling up short as Horralain stepped in the way, hammer held high. Him, they certainly recognised, I could see it in their faces.

"Asylum," shouted one of the scabs, a tall woman with dirt lining her every wrinkle. She dropped to her knees before me, her eyes on me rather than the giants between us. The other scab, a man with a grimy black beard, followed suit. The soldiers chasing slowed to a halt, clearly nervous and rightly so. "Please. Grant asylum. We're..."

"Prisoners," I interrupted. "Scabs from the Pit." The woman's eyes searched my face and found no recognition there. I had been famous in my time down in the Pit, or infamous at least, but I think the changes wrought upon me were too great. I was much older than when I had left, more scarred, harder, and built like a warrior. My eyes flashed and much of the rest of me was hidden in shadow thanks to Ssserakis. Imiko later said that I looked like some sort of dark queen sitting in judgement. I suppose she was not far wrong.

"We're innocent." A bold claim, and a lie.

"Nobody from the Pit is innocent." I said it quietly, yet the words seemed to carry. It was not Vibromancy, but that everyone nearby was straining to listen as though my words held more weight than the swords the soldiers carried. "I know first-hand." I stood, hiding the pain it caused me, and a black cloak of shadow billowed out behind me. I have called Ssserakis many things over the years, but I cannot deny the horror had a flair for the dramatic and it certainly used it to further my reputation. Hardt and Horralain stepped aside as I walked past them. Hardt gave me a nod, a subtle sign of what I should do; north on the moral compass. He had been down in the Pit for far longer than I; he knew many of its inhabitants.

Guilt and innocence are absolutes, but punishment should not be universal. Stealing an apple is the not the equal crime of murder. It was long said that only the worst criminals are sent to the Pit. Murderers, thief lords, rapists, those of us guilty of war crimes. It is not entirely accurate. The Pit was simply where prisoners were sent to be forgotten. Hardt served his kingdom for years as a privateer, a pirate in all but name and employment. He was sanctioned by the Terrelan Empire, until the crime came to light in the presence of foreign dignitaries, and then he was sent to the Pit for his part in the murders he committed and the ships that he scuttled. Forgotten, and no longer an embarrassment. How many others suffered similar fates for crimes they were ordered to commit? How many scabs were soldiers who deserted their units rather than participate in a war that saw cities razed and civilians brutalised? How many prisoners had served their time down there in the dark?

Asylum. Another word for shelter, protection from persecution. Silva had granted me asylum once. She'd prevented the executioner's blade from ending my life. A life saved, though she never told me what the decision cost her. That was the thought in my mind right at that moment, that Silva had once given to me what these two scabs asked for. She was making me a better person, even months after I had killed her.

"I grant asylum." The words slid from my mouth and the importance hung heavy in the air. Asylum is most often granted by a state, not a single person. Without even realising it, I had just started my own little kingdom, right there in the heart of Terrelan.

"This is treason!" The boldest of the soldiers shouted, rushing forward sword drawn. I couldn't back up, couldn't show weakness or fear, yet I also couldn't fight. It was taking all the will I could muster just to stay on my feet, and though Ssserakis was doing a good job of making me appear sinister, the horror was not strong enough to do much else after holding back Aerolis and the toll the magic had taken on my body. Luckily for us both, Horralain was there.

The thug stepped past me, moving me aside with a gentle push, and stepping into the oncoming soldier. He brushed aside the sword stroke with the haft of the hammer, and pivoted it, slamming the head into the soldier. Shatter lives up to its name. The soldier shattered into chunks of bloody flesh. More than a few people lost their stomachs that day, and I was the only one with Sources as an excuse. To his credit, even Horralain looked horrified with the

consequences of his single hammer blow. In the confusion
that followed, more of the scabs broke free from their
guards and ran toward us. Horralain held his hammer up
as a ward, but he needn't have bothered. More men and
women threw themselves at my feet and begged for my
protection. Suddenly I found myself offering asylum to
not one or two, but fifty inmates from the Pit. Some offered
meagre belongings in exchange, while others offered their
fealty. It made me smile that one man offered a particularly
long length of rope from around his waist. Whether he
knew it or not, he and his rope had been instrumental in
our escape from the Pit years earlier. Perhaps even stranger
than the scabs, many of the soldiers came forward as well,
laying their weapons on the earth and offering service in
return for home and protection. I will admit, this confused
me somewhat. It was not until I took the time to speak to
some of the soldiers, that I discovered the Pit was as much
a punishment for them as it was the prisoners. Men and
women of the Terrelan army were sent to the Pit for life, to
carry out the full term of their careers underground, or close
to it, guarding nothing. The Pit had been run by the inmates,
and most of the scabs never even saw a soldier after they
were sent into the lower levels. Many of them wanted out, a
new career or maybe just a new master.

By the time that day was done, I had one hundred
and sixty-two members of my new little kingdom. Soldiers
and prisoners, and many had trades they could still
remember working. I should have looked more closely at
those I was accepting into my service. I would have noticed
one of them was off. One of the scabs did not belong. For a
start, she was far too beautiful to have spent time down in
the Pit.

CHAPTER SEVENTEEN

In the days that followed I let Tamura take up much
of the heavy lifting in regards to organising my new little
kingdom. It was more like a collaboration between Tamura
and Imiko, as most people needed someone to translate
his mad ramblings into something approaching workable
orders. The old Aspect was a natural, easily listening to
others and directing them where they were most needed,
and where they could benefit us most. Before long we had
scavengers out for food, foragers picking their way through
the forest, people with axes chopping down trees, and small
patrols to act as an early warning, should the Terrelan army
turn up in force. I hoped they wouldn't, we were not ready
for such a conflict. I was not ready for such a conflict. But
our enemies rarely wait for us to be ready.

We had moved into the city I raised from the earth,
occupying the ground levels and keeping close to one

another. There were no windows in any of the rooms and all were interconnected, such is the problem of occupying a city that was built underground and never intended to see the light of day. Luckily for us, the scabs from the Pit were nothing if not experts at digging, so we set about shining light onto the upper levels of the city, while the lower levels would remain in darkness. Most of the city was still buried and unexplored. There were imps down there somewhere, and Damned too. Enemies infesting the lower levels of my empire. I had two choices. Either we sealed off the lower levels as best we could and ignored the problem, or we ventured out into the dark to deal with the monsters beneath us. You can probably guess which option I chose. I've never been very good at leaving a thing alone.

Somewhat predictably, not many of the scabs were willing to join my little expedition into the dark. I couldn't blame them, they had so recently escaped a life without light, most of them spent as much time as possible outside, staring at the sky in wonder. Though there were a few who had a very different reaction. Some of the scabs feared the sky and the daylight. They had spent so long down in the Pit, the idea of freedom, of open space where walls cannot be seen, scared them. I could feel the fear and detect its cause without even being told.

My bond with Ssserakis was deepening, and with it came a deeper connection to my horror's powers. I think it was that deepening bond that allowed Ssserakis to control my shadow more easily. What once had been a draining struggle, was now easy for it. I wore my own shadow like a cloak, hood pulled up so only my flashing eyes could be seen in the depths of that darkness. It was an image I was keen to maintain. Shadow is an odd thing when made tangible by magic. It felt like silk beneath my fingers and flowed easily while also clinging to my form, yet Ssserakis could dismiss it at will and it would simply fade away, my normal shadow returning.

Horralain was, of course, the first to my side when I announced I was heading into the depths of the city. Hardt attempted to join us, but I convinced him otherwise. Isen had died down there, and it was a pain Hardt did not need to revisit. Besides, I knew there would likely be killing involved. The Damned would not be cowed or parleyed with like the feral pahht. They were vicious and animalistic and would attack us on sight. We had no choice but to exterminate them like the pests they are. We terrans share far more than we would like to admit with our ancestors. We are good at making war and confused by peace.

By the time we set off, my little group of explorers was ten strong. Horralain and I, six soldiers eager to do something other than patrol, and two scabs who seemed more scared of the sky than the dark. One of the scabs claimed to be a cartographer, at least in her earlier life, and volunteered to map our progress. We took chalk to mark our way, torches to light our way, and weapons to cut our way.

I went first, much to Horralain's grumbling. It was his job to protect me after all, but he soon relented when I made it an order to stay behind me. Besides, I could see in the dark, he could not. With the torches to my back, I let Ssserakis' sight guide us. My horror painted the tunnels in black and white, details clearly defined but devoid of colour. With that sight I could see dozens of feet down the corridors of the city, far more than any torchlight would reach. I am told Photomancers can achieve a similar effect with their magic; they can sap colour from sight, or bring those colours bursting to life so much more vibrant than before. They see in spectrums the rest of us cannot even begin to understand. It is perhaps why so many of them are driven mad by their magic. Photomancy rejection takes an interesting form. The Sourcerer begins to blur, then their colours separate in seven different versions of themselves, each cast in a different hue. Eventually all seven of their forms simply shatter, and they become one with the light. I'm not sure what that means, but the result is like any other rejection. They die. Painfully.

Progress was slow as we checked every room, our cartographer making notes as to possible purposes. Some were designated as living quarters, others as places of industry or storage. I'm not sure what qualified each room for its intended purpose, but then it's a ruler's job to delegate tasks to those best suited to them. My own version of rule was not so much delegating the tasks, as allowing others to take them upon themselves. It seemed to work out well in the beginning.

I was not as graceful as I would have liked, especially considering I was ahead of the others with their torchlight illuminating my every move. My left arm was heavy and awkward. Hardt had advised resting it in a sling to take some of the weight off, but I could still move the arm itself, only the hand and wrist and much of the forearm were stone. It was useless, but I would rather have it free than strapped to my chest. I carried a Sourceblade in my right hand, short and perfect for close confines, sharp as a razor. It glowed with an inner light, Kinemancy and Pyromancy mixing together inside. A sword that could burn and cut at the same time.

Sound echoed strangely down there, making it tough to determine the source. Our own footsteps rang back at us, and more than once I had to quiet our party to hear what sounded like whispers so far away they might have been the whistling of the wind. But there were words buried beneath the noise. Old words. A language I didn't know. One so old even Ssserakis did not know it.

It was quite a surprise, at least to the others, when we found the first of the faces carved into the walls. From that point on, they were a regular thing, a new face every dozen paces or so, almost terran, but not. Some of the soldiers were unnerved, I heard at least one talk of going back. I snapped at him for silence and told them they were just carvings, no matter how lifelike they might look. Of course, I knew it wasn't entirely true. With Ssserakis' sight I could see further than any of the others, and with that sight I could see the faces had their eyes closed, at least until we drew close. Just out of range of the torchlight, their eyes snapped open, and seemed positioned in just such a way that they were staring at us no matter where we stood. The others didn't need to know, so I did not tell them. But I was certain that once the city was fully explored, I would have every one of the faces chiselled out of the walls.

"Some sort of Geomancy?" I whispered to Ssserakis.

The horror laughed. *Far older than magic. Not everything dies as you know it, Eskara. Some things live forever in one way or another.* The horror had the truth of it. The faces were alive, yet not living. A true oddity of the world.

For hours we searched that city, and even then, we only covered a tiny section of it. On the fourth level down from the surface, we found bodies. One or two at first, but soon more. They were small things with grey flesh and tails. Heads with no ears. Imps. Through my innate Necromancy I could tell they were freshly dead, no more than a few days.

Some were eviscerated, others showed clear signs of being
gnawed upon. One thing was abundantly clear to me: In
raising the city, I had broken it apart in many places. The
barriers the imps had built to block off the Damned and
protect themselves were broken. There was a war happening
beneath our feet, one the imps could not hope to win.

Another floor down and new noises started echoing
along the tunnels toward us. Our cartographer was making
marks on a nearby wall when she heard it, a shrill scream
barely audible to us. She backed up, placing herself in the
centre of our little group. We heard it again, louder this time,
maybe closer. I could not tell which direction it came from,
sound echoing underground is often distorted that way,
confusing our senses. And terran hearing is far from perfect.
We are a people who rely on our eyes most of all, and the
tahren do like to mock us for it. Horralain moved in close
and I stepped away, growling at him not to crowd me. There
was something familiar in the scream, a noise I recognised
but had not heard in a long time. That knowledge gnawed at
me, recognition so close yet just out of reach.

*Would you like a hint? That Ssserakis recognised the
noise was already a hint.*

When it came again, I realised it was no scream. It
was a howl. Our little group closed ranks, soldiers watching
each other's backs, weapons raised and ready. The noise
came again louder, closer. Hunters moving in for the kill. We
were prey. I do not like being prey.

"We should go back to the stairs," said the
cartographer in a shrill voice that bordered on the edge of
panic.

*Running is for prey. A true predator lays a trap and forces
the prey into it.* I couldn't help but feel we were already neck

deep in the trap.

"Even the deadliest of predators is prey to something deadlier." The words were meant for myself and my horror, but the others heard them. Whether they took as them as condemnation that we were all fucked, or as reassuring that we were mightier than whatever was coming for us, I don't know. Certainly, none of us broke and ran. That was good, we terrans are followers at heart, pack animals clinging to our herds. If just one of us had broken and run, the rest would almost certainly have followed. Courage held up by bravado and company and nothing else.

The howl came again, so loud it hurt my ears. The others, too, found the noise painful, and I could see how close panic was to setting in and taking control. I could feel the fear, and it was delicious. "We used to hear stories down in the Pit, Horralain," I said. "That you had once wrestled a Khark Hound. Were they true?"

Horralain looked pained, as though suddenly being the centre of attention hurt him. "No." The word slid slowly from his mouth. "I hit it with a rock while the others went at it with picks and shovels."

I smiled at him and then turned it on the others. "A rock and some picks. And we have a bloody great hammer and a thicket of swords. I think we can take a Khark Hound, no problem." Laughter, even forced, can do much to bolster courage. A few chuckles rolled around, half-hearted at best, and the fear lessened a little, though not enough. I couldn't blame them, not really, I knew what we were up against.

When I noticed them for the first time, it was at the furthest edge of what I could see, and even then, they were little more than indistinct shapes waiting out in the gloom. I don't know how long they had been there, watching us, but

Khark Hounds have a savage intelligence to them. They are not quite the mindless beasts they appear. There were two of them and they filled the tunnel. Two great slavering maws, and eight eyes all trained on us. Ears twitched our way and backward, keeping track of many sounds all at once. They were waiting. They were hunting us.

"The howling stopped," one of the soldiers said. "Have they gone?" Fear often makes us cling to vain hopes.

"No. They're here. Watching us," I said. Khark Hounds are voracious hunters, moving in packs and tracking prey over long distances. They have no noses, and their faces end in a squat muzzle bursting with jagged-edged teeth, but their hearing and eyesight is unmatched in either Ovaeris or Sevoari. Like all creatures of the Other World, they are a nightmare given savage form; a nightmare of the perfect hunter maybe.

Minions and beasts. I kept them as pets, trained to hunt down the places where Norvet Meruun's tendrils spread.

"Any suggestions on how best to fight them?" I asked quietly.

Fight them? I dominated them.

"Helpful."

"Who are you talking to?" asked one of the soldiers, an older man with dark, wrinkled skin.

Horralain grunted. I'm not sure if the exclamation was meant for me or the soldier, but it certainly put a stop to people asking about my conversations with myself.

I'd never actually fought a Khark Hound before. I'd summoned many in my time, using them to great effect harrying the Terrelan army as it advanced upon Vernan, but summoning a monster, and fighting against one are two different things. I remembered the tactics I had seen soldiers employ against my own summoned creatures, spear and bows for the most part, and acceptable casualties. Losing even a single member of my team seemed unacceptable to me. That is the problem when you start thinking about soldiers as people, they are much more difficult to send to their deaths. One of many reasons I made for a terrible general.

The tunnel was maybe ten feet high and almost twice that wide. A large space, but we would struggle to surround an attacking pack of hounds. I was still considering options when our time ran out. An ear-splitting howl ripped the air to pieces and with Ssserakis' black and white sight, I could see the monsters in front of us leap into a loping run. The howl was answered, a second group I couldn't see. I realised then that we were surrounded. I let my Sourceblade puff out of existence and raised my right hand, forming a kinetic shield that blocked the tunnel in front of me almost entirely.

"I'll hold this side. Deal with the ones behind us!" I shouted.

"They're behind us?" The cartographer's panic spread instantly, and my group of soldiers became a milling chaotic jumble of steel, flesh, and fear. They barely had time to turn before the monsters reached us.

Everything happened at once. Two Khark Hounds hit my kinetic shield with all the force of two running monsters, each weighing maybe ten times what I did. A kinetic shield disperses the energy striking it as best it can, but the force must go somewhere. I would have been barrelled over in an instant if not for Horralain at my back, steadying me with his own considerable weight. The hounds rebounded, momentarily dazed by the arrested momentum. Their confusion didn't last. A terran might have stepped back,

considered the problem and given me respite from the
onslaught. But Khark Hounds do not relent, they threw
themselves at me again and again, scrabbling claws at my
shield, a frantic attempt to find any way past my defences.
Behind me, the first of my soldiers died. They had no
shield to hide behind and one of the hounds leapt forward,
grabbed a soldier by his sword arm and wrenched him off
his feet, dragging him away into the darkness where the
monsters behind us could tear at him without intervention.
None of his comrades dared go after him. They formed into
a tight rank of steel pointed into the dark, hoping it would
make a difference. Fools.

Fear takes many forms. Through Ssserakis, I have
tasted them all. Terror is an interesting one. It was like force
feeding Ssserakis; so much strength so quickly it seeped
out into me. New strength flooded my limbs, giving me
confidence. My cloak dissolved and Ssserakis sent shadowy
spikes into the stone beneath my feet, anchoring us against
the onslaught tearing at my shield.

"Help the others," I growled the words at Horralain,
waving my stone arm at him. He hesitated a moment, his
jaw working back and forth as he tried to decide whether to
follow my orders or not. Eventually he hefted his hammer
and strode off to meet the attack coming from behind me.

The two hounds in front were still scrabbling at my
shield. They resemble wolves in many ways, though far
larger and more terrifying. Their shoulders reach as tall as
a fully-grown man, and that meant they towered over my
smaller height. Each beast had a mouth full of teeth, and four
eyes set two to either side of its head, all filled with savage
malice. Ears on top of their heads swivelled back and forth
in a constant motion. The beasts are often called Razorbacks,

and it's a name that is well earned. Bony shards, each sharp as a blade, breached the skin of the monsters all along their backs, forming a natural armour and weapon both. I could see them both so clearly as they tore at my shield, snarling and snapping, desperate to get through. It would not take much for them to tear me apart, and in truth there was little keeping them from doing just that.

I could hear the fight behind me, and it did not sound as though it was going well. The cartographer was screaming, high-pitched and incessant. Soldiers were shouting, mostly impotent threats to bolster courage. Horralain was grunting with some effort. Whether we were winning or losing, I couldn't help. All I could do was hold back the two monsters trying to tear us apart, certain in the knowledge that if we were attacked from both sides at once, we would all die.

Did I mention the intelligence of Khark Hounds? It did not take them long to find the edges of my shield. I could not contour it to the tunnel's shape exactly, and once they found those edges, I knew it would soon fall. Rather than let them tear my shield from my hands, I acted. I dropped the shield and released a pulse of kinetic energy at the same time. Behind me, the cartographer was caught in the blast and thrown into the backs of the soldiers. In front of me, the hounds took the blast head on. The first had been up on its hind legs, scrabbling at the top edge of my shield, and the blast knocked it over and sent it sprawling. The second of the monsters had been on all four legs and weathered the pulse easily, powerful claws gouging into the stone beneath it. I may have ruffled its fur and bloodied its snout, but neither was enough to stop a Khark Hound. Neither was enough to even faze the beast.

I barely had time to react as the monster threw itself on me, but I just about managed to throw my left arm in its way. It was not really conscious thought that made me do it, but rather a need to protect myself. In time of crisis, we terrans usually put our arms in harm's way before the rest of us. Teeth locked around my stone arm, jaws clamping down so hard flesh and bone would have snapped. But my petrified arm did not. Of course, having a stone arm didn't really save me. Before I could think of striking back, I was wrenched off my feet and thrown side to side as the Khark Hound ragged me about like a child.

What happened next is a blur. Perhaps you have a seen a dog savage a rabbit or other small animal? Now imagine you are that animal. I was whipped side to side so quickly my eyes could not keep up. I was smashed against the wall and the floor, and my shoulder wrenched from its socket. A dislocated shoulder is pain stacked on top of pain, but I couldn't even scream, such was the ferocity of the attack. I might even have blacked out for a moment or two, it's hard to say. For all my skill and power, I was beaten so soundly by a couple of monsters I learned to summon when I was ten years old. There is little like a sound beating to put life in perspective.

Horralain saved my life. The big thug charged the Khark Hound, hammer held high. He couldn't swing it, of course, not while the monster held me in its jaws, but Horralain is a big man and big men are considered threats even by monsters. The hound considered me dead, or close enough to it that I was no longer a threat. It tossed me aside and I collided with the tunnel wall, collapsing into a broken heap, barely able to get a coherent thought to stick in my head.

In blurred relief, I saw my stone hand in front of me. I was pushed up against the wall, where it sloped outward, half collapsed to the side and feeling boneless. Yet I could see the fingers of my stone hand slowly clenching and unclenching. They stopped as I blinked away the fuzzy confusion, and when I pulled my arm close the fingers were still once more. The hand and the rest of my forearm was blessedly free of pain, but my shoulder felt like fire under the skin. My arm slumped at an odd angle and though I could just about move it, the pain that brought on was dizzying. At that moment I wished I hadn't argued against Hardt coming along

What are you doing?

"I have to fight." The words slurred from my mouth.

Idiot. Don't fight these creatures, they are nothing to us. Dominate them.

"I…"

We are not prey, Eskara!

Horralain was still fighting, swinging Shatter and then bringing the haft up to guard against reply. I watched groggily as one of the Khark Hounds locked teeth around the hammer's haft and ripped it from Horralain's hands. As strong as the big man was, there was no matching strength against a monster of such size. The other hound was on its feet again, stalking, making ready to pounce on him. Behind us, another soldier was down, bleeding everywhere. The other soldiers were gathered close, holding onto each other for protection and courage both. The cartographer was curled into a ball against the tunnel wall, holding her knees and shaking with each great sob she let out, her precious map lying forgotten before her.

I watched as both Khark Hounds went in for the kill.

Horralain acted faster than I would have thought possible, punching the first of the monsters where its snout should have been, and then stepping back from the other and reaching out, somehow gripping hold of its muzzle and forcing its jaws shut. It was a losing battle. No matter what the rumours down in the Pit said about him, no man could wrestle a Khark Hound and live. Horralain was facing off against two, and all to protect me.

Three times Horralain tried to kill me. Even to this day I still bare the odd croak in my voice from that first attempt, some damage he did to my throat that has never fully repaired. But then, since I had recruited him, I could count as many times that he had saved my life. He was a savage brute with no moral compass save for the one I gave him, yet he had thrown himself into the fight against these monsters to save me and to save those with me. He'd followed me into battle against a Djinn, a creature that was all but a god. He'd even tried his hand against the Iron Legion for my sake. I couldn't just watch him die, torn to pieces by monsters. At the very least, I had to try something.

Pushing away from the wall, I slipped around Horralain and stood against the first Khark Hound as it crouched to pounce. Two of its malevolent eyes fixed on me, the other two keeping Horralain in focus. Blood dripped from its teeth, and the growl that rumbled from its throat very nearly had me pissing myself. Just because I was carrying the embodiment of fear inside of me, did not mean I couldn't wet myself in pure terror.

"STOP!" The word tore its way free from me in a scream. I reached for the Impomancy Source I carried inside, but pain has a way of shattering concentration and I could not draw on any of my Sources.

The Khark Hounds stopped. The beast that had been about to pounce straightened up to its full height and took a single step forward. Its face drew so close to mine I could no longer focus on it. The smell was oddly pleasant, a sweet odour somehow masking the gore on its muzzle. A furious growl started somewhere in the pit of that creature and rumbled out through its clenched teeth. I was certain I was about to die. More certain than I have ever been. This beast was no terran to be cowed by my flashing eyes and bravado, it was a nightmare given terrible form. But then, so were we.

Shadowy wings unfurled behind me. The darkness beneath my feet boiled and rose up in plumes like black fire. The shadow passed over my skin, mottling it in twisting patterns. Ssserakis made me look like a lord of Sevoari, and the hounds responded.

The first of the monsters, the one staring at me, took a single step backward, claws scraping across stone. Then it bowed its head, exposing the back of its neck to me. A few moments later and the other Khark Hound broke away from Horralain and copied the actions of the first. I heard frightened squeaks of alarm behind me, and a few terrified threats as another of the beasts skirted the soldiers and approached us, also bowing its head.

Horralain moved slowly, picking up Shatter from the ground and hefting it, preparing to strike. I held up my left hand, the only part of me the shadows didn't touch, and shook my head at the big man. The Khark Hounds were no longer a threat. They were mine now.

The others weren't happy that I kept the Khark Hounds, they had killed three soldiers in total, and very nearly did the same with the rest of us. I was advised to kill them and end their savage existence. I ignored that advice.

Three Khark Hounds were worth more than seven soldiers. I didn't consider the morale issue. Soldiers talk, rumours spread, my hounds were never well liked, and I earned quite a bit of discontent from my new subjects by sparing them.

I also earned a new aspect to my reputation. We went down into the dark depths to explore. I came out flanked by three great monsters, the likes of which most people hadn't seen since the end of the war. More than that, they were mine, even without an Impomancy Source. To my knowledge, no other Sourcerer has ever managed to command a creature from the Other World without the aid of an Impomancy Source. It was a feat unique to me. Of course, I should say it was unique to Ssserakis, but no one else knew of the horror I carried inside.

They called me mad, as I was too often caught talking to myself. I was named a dark queen. Monsters, nightmares listened to me, did my bidding. A stone arm, flashing eyes, a shadow that warped itself to my will, and the power to raise a city out of the earth itself. It didn't matter that only half of the rumours were true, and it mattered even less that those which were accurate were not entirely my doing. The responsibility and the blame were laid squarely at my feet, and I made no attempt to dispute them. I accepted the rumours, good and bad, made them a part of myself.

They called me mad, a dark queen, and I used their insults to define myself. There is a power in being what other people expect, just as much as there is power in being unexpected. Some people joined my cause out of a desire for something new and different, others joined me out of fear; the fear my growing reputation had put in them. Still others joined me because of the promises I made. I was quite open about it.

War.

CHAPTER EIGHTEEN

MORE AND MORE PEOPLE ARRIVED AT MY little city. Some were survivors of the Pit, somehow finding alternate routes to the surface, or surviving a pitch-black swim even after days trapped by the rising waters. That is a trial I cannot imagine, and yet a few people did just that, a testament to their will to survive. Others were looking for a fresh start, and thinking my city somehow held the key to a prosperous life they couldn't find elsewhere. Others still, were criminals, fleeing justice and finding sanctuary in a city full of criminals. I let the others put them to work, I had no heart for it. I have never wanted to rule anything but my own actions, and I've struggled with those often enough.

I delved deeper and deeper into the ruins beneath us, looking for something, though I could not say what. I think, perhaps, it was escape I was looking for. Responsibility has never sat lightly on my shoulders, and people were looking to me for rule and guidance. Down there, in the gloom, it was comfortable. Despite the monsters, and the weight of rock above, I felt safer down in that ruined city than I did up in the freedom on the surface. It staggers me to think just how much things had changed. As a prisoner down in the Pit, I longed for freedom, to see the sky again. Now, I longed for the dark, the close confines of rock around me, of walls I could see and feel. Maybe it was Ssserakis' influence on me, but I think it went deeper than that. I was running away. Again.

Horralain never failed to come with me, a second shadow of sorts, and a tireless defender. He never complained, nor questioned, and rarely left my side. Ishtar followed me down into the dark once and I was glad of her jovial company. Her mocking never failed to put a smile on my face, but it was not my company that drove her to follow me down there.

The Terrelan Empire has always been quite xenophobic. The people are intolerant of the differences in others, and it is a truth of our culture that has been nurtured by rulers for hundreds of years. I saw no pahht or tahren when Orran still existed, and the garn were even more mysterious still. No. Terrans, as a whole, are not so welcoming of differences. Maybe they are a little more so in Polasia, but then it is an empire founded and thriving on trade and cannot afford to discriminate. Make no mistake, the other peoples of Ovaeris are not so different. I've been to Urengar, a tahren city built in the caverns of a dead volcano, and I've seen the jungles the pahht call their homelands. Do you know how many terrans I saw in my time there? Not many. So few, I was considered an oddity. The truth is, none of our peoples are so cosmopolitan. They do not like to mix unless forced to, such as in Polasia or Ro'shan. Yet, we are all made better by the diversity. Ishtar soon found the stares and whispers of the Terrelans who joined us more than she could bear. More than once I had to stop her from using her swords to reply to bigotry. I did it for the sake of peace, but I wonder if I might have been better served letting her teach the fools a final lesson.

Imiko followed me down there one time. The thief had still not shed her melancholy, and even the ringlet had taken to abandoning her in favour of more active people to bother. She was quiet for so long as we stalked those halls, I almost forgot she was there.

"Do you miss Ro'shan?" she asked out of the blue. I turned to face her, ordering one of the Khark Hounds to continue as a scout. "Feels like so long ago, doesn't it?" I found myself having to look up at Imiko. I couldn't say when she had gotten so tall, but she seemed to tower over me. "I left a lot of stuff up there. Money, food. Friends." There was a sadness to her words that went deep, and something else too, a pleading edge.

Silva once told me there was a sadness in me she could never touch. Ishtar said my anger was an unquenchable fire that would burn every bridge I tried to make, and me along with it. People will always try to tell you what you are, what you are made of, where you belong, and what you should do. Fuck them all! I forge my own path. I will not allow others to tell me who I am. I will tell them. I'll tell the whole world. I will scream my defiance into the face of every single person in this world before I allow them to dictate my fate. That has always been my way. But it was not Imiko's. She needed comfort.

Without warning I lurched forwards and wrapped

my arms around the thief. She stiffened and let out a squeak. That hurt a little, I'll admit, as though she didn't trust me, couldn't be sure I wasn't about to hurt her. I held Imiko tight for a few moments, and eventually she relaxed and returned the embrace. When we pulled apart, there were tears in her eyes, and a grateful smile on her face. I had no words that could help her sadness, and I could not bring back what she had lost. Worse yet, I knew she had lost it because of me. So, I offered what I could. Myself. In that brief embrace, I assured Imiko I would be the rock that she could lean on, no matter what. Sometimes, people need actions far more than words.

"Thank you," Imiko said, wiping her eyes. I gave her a smile and hoped it didn't look insidious. Flashing eyes, a pale complexion, and face in constant shadow could make anyone look a little ghoulish, and my scars only served to help the matter.

When Tamura came with me, he looked upon the dark depths with wonder. I think it must have looked oddly familiar to him, but his addled mind could not remember when he had last been there. We met some imps that day, and the crazy old Aspect kept muttering about shrooms, but nothing he said made sense to anyone but himself. I had to stand between the Khark Hound and the huddling imps to keep it from attacking them, and it took Ssserakis manifesting our wings once more to finally convince the monster to back away.

There were a dozen imps, huddling in a corner of a large room. They were filthy and frightened and bloody. And they bowed to me, holding up hands just as they did the last time I was there. I touched a single finger to each upturned palm, and the imps chittered excitedly. We left them there, certain they were harmless. Imps may be nightmares, just like every one of the denizens of the Other World, but not all nightmares are dangerous. Some are just misunderstood.

Finally, Hardt ventured into the depths with me. He had camped outside the city for a long time, refusing to set foot within the halls, even the bits that were now above ground. Fresh grief was etched in the lines of his face. It took a lot for him to brave the ruined Djinn city once more. I always felt so very small between Hardt and Horralain. Both were considered giants for their stature, but it was more than just physical height and build. They were larger than life.

"Is it strange that I feel small beside you?" Hardt asked me as we paced along the corridors of broken stone.

With each foray, I found more of the Damned down there, swarming the lower halls in a mass of chaos and violence. My shaking of the city had woken them all up from whatever prolonged slumber they had entered into. Of course, even a host of Damned were little match to a couple of Khark Hounds set loose. I had two of the beasts with me that day, and they kept easy pace with the rest of us.

"Yes." The answer needed no consideration. "It would take about three of me to fill one of you, Hardt. Besides, you don't get to say you feel small when I have to look up just to see your chin. Not that I can even see that anymore, underneath that thicket."

Hardt scratched at his blossoming beard. Why he chose to stop shaving is beyond me, but men often seem inordinately proud of their ability to grow hair on their faces. "I mean to say, I feel useless, Eska. The enemies you fight now. Djinn and Rand, the Iron Legion, Aspects, Sourcerers. I can't help you fight them. The Iron Legion proved that well enough. Put me down with a glance and I needed you to save me."

I shrugged. "You never liked to fight."

"But I could, if it was needed. Down here I fought against the Damned. Protected everyone. But what can I do now? What good am I to you now? I can't protect you anymore."

It all seemed so foolish to me. "You bloody idiot."

"What?" Hardt seemed genuinely hurt.

"You think I need you to protect me?" I rounded on him, anger flaring. "Poor *little* Hardt. Always there to protect Eska when she gets into trouble. Is it such a bad thing I can get myself out of trouble now?"

"That's not really…"

"It must be hard for you to see me actually standing on my own feet, in front of the world instead of hiding behind your bulk." That was harsh, and I hated myself for saying it.

Even in the gloom I could see him grinding his teeth. "Yeah, you've done a great job so far."

"And what the fuck does that mean?"

For a moment neither of us said anything, though in truth we were not so much speaking to one another, but rather shouting. "Just look at yourself, Eska. Look at what you've done to yourself. What you've become." He took a big step forward and reached out. I didn't flinch away. Hardt gripped hold of my shadowy hood between thumb and forefinger, wincing as the cold of that shadow bit into his skin. "You conceal yourself in this… shadow. Your eyes aren't terran anymore. They're… I don't know. Like a Djinn or something. You turned your own damned arm to stone, Eska! And don't think I haven't noticed you talking to yourself, arguing with yourself. Normal people don't do that!"

Anger begets anger. It is a defensive tactic, I think. When we are beset by uncomfortable truths, rather than face them, we find it so much easier to point out uncomfortable truths in others. Minor issues are blown out of proportion, and festering slights come to the forefront in boiling accusations and insults. Otherwise indelible friendships have been shattered by an ill-timed argument. Trust me on this. I have lost too many friends for the sake of letting my pride rule me.

He doesn't understand. "You're right, Hardt. I'm not normal!" The words were flowing thick and fast now, a current that could not be stopped, and with it rode anger and spite, and maybe some resentment too. I wish I had said none of it. "I'm a monster."

"I didn't say..."

"All these things you say I've done to myself are the price of power." The darkness rose around me like a palpable mist, dimming the torchlight. "And don't for a moment think the rest of you, my *friends*, haven't benefited from my sacrifices." I didn't mean the words, but I couldn't stop them. I wish I had stopped. I wish I had never started. It was all lies. Misdirected anger thrown at the one person who didn't deserve it. "You crawl along behind me, basking in my accomplishments because you're too moon-damned scared of finding your own fucking lives! If it wasn't for me, you'd still be wallowing in the Pit, kissing Prig's arse in the hopes he'd let you live another day!"

"Benefited?" Tears rolled down Hardt's lined cheeks and he suddenly looked old and weary, the vitality leached out of him by this torrent of anger. "You think I benefit from this crusade of yours? Like Isen benefited from it?

Like Kento benefited?" Those words hurt. Not just me, they hurt us both. My daughter was a rift between us that never healed, and he wielded her fate like a knife, plunging it into my chest. I felt my throat tighten and my chest ache. Tears welled in my eyes, reflecting the lightning in them back at me as shards of disjointed light. But I refused to let those tears fall.

We don't need him. "You're right, Hardt, I don't need you!" *We've outgrown him.* "I've moved past you." *He should just leave.* "So why don't you just take your overgrown fucking arse back to the surface before I kick it all the way there!"

I don't know how long we stood there in silence, staring at one another, Horralain and the Khark Hounds forgotten. It could have been seconds or it could have been hours, time lost meaning in that charged confrontation. Hardt's jaw worked like he was gearing up to say more, but then his face hardened into a grimace and he shook his head, storming past me, back the way we had come.

I waited for as long as I could. My left hand, as well as my right, was clenched into a tight fist, and I didn't realise how odd that was. As soon as Hardt's footsteps had faded I stormed ahead into the darkness, tears still welling and threatening to fall at any moment. Horralain made to follow me, but I sent him sprawling with kinetic push. Once the darkness was complete, I drew in a deep breath. And I fucking screamed. There were no words. It was a cry of pure emotion, emptying out of me in a way it couldn't with words. The walls, floor, and roof of the tunnel cracked from the force of a kinetic shockwave I did not mean to let loose. And I cried. Great wracking sobs of pain, of anger, of regret.

I've heard it said that life has a habit of kicking a

person when they are down. It's crap. Life is not some sentient, callous overlord looking to magnify our pain. Each of our lives are full of friends and enemies, often ones we didn't even realise we had, and they are ever watchful for when you are reeling and injured. Friends will, of course, rush to aid you in such a state, assuming you haven't pushed them away. Enemies, on the other hand, will jump on you when you are at your most vulnerable. It is not life that kicks us when we are down. Most often, it is our own choices that do the job, coming full circle to teach us the error of our ways.

My heart wasn't in the exploration after my fight with Hardt. We wandered the darkened halls for a time, but in truth it was just to give my friend time to make his way out. I didn't want to come across him as I retreated to the surface. Eventually I sent the hounds off to hunt, and turned back, my feet trudging with every step. My anger was still there, simmering, but a weariness had settled over me. Part of me wished to collapse right there and then, huddle up against a wall and cry until I couldn't anymore. It was a rather large part of me, truth be told. I soldiered on, dragging my feet, Horralain dogging my steps. Despite my violence against the man, he did not leave me, nor even complain.

"People follow strength." As always, Horralain's words came slowly, as though each one was measured from every angle before leaving his mouth. He couldn't see my ghosts, but Deko laughed at the words. It's strange that most of my ghosts were solemn things, almost emotionless save for the melancholy. Deko, on the other hand, was as hateful in death as he had been in life. He sneered and made threatening moves toward me, as though an impotent ghost could scare someone who carried the embodiment of fear inside of them. "It's nature. Can't blame a person for lining up behind someone who has what you lack. It's how we survive. Together."

This one is more astute than we took him for.

By the time we reached the surface I was caught between rage and despair. I wanted to hate Hardt for his assumption that I ever needed protecting, but at the same time, I wanted to hate myself for the words I spewed at my friend. I didn't mean them, not all of them anyway. I did still need Hardt, not as a protector, but as something far more vital. His friendship and guidance kept me centred, and his strength was something I had come to rely upon, to lean upon. I don't mean his strength of arm, but his inner strength. I might have been leading this ragtag bunch of soldiers, prisoners, and misfits, but Hardt had been there since the very beginning, holding me up, lending me the strength to go on. That is what I should have said to my friend. I should have told him how much I needed him, in ways far more vital than being a pair of fists. Instead, I insulted him and drove him away. Ishtar was right about me. I am a fire who only knows how to burn bridges.

So caught up in my spiralling melancholy was I, that I barely noticed the woman waiting at the entrance to the city depths. She called herself Nic and she was stunning. Far too beautiful to have spent any time down in the Pit. Glossy black hair and flawless onyx skin, eyes full of malice, lithe body tense as bowstring. I stumbled past the woman as if she wasn't there. Only Horralain's ferocious attention to preserving my life saved it.

The first I knew of any treachery was a loud grunt by Horralain, and the ground beneath my feet shattered to rubble. I struggled to keep my footing, stumbling forward even as I turned. Nic was there, hate in her face and a blade in her hands. The knife was a curious thing, as long as my forearm and with a jagged edge that would tear rather than cut. Her eyes fixed on me even as Horralain, stood between us, hefted his hammer for another strike.

Horralain was fast, far swifter than any man his size had right to be, but she was quicker. Even as my protector raised his hammer, Nic rushed forward, slipping inside his guard, and plunged her knife into Horralain's chest three times. Her eyes never left me, fixed on their true target. Horralain grunted in surprise and pain, blood gushing from his wounds, and then Nic tossed him aside as though he weighed nothing, sending him crashing into a nearby wall. He didn't rise.

That was when I knew the true identity of my attacker. I should have seen it earlier, should have seen past the lie. "Well that's a week worth of infiltration wasted." Her voice dripped with hate. "At least this way I get to watch you die instead of knifing you in the back."

"Coby!" I spat her name with as much malice as she directed at me. A glance toward Horralain revealed that he wasn't getting up any time soon. His body twitched and a big hand clutched at his chest. There was a lot of blood, too much even for a man of his size. Too much blood. Too much death. Too much loss. Another of my allies, of my friends ripped away from me. All the anger, all the pain, all the hate I had felt underground came rushing back in and I screamed in animal fury.

This creature is dangerous. There is no fear in her. The rage eclipses all else.

Without needing to think about it, I formed a Sourceblade in my right hand. It was a long, slender weapon, good for keeping a knife fighter at bay. I wrapped both hands around the hilt. It didn't even occur to me, at the time, how odd that was, but then it was not the first time I had managed to move my stone fingers.

I blinked and Coby changed. Gone was the woman of raven hair and skin. Silva stood before me, as radiant as she had ever been. Her hair glowed with the dying light of the day, and her eyes were the endless, shifting blue of a sapphire. I wanted to believe. By the moons, I wanted to believe it was her. I wanted to drop my sword, run to her, wrap my arms around her. I wouldn't even have cared if she'd come for vengeance. If it had been Silva… If it had truly been Silva, I would have taken her in my arms and never let go. I wanted to believe it was her. I would have ripped the world asunder and myself with it to make it real. But it wasn't real. I couldn't believe. It could not be her. I knew it couldn't, because I had killed her. Because the hate I felt for myself was a constant reminder that Silva was dead, and it was because of me.

"You don't deserve to wear her image, Coby," I screamed.

Silva's face contorted into a snarl of rage that seemed so alien on her features. "You didn't deserve her!" Coby snarled. Silva had never snarled like that. She had never stood like a cat ready to pounce. She had never held a knife dripping with the blood of my friends. Coby make a mockery of the woman I loved. A hateful, twisted image of a woman who had only ever wanted to help others. And seeing her look like that twisted a knife in my guts.

The shouting would bring people to investigate. While I knew the backup would be nice, I also knew that no one stood a chance against Coby. All that attention would bring would be collateral damage, and no one else deserved to die for my transgressions. Coby was there because of me, and she had already killed one of my friends. I would not let kill another!

There would be no reconciliation between Coby and I. There could be none. She disliked me from the start, jealous of the attention her twin sister gave me. Jealous of the love between us. Do'shan had opened a wound and let it fester, and now there was nothing but hate and rage between us.

"Why did you kill her?" I have a feeling that question had burned away at Coby, eating away at whatever sanity she had left. The desire to know what had gone wrong.

"Does it matter?" I had my own anger to vent. "You knew she was going to die. Your fucking mother sent her there to die!"

"For a cause. For a reason!" Coby spat, still wearing Silva's face. She did not deserve to wear that face. "To rid the world of the Djinn. Because of you she died for nothing. You betrayed her!"

Only a fool argues against the truth, for even if you win, you are still a fool. "I didn't want her to die, Coby. I…" Pointless words. Excuses without meaning. Wasted air. Neither of us cared about intention. Silva was dead, and we were both in pain. We were both nothing but pain. Perhaps if things had been different between us, we could have worked through that grief together, but Coby was a creature of spite and malice and jealousy. And I'm not sure I was any different.

No words could resolve the conflict between us, but sometimes a blade can cut straight to the heart of the matter.

I have had many enemies over the years across many conflicts, but few could match up to the sheer violence of that brief fight. I had the benefit of skill. It's not often I can say that about a duel, but Coby was not well trained in the art of the blade work. Of course, her speed and strength went far beyond anything even the mightiest terran could hope for, and often it was all I could do to keep her from closing in and overpowering me. I kept her at bay with timely slashes and gouts of flame. Every time I blinked or lost sight of Coby for even a moment, she changed. One second, I was fighting Silva, and the next, it was a Polasian man with arms like Hardt's and a jaw like granite. The next time our blades met, she was a child, barely as tall as my waist and snarling with the sort of fury one can only expect from a toddler who has not yet learned restraint. It was off-putting, but then that was the point. Coby bent not just her own strength and speed upon me, but also the power given to her by Mezula. She used it well and more than once I was caught off guard by the shift. When I blinked and saw Tamura in front of me, I admit I hesitated. With Silva's image, I knew it couldn't be real, no matter how much I wished for it. I had killed her myself. But for a brief flicker of a moment I saw Tamura and my mind asked, what if it was real? That hesitation almost cost me my life. It would have if not for Ssserakis' intervention, whipping out with my shadow so quickly it very nearly severed Coby's arm. The Aspect leapt backward, eyes narrowed to the trick. It wouldn't work again. Coby was nothing if not adaptable. And all the while, Horralain bled out, slumped against the wall of the entrance to the depths. Dying.

As we fought, a storm rose around us. My melancholy retreated and my ire grew, the anger fuelling my lightning. It licked at us both as we traded blows, but the storm was mine, was me, it could not harm me. Coby, on the other hand, simply didn't seem to care. Lightning burned across her skin, and my blade often followed it, drawing red lines across her. But every time I blinked, every time her image changed, the wounds were gone. I realised then that I couldn't win. How I could I hope to beat a creature I didn't understand. My strikes meant nothing to her. My magic all but useless. More than once I tried hitting her with a kinetic blast that would have dashed a man of Hardt's size into bloody pulp, yet Coby took the full brunt of those blasts and barely moved.

There was but one piece of good news. Even as I couldn't beat Coby, she could not get past my layers of defence. Between my blades, my magic, and my horror, I kept her at bay long enough for people to come and investigate the noise. Before long we had an audience, and with them came people I could trust to help. Ishtar and Tamura turned the tables on Coby. As strong and fast as the Aspect was, even she knew her chances of taking on all three of us at once were slim.

"You can't hide behind your minions forever, Eska," Coby snarled, already backing off from the fight. "Eventually I'll catch you alone. You know I will." Before I could stop her, Coby launched herself sideways, crashing through a stone wall as though it were nothing to her. She snaked her way into the crowd, as I gave chase.

"Don't lose her!" I shouted. "Don't take your eyes off her." It was useless, of course. Hidden amid the crowd, all it took Coby was a moment, hidden from all eyes, and she was someone else. Anyone else. Still, I forged my way into the crowd for a while, shoving people aside with my stone arm, and casting every which way, trying to catch a glimpse of the Aspect as she fled. Useless. She was gone, for now. Coby had failed to kill me, but she had done something almost as good. She had taken away my staunchest protector.

My bodyguard lay dying with huge gashes torn out of his torso, blood running out of him like a river. I call Horralain my bodyguard. I once called him a monster, a thug, a lackey, a beast. One thing I never called him while he was alive, was friend. I name him that now. He was not a kind man, nor a good person. But he was my friend and I miss him as I miss all those who I have lost. All those who have been taken from me.

I sent Imiko to find Hardt. Someone had seen him storming out of the depths hours earlier, but no one had seen him since. Tamura fretted over Horralain's wounds and said, *Only the living can die.* He looked to me as he said it and I knew what he meant. Josef was the Biomancer with the power to heal, knit flesh and restore good humours. I was the Necromancer, and my magic lay not in healing the living, but preserving the dead.

We all watched Horralain die. Words were already beyond him, but he was not beyond fear. Right up until the end I could feel it, yet I could do nothing about it. I was there, watching him, holding his hand the moment that he died. Another friend stolen from me. I saw something leave him then, a wisp of energy, a faint blue light that was all his. It was an oddity about my Necromancy that I could see the moment his spirit left the body. And I knew with a horrifying certainty I could stop it. But I also knew that it wouldn't be him, not really. Whatever I put back in his body would not be Horralain. It would be piece of him, bound to me, to my magic. A sick mockery of the man. I wouldn't do that Horralain, to my friend. I wouldn't do it to anyone. Instead, I turned away to find the ghost of Deko laughing at

Horralain's corpse. Well, that was a bit too much to take. It's fair to say I let my anger get the better of me.

I reached out with my good arm and gripped the ghost by the neck. The surprise on Deko's fat fucking face was worth it. The ghost thought he was beyond the mortal world. He was wrong. Necromancy, my innate magic, raised the ghosts around me, drifting reminders of my guilt in their deaths. Well, it was time to stop feeling guilty over Deko's death. Rarely has anyone deserved it more. Necromancy made my ghosts, and I could use the magic to unmake them, too. I heard gasps, a few hushed whispers. Caught in my grip, Deko's ghost became visible to everyone. Most of those in our little community recognised the Pit kingpin. They recognised, too, the fear on his face as I unravelled his ghost. Lightning crackled around me, summoned by my anger and hatred, and Deko thrashed and flailed, but he had no form and could do nothing but fear the end as I crushed him for a second time. I could have done it in an instant, but I didn't. I drew out Deko's second death long enough that I felt the satisfaction of it. Long enough that the satisfaction turned to guilt and disgust. Eventually I let him fade into oblivion. In truth, I wish I hadn't done it. I gave Deko's ghost a few moments of terror, and then nothing. It would have been a far greater punishment to bind him to the world for eternity, forced to witness everything and never again affect anything.

When all was done, the people dispersed back to their work, and my friends came to comfort me. There is no comfort for the guilty. None of them could see Horralain staring down at his own body, or the confusion on his brutish features. None of them could see the sadness in the eyes of his ghost.

CHAPTER NINETEEN

JOSEF WAS ALWAYS THE PATIENT ONE. WHERE I would run off and attempt something with barely a thought of a plan, Josef would consider it from every angle, and plan for every possibility. Of course, I often dragged him astray. I would brook no argument, rushing headlong into my schemes and adventures. Josef would simply rush to catch up, dragged along in my wake. Some tutors named me a good influence on my friend, and others damned me as a bad influence. They were all right. We all influence everyone we touch, sometimes for the good, sometimes not. That is the nature of life. Heroes and villains are for stories. In the world outside of songs and books, we are all just people.

Months of study and experimentation passed. Thousands of deaths weighed heavily on Josef's conscience. I would say it was not his fault, that he was forced into it every time. He didn't want to take a single life, yet he was made to take two hundred and sixteen over and over again. Every time, the experiment failed. Every time, something was missing. No matter how many tweaks the Iron Legion made to his plan, there seemed to be no resolution. Of course, that didn't stop him from trying, and Josef's conscience paid the price along with all the innocents that he was forced to kill. He saw them all, every man, woman, and child. Every screaming face contorted in pain, and every weary acceptance of an end long in its coming. It broke him. Again. How could it not?

In my arrogance, I always thought myself the stronger of us. I never broke. Well, almost never. Josef was broken time and time again, through actions both his own and those done to him, and the consequences of those actions. But every single time he put himself back together again. I might have the strength of conviction, but Josef always had me beat in resolution.

These are not my memories. They are Josef's.

Josef sits at the desk and pulls a new book in front of him. Loran is gone for now. He regularly leaves for a day or two, and during those times Josef is free to do what he will. There's no trouble he can get up to. All the Sources are hidden away, and the entire complex is underground, sealed by Geomancy. There's nothing for Josef to do but read. Which is fine because he enjoys reading.

He reaches across and picks up the pasty the tahren steward, Inran, has brought him. He takes a bite and grimaces. It tastes of nothing. No, that's not right. It has flavour. It used to be a flavour Josef enjoyed, but not anymore. He neither enjoys, nor detests it. It is flavour without taste. It's not the pastry's fault. It's his fault. Something is happening to him, something he doesn't want to admit, doesn't want to think about. He's changing. He cares less, feels less. At least when Loran drugs him, he can blame the Sweet Silence. He can hide in the fog. At times like this, he has no drug to blame. Something is happening to him. Something bad. Something he can't contemplate. Read the books. A distraction.

Josef flicks open the cover of the book and stares down at the words. This is not an encyclopaedia or Sourcery manual. It's a journal. It's Loran Orran's journal. It had been hidden away on the shelves, just another book. Only it wasn't. Maybe with this he can understand the Iron Legion a little better. And maybe if he understands the man, he can escape the monster.

Year 607-O 12th of Raneese

Progress! After years of experimentation and dozens of lives, I have finally succeeded in implanting Sources into two separate subjects. ~~Josef Yenhelm and Esk~~. I can't do it. I can't refer to them by name. Not after what I've had to do to them and not after what I am going to have to put them through. They don't deserve it, I know that. But I don't have a choice. This must be done. It's the only way. If I don't bring back the Rand and the Djinn, there is no way to close the portal, and if it isn't closed, there is no way to prevent the second cataclysm. No names. They are Terran 24 and Terran 25, and they survived the procedure.

Terran 24 is male, roughly 12 years old. From the Orran side of Isha, though I'm still certain that makes no real difference to acceptance ration. Fair skin and no previous major injuries. His attunements are Biomancy, Geomancy, Empamancy, Kinemancy, Morphomancy, and Aeromancy. He is a 5th tier Sourcerer.

I injected Terran 24 with a Biomancy Source mixed in a plasmatic solution of 1:3. Bleeding occurred around the eyes and ears, and the subject had to be restrained to control the spasms.

Terran 25 is female, roughly 11 years old. From the Orran side of Isha. Fair skin and suffering from extensive previous injuries to the abdomen and arms. Biomancy has been used on Terran 25 repeatedly to heal the previous injuries. Her attunements are Pyromancy, Impomancy, Portamancy, Necromancy, Kinemancy, and Arcmancy. She is a 5th tier Sourcerer.

I injected Terran 25 with a Necromancy Source mixed in a plasmatic solution of 1:3. Bleeding occurred from the mouth, eyes, and nose.

They both survived and appear to have retained their faculties, unlike the failure of Terran 22. That poor boy. I can undo the damage he does to himself, but I cannot undo the damage the injection of Sources did to his mind. Maybe the Rand can help. Once I bring them back.

I have locked their memories of the procedure behind an Empamantic command. Further observation will be needed to determine the level of success. If they survive and retain their faculties, I will need to fashion scenarios for them to achieve the Auguries.

It did not sound like the same mad man Josef had come to know. The passages in the journal speak of a man wracked by guilt over his actions but determined all the same. He flicks through the journal, looking for more entries, and finds one without a date. The handwriting is messy, as though scrawled in a rush or in anger.

Idiots and fools. They call themselves tutors as though they have any knowledge worth teaching. They know nothing, and rather than take the opportunity to learn, to expand the boundaries of Sourcery, they bury their heads in the earth.

I am on the verge of success, I can feel it. Five subjects have survived the procedure and two show real promise. Terran 24 and Terran 25 need to be nurtured and directed, not sent off to die in my brother's pathetic war.

And, of course, Bell and Elsteth and Marrow have complained about my experiments directly to my brother. He'll order me to stop, I know it. He's always loved ordering me about, ever since we were children. But I cannot stop. I cannot allow him to stop me.

I have developed a new technique. It is monstrous. I know it is. Biomancy should never be used this way. It should never be used to take rather than give, but I don't have a choice. The only way to bring back the Rand and Djinn is to balance the equation. Life must be bought with life. I must find out the worth of a single life and this is the only way to do it. It is the only way. It is.

Josef reads more. Flicking through page after page and discovering the truth. It was clear the man writing the passages was growing more agitated with each entry. More agitated and more monstrous.

Year 611 – O 9th of Abaster

It takes something from you. I realise it now. Now it is too late. Now it has taken enough from me that I have perspective.

The lives no longer matter like they used to. I can remember they did, but how did it feel to take a life? I used to feel guilt at using my Biomancy to take another person's life and add it to my own, but not anymore. Guilt is a word with no meaning. A feeling I am now beyond. I have surpassed so many of the terran emotions. Ascended. Yes, I like that word. I have ascended. I am not longer a normal terran. I am greater. ~~I am immortal.~~

The Rand and the Djinn are immortal. Age and time mean nothing to them. But no matter how many lives I have taken, all I am doing is preserving what is left of me, and that is far too little. My flesh sags, my bones ache. My mind is as clear as ever, but the flesh fails it.

The Djinn, Aerolis, said immortality is not possible for a terran. It's a lie, but also a truth. The Djinn may be masters of time, but the Rand are masters of flesh. The Rand have remade terrans before. They can do it again.

The original plan still stands. I must bring back the Rand. Enough of them to remake me. Not as a terran, but as something greater. Something immortal.

Josef shuts the journal with a slap and listens to his own rapid breathing. It feels as though the book is staring at him, judging him somehow. It's just a book. But it's not. It's a descent into madness. He snatches it off the desk and throws it away, listening to it slide along the floor into the darkness.

Is that his fate? Being forced to steal lives from others until he no longer cares? Until guilt is a word with no meaning? No. He can't do it. He can't become that.

Josef stands and calms his breathing, remembering the old techniques the tutors taught him. Deep breaths in and out, slow and rhythmic, in and out. He has to escape. There must be a way to escape. And he will find it.

CHAPTER TWENTY

WEEKS AFTER HORRALAIN'S DEATH AND COBY had yet to show herself again. I wasn't fooled. The vengeful Aspect was still out there somewhere. Hardt had returned, sullen as a storm cloud. We didn't speak, just shared angry glances. I missed him. I needed someone to talk to about Horralain, someone to share my pain and anger with. Ishtar just pushed booze at me whenever I brought up the subject. Imiko vanished the moment I said his name, and Tamura claimed the thug was still with us, as though he could see the ghost who drifted after me. Horralain's spirit was as watchful of me in death as the man had been in life. I considered unravelling him like I had with Deko, to give him a measure of peace in the nothing of true death, but I couldn't. I wasn't ready to say goodbye to another friend for good. I wasn't even sure it was what he would want.

Under guidance from Ishtar, I sent scouts out toward

Juntorrow, the capital and seat of the Emperor's power.
We all knew he wouldn't allow me to fester inside his
empire. Word came back that an army had been raised, two
thousand soldiers at least, and a handful of battle Sourcerers.
It was more than enough to crush my little rebellion ten
times over, but sometimes it's good for a ruler to crush their
enemies into the ground. It makes an example of them,
reduces the probability of others rising. Besides, we were the
first real rebellion since Orran fell. The Emperor intended to
put us down hard. I was ready for it. I knew it was going to
happen. But being ready for something and being prepared
for it are two very different things.

Ishtar told me we couldn't win. Hardt said the same,
though he wouldn't say it to me directly. The soldiers
who had joined me from the Pit were loath to agree with
anything Ishtar said, and most of the time they barely
acknowledged her existence, but on this they agreed. We
were a few hundred people, and only half of those had any
battle experience. I was one Sourcerer. We couldn't win
against an army, nor against an empire drawn against us.
Some counselled surrender, others said we would be wise to
flee into the Forest of Ten and hide amidst the dense trees. I
chose another option. I chose to meet the Emperor and his
army before he reached my city, and I chose to leave all my
soldiers behind.

I marched south with all the bravado I could muster
and gave Tamura orders to keep the home fires burning.
The old Aspect was far better at organising the day to day
affairs of a city than I ever was. I thought Hardt would
stay, leave me to my madness, but the big man joined me
without a word. Ishtar too, though that was no surprise. My
pahht sword tutor was sick of the stares and whispers. She

was sick of Terrelan. I was most surprised that Imiko joined me. She wanted nothing to do with war, of course. I have often thought about Imiko and why she followed along as she did. I believe she was swept up in my wake, lost and unable to realise she would have been so much better off by abandoning me and my lost cause. Things would have gone so much better had all my friends just left me to face down the Emperor's army alone. I suppose that is the truest act of friendship I have ever witnessed. They were willing to follow me into the depths of madness, even knowing it was suicide. They couldn't have known I had a plan, because I didn't tell them.

Many times, I have ruminated about my own reasons for taking the fight to the Emperor and his armies in such a brazen way. I have concluded that war is a part of me. I have often thought that children born in war never truly leave it behind. The Orran-Terrelan war was already well under way when I was born and more than that, I was raised into it. I was raised for it. The tutors at the academy taught me to kill for one simple reason. I am the weapon. War is who I am. I cannot seem to leave it behind no matter how hard, or how many times I try. Even in times of peace, surrounded by friends and loved ones, I still look for the next fight.

Three days south from the Pit we made camp. It was far enough that my city would not get caught up in the battle, and also far enough we would have time to prepare. In some ways it felt a lot like old times, a small group of us battling hardship. But too much had changed. Ishtar worried, always finding a new blade to sharpen and never seeming happy with the result. Hardt grumbled to the others and said not a word to me, even when I faced him and demanded it. Imiko looked sick to her stomach by the thought of what was to come. She had no idea.

That first night I left them to their fire and melancholic company, striking out alone into the darkness. "Are you ready?"

Are you?

"No. But I don't think I have much of a choice. We're running out of time. His armies will be here soon."

I could feel my horror's amusement. *We will crush this weak Emperor into the dirt, and then find the Iron Legion. Nothing will stop us. I swear it.* There was a pause of anticipation and I knew what Ssserakis wanted.

"I swear it also." A savage grin tugged my mouth open, bravado to disguise the pain I was about to feel. "Now let's find our army and bring it across."

I have mentioned before that all magic comes with a price, and the price for Impomancy is pain. I would liken it to giving birth, but the experience differs so wildly depending upon what the Sourcerer brings across. You see, it is not like Portamancy, the Sourcerer uses their own body as a conduit to bring the creatures from the Other World across. And I was intending to bring some big fucking creatures across.

Start small, Eskara. It has been a while since you have done this. I sensed something else in my horror's words. Trepidation. It was not truly for me, that Ssserakis wanted to build up to the bigger monsters, but for itself. It had been trapped in my world for a long time, and trapped inside of me for even longer. Ssserakis feared its control over the creatures of its home might have waned a little. The concept seemed somewhat laughable when I think of it. As long as there was fear, Ssserakis would dominate all but the strongest of Sevoari's inhabitants.

Khark Hounds have always been a favourite of mine. They are large, ferocious, and intimidating, and I have rarely been one for subtlety. However, the hounds do not come across easily. Each Khark Hound claws its way free of the Sourcerer, opening small wounds in the flesh and dragging itself out of the bloody rents, growing to full size only once they are across. All creatures from the Other World start small, as we conduits are small. Even now there is much about Impomancy I simply do not understand, and I very much doubt any of the Rand would be willing to enlighten me on the intricacies. I summoned twenty Khark Hounds that night, each one clawing itself out of my flesh in blood and pain. Ssserakis sealed my wounds with shadowy thread, aiding my healing through some power I did not care to understand, but it still hurt. Each hound joined the others, and before long I had a pack the likes of which had not been seen on Ovaeris since the Orran-Terrelan war.

They should not have listened to me, should have been beyond my control. There is, after all, a limit to the number of creatures an Impomancer can dominate, and losing control of even one almost always results in death. But there was no magic in play there. I severed the link to each of the hounds almost as soon as they were across. Ssserakis worked through me, dominating the monsters. This was my plan. Between us we would bring over an army to fight for me. An army of monsters. An army loyal to me and no one else. One that would never break or show mercy.

When I had summoned my pack of Khark Hounds, I returned once more to the Other World. Most Sourcerers appeared there as a spirit of sorts, ethereal and unsubstantial, but not me. Perhaps it was Ssserakis' influence, or maybe it was the magic I had absorbed over the

years, but I manifested a body in Sevoari, and the creatures
of that world could see me as surely as I could see them. I
let my horror guide me, searching out the beasts best suited
to the war I was intending to fight. Hellions came next,
each one tearing out of my stomach with such pain I was
certain they had split me open. But there were no wounds,
only agony. Eight of the flying monstrosities was all I could
manage that night before the exhaustion caught up with me.
I ordered all my minions to hide in a nearby cave, to wait
out the harsh light of day, while I recovered. I knew with a
certainty the next night would be a greater trial, because I
had even worse monsters to summon yet.

Ishtar came to me that day, the first of my friends
to voice their concerns. "What is this, terrible student? I
thought the plan was to negotiate. Secure your city and
people. Now, I see you are creating monsters."

"I'm not creating them." The words slurred wearily
from my mouth. It was too much effort even standing and
I trudged back towards our little camp. "I'm summoning
them."

"What does it matter? They were not here, and now
they are. You bring them here. Why?"

"To fight."

Ishtar snorted, gripping hold of my shoulder so I
had to stop. I had not the strength left to brush her off. "You
cannot fight an empire on your own, Eskara."

You're not alone.

"I'm not alone." I tried to back away from her,
but Ishtar's clawed hands gripped even tighter. "I have
Ssserakis."

"What is that?"

Wake up, Eskara. Ssserakis shouted the words in my

head and I realised in my exhaustion I had been about to reveal my horror.

"I'm not alone," I repeated. "I have you, and Imiko, and Hardt, and an army from the Other World."

Ishtar gave me a push and I stumbled, somehow staying on my feet. "An army of monsters. This is how you wish to fight your war? Your meaningless war."

"It's not meaningless!" I spat at her. "The Terrelan Emperor destroyed Orran, threw me into the Pit, sent Prena after me."

"All at the request of this Iron Legion." Ishtar grimaced. Her ankle hadn't properly healed, would never properly heal. For a warrior of such prowess, I could see how much it angered Ishtar at times, and yet she made it her own. She was more graceful with her limp than I have ever been.

"And they both have to pay!"

Ishtar shook her head. "You want revenge, terrible student. I understand this. But what you are undertaking is revenge on a kingdom, not a person. The people should not suffer because you cannot find your target. I taught you better than that. I taught you to be precise."

"You taught me to swing a sword."

"With precision."

I let out a frustrated growl. "What is it you want, Ishtar? This is me. This is what I was trained to do, to fight a war."

"There is no war unless you start one. A good mercenary knows this. We fight in wars, other people's wars, but we relish the times of peace."

She doesn't understand, Eskara.

I shook my head, exhausted, and continued towards

our little camp where Imiko and Hardt watched us. "You don't understand, Ishtar."

"And you are doing a poor job of helping me to."

I waved my stone arm at her dismissively and stumbled on. "If you don't like my methods, you're free to leave."

"You are a curse, Eskara," Ishtar shouted after me. I stopped but didn't turn back to her. "You destroy everything you touch. Everyone you touch. My company, my friends, gone. Your big Terrelan monster, gone. Your lover, gone. All because you cannot give up the fight. How many more have to die? How many more do you have to kill before you take responsibility for the war you are trying to start?"

I waited for a few more moments, long enough I was certain her tirade was over, then continued to our little camp. Ishtar was wrong. I didn't start this war. The Emperor did that. He threw me to the Pit, he sent Prena Neralis to kill me. He was sending an army to kill me. He would not stop until I was dead, and I would not give him the satisfaction.

The others watched me as I slumped down next to our fire. Hardt was cooking something over it, a pot of stew, it smelled delicious. I don't even remember closing my eyes. One moment I was staring at the pot of stew, and the next everything was black. When I woke the sun was slipping over the western horizon; I had slept the entire day. It was not the first time. I often slept through the days and found myself more active at night. And the days I was awake, I had spent underground. More and more of my time was spent in darkness than light. I don't think it was a conscious decision, but it just felt natural somehow. Signs of change. Signs I ignored.

Ishtar was gone. Her pack, her swords, her bedroll,

all gone. I looked for her on the horizon, all the horizons, but she was gone. That hurt. I wondered if I could have said something to make her stay. But it was probably for the best. I didn't need her to fight. I didn't need her at all. Oh, the lies we tell ourselves.

"She left," Imiko said when she noticed me looking. "Said what you were doing was madness and we'd all be wise to follow her."

"But you stayed," I said numbly. I loved her for that.

Hardt dumped a bowl of cold stew in front of me without a word, but his glare spoke volumes. I wished he would talk to me again, but I was too proud to break the silence that had grown bitter between us. Too proud to apologise for the rift I had caused. Just like I had been with Josef.

I tried to hide it, but Ishtar's leaving hurt. I'd told her to go, all but called her a fool, but I didn't think she'd actually leave. It reminded me of Yorin, storming off the moment we escaped the Pit, telling me there was something wrong with me. They both said it. They both saw it.

We didn't need him and we don't need her.

"Which way did she go?" I asked.

It doesn't matter. We have more minions to summon.

Imiko shook her head. "She said not to tell you." There was sadness in her eyes. My fault. Imiko had been happy before she had met me.

After the stew, I went back out into the night, and Ssserakis and I continued to raise our army.

There is a list of creatures from Sevoari that have been banned. After all, there must be rules even in warfare. Orran adhered to the rules, as does Terrelan, and as far as I am aware so too does Polasia. Even the non-terran kingdoms

have agreed to the banning of summoning certain monsters.
There is a reason for every one of them. Some, like the
Abomination, will not be controlled. They break whatever
hold the Sourcerer has over them and wreak devastation
upon our world. Others are too intelligent to be allowed in
our world. The lords of Sevoari are on the banned list for just
such a reason. But there are other creatures that are banned
because they are just too destructive to use in warfare. The
Yurthammer is one such creature.

I was sick of playing by other people's rules.

Yurthammers are monstrous creatures of large enough
size that they could crush a house and barely notice. They
have stout back legs, thick with muscle, but not very agile.
Their front legs, in contrast, are much thinner and longer.
Their bodies are bulbous, covered in green scales, their bulk
threatening to overwhelm their legs. There are thick spines
running all the way down their backs and to the tip of their
reptilian tales, that glow with a warm inner light that pulses
through a variety of colours. Despite all of this, their heads
are the most repulsive thing about the Yurthammer. Dozens
of eyes hang on prehensile fleshy tendrils that move back
and forth, twisting upon each other like a tangle of eels, or
hair blown in the wind. They do not blink but focus with
an unnerving intensity. Their mouths are huge, as wide as
their bodies, and open up to show row upon row of curved,
backward facing teeth that open out to engulf their prey
when they feed, dragging creatures into the gaping maw.
They are slow moving beasts. Even a lame child could
outrun one of them, so you might wonder why they are
banned. What use could such a thing have in the field of
war? Well, it certainly helps that they can belch pockets of
clumped poison gas that is so corrosive it eats through metal

and causes skin to boil on the bone. Whichever long dead
terran dreamed up Yurthammers had a strange imagination.
The Rand are even odder for believing it would make a good
inhabitant of the Djinn's fledgling world.

I had never before brought a Yurthammer across
and had no idea of what to expect beyond the certainty of
pain. They are transferred across with a belch as repugnant
as their own. I have eaten a variety of foods in my life,
including cave fungi, and a garn delicacy called urun, which
I later discovered was actually the egg sacks of garn that
had not been fertilised. If that does not convince you of the
strangeness of their people, I do not know what will. My
point is this, the belch of bringing across a Yurthammer is by
far the most disgusting thing I have ever tasted, and it burns
like liquid fire on the way up too. The revolting gas then
quickly expands and coalesces into a creature that smells just
as bad. I sometimes wonder if that is the true reason for the
monsters being banned, not the devastation they can wreak,
but the smell of them.

I brought five Yurthammers across that night.
Ssserakis pushed for more, having taken me to a place in
Sevoari where a pack of thirty of the beasts lounged, but I
could stand neither the effort, nor the smell or taste for one
more moment. For the second morning in a row, I stumbled
back to our little camp and collapsed into my bedroll. At
least on that second day none of my friends abandoned me.

CHAPTER TWENTY ONE

How many people had Josef been made to kill before he seized upon his chance to escape? Too many. We all like to think we are only what we make of ourselves, but the truth is we are often what others make of us. Josef was made into a murderer, and only the hope of escape kept his sanity, tattered as it was, together. He wanted to escape, to flee the Iron Legion and his machinations. Josef wanted to find me. Even estranged as we were, he never lost that desire. I think, perhaps, it was because he recognised that only together could we hope to stand against Loran Orran.

This is one of Josef's memories.

Another failure. Another Source shattered. Another two hundred and sixteen deaths, their live force stolen and channelled into the Source. These ones had mostly been

terrans, but not all; the Iron Legion had found pahht and
even some tahren to sacrifice on his altar of madness. Josef
tries to care. He wants to care. He reaches for the guilt he
knows should be there. But it isn't. He has just murdered
two hundred and sixteen people, and he doesn't care. Every
life he takes steals a bit of himself with it. He is becoming
something else, something monstrous.

Loran is not angry; he does not get angry. But he is
disappointed and that is worse. He stares at Josef, eyes icy
with resentment. Josef knows what he's thinking. Loran is
beginning to wonder if he had been wrong, if Josef isn't the
chosen one at all. What will he do if decides Josef is useless?
Will he kill him? Would that be so bad?

There are always bodies. After each failed attempt at
resurrecting a Rand, the lives of two hundred and sixteen
people have been snuffed out, but their corpses remain.
The cells below the laboratory need to be emptied to stop
those bodies rotting and spreading disease to the rest of
the prisoners. And new prisoners are needed, always more
prisoners needed. This is it! Josef has thought it through,
planned it all out. This is his only chance to escape.

A group of terrans will soon arrive, soldiers or
mercenaries. Loran hires them to take the corpses away and
bring in new prisoners. It's the only time the laboratory is
open to the outside world. He tried to walk out once, while
the soldiers were down on the prison levels, but there are
golems guarding the passageway and threw him back.

Josef sneaks away from the Iron Legion. Loran cares
little where he goes when there is not an experiment to be
attempted. There is no light down to the prison. No torches
or lanterns. No need for them. But Josef knows the way.
Years in the Pit taught him a thing or two about coping in

darkness. He's memorised it, every step and wall, every door and ramp. He feels his way down, one hand trailing against the cold stone of the wall, following the contours.

Row upon row of cages are set into the very walls of the prison levels. Metal bars treated against the rigours of time set into the rock above and below. Each cell has a section of metal bars that can be swung open and locked closed.

In the darkness, Josef fumbles around the prison level until he finds an empty cell. The lock yields to him instantly. It was not left unlocked, but that doesn't matter. Josef had absorbed the Source from the sword Neverthere. He had absorbed an Ingomancy Source. The magic of manipulating metal had never been one of his attunements, but that did not matter anymore. It was now innate, a part of him whether he wanted it or not. Once inside, he pulls the door closed and uses his innate Ingomancy to fumble the lock closed. Then he lays down on the cold stone floor and centres himself, reaching for the other power inside of him. The power the Iron Legion long ago forced upon him.

Biomancy is the power of flesh, of blood and bone, of life. It can be used to heal, to bolster a person's energies, and it can be used to kill, to sap the life force from a person or nurture infections. But Josef has discovered a new use. He goes still and slows his heart and breathing both. He slows them so much, it looks as though he is entirely still. Then he uses his innate magic to force an unhealthy pallor to his skin. Then he waits.

Eventually the soldiers appear, bringing with them light and conversation and laughter. Despite the gruesome work, they are jovial, joking about which of the corpses would be eaten first. A gruff male voice claims the younger

the body, the sweeter must be the taste, and says he has seen
the monsters pick the youthful flesh first. Another voice
counters, claiming to have seen older bodies eaten first as the
younger ones keep longer. The first replies that the monsters
didn't care if the rot was set in deeply. Doubt creeps into
Josef's mind. It is no longer doubt as to whether his ploy
would succeed, but whether he wanted it to.

"Another one here," says the gruff soldier, turning the
torch to shine light into Josef's cell. He has his eyes closed,
but bright light cares little for eyelids. Josef hears his cell
door swing open on squealing hinges. "Poor fucker. Almost
looks fresh."

"They died only yesterday." A woman's voice,
with the fluid accent of a Polasian. "That crazy librarian
sometimes lets them rot for days before calling us."

"Quiet!" The second male voice is urgent and fearful.
"If he hears you…"

"He never comes down here," says the woman again.
"Except maybe to kill a few more worthless fools."

Josef feels a strong grip around his wrist, and he's
pulled along the floor. "Just make sure we lock the cells
when we bring in the new ones." the gruff soldier grunts as
he drags Josef over the lip of the bars. "If any of these poor
fuckers get out, we'll catch hell for it. He might even throw
us in here with them." The soldier and another person grip
Josef by shoulder and leg and tossed him onto a heap of
dead bodies lying on a cart. Then they continue down the
cells and pile four more bodies on top of him before deciding
that the cart is full enough for a single trip.

The soldiers push the cart through the Iron Legion's
dark halls and Josef keeps still and silent. The stench of
death surrounds him, gets inside his clothes and under his

skin until he is certain he'll never smell anything else ever
again. He feels the weight of the dead pressing down upon
him and it feels right, fitting. He killed them, and now they
were crushing him, pinning him down and crowding him
on all sides. He feels something wet drip onto his cheek
and ignores the sickening way it slowly trails down his
skin. Through pure will he stops himself from reacting and
remains still and silent. And then the cart passes out of the
laboratory and Josef glimpses the sky. It's bright blue with
wisps of white cloud. Lursa is in dominance and plainly
visible despite the light of day. He feels again. Something
deep in his chest. Hope. Embers he thought long since
crushed under the Iron Legion's boot, spark to life once
more. He can escape. He has escaped. He's free.

　　Josef continues to wait, though he aches to throw
off the corpses pinning him down. The soldiers mention
monsters a few more times and they escort the cart. Then
they stop and the cart tips up. Josef tumbles out with the
dead, landing in a painful, wreaking pile of splayed limbs
and cold flesh. Then the soldiers retreat as quickly as they
can.

　　His patience and will fray with each moment, but
he waits until he thinks the soldiers are gone so they don't
see him. He's in amongst cracked and ruined buildings, the
remains of a city long since destroyed. A howl echoes around
the crumbling stonework of the buildings.

　　Panic! Josef's concentration slips and his heart
thunders in his ears. He scrambles out from underneath
flaccid flesh and shoves his way free of the corpses. A second
howl splits the air, answering the first. Josef finally pulls
his way out of the pile of bodies and stands. The day is
bright and cold, and as he stares around, he recognises the

crumbling ruins around him. This is Picarr. He's standing
in what remains of Cellow Street, where tailor shops once
stood proudly displaying the latest fashions in their glass
windows, and there was a chandler who's shop always
smelled wonderfully of herbs and tallow. He had had grown
up here, just a few streets away within the academy. A third
howl rings through the air, closer than the last, hauntingly
familiar and utterly terrifying.

Stone *clacks* against stone to his left and Josef spins
around. A Ghoul perches atop a crumbling wall. It's the size
of a large man with grey skin. It wears no clothes but has
strips of cloth wrapped around bits of its arms and legs and
chest. Its head is skull-like, sunken flesh around a mouth full
of sharp teeth, a nose that is little more than pits in the flesh.
It has no eyes and a length of yellowing cloth is wrapped
around the top half of its head. It sniffs, its head jerking
about as it searches. Then it focuses on Josef and opens its
mouth. Thin tendrils of drool drip down from grey lips. The
Ghoul goes down on all fours and pounces.

Josef runs. Ruined buildings pass as hazy blurs of
grey and brown. The sounds of the Ghoul chasing him are
distant things, and he barely hears them over his thumping
heart. He swings to the left, ducking into the remains of an
alleyway with high, crumbling walls. The monster behind
lets out an animal bark.

Another Ghoul leaps out of a window to Josef's left
and he throws himself right, his shoulder slamming against
the stone wall. Hands with black nails slam down where he
had just been, and Josef flees. He's breathing hard, a high-
pitched squeal whistling from his mouth but he can't stop
it. At the end of the alleyway he turns right and sprints. He
used to know these streets well enough he could navigate

them with his eyes closed, but he can't remember them now.
He can't think. His mind is gripped in a panic that screams
run at him over and over and nothing else.

He's faster than them, leaves the Ghouls behind him.
They scramble along remains of buildings, climbing walls
and leaping gaps. They don't like the ground! Another
Ghoul leaps up onto a wall ahead of him and Josef turns
left, careening down an alleyway. He kicks a rock and trips,
skinning his hands against the ground, but doesn't let it stop
him. His palms sting and his toe is pulsing agony, but he
throws himself forward and keeps running.

The buildings on either side are mostly intact, high
walls obscure his vision. At the far end of the alley is a
mound of rubble, but he can leap over it into the street
beyond. Then another Ghoul drops from the wall above
him, landing in front, blocking off the alley. With a scream,
Josef slides to a halt and turns. He has to go back. He has
to… There's a Ghoul that way too. He remembers something
Eska once said. She said she didn't like Ghouls because they
were too intelligent. Too cunning. The truth seeps in and
Josef realises they forced him into a trap.

Josef falls to his knees and sobs. Tears running free
down his cheeks. He doesn't want to die. He doesn't want
to be torn apart and eaten. But at least the Iron Legion won't
have him anymore. At least he won't be responsible for any
more deaths. At least there's that.

The Ghoul at the far end of the alleyway barks out
a harsh sound and charges, scuttling forward on all fours
with reckless abandon. Josef watches his death coming and
accepts it. There's nothing to do. Nothing he can do. The
Ghoul bashes into him, knocks him down and tramples
him. Hard feet kick him as it passes, talons tearing through

clothing and gouging his skin. He lays there, staring up at the sky between two rooftops, waiting for his death. Waiting. Waiting. Still waiting.

"What did you think was going to happen?" The Iron Legion moves into view above Josef, staring down at him with harsh eyes. "Fool!" He reaches down and grabs Josef by the collar, hauling him to his feet with an irresistible strength.

Josef reaches out with his innate magic the way Loran has taught him to, to suck the life out of a person. He has nothing left to lose; he might as well try. Try to ride the world of the Iron Legion. His hand touches Loran's face and… Pain rushes back along the Biomantic link. He finds no well of life force inside the Iron Legion, only pain. A freezing agony that is far more death than life. He recoils, collapsing backward, but caught in the iron grip of Loran there is nowhere he could go.

"Well." There's a new, harder edge to the Iron Legion's voice. All sympathy burned away, leaving nothing but cold calculation. "That was quite revealing for both of us, wouldn't you say?"

Josef shakes his head. He can't meet Loran's gaze. He can't understand what just happened. "What are you?"

A cruel smile spreads across Loran's face. "I am the future. You are the past. More importantly, now I know just how little you can be trusted." The Iron Legion waves a hand and a portal opens in the alleyway, the space beyond it is dark with flickering yellow light. Loran throws him through the portal, and he crashes to a heap against cold stone floor. He's back in the laboratory, down in the prison levels once more. The Iron Legion follows him through the portal and snaps it shut behind them. A few paces away, the soldiers wait, lanterns providing the only light in the darkness. They're caught between fleeing and grovelling, but Loran pays them no mind.

"Do you remember the rules, Yenhelm?" There's anger in the Iron Legion's voice now, and an odd urgency. "What would happen if you resisted or tried to escape. I promised people would die. I promised you would kill them."

Josef shakes his head, already dreading what was about to happen and unable to find his voice. He doesn't want to kill anyone. He doesn't want to lose any more of himself.

"Well a promise is a promise." The Iron Legion reaches out a hand and a nearby prison door rips open, the lock protesting for only a moment before giving. A man lays inside the cell, gaunt and malnourished, but still alive. A purple haze forms underneath the man and he's lifted and carried through the cell door by the Iron Legion's Kinemancy. Loran drops him before Josef. "Do it, Yenhelm."

Josef shakes his head again, tears rolling down his cheeks. He's scared and tired and… and helpless. He can't do it. He can't fight the Iron Legion anymore.

"Last chance, Yenhelm. Kill him. Or I will. Then I'll kill ten others and we'll start again. Their lives mean nothing to me, I can always find more." There's no lie to his words. No bluff or bravado. The Iron Legion will do it. He'll kill hundreds to force Josef's compliance.

Josef reaches out and puts a hand on the man's cheek. His flesh is clammy to the touch, dirt smeared and sunken, but still he looks up at Josef with pleading eyes. It's the only way. To save others. To save the lives of ten other people, Josef has to do it. He has to kill once more. He weeps as sucks the life out of the man and then lets the corpse drop to the stone floor. A part of himself was torn out, he felt it. Even as he took the life force of this man, he felt a part of his soul tear free and vanish.

"Excellent," the Iron Legion says. Josef collapses onto his knees and sobs. For the life he has taken. For the part of himself he has lost. He weeps. "I have to go. I may be gone for a while and you've proven yourself untrustworthy, Yenhelm. So…" Loran again grabs hold of Josef's collar and drags him towards the vacated cell, tossing him inside as though it took no effort at all. With a wave of his hand the cell door twists and fuses together so no key could open it. "Your privilege of freedom is revoked. I'll make certain Inran remembers to feed you occasionally. You can wait here until I return."

With that, the Iron Legion turns to the nearby soldiers. "What are you doing? Continue. These cells won't fill themselves." Loran waves his hand again and tears open a portal, stepping through it quickly and letting it snap shut behind him.

CHAPTER TWENTY TWO

JUST FIVE DAYS AFTER WE SET UP CAMP, THE Terrelan army appeared on the horizon. Thousands of soldiers marching in ranks, mounted troops on trei birds, Sourcerers flying the glowing blue banners of the Terrelan Magic Guild. It was a force to be reckoned with, and no mistake. They knew what they were getting themselves into, their scouts had been watching us for the better part of a day, and they could see the bulk of the army I had summoned across from the Other world. Yet still they came. I will take nothing away from them for that, it must have taken quite a bit of courage to march against such monsters as I controlled.

Hardt still wouldn't talk to me, but I could see the worry on his face. These were his people arrayed against us. It doesn't take much to make a person question whether they are on the right side of a conflict. His position was clear, he wanted no part of the fight, and only stayed beside

me out of loyalty. It is strange to think that he remained
so loyal yet refused to speak a word to me. I could have
used his counsel. Perhaps with it, I might have avoided
what happened next. I would wager most tragedies could
be avoided by listening to the words of those who preach
pacifism. Unfortunately, they tend to preach it at a much
lower volume than those who preach war.

My army gathered the night before in its full force.
Eight Yurthammers, almost one hundred Khark Hounds,
twenty-two Hellions, and a lumbering beast as tall as a
house and coated in whipping tendrils of bone dripping
with venom. I had never before seen that last monster
and had no name for it at the time. I named it a Horain as
some sort of misguided tribute to my fallen friend. I think
Horralain would have laughed to know I named a monster
after him, but then his ghost rarely visited me anymore. In
sheer numbers we were dwarfed by the size of the Terrelan
army, but what I had summoned was an army that should
have taken twenty Impomancers. My monsters were more
than a match for the paltry force the Emperor sent against
me. Or so I believed. Pride has always been one of my
failings.

Flags went up on the other side of the grassy plain
upon which we gathered. The Emperor wanted to talk. I
was in no mood for words, but I wanted to see who was
responsible for the fall of Orran. The man who had signed
the order to send me into the Pit. The fucking bastard who
had sent Prena Neralis to murder me. I wanted to look
him in the eyes as I told him he was going to die for all
the atrocities he had committed. So, I raised a flag of my
own, a strip of white cloth attached to a stick, and walked
onward. Imiko joined me, but Hardt stayed behind with the

monsters. Maybe because he still refused to talk to me, or maybe because he believed that the little thief would provide me greater stability than he could. Hardt has always had an annoying habit of being right.

I'd never been in any sort of parley before. I fought for Orran in the war, but I was nothing more than a weapon, pointed and told to kill. Things were different for those in charge, there were rules to these sorts of things, and I didn't know them.

"So many of them," Imiko said, her voice quiet with awe. "I don't like this."

"Then leave." The words came out harsher than I intended, and I didn't slow my stride. Still, Imiko kept up with me with ease, her longer legs easily matching my pace.

Three men on trei birds stopped before us, one still holding a white flag. They did not dismount. I passed my own flag to Imiko and met them with my usual bravado.

"I am Field Marshal Eres," said a man wearing an impeccable black uniform that almost matched his skin. His eyes were sharp underneath bushy brows that threatened to engulf his face, and his hair looked slick with oil. The trei bird beneath him fidgeted, but he kept his composure. I wondered how easy it would be to make the beast bolt with him still atop it. In response, Ssserakis made my shadow cloak a little darker so my face was only lit by the flashing of my eyes.

"My name is Eskara Helsene." My own clothing was not nearly as well-maintained as the field marshal's. After all, I had been wearing it for nearly ten days, but I wore a sturdy outfit of red and brown that deepened in the shadows Ssserakis wove about me. "Where is the Emperor?"

The frown on the field marshal's brow deepened

slightly. "He's not here." A deep voice, not unlike Hardt's though without the warmth. "The Emperor is back in Juntorrow." He said the words as though to a simpleton and I felt my ire rise.

They mock us!

"He does not even have the courage to face me?"

I felt Imiko's hand on my shoulder and shook it free.

The field marshal watched me from beneath his bushy brows. He was not even armed. "The Emperor has entrusted me to deliver his terms."

"Terms?"

"Yes. The terms of your surrender. Hand yourself over, bound and bereft of your Sources, and all others are pardoned and free to go about their lives. The Emperor only wants the Orran Sourcerer. No one else has to die today." He glanced up at the monstrous army that waited behind me, and though he kept his face tightly schooled, I could feel his fear. "How do you respond?"

Separate his head from his body and send it back to this cowardly king. That seems a fair response.

I grinned at Ssserakis' words. The third man in the field marshal's group was a Sourcerer, wearing the glowing blue emblem of the guild. They were, no doubt, to protect the field marshal should I attempt to cut negotiations short, but no one Sourcerer was a match for me.

"Your army will die here, Field Marshal." I said the words with such unabashed confidence, as though nothing could touch me. "And then I will march my monsters on Juntorrow and level every building, burn every home until the Emperor crawls out of his hiding place to face me!"

Nothing can stand in our way.

Field Marshal Eres shifted his grip on the trei bird's

reins and glanced toward his Sourcerer. The man shook his head slowly, a sad look on his face. "This is no way to fight a war," the field marshal said, nodding past me towards where my monsters waited.

Again, I grinned. "I can feel your fear. Run! And maybe I will spare you and your men."

With a sigh, the field marshal pulled his bird around and kicked it into motion. The Sourcerer and flag bearer followed. Lursa stared down at us, despite the bright sunlight, and I couldn't help but feel the moon was accusing me somehow.

Imiko tugged on my arm again and this time I turned to face her. She recoiled from whatever look she found on my face. "What are you doing, Eska?"

"Fighting a war."

"Against who? I understand you want revenge against the Emperor, but he isn't here." She was pleading.

"Then I will crush this cock-headed fool he has sent against me, and any other he puts in my way. I will tear Juntorrow to the ground to find him!"

Imiko shook her head. "You're waging a war against an entire kingdom just to get at one man. Ishtar was right, Eska. This is madness."

She is a fool. If an army is in your way, you crush it.

"These people are just trying to protect their kingdom, and their families. They're not your enemies." Imiko shook her head and tears fell free.

"They're Terrelans!" I snapped.

"So am I." She sniffed and wiped her eyes with the back of her hand. "So is Hardt. So are you, Eska. You want to depose the Emperor, to kill him. Fine. I'm sure he's a horrible man. But slaughtering anyone he puts in your way is not right. These people don't deserve it. The people of Juntorrow don't deserve it."

"They're his army. His weapon." Her words had stirred something inside, and it felt a lot like guilt. Guilt for something I had done long ago under the banner of war. Actually, it was guilt for a lot of things I had done. It was a feeling I had long ago buried. But burying your past just means it's still there for someone else to dig up and reveal to the world once more.

I was a soldier, ordered to kill by the people in charge, the people I trusted, the people who had raised me. Pointed at a target and told to bend my power upon it. By fire and horror and everything else at my disposal, I killed hundreds during the Orran Terrelan war. They were my enemies by the simple act of being on the other side of a conflict that, in truth, should never have been ours. Orran started the war, for land and power and unification. I was trying to start a new war, for even worse reasons. My ghosts crowded in around me, swirling faces raised by my guilt and brought into sharp focus by my turmoil. My old mantra echoed in my head; I am the weapon, but it no longer dispelled the guilt or doubt. It rang false.

Do not listen to her, Eskara. You swore to me and I to you.

Ssserakis was right about that. I promised I would fight. I swore I would win. But I didn't realise who I was truly fighting against, or even what I was fighting for. I was on the verge of starting a war nobody wanted, not for power or land, not even truly for revenge. I was starting a war because I didn't know what else to do. What a horrifying realisation that was to make. After everything I had been through, everything I had suffered… It dawned on me then that I wasn't the hero of my own story. I was the villain.

My vision blurred from my tears and I let out a ragged breath. The field marshal re-joined his troops and there was movement in the ranks. My monsters waited for my signal.

"We can still run away," Imiko said, clutching my shoulders. I don't know if she could see my inner turmoil, but that contact helped me steady me. "You can create one of those portal things and we can run. You don't have to fight."

I looked up my friend, the woman I considered a sister, and smiled. And nodded. Imiko was right. I was on the verge of starting a war, and she had talked me down. I will always owe her for that. Not that it mattered.

A dull thudding percussion echoed across the field, followed by another and another. Swirling green masses passed overhead as the Yurthammers began their toxic bombardment.

CHAPTER TWENTY THREE

I STARED IN MUTE HORROR AS THE GASEOUS projectiles sailed above me, trailing green wisps behind them. The impact was not violent. What the Yurthammers belch out is concentrated toxin, bound in mucus. The poison bombs crashed down on the Terrelan troops and split apart into clouds of vapour tinted a sickly greenish yellow. Screams followed as the men and women of the Terrelan military found out exactly why Yurthammers are banned.

"No," the words slipped out of my mouth as a whimper.

"Why?" Imiko asked, her own voice just as quiet.

More percussive thumps sounded as the remaining Yurthammers unleashed their toxic loads, and more gas clouds sailed overhead. The beasts would take many minutes to generate enough toxin to release again, but their damage was already done. A howl sounded and large packs of my Khark Hounds leapt forward into a loping run.

"Eska, stop!" Imiko clutched my arm so hard it hurt.

"It's not me." Useless words, but I uttered them anyway. "I didn't do this. Ssserakis, stop!"

My horror was silent for a moment. *No.*

"Eska, you have to stop this." Imiko tugged on my arm again. "Didn't you listen to a word I said? Don't you care?"

The packs of Khark Hounds tore past us, panting and barking in a flash of spikes and fur. I tried to stop them. I drew on the magic of my Impomancy Source and sent a command to every monster nearby, a mental scream at them all to stop and retreat. Ssserakis blocked me. The horror had ordered the attack when it sensed my will faltering, and now it was in control. Not I. I was helpless to stop them. No longer in control. I didn't understand how my horror could do that to me. It knew what I had been through. It had been there with me for all of it. And now it wrenched control away from me, making me helpless. It betrayed me! Just like Josef had. Just like Silva had. I thought I could trust it. I believed we were one. One mind, one soul. But just like everyone else, Ssserakis betrayed me.

Maybe a hundred soldiers died in the first salvo from the Yurthammers, those who could not drag themselves to the safety of fresh air before the toxin did too much damage to their skin and lungs. More died when the Khark Hounds hit. A single hound can take down half a dozen soldiers in a flurry of claws and teeth and bladed spines, but fully half of the beasts I summoned were committed to that first charge. Fifty Khark Hounds attacking in packs, barrelled through the lines of the soldiers turning ordered ranks into frenzied chaos. I must hand it to the field marshal though, he pulled his troops together and organised a proper defence; he had fought against the denizens of the Other World before. He also sent a unit of trei bird mounted cavalry to charge at me, hoping to end the battle in its infancy.

"Ssserakis, stop this!"

"Who are you talking to?" Imiko was frantic.

No. You started this, Eskara. You swore nothing would stand in our way. Your vengeance, then mine.

"There has to be a better way," I said, ignoring Imiko's aghast look.

"There is!" she said.

There is. There is always a better way. You could spend eternity looking for it, or you can choose the path in front of you now.

"I choose to look for another way."

And I choose this path.

A horrifying screech sounded from behind us as dozens of Hellions took to the sky. All around us a battle waged, monsters and humans fighting and dying in my name, or against it, and yet I stood at the centre arguing with my horror. It was a pointless argument. There would be no convincing Ssserakis of other action, and the ancient horror held all the cards. For the first time in my life I chose not to fight, only to have that choice ripped away from me.

Five cavalry soldiers, mounted on charging trei birds, bore down toward us. You may have never seen a trei bird in combat, but they are even more deadly than the people riding them. With slashing claws and a beak that can pierce metal or break bone, they are trained to lash out while their rider swings with spear or long axe. Even from a distance I could see the metal barding they wore was warded against various Sourceries. And I was out of time.

"I'm sorry, Imiko." I turned away from my friend, putting myself between her and the cavalry charge. They might take me, but I would not let them take her. I formed a long Sourceblade in my right hand, and I saw my left hand curl into a fist, though I still could not feel it.

My shadow flared, the cloak whipping around into two great black wings, lightning arcing between them. Then Ssserakis lifted my wings high and thrust the jagged tips over my shoulders and down into the earth. They erupted a few paces further on as spears of darkness and two of the trei birds impaled themselves upon cold shadow, their momentum arrested, and their riders pitched forward to roll on the hard earth. My wings faded into nothing just as the first of the remaining cavalry reached me. I released a kinetic shockwave that pushed it off course. The bird stumbled, its right leg snapping, and it went down for good. The final two cavalry veered off to avoid their downed comrades, then came around for another pass, charging at me in a pincer.

I chose the bird coming at me from the left and leapt towards it, pushed by a kinetic blast. It's fair to say the move wasn't expected, but man and bird both recovered well. The soldier struck at me with his spear, and the bird snapped its beak at me. I parried both with Sourceblade and stone arm, and let Ssserakis strike out with my shadow, slicing the bird's neck. It continued for a couple of dozen paces, bleeding all over the hard-packed ground, before finally collapsing.

The final member of the cavalry unit completed her charge, long axe swinging in an arc that would cut me in two. I dropped my Sourceblade and formed a huge shield as tall as I was, and twice as wide. My shadowy wings burst out of my back once more and speared into the ground, bracing me against the force of the charge. Bird and rider both hit with a sickening crunch. Even braced, I felt the force of the impact travel up my arms. Neither rider nor bird got back up again.

Hellions screamed overhead, and Khark Hounds raced past us. This was no organised assault, it was chaos. Ssserakis had ordered the monsters to attack but had given them no orders. Even now I could see the Terrelan soldiers starting to form a resistance, the instructions of how to attack the hounds being relayed, and their efforts backed up by the Sourcerers from the guild. At the same time, I could hear the Yurthammers rumbling as they readied for another volley of toxic gas.

I ran back to where Imiko waited. She was not born for battle and had no idea where to run. Panic had gripped her entirely and she had frozen. I had to get her to safety before things got any worse. Unfortunately, I was already out of time. Just as I reached Imiko, the Yurthammers began dying.

The first of the giant monsters collapsed in a scream of pain, an explosion of gas, and a river of blood. Another followed, and I could see two more panicking and letting loose similar screams of agony.

What is this?

There were small shapes crawling over the Yurthammers, multi-legged things that shone like metal catching the sunlight. Each one looked like a disc with legs and each of the legs ended in sharpened blades that gouged and dug into the flesh of my monsters. And there were hundreds of them. Thousands, maybe. A legion. The remaining Khark Hounds received similar treatment. They tried to fight back, but there was little even their teeth or

claws could do against constructs formed of solid metal. The
Horain fared slightly better, flinging the constructs away and
crushing them into the earth, but their numbers were too
great and even that mighty beast started to falter, cavorting
about in pain as the iron legion tore it apart piece by piece.

He's here!

"What's going on?" asked Imiko.

"You were right," I said wistfully. "We should have
run."

No! We fight.

I glanced back towards the Terrelan army. They were
still struggling with the Khark Hounds and Hellions, but
their soldiers had pulled together. Without backup, my
monsters would not last for much longer. A unit of archers
pushed past the front lines and raised their bows to the air,
a guild Sourcerer was with them and with a wave of their
hand, the bows began to glow, the sign of an Augmancer
making deadly projectiles even more so.

"This battle is already lost." I was certain of it. The
Iron Legion had once again outmanoeuvred me. My army
would be destroyed before long. I could not hope to fight
both him and the Terrelans.

We can still beat him. There was little conviction in
Ssserakis' voice. I think the sight of so many of creatures
of Sevoari being reduced to body parts put the battle in
perspective for both of us.

I dropped my Sourceblade and raised my right
hand to the sky, forming a kinetic bubble around Imiko
and myself. I infused the shield with Arcmancy as well so
it would block both physical and magical attacks. It was
all that I could do. The archers loosed and drew again, and
arrows shattered themselves upon my shield, but Imiko

winced all the same.

"Hardt!" Imiko squeaked the word and I saw the same thing she did. The Iron Legion strode past the dying Yurthammers as if they weren't there. His constructs, a metal legion of insectoid golems, continued the slaughter and kept him safe. One ambitious Khark Hound leapt for the man, but a handful of the legion rose up and knocked it aside, tearing the hound to shreds for its audacity. Hardt was clearly the Iron Legion's target and the big man was backing away slowly, hands balled and held ready.

Another volley of arrows pounded into my shield, shattering under their own force. Imiko and I watched in helplessness as the Iron Legion closed on Hardt, and his legion of golems surrounded my friend.

Hardt did what anyone would do when cornered and breathing their last few breaths: he attacked. He leapt at the Iron Legion, fist already swinging, and didn't even reach his target. Two of the constructs leapt on him, bearing him down to the ground and wrapping metal legs around his body. He collapsed, constricted and unable to move, and the Iron Legion simply stepped past him, and turned his attention to me.

"Do something!" Imiko hissed even as another volley of arrows struck my shield. I could feel Ssserakis seething inside, but even my horror knew I would not drop my shield and let Imiko die. Besides, the Iron Legion's threat was implicit. If I tried to fight back, Hardt would be killed.

"Surrender, Helsene," the Iron Legion's voice carried over the battlefield as though there weren't the sounds of chaos trying to drown it out. "The Emperor wants you alive. He said nothing about your friends."

Hardt screamed in pain as the metal wrapping him

squeezed him tighter.

Choices are odd things. We make them every day without even thinking about them, but when something really matters, we often find ourselves hesitating. A delay tactic, hoping that something unexpected will happen that will take the choice out of our hands. Another volley of arrows crashed harmlessly against my shield. The Iron Legion reached down and dragged Hardt onto his knees. His face was drenched in sweat and tears and screwed up in pain. His left arm was bent at an unnatural angle and was clearly broken. Still the metal constructs clung to him, their legs pulling tighter.

"Do something," Imiko's voice was little more than a whisper.

"I do not believe he can take much more of this, Helsene," the Iron Legion's voice carried to me easily, boosted by his magic.

I lifted my left arm, as always struggling with the weight of it, and opened a portal inside my shield. It tore open with a ripping noise like wet cloth pulled apart. "It doesn't go far, but it's as far north as I can put you." I smiled at Imiko, but it was a sad smile. "I'm sorry. This is all my fault."

Imiko stared at me with wide eyes. She was shaking, sweat beading on her forehead. Fear pulsed from her in waves and standing so close she felt like a furnace. "What..."

"Get back to the city as quickly as you can. Tell Tamura what happened. He'll get everyone to safety, maybe hide them in the forest." I saw tears in Imiko's eyes and felt my own well up in response. "No one else has to die for me."

Imiko glanced between me and the portal. I was

struggling to keep it open along with the shield, but I didn't rush her. I knew it would be the last time I saw my friend, and I knew how much I would miss her. I didn't want to say goodbye. "What are you going to do?"

I would have hugged her if I could have, but I needed to keep the shield up, at least until she was safe. The arrows had stopped, but I could still see the archers with their bows drawn and ready. My Khark Hounds were all but defeated, and the Hellions had already quit the battle, flying off now that they were released from any control.

"I'm not going to let Hardt die. Not for me." My voice trembled.

Imiko bit her lower lip and nodded, stepping backwards towards the portal. Tears rolled down her cheeks. "I'll tell Tamura. He'll know what to do. We'll find you."

I smiled and nodded, and Imiko stepped backwards through the portal. As soon as she was through, I snapped it shut and lowered my hand, letting my bubble disperse. I turned my attention to the Iron Legion where he held Hardt captive.

If we get in close, his minions won't be able to help. You distract him and I'll strike.

"Surrender, Helsene. You know I'm not bluffing." The metal constricting Hardt tightened even further and my friend collapsed sideways, unable to breathe, let alone scream, despite the pain. There were footsteps behind me, soldiers from the Terrelan army closing in, weapons held at the ready.

Once before, I had surrendered to the Terrelans, though not willingly. At the fall of Orran, Josef had blindsided me, knocked me down and distracted me long enough for Terrelan Sourcerers to shove Spiceweed in my mouth. This time I did it willingly, and with a little more dignity, though it is hard to retain dignity when retching so hard you burst blood vessels around your eyes. I chose to surrender, and even on my hands and knees, vomiting up my Sources and my breakfast both, the soldiers kept their distance.

When I was done, I stood and continued forward, leaving my Sources behind in the sticky grass. I crossed the distance between the Iron Legion and myself, with Terrelan soldiers following close behind.

Get us closer, Eskara. He'll let his guard down now that your magic is left behind. Get me close enough to strike.

I wiped my mouth with the back of my good hand and then held my arms out to the side as I approached. The Iron Legion narrowed his eyes and stretched out a hand towards Hardt, ready to crush him with a twitch of his fingers.

"I surrender." My shoulders slumped with exhaustion as the words left my mouth. I had been holding it together so tightly, tension stacked atop tension, but those words were an admission. I was done. The Iron Legion knew it, the Terrelans knew it, and I knew it. Years of fighting them, of running from them, of planning my revenge. It was all over. I was done. They had won.

Just a little closer.

The Iron Legion took a step forward. Hardt was still lying on the ground, in agony and barely able to draw enough breath to stay conscious. But he was conscious, his eyes fixed on me and I could see the pain there. And oddly, pride as well. The Iron Legion took another step closer.

I often wonder what might have happened had I been stronger, more capable. If I had let Ssserakis have its way.

But I made a promise to myself that I would not let Hardt die, not for me and not at the hands of Loran Orran. I looked inside myself, found the space that Ssserakis inhabited within me, and walled it up, cutting my horror off from my shadow. The world around me seemed to brighten a little, the light bringing everything into sharper focus than before.

Ssserakis raged. It wasn't just the missed opportunity, our mutual enemy was so close, and I had removed any chance we had of striking out at him, but the horror resented the cage I trapped it in. Ssserakis had become used to controlling my shadow as it saw fit, a way to influence the outside world at any time. I took that away. I can't even blame Ssserakis for the rage it let loose, I have been caged enough times myself, and I have always hated my captors and found ways to fight back.

"What have you done to yourself, Helsene?" the Iron Legion said as he stepped forward. He was within striking distance now and I felt Ssserakis batter against the walls I had locked it behind.

I lifted my stone arm. "Made a deal with Aerolis. The terms were steeper than I realised."

"Djinn are not to be trusted."

I grit my teeth. "Neither are you. Let him go."

The Iron Legion glanced at Hardt and waved a hand. The metal bonds holding my friend released a little, enough to let him breathe deeply again, but they kept him bound. "His fate is for the Emperor to decide. The same as yours." The Iron Legion sighed and looked suddenly tired, his expression softening into the grandfatherly smile I remembered of old. "I gave you your freedom, Helsene. You should have taken it. Instead, you made a statement and now Aras Terrelan wants you." Loran shook his head. "He is not a kind man."

"Where is Josef?" I spat the words at him.

"Caged. Though in no danger, unlike you." The Iron
Legion looked up as the soldiers drew closer. "Her power is
gone. You can restrain her now."

The Terrelans rushed forward and strong hands
grabbed hold of me, pulling my arms behind me and
securing them with chains. I took some small satisfaction at
the murmur of surprise when they realised my left arm was
made of stone. They still chained it to my right. I kept my
gaze locked on the Iron Legion the entire time, focusing all
my hatred and Ssserakis' into the glare. He met my flashing
eyes without flinching.

"Once before, I told you I hoped we had no cause to
meet again, Helsene. Now I am certain we won't. He will
destroy you." A sad sigh escaped his lips. "Goodbye." With
that, the Iron Legion turned and walked away through the
carnage of my army, his hands buried in the folds of his
robes and his back bent under the weight of his unnatural
years.

The Terrelan soldiers held me there until the field
marshal arrived. Then both I and Hardt were dragged away,
bound and unable to do anything to escape the tortures
planned for us.

CHAPTER TWENTY FOUR

THERE IS NOTHING QUITE LIKE SOLITARY incarceration to give a person time to think. Josef was not truly alone, of course, there were occupants in nearby cells and many of them spent much of their time, at least at the start, howling their indignation or begging for their freedom. Wasted words. The other prisoners could do nothing and did not care. Josef did not care.

It is a terrifying thing to strip a person's benevolence away from them. Even more so for someone like Josef who only ever wanted to help others. To look inside for his compassion and find that he no longer cared should have broken him, except that he no longer cared.

This is one of Josef's memories.

He could feel them. Every single prisoner on this

level had a spark to them, a little light in the darkness. Not a real light. There was no light. But they had a Biomantic light. Josef closes his eyes and concentrates, letting his senses mingle with his innate magic. There are thirty-one of them. Ragged souls, malnourished and rotting. Some are injured, others have simply lost their senses and no longer even know where they are. Or what they are. They are broken. But Josef could fix them. A nudge here, a push there, chemistry moved back into alignment, pathways corrected. He could fix them. But why should he? He can't find the effort. He doesn't care.

One of the men still screams. He's two cages over, a big man and still healthy. He kicks at the door to his cell and screams even though his voice is raw from the effort. Josef wants the man to shut up like the rest of them. To sit down and accept his fate. If only he were closer. If only he could reach the man, he could shut him up. He could suck the fight right out of him and leave him quiet. Dead.

Josef turns his senses inward and probes his Biomancy. He has always imagined his Sourcery as a sort of well. When he swallowed a Source, the well filled with magic and he could take from it at will. It would run empty eventually, of course, and if it did rejection would set in, but he was careful never to let that happen. When he regurgitated the Source, the well ran dry, the waters draining away in an instant. But there was no well inside him anymore. It had overflown, the waters engulfing everything around it. It was no longer a well, it was a lake, vast and deep. And always there.

His palms no longer hurt and though the skin on them feels new and raw, there is no evidence that he ever skinned them. His toe no longer hurts. It has not been so long since his attempt at escape, he should not have healed so quickly. He reaches up and traces a hand along the scar at his throat. Yorin had cut his throat and the blade had bit deep. No one should have survived that sort of wound. But he did. He survived and he healed.

Josef wraps his hand around his little finger and braces for the pain. He wrenches it to the side and hears it snap, feels the break as a rising wave of pain and nausea. He screams, adding his own voice to the other man's.

"Shut up!" someone hisses in the darkness.

Josef waits. He can feel his finger realigning, the bone knitting back together. With his Biomantic senses turned inward, he can feel it happening at a rate that should not be possible. And the waters of his lake are barely touched. He counts out the time in his head. Four minutes. Four minutes for a broken bone to heal as though the injury had never been.

He puts the heel of his hand in his mouth and bites down hard. Again, the pain, though less this time. He was expecting it. He was bracing against it. He was numbing it somehow, another use of his Biomancy he hadn't even realised was possible. The blood in his mouth is sticky and metallic and he spits it out. His flesh knits back together in seconds. Before a minute is up the wound is completely closed.

It's the Iron Legion's technique at work, Josef knows for a certainty. His innate Biomancy has been there ever since the Pit. No, even before that. It's been there ever since Loran first experiment on he and Eska. He injected them with Sources and changed them forever. But ever since Josef had started draining the life from his… Victims. They were victims and he would call them such. It sparked to life a brief flicker of guilt that he clung to, knowing it would not last and that when it disappeared, he would be truly lost. Somehow, draining the life from others was strengthening Josef, causing his well to overflow into a lake. Even though he was channelling that energy into Sources, a part of it stayed with him.

What about the Iron Legion though? He had developed the technique. He had been using it for years before now. How long had he been draining the life from people, adding their power to his own? How many people had he murdered? How strong was he really?

Josef saw his reserves as a lake, but then the Iron Legion must have an ocean!

It was hopeless. It had been hopeless from the start. Josef drew his knees up and hugged them to his chest. There was no way out of this prison. The Iron Legion countered him at every turn. His power was too great, too unfathomable. He would not let Josef go. He would not let Josef stop. And with every life taken, Josef cared a little less.

He sobbed, tears rolling down his cheeks. A broken thing like all the other prisoners. There was no hope. There was no respite. He had no fight left. The Iron Legion had won.

CHAPTER TWENTY FIVE

I DON'T REMEMBER MUCH OF THE JOURNEY TO Juntorrow. I think I have blocked the details of it, for it was without a doubt one of the worst times of my life. Hardt's arm was set and he was marched along in manacles, kept under constant guard. He had it easy. The Terrelan soldiers blamed me for the deaths of their friends and comrades. Over five hundred dead and as many injured. They were right to blame me, it was my fault. That doesn't mean they were right to take my shoes away, tie me to the back of a horse, and force me to march along at speed or be dragged. The vanguard set a gruelling pace and I was forced to keep it. Each day was a monotonous agony of marching on blistered, bloody feet, dragging myself along beyond the limits of endurance. I was given a few sips of water each morning and when we made camp, barely enough to sustain me, and my throat felt like fire. They fed me once every

two days and only on the scraps soldiers left behind. I was
insulted, spat upon, tripped, and even punched by some of
the more vicious soldiers. The field marshal did nothing to
stop his troops.

By the time we arrived at the outskirts of Juntorrow
I was already on the verge of giving up. I felt like I had
nothing left. The only thing keeping me on my feet was my
own stubborn defiance. I refused to die, and the Terrelans
refused to kill me. It's their way, and the Red Cells are there
to force the issue. I mention this, because as bad as my
forced march to Juntorrow was, my stay in the Red Cells
was worse. Though at least there wasn't much in the way of
walking. Something to be grateful for, I suppose.

Whenever we stopped, I slumped. Whenever I
slumped, someone hit me. We stopped outside of Juntorrow
for hours and I earned more than a few new bruises. I
briefly caught sight of Hardt and he was hunched over and
bleeding from a cut on his head, his left eye swollen shut. We
met each other's gaze for just a moment, and I found myself
standing a little taller. Then, someone punched me, and I
found myself on the floor instead. When tied to horse and
it starts moving, you start moving. It's wise to make it your
choice, especially when you're entering a city of cobbled
streets.

News of my arrival had spread. The people of
Juntorrow shouted and jeered, some even throwing things
at me. I took a stone to the face that sent me reeling and
had to struggle to get back to my feet before the rope pulled
taught. Their hate of me seemed a disproportionate thing.
My actions could not have affected the citizens of Juntorrow
to such a degree, but then I suppose it didn't need to. Maybe
there had been lies told about me, news reported that turned

me into an invading despot. Perhaps they hadn't even heard of me at all but jumped on the opportunity to throw mindless hate my way. People are like that sometimes, cheering on the suffering of others, often as a way to forget their own. I weathered the assaults without complaint, but my hatred and anger kindled inside once more.

Ssserakis remained utterly silent. I was no longer blocking my horror from manipulating my shadow, but it was absent somehow. I couldn't even feel it inside. That saddened me far more than the fools shouting vitriol at me.

Eventually we arrived at the gates to the Terrelan palace itself. We stopped there. I slumped and someone punched me in the kidney. As if it wasn't hard enough to find any comfort, a punch to the kidney only serves to compound the issue. Though I must admit, my pride rose a little then. To think I was important enough to warrant an audience with the Emperor himself before they dealt with me for good. I didn't understand the truth yet.

The field marshal turned back to me. He didn't smile, as some people might have, but there was a savage satisfaction in his eyes, along with some pity. There is little that raises my defiant streak quite like pity.

The gates were opened, and I was marched through with a combination of being pushed and dragged all at once. The Terrelan royal palace is a grand, sprawling thing that overlooks Juntorrow from a raised hill near the centre. It is a marvel of gleaming stone, stained glass windows, and towers. The tallest tower stood apart and alone at the zenith of a hundred polished white steps, it rose like a dark grey monolith at the centre of the palace. The Emperor's tower. It's said he could see all Juntorrow from the rooftop. A commanding view of his empire. I assumed that was where they were taking me, to be humbled in front of their ruler. Instead, I was pushed to the side, away from the tower and towards a squat, ugly building that looked out of place amidst the glory of the palace. It was an apt appearance. The soldiers pushed me towards the dungeon. Towards the Red Cells. I tried glancing behind, attempting to look for Hardt, but was cuffed about the head. My dignity was well and truly gone now.

I was led into the darkness, lit only by flickering lantern light, and down into the depths. It was like returning home. Beaten and chained, led deep underground, my magic stripped from me, and nothing to look forward to but torture and death. The circle was complete. But unlike the Pit, there was no great cavern down in the Red Cells, no scabs nor digging, no rough-hewn walls or discarded tools. Down there were stairs, ordered corridors with equally spaced doors, and screams. Some were the wails of the damned, people long since devoid of sanity, and others were of true pain brought about by torture at the hands of seasoned professionals. It was not long before I was adding my own screams to the cacophony, and they were never torn willingly from my throat.

The field marshal was gone, but the soldiers who led me were no less rough with their treatment, and they even pulled me aside to give me a last beating before finally shoving me into my new home. One thing to be said for having an arm of solid stone, it does a good job of protecting your vitals when you're curled into a ball receiving a kicking. Eventually they opened a door and tossed me inside, slamming it shut behind me. I crumpled against a wall and didn't bother getting up. I'm not even sure I could have. Something felt broken inside, a rib maybe, and the pain was so excruciating even lying still was no respite. The darkness was complete and Ssserakis provided me no night sight. I closed my eyes and found some small measure of escape in the oblivion of sleep.

I woke to light spilling into my cell from a small hole set head height in the door. For the first time, I could clearly see my new home and it's fair to say I'd lived in better. My cell was no larger than a cupboard, and even as short as I am, I was unable to stretch out fully in any direction unless I was standing. There was a bucket in one corner, and I was certain much of the unpleasant smell was coming from that direction, and above me hung a rope tied into a noose. That was it, nothing else in the cell but me and my pain. No window, no cot, no ratty blanket to sleep under, not even any straw to protect me from the cold stone floor. Everything in that cell was there to make the noose seem more tempting.

Something passed in front of the hole in the door and obscured the light. I saw eyes peering at me for a moment, and then the sound of a key turning a lock. Then, the door pulled open. The light that flooded in nearly blinded me, despite being dim, and I pushed myself further back against the wall, shielding my eyes with my good arm and groaning in pain as my body reminded me I had a broken rib.

A figure limped into the cell and stood between me and the door. I recognised the sharp features and glossy black hair, along with the gold on black uniform. Prena Neralis had come to visit me. She wore a new sword at her hip, a plain thing of silver steel that lacked both the grandeur and power that Neverthere had shone with. I attempted a mocking laugh, but it came out as a cough that wracked my body with new pain. Prena said nothing, only watched me through cold, harsh eyes, her hand resting on the hilt of her sword.

A second figure passed in front of the door, this one wider than Prena and a little shorter. He had a dangerous smile on his face, accentuated by the dark beard streaked with grey. He wore a fine suit of red on black and carried no visible weapon, and he walked like a man in charge of things. There is a way that people of power move, as though the whole world revolves around them. They expect things to move out of their way and so walk without concern or respect. I have known many people like this over the years and I have hated all but one.

"It's good to finally meet you, Eskara Helsene," the man said in a voice like a crackling hearth fire, all warmth and light hiding the dangerous heat of the flames. "I've heard a lot about you for quite some time now."

"Should I care who you are?" My voice was a rasping croak and I tasted blood on my lips.

"Oh yes." That smile and the way he looked at me… the memory of it still makes my skin crawl to this day. Like a beggar staring at a banquet, unable to decide which delicacy to sample first. I hated the way he looked at me as much as I hated the man himself. "We've been at odds for as long as you've been alive. You've been my enemy, my prisoner, my quarry, a thorn in my side. Prena here was quite beside herself when I gave the order to leave you be."

Prena grunted and her face contorted into a snarl.

"I know," the man continued. "But Loran is an ally and I respect his requests where I can. But then you returned to Terrelan and attacked my soldiers. Well, Loran's protection only extends so far, I'm afraid. I'm quite glad you came back, though. I've been wanting to get you down here for quite some time."

It dawned on me then, my mind working slowly, who I was talking to. Well, the talking part was over for me. I had just about enough strength left to push onto my knees and swing my stone fist at the Terrelan Emperor. I knew it wouldn't kill him. Finally, I was face to face with the man I had so long ago sworn to see dead, yet I was at his mercy. I couldn't kill him, but if I could just land a punch… if I could just hurt him, even for a moment, even if all I left him with was a stinging bruise, it would be worth it! The fucking bastard had me, but I could still teach him fear.

A boot connected with my face and I sprawled back on the floor of my cell, blood in my mouth and agony in my face to go along with the incessant pain in my chest. Prena had been waiting for me to make a move, waiting for the opportunity to put me in my place.

I'm ashamed to say I was spent. I curled into ball and moaned from the pain, unable to summon even the energy to drag myself away from two next boots Prena lashed out with. The only consolation I can drag from that kicking is that it hurt her too. Whatever damage the Iron Legion had done to Prena up on Do'shan, it left her with a limp and a weak left leg. Small victories. It's important to look favourably on even the smallest of victories when in the position I was down there. Anything you can cling to to keep you going. To keep the misery and despair from crushing you out of existence.

"That's enough," said Emperor Aras Terrelan in a voice thick with command. Prena obeyed without hesitation and took a step back, certain I would be causing no more trouble, that I was past any point of resistance. She was right. I had no resistance left in me, no strength for anything but a mewling crawl into the corner of my cell. But there was light, and where there was light there was shadow.

"Help me," I whispered the words, but I needn't have said them at all. Ssserakis didn't answer. I could barely even feel the horror inside save for the icy pit in my stomach. It had abandoned me. When I needed it most, Ssserakis abandoned me to my enemies.

"Begging already?" the Emperor scoffed. "I had hoped for a bit more resistance out of you." He rubbed his hands together, staring down at me with hungry eyes.

"I want to share something with you, Eskara." The Emperor of Terrelan took a step forward and squatted on his haunches before me. Prena tensed, the man was within striking distance, but I could not even summon the strength to lash out at him. My left arm lay out in front of me and I could just about see the stone fingers curling into an impotent fist. "You're never leaving here. Prisoners never leave my Red Cells. But you can take the easy way out any time you choose." He glanced up at the noose hanging above us. "I hope you won't go quickly, but eventually you *will* choose the rope. Some people don't make it to the first day, choosing to spare themselves the pain. Others get through the first day, and then realise that worse is certain to follow. The noose starts to look quite inviting, I'm told. Occasionally we get a truly rare person down here." The man bit his lip and smiled. "They are my favourites, the ones who resist. There is something… special about being the one to snuff out the fires of their resistance."

I glanced at Prena. She looked uncomfortable, fidgeting as though the Emperor's words made her uneasy. When I looked back to the Emperor, his eyes were shining in the darkness.

"I know what I am," the Emperor continued. "And I know it should be beneath me. The pressures of running an empire are... myriad. The responsibilities are crushing. I have been Emperor for thirty-four years. I have fought and won two wars. I have sacrificed for my empire, forged new alliances, brokered trade deals with creatures I should not have to deal with." He drew in a deep breath and let it out slowly. "I am under great pressure, as any ruler is, and so I have found ways to calm myself. I know these methods should be beneath me, that they are not befitting of a man of my station. But I enjoy them. I enjoy torturing people, especially those who have set themselves against me. Those strong enough to hold out against the torture. For a while, at least.

"I believe you have that fire in you. I can see it in your eyes, the way they flash like a storm in a bottle, and the darkness in between those flashes is even more striking. You'll resist. You'll fight." He reached out a hand and stroked my cheek. I tried to jerk away from him, but my head hit the wall and bright spots danced in my vision. "But one day, I will know that bittersweet pleasure of finding you swinging from your rope, purple and bloated and broken." The Emperor drew in a ragged breath and his eyelids fluttered. "Please, hold out for as long as you can. Please."

I lunged, snapping my teeth shut in an attempt to take off a finger or two, but the Emperor was swifter than I gave him credit for and pulled his hand back. He did not strike me, nor even order Prena to do it for him. Physical brutality was not the man's way. He knew it had its uses and employed it when necessary, but his tortures went far beyond the simplicity of a beating. With a smile, the Emperor stood easily and sauntered back towards the door.

"Until tomorrow, then. Oh, the anticipation of that first scream. The cadence and pitch, the hopelessness as you realise…" His voice trailed off as he moved away down the corridor.

Prena remained, looking down at me through a stare that was either pity or disgust. Maybe it was both. I could see something else as well, an indecision. It took a monumental amount of effort for me to uncurl, and even more to make it to my knees, using my stone arm as a crutch to hold myself upright. I wanted to get to my feet, to face her, but that was beyond me.

"Use the rope," Prena said once it became clear I was not anywhere close to being on my feet. With that, she turned and walked out the door, shutting it and locking me in near darkness once more.

I looked up at the rope, the thick cords of it standing out in the scant light shining in from the other side of the door. It was the only thing in my cell that was lit, a shining, temping beacon. I'd be lying if I said the call of the void didn't make itself known then. Lesray Alderson's *gift* from a time so long ago it seemed a different life, a far happier life that couldn't possibly belong to me. Before the academy had turned me into a weapon, and before the war had turned me into a killer. Before the Pit had turned me into a prisoner, and Josef had made me choose between my best friend or my freedom. Before the Rand and Djinn had turned me into a pawn in a war neither side could ever win. Before Kento had turned me into a mother, and Silva had taught me how to love, and how to betray.

There was little to do down in my cell other than ruminate on my past and the decisions, and mistakes, I had made. On the friendships I made and ruined. On the people

I loved, and where my leadership had led them, what it had made of them. Hardt shared my prison, I was certain of it. He was down in the Red Cells, awaiting torture, just like I was. I imagined him staring up at the rope. How much would it take before Hardt gave in? How long could he last? I wagered it would be longer than I.

My other friends soon intruded into my thoughts as well. Imiko had gotten away, I would accept no other possibility. She had run and reached the ruined city. Somehow, she'd found Tamura. They had fled to the forest and the safety of the trees. They had to have made it. They had to. Part of me hoped they'd come for me, somehow storm the gates of Juntorrow and break into the palace, before freeing me from my cell. A stupid, fanciful dream that would see my friends dead long before they reached me. A larger part of me hoped they'd stay away, embark on a life without Eskara Helsene dragging them down with her. I hoped Ishtar had made it out of Terrelan as well. She would find no hospitable welcome in the Terrelan lands, only suspicion and outright hatred. But there was no one more capable than Ishtar, and I believed she would find a way back to Polasia.

That left Josef. Taken by the Iron Legion. I didn't even know if my friend was still alive or not, what the Iron Legion might be doing to him. I must admit, even in my wildest nightmares, I did not come close to the truth. Perhaps my imagination was lacking, or perhaps I simply could not fathom the reality of his situation. I thought about Josef a lot, especially on that first night in the cells.

Spending too much time with only your own thoughts for company is dangerous. They start to swirl and circle, becoming ever more damning and heaping more and more guilt upon you. It was too much to take, too much turmoil, too much pain. My gaze slid to the rope over and over again. All I had to look forward to was torture. They wouldn't kill me, it wasn't the Terrelan way, due to laws set in place centuries ago, circumvented in the cruellest fashion possible. The Terrelans didn't kill their prisoners, just convinced them to kill themselves. I was in their clutches, well and truly caught with no way out, and it would be a kindness, both to myself and to the whole world, to just stop it there and then. No more pain. No more torture. No more mistakes causing the world and its people harm. The others would be free of me, of the things I put them through, and I would free of everything. It would be over.

"Ssserakis?" I asked of the darkness, my voice quiet, timid like I had never been. I received no reply. The horror was inside me still, coiled tight around my heart and soul, but it ignored me, a different sort of torture. Punishment for the promise I had broken.

For the first time in as long as I could remember, I felt alone. Truly alone. No friends, no horror. Nothing but empty darkness. That scared me more than I can explain. More than the threat of torture or the lingering stare of the Emperor. I was terrified of being alone. Tears welled and I started to cry, at first, they were great, wracking sobs, but my broken rib soon put an end to that, and instead I cried in silence. It seemed fitting somehow.

A deep, dark, desperate misery settled upon me. The type of despair that makes the call of the void even stronger. Again, I found myself staring up at the noose and imagining how easy it would be to just stop. It was with no small amount of surprise that I realised I was no longer alone. Horralain stood nearby, his image pale and soft around the

edges. A silent ghost to keep me company, a friend I had
pressed into service beyond death, summoned now to chase
away the fear of being so utterly alone.

Horralain's mouth moved, but no sound came out.
Ghosts had no voice. My friend had rarely spoken in life,
and when he did, his words were measured and brooked
listening to. There was meaning to his words now, but I
could not hear it.

"I'm sorry," I whispered into the gloom, unable to
take my eyes from Horralain's ghost. "I did this to you. You
don't deserve to be here." It should have seemed funny. Of
all my friends, Horralain was perhaps the only one who did
deserve to be in a cell. I had no idea what he had done to
earn his way into the Pit, it was impolite to ask after another
inmate's crimes, and back then Horralain had seemed the
type of man who would strangle a person rather than talk
to them. But there were plenty of rumours and none of them
were kind to the big man. Even so, he didn't deserve what I
had done to him.

I reached out with my good arm and clasped a hand
around Horralain's own. The surprise on his face was
obvious. Ghosts have no real form, they cannot interact with
the world, nor even with other ghosts. They are nothing
but thought and memory trapped at the point of death
and given pitiable form, slowly eroding from existence.
A terrible fate to inflict upon anyone, especially a friend.
So, I did what I should have done long ago, right from the
start. I unravelled Horralain's ghost and freed his spirit
from the damnation of existence. He stared down at me the
entire time, an unreadable expression on his face. Gratitude
maybe? Pity? Hate? I couldn't tell through the blurred vision
of tears.

And then I was alone again.

CHAPTER TWENTY SIX

BELMOROSE SAID: *THERE ARE JUST TWO reasons for torturing a person. The first is to acquire vital information that would otherwise be withheld. The second is because you're a sadistic fuck who likes to inflict pain.* Nowhere was the truth of his statement more apparent.

There is no concept of time down in the Red Cells. No light, save for that which my captors provided, illuminating nothing but the noose. There is no sound but an incessant dripping of water, and the wails of the damned as they experienced what I was certain to. How long passed between that first meeting with the Emperor and the next? I don't know. Long enough that I had to use the bucket. Long enough that I started to dread what was coming and imagine what they might do to me. It is impossible to truly imagine torture. You can never really comprehend the pain and fear of it, until it is happening to you. I slept, I know that, exhaustion getting the better of me and dragging me down into oblivion. Ssserakis did not wait for me there. No nightmares or existential trips to the Other World. Most people would think that a blessing, but I would have given almost anything to hear my horror's voice once more.

When they came for me, I had barely enough time to open my eyes before a flurry of hands grabbed me, pulling me to my feet. I fought back, of course, but there was little I could do in my weakened state, and even less I could do once my arms were twisted behind my back. I reached for the Arcstorm inside, but its power was diminished. Too long without a Source to draw strength from. Even my eyes had dimmed. Still, one of my captors got a nasty shock that sent him stumbling and I took some small pleasure in that. It was short lived as I received a backhand to the face that had me spitting blood.

I was pulled to a halt and a hand grabbed hold of my chin; an ugly face shoved up close to mine. The man was old, wrinkled skin like dusty onyx and a white beard that was so tangled it looked like a bird's nest. His uniform was clean and pressed though, black on black, the colours of the Grave Watch. Even I had heard of them. The Emperor's loyal dogs; men and women without scruples or morals. In any other profession people like that would end up down in the Pit, but as long as they were loyal to Aras Terrelan, they were more useful to him free. I was under no false impressions; my guards were killers and worse.

"Do not do that again," the old Grave Watch man said in a voice that whistled through missing teeth. "His majesty wants to tend to you himself, but that don't mean we won't play rough if you struggle."

I stared at the man, putting as much venom as I could

into the dim flashing of my eyes. Silence held for a few moments, then he looked away and started on again, the others holding my arms pushing me forward. Even at my most vulnerable, people have struggled to meet my gaze. Again, small victories.

The dark corridors passed in a blur of hazy lantern light and rushed footsteps. I saw other cells, doors locked and the occupants within either silent or screaming. My guards joked as they hustled me along, something about the city being in an uproar, its people demanding to see my corpse. Again, I was struck by the oddity that the people of Juntorrow hated me so. It really shouldn't have surprised me; Terrelans have always been a people who are easily led, and the Emperor had declared me an enemy of the empire, a dissident who wanted nothing more than to throw the people into another war no one wanted. I suppose Orrans were not so different, really. The truth is, the only real difference between Terrelan and Orran, back when it still existed, were the markings on a map.

I was moved down a winding stairwell, pushed along and held by the arms behind my back and a hand on what was left of my blouse's collar, then down another blank corridor of dark stone. Finally, the old Grave Watch guard opened a door and I was shoved inside. A single chair, set into the floor, sat at the centre of the room and I was pushed toward it. The Grave Watch wasted no time in forcing me down into the chair and then securing the iron manacles in place over my wrists. They had a little trouble with my stone arm and had to adjust the size of the manacle, all the while exclaiming at how odd such a thing was. I offered no explanation.

There was nothing else in the room. It was large for

all it contained, easily five times bigger than my cell, and a single hook was embedded into each wall, a lantern held on each, bathing the room in dancing light. The Grave Watch gathered near the door and continued to talk amongst themselves. They spoke of people they didn't like, people they'd like to know better, of many other inconsequential things. The wait frayed my nerves. I have never liked being tied down or constricted, and the chair I was strapped to left me little room to move.

Eventually the Grave Watch heard footsteps and took their places; two by the wall behind me and the third standing to attention next to the door as it opened. Prena stepped through followed by the Emperor and an ancient, withered old man I did not know. The Emperor smiled, Prena scowled.

"Oh, this is most excellent," the Emperor said in that energetic, charming voice of his. "I can already see there's some fire in your eyes. It's amazing what a little rest will do for a person's humours." The door swung shut with a damning finality. I saw Prena shake her head, a pitying glance sent my way. "Now," the Emperor continued. "I'll be dealing with your stay personally. This is master Tivens." He placed a light hand on the ancient man's shoulder. "He's my tutor in such matters. Fifty years' experience in the arts. Don't worry, he'll stop me if I get carried away."

"Fuck you, you cunt!" I put as much venom as I could into the insult, but the Emperor just laughed as he produced a pair of heavy iron pliers.

"We'll get right to it then." The warmth in his voice vanished, replaced by a sinister air. "I am quite pressed for time, what with having an empire to run. And you really thought to challenge me for it. Idiot girl."

The two Grave Watch behind me moved forwards. One grabbed my right hand, forcing my fingers to splay out on the arm of the chair I was strapped to, the other placed hands on my shoulder, pushing me down into the chair. The Emperor approached and set the pliers around the nail of my index finger. He gripped tight and pulled a little and the pain started. Tearing, ripping. Like hundreds of needles stabbing into the skin.

"Did you know," the Emperor said, lessening the pressure. Already my breathing was coming fast and ragged as I tried to brace for the pain I knew was to come. "There are over twenty different screams of pain a person can produce."

I glanced down at my right hand. The pliers were still in place, but there was no blood yet. I could feel my own fear making my heart race. I should have been able to taste it, to draw strength from it through Ssserakis, but my horror remained silent and distant, as though it were not even there. The Emperor was still talking. The fucker really liked the sound of his own voice.

"… varying in tone and pitch. Each is produced by different stimuli. But what's really interesting, is that each person is different. Different stimuli producing the same screams."

I groaned. The anticipation of the pain was unbearable.

"Am I boring you?" the Emperor asked.

"Ye—" My reply ended in a scream of agony as my fingernail was slowly ripped from its bed.

He waited for my scream to die down. It took some time and he smiled at me through all of it. When I quieted, he started again. "I want you to know how close you came," he said, his voice gone cold again. "You might have realised the army I sent against your monsters was somewhat diminished." Two thousand soldiers was a smaller force. At the fall of Orran, the Terrelan army had numbered well into their tens of thousands. "I'm afraid that was all I could muster on such short notice. So many of my troops are forced to spend their time maintaining peace in the empire. Oh, I say Orrans have been integrated into what is now Terrelan, but it's not entirely true. There is resistance. And it is all your fault."

I shook my head, trying to clear away the fuzzy edges left by the agony. Trying to understand his words.

"The last of the Orran Sourcerers. A rebel fighting for independence, for freedom, for rights. That's what they call you. Eskara Helsene: survived the war, escaped the Pit, thwarted my Knights of Ten, returned and pulled a city from the earth." He paused and chewed at his lip for a moment. "They have unified around you, around your name. Rebel factions have been popping up all over old Orran, and seditious whispers have even been heard over on the Terrelan side of my empire." He sighed. "That is where most of my troops are focused, on keeping the peace. But I intend to use you to put the rebels down for good. If I executed you, my own people would turn against me for breaking tradition, and I would only succeed in turning you into a martyr. But, when you take the noose and end your own life, I will show your broken corpse to the world. Bereft of their unifying catalyst, the rebellious elements will break down." He approached me again and set the pliers to my thumbnail. I'm ashamed to say I let out a whimper. I knew the pain was coming and I didn't want it. I didn't want any of it. "But don't for a moment think I want that to happen quickly. My empire will survive these rebels for as long as is needed, for as long as you can hold out."

By the time the Emperor was done with me that day I had no nails left on my right hand. I think he would have moved onto my left, but one look at the solid stone of my arm convinced it would be a fruitless endeavour, and the Emperor hated doing anything that wasn't to the purpose of breaking my spirit. My voice was raw from screaming out my pain, and none of those wails were drawn voluntarily. They were ripped out of me just as my nails were. And each time that hateful fucking bastard drew pleasure from my pain. Master Tivens gave *helpful* pointers and occasionally tutted at work he considered sloppily done. I would have ripped out his throat if I had been free. Each time the nail was gone, dumped on the floor like the worthless, bloody flesh it was, the pain ebbed from a sharp agony to dull, throbbing ache. Each time the nail was gone and I could think once more, I hated everyone in that room. The Grave Watch, Master Tivens, Prena, and the Emperor. My rage knew no limits. I tried to reach for my power over and over again, but there was no strength left to it. My Arcstorm was there, but I could not even summon a spark. Ssserakis was coiled tight, its power to manipulate my shadow withdrawn from my use. I had nothing left to fight with. And they knew it. They knew I was powerless. They counted on it.

Drenched in cold sweat, shaking from the pain, and babbling whispered curses. That is how the Emperor left me on that first day. His work done, he handed the pliers to one of the Grave Watch and strode from the torture chamber with Prena falling in a step behind. At least she had the good grace to look sickened by what had been done to me. Master Tivens wrapped my right hand in bandages and forced me to drink water that tasted of herbs, then he too left. The Grave Watch unfixed my manacles and led me back to my cell. I say they led me, but mostly they dragged me. I struggled to put one foot in front of the other. Back in my cell I found bread and water waiting for me. One thing I will say about the Red Cells, they fed me well down there. How else would I keep my strength up to withstand the Emperor's ministrations?

That first day was a bad one. The days that followed were even worse.

CHAPTER TWENTY SEVEN

THIS IS ONE OF JOSEF'S MEMORIES.

Another prisoner is dumped in front of Josef, this one wearing the faded robes of a monk, the symbol of Lursa on his breast. The Orran empire had always considered worship of the moons heretical. They had always considered any form of worship heretical. Terrelan, however, had welcomed believers of both Lursa and Lokar, and claimed it was their prayers that brought the moon showers. Josef places his hand on the man's shoulder, and draws the life force out of him, channelling the power into the metal sceptre and the Source affixed to the end. The body slumps away from him, dead flesh worthless.

A sliver of Josef screams inside, as it does with every life taken, but that part grows smaller, quieter. In his drug-induced haze there is nothing that small part of Josef could do but watch and shrivel a little more with each death.

"Next," Loran says, making a small note in his book. He flicks his fingers and opens a portal, an invisible shove sending the body of the monk through it. The soldiers grab the last of the nearby prisoners and pushed her forward.

Things have changed recently. The experiments are happening more frequently, Loran's supply of prisoners has been all but exhausted. Now, they are used as soon as they are brought in. No, not used. Killed. Murdered. Josef has to remind himself of that. But it's becoming harder and harder to care.

The Source affixed to the end of the sceptre glows now, a flashing yellow light pulsing from within. There are no more prisoners left. The poor woman with buck teeth and watery eyes looked barely old enough to be called an adult, but that didn't matter to the Iron Legion. And Josef found it didn't matter to him either. Not anymore. They were all the same once their life was drained from them.

The two hundred and sixteenth body drops and Josef channels her spirit into the Source. It glows even more brightly than before, a high whine filling the room as the dead Rand within the Source returns to life. Josef tries to care about that as well, but he doesn't.

In the gloom of the Iron Legion's laboratory, a second Source begins to glow. Upon his writing desk sits a large Source with a flat side. It is too big to swallow, making it completely unviable to be used in Sourcery. Loran turns his attention to it, to the soft blue glow burning within the crystal. He glances back toward Josef, still holding the sceptre, the Source affixed there shining so brightly it hurts to look at. Then both Sources shatter in a scream that echoes about the laboratory. The light fades and they are left once more in the dim, flickering glow of lantern light. Another failure. So many failures. So many lives spent for nothing.

The soldiers cower. Their good humour evaporated when Loran started involving them directly in his experiments, and Josef sometimes hears them talking about running. But the pay is good enough to keep them around no matter the atrocities they must commit to earn it. Inran lets out an audible sigh and turns towards the broom leaning against the far wall. It was ever the little tahren steward's job to clean up after Loran, and he often complained about finding shards of Source for weeks after each experiment.

Josef stands, holding the empty sceptre, numb from the Sweet Silence Loran drugged him with, and from the consequences of so many lives taken. He can feel the strength of his innate Biomancy growing all the time now. Each experiment, each life taken makes him stronger. He cuts himself from time to time, to see if he still bleeds. He does, but only a trickle. The wounds close in moments and don't even leave scars.

The room shakes. It's a subtle thing at first, but the tremors grow even as Josef focuses on them The room, the halls nearby, the cells below, the very earth around them is quaking. It's not a natural tremor, Josef needs no Geomancy Source to know that, but instead it was coming from the Iron Legion. Loran's face is tight, jaw clenched, and eyes screwed shut. His hands are balled into fists and shaking. Every bit of the man is too tense, taught like a bow string, and power flows out of him. It's not just Geomantic tremors, sound travelled bizarrely in the laboratory, one moment booming and the next, all but silent. One of the soldiers gasps as his sword twists and curls like rope caught in the wind. Portals snap open, leading to some unknown realm, and vanish in an instant. Golems break themselves free of the very rock around them, all reaching up from the floor or walls, half pulling themselves free before crumbling to chips of stone and dust. Josef feels a tide of rage sweep over him and, even numbed, he feels angry enough to scream, and then it's was gone.

Two of the soldiers collapse, hands pushed against their heads, sobbing from the tumult. Inran braces against the wall, just a few paces from the broom, his head twitching from side to side as though trying to smell the threat.

Josef glances down at the sceptre in his hand. It was unornamented, solid metal and weighty even without a Source affixed to the end, certainly heavy enough to inflict damage to an unprotected skull. The Iron Legion's back is turned, his magic flaring out in uncontrolled bursts. His shield might be suffering the instability too. There's no better chance. Josef will get no better chance to end it all, to free himself and all the others still trapped in the cells below. But he doesn't take it. Because it doesn't matter. He doesn't care enough to try.

"All for NOTHING!" the Iron Legion roars and the sound booms around the laboratory knocking everyone off their feet and making them all cover their ears. Inran is affected worst of all. Tahren hearing is much more sensitive than a terran's and the little steward is knocked unconscious by the burst of sound. "All these years of planning. All my experimentation. Made useless by an oversight!" The Iron Legion turns furious eyes on Josef. "Chosen one. Chosen ONE!" Again, a burst of sound accompanies the word and Josef groans from the pain.

The Iron Legion advances on Josef, stalking closer. "It was never about one at all, was it?"

Josef groans again, the only response he can manage, and he can't even hear that over the booming of the Iron Legion's voice.

"That is why you succeeded where all my other candidates failed. That is what makes you special. Not a chosen one, but a chosen two!"

"Eska?" Josef forces the word past gritted teeth.

"Yes. Helsene. Apart, you are useless. There is no escaping the laws of existence, Yenhelm. The Rand and Djinn are linked, inextricably paired. I cannot bring back the Rand without also bringing back the Djinn. Do you understand what that means?" Josef feels strong hands gripping hold of his tunic, shaking him, but the light had grown so bright it hurts even through closed eyes. "Twice as many lives needed for each resurrection. Twice as many chosen ones needed."

"No!" Josef fights through the pain and the haze. Tries to make his words mean something. Tries to protect the only person he can still care about. "Leave her alone."

The assault ends. The laboratory falls dark and silent in an instant, and the shaking subsides. With the pressure gone, Josef rolls onto his side and throws up, tears streaming from his eyes and stomach heaving.

"It's too late for that," the Iron Legion says in a mournful voice. He sinks down next to Josef, legs folding beneath him. Suddenly looks old. The weight of his years, both natural and not, have settled upon him. His hair stands up in thin clumps, only white wisps remaining. His skin is wrinkled and mottled with dark brown marks. His ears are too large for his head and two of his teeth had already fallen out, leaving gaps hidden behind sagging lips. "I gave her to that fool of an emperor."

Josef turns away from the Iron Legion and lets out a secret smile. At least she is free of the Iron Legion. A small compensation, but anything would be better than this torture.

"She hung herself twenty-two days ago," Loran continues. "The Red Cells get to everyone eventually."

Josef laughs but there's no humour in it at all. It's a manic thing that he can't stop.

"I'll have to start again," Loran says. "Expedite the process somehow. I know how it works now. I can make it work again."

Josef continues laughing, a madman's cackle.

The Iron Legion rips open a portal and shoves him through it. Josef is still caught in the hysteria, the laughing shaking him all over. He laughs so hard it hurts, so long he can't tell if the tears streaming from his eyes are out of joy or pain or grief or madness. One thing he does know though, something the Iron Legion does not, something he will keep from the man no matter what is done to him. Josef can feel it, deep down within himself, within his soul. He can feel Eska. He can feel that she's still alive.

CHAPTER TWENTY EIGHT

HOW LONG HAD IT HAD BEEN? I FORGET.
Time lost meaning down in the Red Cells. Days bled into
one another, punctuated only by those hours spent with the
Emperor and his ministrations. He varied his methods, and
I will not go into them. I have no wish to relive them all, and
you have no need to know what was done to me. Torture is a
harsh word for a reason.

At the end of each day I was escorted back to my
cell, carried, more often than not, and I would find food
and water waiting for me, my bucket emptied. Each day I
would eat and drink, and then bereft of anything to do, I
would stare up at the noose in my cell, trying to summon
the courage to use it. Some people would call it cowardice
instead. It is not that. It is never that. It is simply the effect of
having nothing left to give, of seeing no way out but death.
The only end to the pain.

Each night one of my ghosts would come to me.
I think I summoned them, dredging them up from the
throng that followed me, to provide some measure of
companionship and comfort. They were all people I had
killed, or at least those I was responsible for. Many of
them I recognised; scabs from the Pit, Ishtar's mercenaries,
Terrelan soldiers who died because of my little rebellion. I
understood my innate Necromancy better because of those
nights. I came to understand that I was using it to raise my
ghosts, using it to sustain them, without even realising. My
guilt over their deaths manifested through a magic I had
not, until recently, even known I possessed. Looking inside
and studying that power passed some time, and I had a lot
of time. Each night one of my ghosts would come to me,
and each night I would unravel it, giving the poor soul the
final rest I had unwittingly denied from them. I like to think
of it as a form of penance. Mistakes are ever easy to make,
and paying for them always more difficult. Each one left
something with, something of themselves, or at least who
they used to be. Memories. I learned to absorb memories
from the dead.

It was not quite like the memories of the Djinn I
absorbed through lightning. That had been like a vision
forced upon me. I could do nothing but experience it in the
moment, feeling as though I were living it. The memories
I absorbed from the dead were different. They were
impressions, a picture and the emotion imprinted upon
it. One of the old huntsmen from the Forest of Ten left me
a memory of his father and the way he used to smell of
woodsmoke and leather. A Terrelan soldier left me a memory
of her first child stubbing his toe and wailing for his mother.
One of Ishtar's mercenaries gave me a memory of the whole

company drunk in a tavern singing bawdy songs and drinking until their whiskers curled.

Magic was in me, I realised. Part of me. Whatever the Iron Legion had done to Josef and I, it had given us both something. I realised now that I absorbed magic. I call my Necromancy innate, as I had been changed using a Necromancy Source, but I had absorbed an Arcstorm and the magic that powered it. Or at least, I had absorbed a part of the storm. It was in me still, though so diminished it was barely a flicker. My eyes no longer flashed, and all I could find when I looked within was the shadow of the storm, the memory of it. But it was not gone. Nor, too, was the Geomancy I had absorbed when I pulled a city from the earth. Though the magic had been seconds from killing me, I somehow retained some of it inside, enough to move my stone arm. It was not much, though I think that was more because of weakness and condition, but I had enough strength left in me to curl and uncurl my fingers. It gave me hope, of a sort. The only hope I had. That one day, should I somehow survive the Red Cells, I might have full use of my arm once more, even if I would never be able to feel it again. It was not gone, only changed.

The loneliness ate away at my resolve. I realise now I have never been good at being alone. I had never been alone before. Not since leaving Keshin all those years ago. I was alone now. Ssserakis continued to ignore me, but my horror was there. I could feel it, feel the chill of it. It was not gone, but it had abandoned me. That loneliness did more to break me than anything the Emperor ever tortured me with. Almost. That statement is almost true.

How long had it been? Long enough that my nails, ripped from my hand on that first day, had grown back.

That the sky and sun and moons were a fading memory. My clothes had turned to sweat stained rags that barely covered me. Long enough that the Emperor had torn all but one of his precious screams from me. He seemed disappointed every day. Every day he couldn't find that final scream, and every day it made him more vicious.

The Grave Watch escorted me to my torture chamber once more. I knew their names now. Rork, the tall one with a bushy moustache. Picklesten, the man of few words and few teeth. Clews, the shortest of the three and the one with the quickest tongue. They no longer joked at my expense. I think, in some way, I had earned their respect. I never tried to run from them or fight them, mostly because I knew it would do no good. I did not attempt to bargain or threaten. I did not make their job any more difficult. Each day I walked to my torture, and some days, those I could, I walked away from it. It really depended on what the Emperor had done to me. Despite the torture, despite the scars and the injuries that have never fully healed, despite the pain and humiliation. Despite it all, I persevered. How long had it been? I do not know. Long enough to earn the respect of some of the most hardened soldiers in the Terrelan military. Long enough their mocking stares turned to pitying looks. They strapped me into my chair, as they did every day, and then took their positions. They might have learned to respect me, but they were still my captors, and I was still a prisoner in the process of being tortured to death.

Torture is a delicate art, or so I've been told by those with the knowledge of it. Everyone breaks, given enough time and pain to do so. But in order to extract information from someone, it is important to take just enough from them. They need to give up, to lose themselves and all hope of escape, but they cannot lose the will to live. It's important to leave them with that, or they have no reason to give the torturer what they want. Of course, that's a moot point when information is not the goal. When the goal is to convince the subject to take their own life, the torturer can take as much as they want, do as much as they want. All they need to leave the poor soul with, is enough of themselves left to take the final act of release.

Prena entered the room first, as always. Her position as First Sword was lost to her when the Iron Legion took Neverthere. Now she was the Emperor's bodyguard, following him around and paying witness to every monstrous action the man took. Aras Terrelan swept in behind her, a frown on his rugged features.

"The people are restless, Eska," the Emperor said. "That's what your friends call you, isn't it? I had a wonderful chat with that big one earlier. He resisted, I'll give him that, but somewhere in all the screams his tongue loosened. Oh, the things he told me about you."

A younger version of myself would have damned Hardt for the betrayal, for revealing my secrets to the worst of my enemies. I was not that young, foolish girl anymore. "You have me. Let Hardt go." I didn't bother straining against my restraints, there was simply no point.

The Emperor scoffed. "I have you both. I see no reason to let either of you go." Master Tivens arrived, lagging behind the Emperor as his age slowed him down. It also might have had something to do with the large black bag he carried. When he set it down, I heard heavy tools settling within.

"The people are growing restless, Eska," the Emperor said again. "They have not forgotten you." He shrugged. "I

don't let them forget. Not a day goes by when there aren't
people outside my palace demanding to see the Corpse
Queen."

And there it was. I have had many names over the
years, but none have stuck with me quite like that one.
Perhaps because none have fit me quite so well. Perhaps
because it was not given to me by my parents, nor any king,
not by the Rand or by the Djinn, or by any other creature
of power. It is a name that was given to me by the people,
regardless of whether I had earned it or not. It did not take
me long to grow into the name.

"That's what they're calling you. The Corpse Queen.
It's quite dramatic, though not very inventive, I suppose.
The woman who would call herself queen, soon to be a
corpse." The Emperor strutted about the torture chamber
for a few moments, trying out my new name in a variety of
mocking voices. Eventually he shrugged. "You'll fit it soon
enough. Though not too soon. I still want my final scream
out of you, Eska. I just need to find the right stimulus."

"I won't do it," I said, my voice weary and quiet. "It
doesn't matter how many screams you shake loose, Aras." If
the man insisted on using my name, I'd damn well throw his
right back. "I will never use that noose. If you want me dead,
you'll have to kill me yourself."

Again, that arrogant shrug as he pranced about
in front of me. "Not before my last scream. You'll have a
funeral to rival a king's, Eska. I'm going to mount your body
on a wooden throne and parade it through the city. The
people will come and watch and shout, and probably throw
things. Commoners love to throw things. And once you've
done a full circuit of the city, I'll set fire to the throne and
whatever is left, and the whole of Juntorrow will watch you

burn."

"You're going to parade my body through the streets for your amusement?"

"Oh no, not for me. For the people, Eska. They demand it." He said the words as though speaking to a simpleton. As though it were madness that I didn't understand. And I was the one who was being called a monster. "Now then, let's get to it."

I shied away from the man as much as I could while strapped to a chair. I curled my fingers up, pushed myself as far back into the chair as possible. It was an involuntary reaction. After so much pain, so many days of torture... I knew what was coming and I feared it, dreaded it. I had scars, some old, some still fresh, some wounds not even closed yet. Some I wore on the outside, and others on the inside. Weeks of torture, maybe months, I couldn't tell. It conditions you. You expect the pain. You know it's coming, and there's nothing you can do about it. I didn't want to give the Emperor the satisfaction of seeing me shy away, tremble in fear. I didn't want him to see my tears as the expectation of pain took hold and the terror made a mockery of my defiance. I didn't want to plead for a respite. But I simply had no resistance left. He had torn it all away. As the Emperor opened Master Tivens' bag and rifled through the contents, I begged him. Perhaps there is the truth of it, I was already broken. I begged him to stop before he even started, and I have never been more ashamed of myself.

It was not the first time the Emperor had considered the *problem* of my stone arm. There was no feeling to it, little movement. It was solid stone, but a part of me. Once before, the Emperor had chipped away at it, growing increasingly frustrated as he realised that I felt nothing. But there are some pains that go beyond the physical. Some agonies that have nothing to do with injury.

The Emperor drew a hammer out of the black bag. I had seen the type before. It was the same kind of hammer Prig used to drive the marker into the tunnel walls. A rock hammer.

Panic set in. Fear driving me to thrash about, but the manacles attached to the chair held me tight. Two of the Grave Watch, Rork and Picklesten moved forward and held me down in the chair as the Emperor took a few practice swings with the hammer, a gleeful smile on his face all the while. I babbled, pleaded, begged. I searched the faces I could see. Clews looked away, Master Tivens wore a thoughtful frown. Prena's jaw clenched, her mouth turned down and her eyes full of pity as they met my own. I begged. I begged!

"Help!" My plea fell on deaf ears, only causing Prena to look away. But I felt something inside. No, that's wrong. Not felt. I heard something. A voice calling across a vast distance, so far away all that reached me was the impression of sound.

The Emperor leaned over beside me. "No one is coming to help you. Now, I suggest you hold still." He rested the head of the hammer on my arm, just below the elbow, a couple of fingers from where it turned to rock.

Again, the voice so far away. A whisper and nothing more.

"Please," I said, shaking my head, tears streaming from my eyes. "Please don't."

Emperor Aras Terrelan smiled and raised the hammer above his head.

Eskara.

I screamed. And it was the last one the Emperor wanted from me. And the last he would ever get from me.

There is a special kind of horror that comes with losing a limb. With knowing that a part of you is gone and is never coming back. I could argue I had lost the limb long before that, when it turned to stone, but that was different. The arm had still been there of a sort. The flesh was gone, the feeling was gone, but the arm remained. Not anymore. It was gone. I would never again pull someone I loved into a full embrace. Never again hold a knife and fork in hand. Never again would I wield two blades at once. These were all things I had not been able to do for some time, but it suddenly seemed real. My left arm was gone. It ended in a jagged stump of fractured stone just below the elbow. I felt lighter, and oddly more weighed down than ever before. It was gone.

I kept poking at the stone, running my fingers along the edges, picking at notches. I couldn't help it. Huddled in my cell, face tired from the tears, eyes raw and painful. All I could do was fiddle with the stump of my arm and stare up at the noose.

Eskara. Again, the voice inside, so faint I was certain I had imagined it.

"You left me," I sobbed. I waited a long time for a reply, holding my breath.

Let me out. The voice startled me as I was dropping off to an exhausted sleep. I waited to see if I heard it again, but there was nothing but silence in my cell. Even the screams of my fellow prisoners seemed far away.

A sob broke free and I swallowed it before it could lead to any more. Ssserakis was still there, inside

somewhere. Hiding from me. And I was so sick of being
alone, so I went looking for my horror. I closed my eyes,
concentrated on my breathing, and meditated the way I
had been taught. The way the tutors at the academy had
instructed me. The way Tamura had reminded me. I looked
inside, deeper and deeper. I looked until I found my horror.

I opened my eyes to a place filled with light. That's
not quite right. I didn't open my eyes. I was just there. It was
a place inside of me, a part of me. A land of light so bright it
should have hurt to see. Featureless save for a single spot of
shadow, floating there, surrounded by searing light.

"Ssserakis?" My voice echoed in that broad expanse.

Let me out. The voice was clearer in that space, but no
less quiet. I had to strain just to hear it.

"You left me alone!" I cried. I couldn't help the
accusation that crept into me voice. My horror had hurt me.
Abandoned me when I needed it most.

No.

I moved closer to the spot of shadow and saw a thin
tendril try to reach out of the ball, only to be seared away by
the light.

"You left me!" I accused again, tears rolling down
my cheeks. I took another step forward and another tendril
reached out only to be burned away.

You left me.

Another step closer and I was staring at the little ball
of floating shadow. It looked so small and helpless in the
light. Ssserakis. Lord of Sevoari. My horror. I reached out
a hand, the only one I had left, and cupped it around the
shadow. And everything changed.

Where before there had been light, there was only
darkness. I stood at the centre of it, glowing softly, and all

around I could feel fear. "Ssserakis?"

You trapped me here, Eskara! There was pain and hurt in the horror's voice.

"You left me."

No. You trapped me here to stop me from fighting back.

Ssserakis was right about that. That expanse of light had not been a hole for the horror to hide in, it had been a prison. But my horror was also wrong. I hadn't trapped it there to stop it from lashing out at my captors, but to spare it the pain of my torture. I knew it for a certainty then.

Ssserakis laughed. Not a harsh sound. There was surprise in that laughter. Shock. *I am a lord of Sevoari. I have lived hundreds of your lifetimes. I am the terran incarnation of fear itself. And you walled me away to protect me? To spare me your pain.*

"You feel what I feel. I realised that when I was raising the city from the ground. You tried to shield me from my own pain."

It was more than you could handle.

Fresh tears welled in my eyes. "It was my fault. My pain. My choice. You shouldn't have to feel it too."

In the darkness I couldn't see Ssserakis, but I felt my horror draw close. I felt it wrap around me. The closest thing to an embrace I had felt in so long. I needed it.

"I need your help. I can't..." The tears ran from my eyes and I shook with the violence of the sobs that hit me. "I can't fight them." That admission took a lot out of me. I have never been good at admitting to weakness, not to myself and definitely not to others. But the Emperor had broken me, and I needed help putting myself back together.

Yes, you can, Eskara. We can fight them together.

I slept then. A deep sleep unmarred by nightmares or

fears. A sleep that I could lose myself in, knowing that I was being watched over and protected by someone I could trust.

I woke to the darkness of my cell, but it was different. I could see. The bare room was lit in shades of black and white, not a hint of colour. Ssserakis' sight. Dark sight. Of course, being able to see in the dark is of little use when there is nothing to see. Bare stone floor, a bucket half filled with piss, and the noose. I focused on that rope, eyes narrowing, it was lit brighter than the rest of the room, the light from outside my cell focused upon it.

You don't need it, Eskara. You never needed it.

Ssserakis was right about that. I looked upon the noose with new resolve. It was no longer a way out. It no longer called to me. It was a symbol. A symbol of what the Emperor had tried to do to me. Of what he tried to turn me into. A symbol of all the pain and suffering he had heaped upon me. Of the torture and the screams ripped from me. That noose was a symbol of how the Emperor had broken me. Some people might have raged at that, bent their new resolve against the noose and torn it down leaving shreds upon the floor. The thought occurred to me, to turn that old symbol of my broken self into a representation of my new strengthened resolve. But no. I had a far better use for it.

I stood and almost fell. More than just the weakness of months with little food and no exercise save for bracing against pain. It had taken me weeks to compensate when my arm had been turned to stone, with the extra weight it put upon me. Now it was gone, and I felt too light.

I can help. Strength flooded me. My limbs felt less leaden and I stood straighter, my head clearing a little.

"Thank you." It felt good to know Ssserakis was there

once more. More than the strength my horror gave me. The company. I wasn't alone anymore.

You're missing an arm. There was surprise in Ssserakis' voice.

"The Emperor took it."

Then we'll take his head! Where are we?

"In his dungeon. The Red Cells. Below the palace."

Such a fool to keep us so close. We'll make him regret that. We will bring his palace down and crush his empire while he watches.

I didn't argue. I would happily watch the Terrelan Empire burn, along with everyone in it. I struggled to find any compassion for the people who revelled in my torture, the people who begged for my corpse. They named me the Corpse Queen, called me a monster. I would show them a monster. *We* would show them a monster.

"Hardt is here somewhere. I have to find him."

He is a weakness, Eskara. If not for him, we would never have been captured. You already sacrificed us once for him…

"And I will do it again if I need to. We're getting out of here, Ssserakis, but we're taking Hardt with us."

My horror was silent for a moment. *This Emperor must die. You cannot hide your anger from me, Eskara, nor your pain. I can see what he did to you.*

"He will pay. They all will." I looked up at the noose above me. "Cut it down." My shadow became an oily patch splayed against the far wall. It snaked upwards and sliced easily through the rope. I tied it around my waist, struggling now I only had the one arm. Trust me when I tell you that tying a knot with only one hand is a true challenge. I approached the door and looked at it in the dark sight. A slab of hard wood, banded in iron, a sturdy bolt lock. More than enough to stop a Sourcerer with no magic. But nothing against an ancient horror of fear and shadow and ice. Dark wings burst out of my back and reached over my shoulders, plunging into the wood of the door and ripping it from its hinges before tossing it away down the corridor beyond.

I was free, and I was angry.

And the world would pay!

A lantern hung opposite me, a soft yellow glow flickering within. That lantern had been my only source of light for so long, always shining upon the noose now tied around my waist. I plucked it from its hook and carried it before me. I didn't need the light to see, but it was another symbol of my incarceration.

Footsteps echoed along the corridor. "There will be many of them. Soldiers between us and the Emperor. Are you strong enough?"

Ssserakis laughed. *You may have kept me trapped, but I was surrounded by fear. I gorged on it. Yours. Theirs. This place's. Can you feel it? Fear seeps from the very walls. It pools beneath us and flows around us. This place has seen more fear than you know. It is drowning in terror.* There was a satisfaction in my horror's voice. It approved. *I will lend you everything I have to tear down this palace and the fool who calls himself king, but what of your power?*

I shook my head. "I have nothing left, Ssserakis."

You think they have stripped you of your power. They haven't. They can't. It is a part of you. They could no more take it from you, than you can give it away. Use it! Use my power and your own. We will make them pay together.

"She's free!" The shout echoed down the corridor. "The Corpse Queen has escaped. Get reinforcements." A man started down the stretch between us. He carried a wooden blackjack in one hand and a burning torch in the other. "Get back in your cell." I had already decided I would die before I allowed them to put me back, but they would die first. "Get back in your cell and we'll pretend this didn't happen." He stopped to glance down at the door lying before him, ripped from its hinges, huge rents gouged from it. "How did you..."

Now!

I lunged towards him, crossing the ten paces between us at a flat sprint my body should not have been capable of. I recognised the man in that moment. Clews, one of the Grave Watch who escorted me to and from my cell each day. A man who stood by and watched my torture day after day after day. He no longer mocked me and called that a kindness, but he was as responsible for my suffering as the Emperor himself. They all were. All the Grave Watch. All the soldiers. All the people of Juntorrow. All of them!

Clews raised his blackjack, but it was a stick and I was a monster. Black wings brushed the weapon aside and I slammed them into the man, twisting him about and driving him against the corridor wall. The bladed ends of my wings, talons of shadow, sunk into his chest and Clews gasped in pain, unable to even scream as the wings pierced his lungs. Blackjack and torch dropped from his limp arms and Clews shook as death reached up to claim him.

"No!" I dropped the lantern and reached up with my arm, gripping hold of Clews' neck. "You don't get to die!" I screamed it at him.

Necromancy is a poorly understood school of magic. Attuned Sourcerers are rare, and even at its height the academy had only one tutor. By the time I was attending the academy, so much of the school's arts had been lost, and they were not willing to teach a young girl how to control death itself. Of course, that didn't stop the Iron Legion from injecting the magic into me. I had spent much of my time in the Red Cells studying that innate Necromancy. Every time I unravelled one of my ghosts, I learned more about it. How to control it. What it could do.

I pinned Clews into his body at the moment of his death, not allowing his soul to escape. His body died, but he did not. Trapped between life and death, and mine to command. I gave him an order, one so simple to carry out. and I turned his unlife into a curse he could spread.

"Kill them!" I hissed the words and they became Clews' only purpose. "Kill them all and spread my curse."

I stepped back from Clews, my shadowy wings sliding out of his flesh and dripping with blood. For a few moments my Grave Watch captor swayed on his feet, staring at me with damning eyes. I think maybe he fought against my command. He lost. Footsteps and shouts echoed down the corridor and Clews turned towards them and sprinted away in a headlong rush. It wasn't long before the screaming started. This time it wasn't coming from the prisoners.

I wandered through blood streaked halls, following the chaos I had unleashed. There were no bodies. Every Grave Watch who fell stood back up again only moments after death and carried out my terrible purpose. How far my curse would spread and how many it would affect, I did not know. They were questions I had not stopped to consider when I wrought it. I had given it a life of its own and set it free to destroy and kill until it ran itself dry. I did not feel pity for the soldiers who died and were brought back. They all knew what they did here. They deserved their fates.

The Red Cells are a labyrinth of corridors and torture

chambers and stairwells. I called out as I went, shouting Hardt's name to a chorus of replies, but none of them were him. Other prisoners begged me to release them. I did, tearing doors off hinges and shearing shadowy wings through the bolts that held them closed. The prisoners stared at me like I was a monster rather than their saviour. I was both, I admit that, but it would have been nice for a little gratitude. I can't blame them. A one-armed woman, my face made ghoulish by my scars and the gauntness, and two great black wings hunched behind me. Anyone would have run from that. In truth it might have been kinder to leave them in their cells. The curse I had loosed upon the world was not too selective in its victims. I told Clews to kill them all and that is exactly what he and all the others were doing. I hope some of the prisoners escaped. I hope some of them deserved to escape. When you're an inmate, it's hard to tell who around you are guilty, and who isn't.

It took some time to find Hardt. He was two floors below me, trapped in his own cell no larger than my own. I called for him at every door and my stomach gave a nervous flutter when finally I heard his voice.

"Eska?" He sounded weak, weary. I saw dark eyes peering at me through the little hole in the door.

"Stand back, Away from the door." He did and I made to tear the door down. My wings did not move.

He is a weakness.

"No. He is my strength. Just as you are my strength. I won't escape without him. I can't."

"Eska?" Hardt asked.

My wings ripped into the door. I was not gentle. In my fervour to free Hardt, I tore the wood to splinters and stood amidst the wreckage.

Hardt stumbled forward into the light of the corridor. He was smaller than I remembered, so much of his bulk wasted away. He held an arm across his ribs and limped. His beard was patchy and matted with filth and his face was a patchwork of wounds and old scars where the torturers had plied their trade. But he was alive!

"Eska!" Hardt slumped forward and wrapped an arm around me pulling me in to a tight embrace, heedless of the wings that still sprouted from my back. "I'm sorry." He sobbed into my shoulder. I would have sobbed back, but my throat closed and I choked on it. "I'm so sorry. This is all my fault." He was babbling, leaning much of his weight on me and only the strength I was taking from Ssserakis kept us all upright.

When finally we pulled apart his face was soaked from tears and he was shaking. I smiled at him and hoped I didn't look as monstrous as I was certain I did. His eyes dropped and horror played across his shaggy features. "What happened to your arm?"

That sob I had been holding in broke loose. "They took it." Tears streaked down my face and I felt like a little girl again, hurt and afraid and running to my big brother for protection. "They took my arm, Hardt. They fucking took it."

He hugged me again then and we spent some more time finding strength in each other. I am not embarrassed by this. I was nothing but glad. So happy to see Hardt again. So happy he was whole. Even if I was not.

It's time, Eskara. Time to tear down this fool emperor's walls and show him what his fear looks like.

I pulled away from Hardt. "I know."

"Eska…" Hardt said and looked at me again, his eyes moving over my shadowy wings. "Is it… Are you in control?" His face made the pain of the question clear.

I smiled and nodded. "Yes." And that was it. We never really spoke of Ssserakis, but Hardt knew I carried something inside. He knew. And he never asked.

"We have to go," I said and started towards the stairwell.

Hardt followed me through the bloody halls, limping but easily keeping pace. "Was this you?"

"Yes and no. I… I've caused a lot of chaos. We'll use the cover of it."

"To escape?"

I stopped and turned on my friend, wiping away tears. "I'm not running."

Hardt opened his mouth, an argument maybe. He didn't give it voice.

"You've met the Emperor. You've had that *pleasure*?" I waited for Hardt to nod. "He won't let me go. He'll chase me. I will *not* give him the chance." I turned back towards the stairs. "Aras Terrelan dies today."

CHAPTER TWENTY NINE

EVIDENCE OF MY CURSE STREAKED THE
halls of the Red Cells. Blood mostly, a severed limb or
two, dropped weapons the evidence of swift and fruitless
battle. No bodies. Not a single member of the Grave
Watch survived my curse. But it spread farther than just
the dungeon. We found the door leading outside hanging
open. It was gouged as though from nails biting into it, and
slick with blood. Outside, the true impact of my curse was
revealed. The chaos had spread beyond my intentions. Far
beyond them.

It was night, and I was glad of the darkness. I'm not
sure how I would have reacted to the light of day after so
long underground. Things had changed since my time in the
Pit. I no longer saw the sky as freedom, and I felt more at
home in the dark. Lursa was dominant, her cracked, red bulk
glaring down at us all. The air split with screams, sounds of

battle, a fire raging somewhere close by, smoke billowed up into the night sky.

"What did you do?" Hardt asked. He had found a body. The hands and mouth were bloody, an odd decaying rot already starting to show, veins turned black and standing out proud along the arms and neck. Signs of my curse. The head was split open.

You made them fear us. Ssserakis wasn't wrong. I could taste the fear on the air along with the ash. It was intoxicating.

"I… uh… don't really know. Just stay close to me. Behind me. And not too close." Ssserakis stretched out my wings to their full span for the first time and even I marvelled at their size. They weighed nothing, made from my own shadow, yet they dwarfed me somehow. Thick and jagged. More like the legs of winged spider than any bird I had ever seen, jagged talons along the length of each one. They crouched around me, ready to protect as quickly as attack. I needed them. With only one arm and no magic save for the Necromancy that was already wreaking havoc, I would have felt quite vulnerable if not for my wings.

A soldier wearing a bloodied Terrelan uniform ran past, not even sparing two escaped prisoners a glance. Two other soldiers chased him, snarling and bloody. One of the chasers slowed to a stop and stared at me. Dead eyes. There was something approaching intelligence in them but locked behind the orders I had given. I didn't recognise the man, but he was wearing the colours of the Grave Watch. He took a lurching step towards me and his mouth twitched.

"Release… me." Blood and saliva and bits of flesh fell from his mouth as his spoke, his voice guttural and barely terran anymore.

Never! Ours to control. A spreading curse converting all to our cause. I never even considered such a thing. I could hear the approval in Ssserakis' voice. It should have made me sick, but my rage would not allow any compassion. Not towards these people. Months of torture had beaten the compassion out of me.

"You have your orders. Go."

The cursed man twitched, fighting against my will. He lost. His body, the curse already clearly standing out in his veins, turned and ran off, looking for more victims.

I heard Hardt shift behind me, but he said nothing. That should have given me pause. Revealed to me how broken Hardt was, that even he would not argue at the massacre taking place on my orders.

We moved towards the palace, skirting the edges of buildings. Other soldiers passed us, some under the influence of my curse, and fewer of them still alive. One man veered away, screaming about the Corpse Queen having escaped. We could see the fires now, a large section of the city seemed to be on fire, the flames spreading, building to building, in the chaos.

"The gate..." Hardt pointed to where the palace gates were open. Beyond them were fires and screams and my curse running amok, multiplying with each death. How far would it spread? I never considered the extent. Juntorrow paid a heavy price for my single callous act. Above the gate, a wooden post sat, an arm made of stone nailed to it.

They deserve the pain and fear. I did not agree, but in that moment, I could not find it within myself to care. The people of Juntorrow had begged for my corpse. They hated me. Assaulted me. And now they would die because of me.

I am not proud of the decisions I made that day. But

I cannot change the past. I was broken and not thinking clearly. These are not excuses. Nothing can ever excuse what I did. Nothing. I offer the words as explanation only.

We rounded a building and the palace steps came into view. The great doors were closed, dozens of my Cursed hammering in an attempt to break it down. Bodies littered the courtyard in front of the steps, some broken things, others charred beyond recognition. From the highest balcony, a man watched the carnage below, flanked by guards and Sourcerers both. Emperor Aras Terrelan. He saw me then and it was obvious he recognised me. I could not hear his voice, but I saw him pointing and I was easy to recognise. A small woman with a savage snarl and one arm, great black wings curling protectively around me.

More of my Cursed lurched into view, they barrelled towards the others, hopelessly assaulting the palace doors. It would take more than a few dozen dead beating their fists upon that metal barrier to break through.

"Watch out!" Hardt's cry was too late as a bolt of lightning ripped through the air toward me. Ssserakis shifted my wings to protect me and I felt the pain of my horror as the energy burned our shadow. The Sourcerer was an Arcmancer, and stood at the entrance to a large building, not part of the palace. Some of my Cursed lay at his feet, smoking ruins that had once been men.

"Don't protect me." My words were meant for Ssserakis, but Hardt took a step back all the same.

Are you sure, Eskara? You have no Sources.

I shrugged and my wings furled behind me. I placed the lantern I was carrying on the ground and stepped past it, holding up my right hand and giving the gesture to the Sourcerer to try again. He was an ageing man, grey of hair and a face just starting to droop from his long years. He wasted no time and let loose another blast of lightning toward me. I didn't try to avoid it.

Memories flooded me, or more the impression of memories. I had a feeling I knew the Sourcerer though it was nothing specific. It was not like Tutor Elsteth's Arcstorm; I recognised it as hers' because I knew her. This man was alien to me. But I felt suddenly as I had known him all my life. His emotions, his memories, all a jumble. And then gone.

I felt the Arcstorm roar into life inside me once more. My eyes flashed, the storm inside and raging. I was breathing heavily as I came around. Still night, still in the courtyard before the palace. Energy crackled around me, tiny bolts of lightning sparking between the talons of my wings. I looked up at the Sourcerer and grinned, savage and feral, and full of malice.

"Thank you. I needed that," I said.

Now?

I nodded. "Now." I leapt and with a single beat of my wings, I flew towards the Sourcerer. He let loose two more bolts of lightning and I felt him once more. I saw him as a young man, proud of his magic, and then a flash of him cradling a child, face ashen and still. There was no context to the memories. No idea what they truly meant to him, and why. Each blast of energy hit me, and I absorbed it, the storm inside raging ever stronger and more violently. I slammed into the man, carrying him back inside the barracks. My wings crashed through the bricks, scattering stone around us, and the talons stabbed into the man's chest and abdomen. He was already dead by the time I slammed him against the far wall and when I withdrew my wings, his body slid down to sitting, a large blood smear behind him, more of the stuff leaking out through his wounds.

The barracks was in chaos, smoking bodies apparent everywhere, cots overturned, whole sections of the walls scorched by lightning. I cared not a whim for that devastation.

"I need a blade." Ssserakis was happy to oblige and shadow twisted around my right hand, forming itself into a small, wide blade. "Sorry about this." I shoved it into the dead Sourcerers midsection and cut through robes and flesh alike, opening his stomach. It was messy work, but I pulled a single Source out of the bloody wreckage. Not a large crystal, at least not by some standards, but larger than I was used to. I wiped it as best I could on his stained robes, and then shoved it inside my mouth. It tasted vile, blood and worse that I refused to think about. I tensed and swallowed it. The taste almost made me vomit, but I forced it down.

Half of the barracks exploded as a lightning storm raged to life around me. It was not quite an Arcstorm, it did not take on a life of its own. No. It was just me, exalting in my power once again. Revelling in the feeling of magic inside and fuelling the Arcstorm that had resided in me since the day I died at Picarr. I reigned it in, but only a little. Lightning crackled around me, constant bolts sparking off my body and my wings, striking anything and everything nearby. Some things were set alight from the heat of the bolts, others just smoked as the power scorched them. I stepped out of the wreckage of that barracks and set my sight on the palace. The Emperor was gone from the balcony, but I had no doubt he was still up there, hiding where he thought he was safe. Nowhere was safe. Not for him. Not from me!

"Eska, what—" Hardt paused at the sight of me.

"Are you alright?" A fair question given my appearance. My eyes were flashing once again, lightning struck around me constantly, and I had blood smeared across my mouth. Someone else's blood.

"You should find somewhere to hide," I said, my voice croaking.

"I'm coming with you."

I stared up at the balcony and plucked the lantern from where I had left it. "You can't. I'm going up there. You can follow behind though."

My Cursed were still battering uselessly at the palace doors as I approached, some had already broken their wrists in their fervour to get inside. "Stand back." I shouted the command and the Cursed turned toward me, the intelligence all but lost from their eyes.

"They obeyed you," Hardt said in wonder. My Cursed waited nearby, almost thirty of them, mostly in soldiers' uniforms.

"They have no choice. My will is theirs'." I drew my Arcstorm back inside, letting the power build and build until I felt as though I were about to explode. Then I unleashed the full fury of it, drawing upon the Source inside my stomach, as a single bolt of lightning directed at the palace doors. They burst open with a crack, the bar on the other side giving way in an instant.

Smoke drifted from the doors, bent and buckled from the force. Through my dark sight I could see men crouching on the other side, bows raised, waiting for targets. I doubted arrows would do them much good. "Go." I said to my Cursed and watched for a moment as they surged into motion and charged in through the doors. Some went down under the hail of arrows, but most ignored their wounds and the screams started once more. I turned to Hardt. "I'd give it a minute or two. They should leave you be, but you don't want to get caught up in that."

I turned back towards the balcony so far above. "What about you?" Hardt waited nearby, not daring to get too close with the storm striking all around me.

"I told you. I'm going up there. Ready?"

Ssserakis laughed. *He will pay for your arm.*

I crouched, my wings unfurling and spreading out high above me. "And everything else." I leapt upwards, my wings beating hard. Once. Twice. It was not true flight. Even with wings so large, I could not have sustained the lift, but it hurled me upwards. Even so, the balcony was high above us. It was a start at least. We gave up on the attempt at flight and my wings drove into the stone of the palace wall, shattering windows and gouging rock. I had only one arm, and that was carrying the lantern, so I relied entirely upon my wings as they thrust into the palace facade and dragged us upwards. No, it was not anything approaching flight. I was more like a giant black spider, crawling its way up the side of the building, leaving scarred, crumbling stone in my wake. I imagine the noise of it was quite terrifying to those inside the palace, though they may have been more focused on the screaming from my Cursed slaughtering their way from floor to floor.

It's fair to say they were expecting me by the time I reached the balcony. With a last push of my wings, I gained the lip and stepped down just as a plume of fire shattered the double windows and engulfed me. Ssserakis shielded me with my wings, but barely in time. I felt the heat of the flames and the searing kiss of them on my face. My chin still bears the scars of that fire, mottled flesh between chin and neck, pitted and annoyingly smooth from where it melted. I often find myself rubbing at that scar, the feel of it strangely both horrifying and compulsive. I screamed at the touch of it, and Ssserakis screamed with me, its shadowy body taking the brunt of the heat.

The flames continued and my wings curled tighter around me, so tight I could barely move. I knew Pyromancy well, had always felt the attunement stronger than any other school, and I knew the Sourcerer could keep up the attack for a long time.

I cannot hold out against fire, Eskara. Forever Ssserakis' weakness, fire is the enemy of ice and darkness both.

Cold rage built inside of me. I couldn't let it end like this, couldn't let them beat me so easily. Not after all I had survived, all I had been through. The very thought of it made me angry. The Emperor winning was more than I could stomach. I stopped caring. They could burn my body to ash, but I would take them all with me! I let my Arcstorm rage with me.

A plume of flame is easy for a Pyromancer to maintain, simple magic but effective. It also has a limited range. The Sourcerer needs to be quite close to their target. It is difficult to remain close with a lightning storm raging around you. I'm not sure if the Pyromancer was struck at all, only that they backed off, the flames subsiding as they beat their retreat. My anger and my Arcstorm were linked in a way I have never quite understood. They feed off each other, growing stronger and stronger until neither can be sustained, and then fade for a time, leaving me numb and raw. Drawing on my Source and turning my mind towards the atrocities directed toward me, my anger and my storm grew until none could stand within twenty paces for fear of being struck.

I stepped off the balcony and into the throne room, the centre of an Arcstorm, my eyes flashing, and shadowy wings poised behind me, ready to strike. Before me stood half the royal guard, thirty soldiers all wearing gold armour with runes glowing pink in the gloom. Armour designed to absorb magic. Two Sourcerers, one to my right, the Pyromancer readying another attack, the other a mystery, and standing next to the throne. Opposite her, stood Prena, eyes hard and damning and locked on me. And beyond them all, cowering on his throne, the Emperor of Terrelan.

"Aras!" I screamed the name.

"She's a nightmare. Kill her!" The Emperor all but screeched in his fearful hysteria. I could taste the terror on him.

Soldiers started forward just as the door to the throne room burst open, my Cursed piling through it. The Pyromancer turned and sprayed flames in their direction, but they were dead things, shrugging off injury and pain. They swarmed the man and carried him down, fists and weapons rising and falling, screams turning to sickening thuds. Others ignored the Sourcerer entirely and rushed on towards the royal guard. The throne room erupted into a chaotic battle where only I understood the rules. Or so I thought.

"Stop!" The Sourcerer standing beside the throne was a Necromancer and his order carried a weight my Cursed could not ignore. Even as more of them forced their way through the throne room doors, the royal guard advanced upon them, swords cutting them down in a one-sided massacre. Two of the soldiers turned my way, braving the Arcstorm, their enchanted armour absorbing the lightning strikes.

They attacked as one, too well-trained to come at me one at a time. I had seen their like before, had fought against them before. Long ago, up on the tallest tower of Fort Vernan, at the Fall of Orran. Terrelan royal guard with their enchanted armour and weapons, leaping through portals and charging toward Josef and I. I had fought them then and defeated many, but I had Sources then, magic at my command.

Now you have something even better.

They thought me weak and slow from weeks or months of torture and malnourishment. They did not count on the fear lending me so much strength. I ducked and dodged sideways from the first of the soldiers, meeting the second head on. I think he assumed his armour would protect him from my wings, but they were not formed from Photomancy and there was no magic at play. My right wing slammed into the man, knocking him to his back and skewering him through the neck and waist where his armour was thinnest. The second soldier was on me in a moment and would have cut me down if not for Ssserakis' reactions. My horror blocked the strike with my other wing and wrapped it around the man, crushing him so fast he barely had time to scream.

Brace yourself.

I crouched down low and Ssserakis threw my wings forward, sending the bodies of both soldiers crashing into the ranks of their comrades. It did little to phase them. With the Necromancer subverting my will, the Cursed could do nothing but stand still while the royal guard tore them to shreds. The throne room floor grew wet with blood as more and more of my minions died, even as others forced their

way through the palace doors, only to fall into the same trap
as the others. The Necromancer needed to die.

We but need to get close. I leapt, shadowy wings beating
hard as they drove me up and forwards towards the throne.
Aras Terrelan let out a screech and the fear sent a jolt of
pleasure through me even as the Necromancer flicked a
hand my way. An invisible forced smashed into me, driving
me sideways to crash against the far wall of the throne room.
Wood splintered beneath the impact and the air was forced
from my lungs. I would have been dead, but for my shadow
absorbing much of the impact.

I cannot sustain your shadow for much longer, Eskara.
There was strain in my horror's voice. Even with all the fear
it had gorged upon and even with the fear of an entire city
nearby as legions of the Cursed slaughtered everyone they
could find. Even then, we were burning through Ssserakis'
power too fast.

My Arcstorm had retreated back inside when the
kinetic wave hit me, so I struggled back to my feet, my wings
giving me stability. The lantern was still in my right hand,
the flame long since gone out, but the glass still miraculously
intact. I reached out and drew on my Source, sending bolts
of lightning ripping through the air, snaking their way
towards the Necromancer by the throne. Again, the Emperor
let out a shriek of warning and the Sourcerer waved another
hand my way, the lightning veering sideways to strike the
wall behind the throne, scoring smoking black marks along
its finery.

A Necromancer, an Arcmancer, and a Kinemancer all
rolled into one. I was running out of ideas; I knew exactly
how powerful a defence those combination of magics could
weave. *Stop trying to use brute force. We have other tools at our*

disposal.

"What?"

Fear. Make her fear us!

"Kill her!" the Emperor screamed again, pointing at me. Neither Prena, nor the Sourcerer moved, and the royal guard were too busy cutting down my Cursed. I could feel their numbers dwindling. Out in the city, the dead were already beyond counting, but here in the palace there were few of them left, and too many being sent back to death.

Ssserakis was right. I didn't need to kill this Sourcerer. I only needed her attention, to distract her from holding back my Cursed. I took a step forwards, letting my shadow pool around me. It rose and flickered like black flames. My wings crouched over my shoulders like a hawk waiting to swoop in and strike. My face was gaunt and ghoulish, my eyes flashed, and I focused my unwavering gaze on the Sourcerer. She glanced my way, but only for a moment, and flicked her hand again. I expected the blow this time and braced against it, one wing held up protectively, the other digging into the floor of the throne room, giving me the support I needed. Another step. And another. The Sourcerer glanced my way again and this time her eyes lingered on me, noticing my focused intent. I knew I had her right then. She tried a couple more times to throw me back with Kinemancy, but each time I dug in and resisted the blow, shrugging it off only to continue my slow pace toward her. The room grew darker, for us at least, I don't think anyone noticed. I could see the sweat standing out on her face, young but lined from stress, hair a slick severe bun tied above her head. I was maybe ten paces away when she broke, turning her attention from the Cursed and hurling her full power at me. It was useless. I absorbed the Arcmancy, letting it fuel the Arcstorm inside and used it to erect a shield around me. Kinemancy may be a kinetic wave, but it is still magic, and my Arcshield deflected her attacks.

My slow pacing continued and the Sourcerer grew more and more frantic, her fear of me giving the darkness a tangible quality. That's the odd truth about that ability of Ssserakis', the darkness does not really exist except in the mind of the person under its sway. Outside of that unnatural darkness, my Cursed surged back into motion and the royal guard suddenly found themselves in the middle of a fight they had not been prepared for.

By the time I reached the foot of the throne, the Sourcerer was a babbling mess, her sobbing barely audible over the sounds of the fighting. She was no threat to me anymore. I'm pretty sure she'd wet herself. Aras Terrelan wasn't far off either. He pushed himself into his throne yet had nowhere else to retreat to. Only Prena stood between us now, hand on sword hilt, but not yet drawn.

"Kill her!" Again, the shriek from the Emperor. We both ignored him.

She doesn't fear us. Doesn't fear death.

"Stand aside." My words were quiet, pitched for menace rather than command. Despite all Prena had done, despite her standing by and watching while I was tortured, I found I didn't wish her dead. Neither did I wish her a long life. I found quite simply that I just didn't care. If she got in my way, I would kill her. If she stood aside, I would leave her and be thankful if I never heard the name Prena Neralis ever again.

I was within striking distance and could remember well the feeling of Prena stabbing me once before, but I would not show fear to her. Especially not when I was so close to my quarry. How long did we stare at each other? I don't know for sure, only that when that contest of will was over, I was not the one to turn away.

"Prena, what are you doing?" Aras Terrelan hissed as his bodyguard turned and walked away. "First Blade Neralis, I order you to get back here and defend me!"

Prena ignored the Emperor, moving to the side of the room. The Sourcerer was curled into a ball next to the throne, rocking back and forth between sobs. The royal guard were up to their necks with my Cursed, desperately trying to survive even as the numbers of the dead swelled with every death.

"There's no one left to save you, Aras. Die with some dignity." He tried; I'll give him that. The Emperor of Terrelan wiped fearful tears from his eyes, straightened his jacket, and launched himself at me, a dagger flashing from his shirt sleeve. I turned aside, letting him stumble past me, his momentum carrying him. Tamura had taught me well how to flow like water, and even emaciated and weary, my body remembered the lessons. I kicked Aras Terrelan in the back on the knee, forcing him down, and whipped the noose from around my waist with my one hand, looping it over his head. Then, with a knee placed on his back, and my hand on the rope, I strangled the life from the Terrelan Emperor.

Revenge. I've heard people say it's never as satisfying as you think it will be. What a load of shit. If it's not satisfying, then you're doing it wrong.

It takes a while to strangle a man to death in such a way and I will admit I was sweating from the exertion by the time I felt the Emperor's life snuffed out. But I wasn't done with him yet. One death would never be enough for that monster. For all the pain he had put me through, for all the pain he had caused to Hardt, for all the pain he had caused to countless others. One death was not enough for him! Necromancy can do many things. I shoved Aras Terrelan's soul back into his body, not quite like I had with the Cursed. I gave him no orders and did not take his will from him, only brought him back at the moment of death.

As I loosened the noose around his neck the Emperor gasped for air, hands clawing the noose up and over his head. On his hands and knees, he coughed and gasped. Not enough! I kicked the man on to his back and knelt on his chest, plucking the lantern from the floor and dashing it against the steps. Shards of glass. I had wielded a shard just like them long ago. Back then I had tried to kill Prig. Failed. Some lessons I only needed to learn once. I plucked one of the shards from the floor, ignoring the pain as it bit into my flesh, and stabbed down into Aras Terrelan's chest over and over again. I do not know how many times I stabbed him. Enough that I couldn't tell which blood was mine and which was his. Enough that his feeble attempts to stop me faltered completely. Enough that his soul once again fled his body.

Not enough!

Again, I forced the Emperor back inside his dead shell of a corpse. I took his will from him that time, a puppet of flesh bound to me and my orders. I took his will, but I left him his wit. A passenger in his own body, forced to watch through dead eyes. Never again to act on his own thoughts, only to my whims. *That* was the final torture I laid upon the Emperor of Terrelan. The man had killed my king, destroyed my country. He ordered me into the Pit, and even when I escaped, he sent his most trusted executioner to hunt me down. He had tortured me for months. He had broken me. Squeezed all his precious screams from me. And yet there I stood, alive; and there he knelt, dead.

CHAPTER
THIRTY

HARDT FORCED HIS WAY INTO THE THRONE
room, wary eyes on the Cursed, but they ignored him. They
ignored Prena too as she slunk away. The Sourcerer finally
gave up her sobbing and I took her pouch of Spiceweed,
forcing some into her mouth and then scooping up her
Sources.

"It's done?" Hardt asked as he approached, eyes on
me not the man standing at my side.

I nodded. "He's dead."

"Doesn't look dead." Hardt towered over us both and
glared down at the Emperor.

"He's dead. But he's still in there." I let a savage grin
slip onto my face. "Dance." And Emperor Aras Terrelan, or
at least the shell of him, began a lurching parody of a dance.
The rest of my Cursed in the throne room joined in. Having
killed the last of the royal guard, there was now nothing for

them to do.

"Stop this, Eska."

I nodded. "Stop." And they did. Obeying my orders instantly. There they waited.

"The city," Hardt said. His eyes kept darting to where the Emperor's corpse waited, his hands curling into fists. Even half starved, much of his muscle lost, Hardt could have crushed the man.

"You can hit him if you like."

Hardt tore his eyes from the Emperor and gave me a disgusted look, turning and moving toward the balcony. It overlooked Juntorrow and from that balcony I could see it was a city in its death throes. Fires spread unchecked. Screams drifted up on the night air. Lursa watched over it all, as red as the streets below her gaze. I had done this to the city. It was not my intention, but that does not excuse the act. Juntorrow was dying, its people were dying, and I had killed it. I had killed them. Even from high up and far away, staring out from the palace balcony, I could see packs of my Cursed tearing down the streets, looking for more death to sow.

Kill them all and spread your curse. Ssserakis echoed my order to that first of the Cursed. *These are the consequences of what they did to us.*

"No. These are the consequences of my mistake." I tried to tell myself the people deserved it. They hated me, begged for my corpse. They wanted to see me dead, to parade my body. I tried to tell myself they deserved it. But the lies rang hollow even in my own head. Not even Ssserakis tried to convince me it was justice. It was vengeance, and I found I did not have the stomach for it.

"Can't you stop it?" Hardt asked.

I tried. But I was too far away. The Cursed could no longer hear my orders, could no longer feel my will. They were a disease, spreading and acting upon that single order I had given. I shook my head. "Not from here."

When I turned from the balcony, I found the Emperor standing close. Bereft of any orders he had followed me and waited. That, too, sickened me. "Fetch the noose," I said. "Tie it to the balcony, put your head through it, and throw yourself off." Aras Terrelan turned to do my bidding.

As I limped through the throne room I found more of my Cursed, many of them wearing the clothing of the nobility, waiting. I think I recognised the princess among the crowd. It is not an idle boast when I say I ended the Terrelan imperial line. "Die." My order cleansed the Cursed from the throne room and all but the Emperor collapsed, their souls finally freed from their bodies.

Such a waste. Think of the things we could accomplish with a deathless army.

I ignored Ssserakis. "I need to be close."

Hardt nodded. "It's going to be a long night." He underestimated the size of the task before us.

By the time we left the palace, Emperor Aras Terrelan was hanging from the balcony. His eyes watched us go, limbs twitching in my direction. He had fulfilled the final order I gave him, and now tried to follow me, bound by my will. He did not die then, for a third time. He remained, hanging from the palace, his body deathless. No one cut him down. I do not know how long he remained there, a broken symbol of my vengeance, body rotting while he watched his empire that he was so proud of fall to ruin.

We walked the city. I gave the order for my Cursed to die whenever I found any. The people recognised me, blamed me, hated me even when I saved them. I kept at it, even when some of the more courageous survivors threw stones along with their threats. For two days Hardt and I walked the streets of Juntorrow giving the Cursed whatever measure of peace I could. I think I may have stayed longer, so heavy was my conscience, but a mob of survivors formed in my wake, and eventually Hardt dragged me away. Always my protector, even from myself.

Juntorrow never recovered from my visit. Too many of its people died, too much tragedy left in my wake. The citizens tried, adversity bringing out the best in them even as I had brought out the worst. But they failed. Juntorrow became a town of ghosts and the ravenous dead. It remains that way even now.

I did not catch all the Cursed, and in my anger, I had released a new power upon Ovaeris. The Cursed are a plague, and it does not matter how long the world might go without a sighting of the deathless, they always reappear. And every time they do so, too, does my name surface. A village falls to the Cursed and the Corpse Queen must have been behind it, bringing ruin wherever she treads. That is the legacy I will always be remembered for, regardless of any good I might have done. And who is to argue I should not be? I unleashed it upon the world. Me. I deserve all the blame.

We set our course north and walked. It was a long way to the Pit, to the city I had bought with such a heavy price, but we had nowhere else to go. I hoped Tamura and Imiko were alive, and yet I feared what the Emperor's armies might have done. There were villages along the way, and we found food and new clothing, but little welcome. News of Juntorrow spread far faster than we moved, and it was difficult to hide my appearance. A one-armed woman with flashing eyes and a shadow that moved of its own accord; the Corpse Queen, murderer of Emperor Aras Terrelan, scourge of Juntorrow, mother of the Cursed. We were run out of more than one village no sooner had we arrived. Still, we found succour in some places.

With the Emperor and his line dead, his control was broken. The Terrelan army fractured, their control over the kingdom splintering. Terrelan broke apart into dozens of disparate states, each claiming independence. Some were ruled by military law, others by the local aristocracy, and some were even unionised into a form of citizen government. It did not take long for the first skirmishes to break out, a prelude to a new war that would eventually consume the continent of Isha. More of my legacy. An empire fallen to ruin, engulfed in strife. No wonder the Corpse Queen is hated and feared in equal measure. But I did it. I swore time and time again, whispered promises to myself each night down in the Pit. I renewed that vow up on Ro'shan, and again on Do'shan. I swore I would kill the Emperor and turn the Terrelan Empire to ash. And I did it. A younger me would have rejoiced, blind to the consequences.

One night we came across a tavern, a roadside inn, days away from the nearest village. Hardt and I arrived there on aching feet. We had secured new clothing, and I had even bathed at the last village, but days on the road made such luxury seem like ages past. The owner had heard of me but put little stock in rumours and tales of small women being monsters in disguise. For once I did not educate him on his mistake. Little is ever given away for free, and though we had no money, the owner allowed Hardt and I to work a day for food and a dry roof. Hardt worked the kitchen and I did what Pyromancers often do by way of work: I made fire where it was needed. I think, in truth, the owner took some pity on me; regardless of winter setting in I did not nearly enough to earn the food and drink that night.

There was music in that tavern, a bard by the name of Reo who played songs I had never heard before. Distant shores and mysterious people, lands unknown and a tragedy for the ages. He held the tavern in rapture with his notes and with his words, and when he was done, he found my table, perhaps drawn there by my flashing gaze. We talked long into the night, even once Hardt had retired to our bed. I told him my story, much more of it than I intended. He made a song of it eventually, *The Fury of the Storm*, it paints me in a favourable, yet tragic, light.

I do not count myself as a vain woman, but neither do I like to think of myself as ugly. In the days and weeks following Juntorrow, I felt ugly. It went beyond the loss of an arm or the ghoulish lack of flesh on my bones. I was a monster. I had done monstrous things. So, when this bard called me beautiful and meant it, I found myself both flattered and charmed. Even I am not immune to flattery, and sometimes even the most endowed of us need to hear that we are worth others' attention.

Nine months later Sirileth was born.

CHAPTER THIRTY ONE

ANONYMITY THROUGH FAME IS AN
interesting concept yet it often holds true. I was known far
and wide, my name spreading beyond the reaches of Isha.
Even the Polasians feared the name, the Corpse Queen. Yet
you could ask a hundred people who the Corpse Queen
was, and maybe five would be able to give my true name.
My reputation was known, my alias was known, most even
knew where they could find me, but my identity was a
mystery. I would wager that fact was the only thing that kept
me alive. I didn't know it at the time, but the Iron Legion
thought I had died at the hands of the Emperor.

When Hardt and I arrived back at our home we found
little had changed. It had grown for a certainty, new life
and new faces abundant in the city I had raised from the
earth. So many new faces I found myself quite lost amongst
them. Tamura ruled in my absence, not with an iron fist, but

with a considerate ear. Imiko held a different kind of rule. I
could not say how, and she would not, but in my absence,
it appeared she had garnered quite the criminal network.
Thieves, thugs, whores, and bandits from all over the nearby
lands answered to Imiko. You may wonder how long had
passed, and I will admit that I certainly did. It had been
more than half a year since I had been taken by the Terrelans,
and most of that was spent down in the Red Cells. My
friends had given Hardt and I up for dead. Oddly, I do not
blame them for it, though I will admit to a pang of jealousy
when I saw Tamura giggling upon his throne as he handed
out orders. It vanished the moment the crazy old Aspect
saw us amid the crowd. Tears rolled down his cheeks and he
leapt toward us, catching me up in a bone cracking embrace,
and flooding my ears with nonsense that almost sounded
like a string of questions.

Within a few days Tamura stepped aside, and I
reluctantly sat upon the throne of my own little kingdom.
I did barely any ruling and left the running of the place to
Tamura and Imiko. I ate well and new flesh filled my bones,
and I became better used to the new balance of my body.
It is frustratingly difficult to perform even mundane tasks
like dressing yourself when you only have one arm, and it
took quite some getting used to. Oddly I could still feel my
arm from time to time, or maybe just the ghost of it. It itched
more than anything, an itch I could never find to scratch.
You have no idea how damnably annoying it is to feel your
fingers itching when you don't even have a hand.

I grew fat with pregnancy, and though I handled it
far better than I had the first time, it was still a chore more
often than not. Ssserakis was not nearly as insistent on action
during the months I carried Sirileth. I still felt my horror's

need for its own vengeance, and its desire to return to its own world, but it did not push me toward either goal even once while I was pregnant. There was a connection between my horror and my second child. I think Ssserakis felt as much a parent as I did.

Sirileth arrived in blood and noise, mine and hers. What is there to say about my second child? Not lightly do I name her a monster, but there was always too much of her mother in her to be anything else. But that is a story for another time. I love her. I have always loved her, no matter what is said about her or myself. I loved Sirileth from the moment I set eyes on her, with all my heart. But I still abandoned her. Some lessons I guess I have never learned. Know this, though, it was not willingly. I left Sirileth in Imiko's care because of a threat I could not ignore.

The Iron Legion had found me.

A messenger arrived in the middle of the night. It was mere months after Sirileth had been born and I was feeding her, my shadow draped around us, hiding my beautiful daughter from the world that would condemn her for her mother's sins. I would have been better off trying to hide the world from Sirileth. My second daughter would settle for nothing less than infamy to eclipse my own. Even back then, so small and innocent, she demanded to be the centre of all attention. Even back then her eyes glowed with an odd darklight, like the corona of the sun hidden behind our moons.

The messenger was a tall man, handsome in that rugged way that somehow defies the dirt and grime of the road they cart around with them. He went down on one knee before me and bowed his head for a moment. A sign of respect, traditions maintained. I cared little for tradition.

"Loran Orran sends his greetings." The messenger's voice echoed around the empty corners of my great hall. It was quite nice to have the place so empty, it was usually a bustling hive of activity and light and noise. There's a lot to be said for meetings in the middle of the night. "I assume I am addressing Eskara Helsene, the Corpse Queen?" He had a well-trained voice, also musical. It reminded me of the bard I had met in that tavern, and the night we had spent together.

Sirileth stirred and I shifted her beneath the shadow draped around me. That, too, is another thing made more difficult by missing an arm.

"Where is he?" I put as much menace into my voice as I could. I will not lie; I had been looking for the Iron Legion. Not just for my own vengeance, and not just for that of Ssserakis'. I had not forgotten about Josef. I could not forget, would not forget.

The messenger caught the tone I used and when he stood, he looked far less confident than before. "I don't know. I was paid to bring a message for the Corpse Queen's ears only. I should mention, I don't understand the content only..."

My patience with the man wore thin and I snapped at him. "Then tell me the message and get out." Sirileth let out a sharp wail, not muffled at all by my shadow.

The messenger coughed. "Yenhelm lives. You can find him where it all began. Wait too long, and I will come for you." He bowed and turned.

"That's it?" Hardt asked, stepping out from the shadow of a nearby pillar.

The messenger nodded and I let him leave. I was a little preoccupied trying to quiet Sirileth once more.

It's time, Eskara.

"Where it all began?" Hardt asked. "The Pit?" The Pit was flooded beneath our feet. There were things living down there, still. Things that could call the deep, dark water home, but no terrans could.

"Not all beginnings are yours," Tamura said. "Go back further and you will see a million beginnings all intersecting."

Hardt sighed. "You could have just said no."

I was busy cooing to Sirileth and rocking her back and forth in a vain attempt to quiet her. "It began in Picarr, the laboratory beneath the Academy of Magic. That's where he experimented on Josef and I."

The ruins of Picarr were not close. Weeks away at least, especially as I would not risk portal travel over significant distances. It was not for myself that I feared to use portals, but for Ssserakis. Whatever lived on the other side, had taken an interest in my horror, and I would not give it another chance to pick Ssserakis apart.

It's a trap.

"This has to be a trap." Hardt agreed with my horror without even realising it. "Why else would he just tell you where to find him?"

I nodded, still dealing with a wriggling baby. Sirileth was never one for sitting still. I had not known my first daughter long, but Kento had been a quiet babe, calm but for the times she needed something. Sirileth could not have been more different, always moving, always noisy. They were, both of them, perfect, my daughters.

"You're going, aren't you?" Hardt asked.

Again, I nodded. "The Iron Legion knows where I am, and for some reason he wants me to meet him." I sighed.

"The fucker isn't going to just accept it if I don't go. There
was a threat implied in that message as well as an invitation.
What we've built here can be torn down. You saw the
powers he can bring to bear. I won't risk it. And I won't risk
her."

*He must be killed. No one from your world should be
strong enough to pull a lord of Sevoari across. There are things in
my world that must remain there.*

I shrugged. "And he has Josef." Hardt opened his
mouth to speak, but I cut him off. "I have left Josef to die
twice now, Hardt. Once down in the Pit, and again when he
was first taken. I have a chance to set him free. I know you
don't… I know what he did." I shook my head. "We've all
done regrettable things. I'm going. I'm going to bring Josef
back!"

That was the end of the discussion, at least as far as
I was concerned. I think Hardt realised it too. He certainly
didn't make any sort of move to stop me. Far from it, in fact.
He insisted on going with me, even when I tried to leave
without him.

I had a maid. Apparently, it's quite normal for women
in positions of power to have maids for their children. Mine
was a terran woman by the name of Galea who looked as
though she could have eaten me and had room for dessert.
But she was good with my daughter and damned useful.
I let Galea take Sirileth from me and place her in the little
wooden cot Hardt had made. She wriggled for a bit, trying
to find comfort in the mound of blankets and missing
the warmth of her mother. My will almost faltered then,
watching my daughter pull faces in discomfort. I had to
wipe the tears from my eyes and take a shuddering breath

before I could speak.

"People will say things about me. Stories." I sniffed and reached down, pulling a blanket a little closer around her tiny flailing form. Sirileth was a small babe, only now reaching the same size her older sister had been at birth. "Some of them may be true. Probably most of them. Never let them tell you I didn't love you. I do. With everything that makes me, I do.

"Listen to Imiko. She's a fucking bitch at times, but she means well. Tamura, too. Crazier than a barrel of eels but there's no one better for advice, if you can decipher it. Hardt will protect you, even when you don't want him to. Don't let his size fool you, he's not really scary at all." Another ragged breath escaped me. My daughter stared up at me with those darklight eyes, her mouth moving in silent incomprehensible words.

"Don't let anyone tell you what you can't do. Challenge them. Break the rules." My breath caught in my throat.

Never let your own fear rule you. Use the fear of others to rule them.

I smiled despite myself. "Never be ruled by your fears. But don't ignore them either. A little fear can be healthy."

And filling.

I drew in another shuddering breath and stood, staring down at my daughter. "Be great!" We have that hope for our children. That they will be better than us, stronger than us, more successful and wiser. We all wish our children will one day step out from the shadows of their parents and cast their own brilliant light upon the world. Well, Sirileth certainly did that. She cast her own brilliant darklight upon the world, and in that light Ovaeris burned. But again, I'm getting ahead of myself.

"Sounds like you're saying goodbye." Imiko, ever one to enter a room in silence. I think she just liked to surprise people. There was steel in her voice these days. She had found that in my absence.

"I am."

"Not coming back?"

"I'll try." There were words left unsaid. I knew I had little chance of surviving a conflict with the Iron Legion, even less so given it was clearly a trap. But there was more, something I had to do even if I somehow emerged victorious. Something I was hiding from everyone, even Ssserakis.

I turned to face my little sister only to find her towering over me, her jaw clenched. "Last time you left me with a kingdom to look after and only an old, mad fool for company. Now you're leaving me with a baby as well?"

"Look after her. Please." No words I could have said would be sufficient. "Look after everyone."

Imiko sniffed, blinked away some tears. "Sometimes I wish I'd never stolen that bloody Source from you."

I smiled. "Time moves ever forward."

"And you've been spending too much time with Tamura." Imiko fidgeted, nervous. Then her stern facade broke and she lurched forward wrapping gangly arms around me. "Good luck. Please come back."

I found Hardt and Tamura waiting for me when I snuck away. Even choosing a back door to my rooms and leaving in the middle of the night hadn't fooled them. Both had travel packs and trei birds saddled and ready.

"And here I thought we'd agreed I was going alone,"

I said.

They'll only get in the way. I didn't disagree.

"You agreed you were going alone," Hardt said. "I agreed I was going with you." He grinned. "And Tamura can't remember who agreed to what."

Tamura narrowed his eyes. "Which is more important; yesterday or tomorrow?" He grinned.

I shook my head at the crazy old Aspect. "I need you to stay, Tamura. Someone must look after this place and Imiko is... You're already running the place better than I could. I just sit around and agree with you."

"It is not foolish to make mistakes, only to repeat them." Tamura finished by swinging up onto the saddle of his trei bird and nodding towards the horizon.

"Tamura..."

Hardt stopped me with a big hand on my shoulder, just like he always had. The familiarity of the contact felt good. It felt like one thing I hadn't managed to ruin, despite everything I had put him through. "He let you leave him behind once before, Eska. Even I can see the meaning behind his madness this time. We're not letting you go alone."

They didn't understand. I couldn't let them face the Iron Legion with me. I couldn't let him hurt them.

I could chase them away. There was humour in my horror's voice, made more apparent by the fact that my shadow did not so much as twitch.

"Fine. We three then." And maybe along the way I could convince them to turn back.

Or kill their mounts and leave them behind.

It was fitting, in a way. The three of us had escaped the Pit together, had been together ever since. Despite my protests, my insistence that they remain behind, it felt right that they would accompany me to the end of my journey.

CHAPTER THIRTY TWO

EVEN MOUNTED ON TREI BIRDS, THE JOURNEY
to Picarr took ten days. It dawned on me, in that time, just
how much the former Terrelan Empire had changed. New
borders had been drawn up and soldiers, wearing newly
coloured uniforms, sat at checkpoints along the roads. They
demanded a tithe from all travellers. We paid them, not
wanting to cause more trouble than we were already in.
They were bandits by another name, sanctioned by the new
state they now served. The unsanctioned bandits we treated
rather differently. We paid them in broken limbs and sent
them scurrying away with the name, the Corpse Queen,
ringing in their ears.

We stopped frequently; villages, taverns, towns. I
think I was delaying the inevitable confrontation, partly
out of fear, and partly because I was enjoying my time
with Hardt and Tamura. We laughed often and hard,

raised drinks to those lost but not forgotten, listened to
Tamura's tales of times long gone. It put a slightly different
perspective on things knowing that he had lived through
all of the stories he told, and given his knowledge of
Belmorose's teachings I will admit I started to wonder
whether the old philosopher's teachings were written by
Tamura himself.

In a small town by the name of Shorelan I met a
woman so beautiful she took my breath away. Her name
was Irilen, and she had perfect brown skin and hair as dark
as my own had once been. When she smiled at me, she
reminded me of Silva, something in the way her lips tugged
at the corners. We never love quite like our first love. It is not
for want or need, or even worth. It simply is the truth. We
throw ourselves into that first love. Every inch, every drop,
every nook and cranny. Every dirty secret and honest truth.
Every bit of us goes into that love. We give them everything
we have. And a bit of that stays with them. Whether they
deserve it or not, a part of ourselves stays with every person
we have ever loved. It is not that we wish to give each love
after that less, only that there is less to give. Too much of
ourselves left behind with the dead or lost or soured parting.
We are finite creatures, and there is only so much we have to
give. I left a part of myself with Irilen and moved on.

More than once in that short journey, I ended the
night by drinking my sorrows away. An escape of sorts,
to dull the mind and the heart. To forget. Often Hardt and
Tamura would turn in before me, leaving me alone with
my drinking and sour reflection. Well, not alone. You never
drink alone. At worst, you drink with your demons. I always
thought it such a shame Sserakis could not get drunk
with me, but my horror treated my inebriation with veiled

disgust, yet watched over me all the same. Some people might think a drunken one-armed woman easy prey, but I taught a lech or two the error of their ways.

My reputation followed us, or perhaps streaked ahead, so we found both it and a cold reception waiting at most stops along the way. In some places, I was treated with open hostility, and in others hushed whispers and pointed glares. Disaster apparently followed in my wake, or I suppose it would be more accurate to say that any bad luck after I visited was attributed to me. The name of the Corpse Queen became synonymous with ill omens and tragedy. At the village of Chorn, I heard the beginnings of a children's rhyme.

Night shall fall and the dead will rise.
The Corpse Queen comes. The Corpse Queen comes.
Hide under your bed and hold your breath.
The Corpse Queen comes. The Corpse Queen comes.
Pray to the moons, pray for the sun.
The Corpse Queen Comes. The Corpse Queen comes.

The rhyme is, predictably, called *The Corpse Queen Comes*. It has grown both in popularity and size over the years. A warning to naughty children to listen to their elders. Do as you're told, or the Corpse Queen will come for you.

Ssserakis spoke to me often yet held itself inside. No dark cloak or black wings, only the light from the sun and moons moved my shadow. My horror was conserving its strength, pulling power from the fear my presence caused in every settlement we visited. It knew a conflict was coming and knew our chance of victory was scant. Still, Ssserakis would fight with everything it had, everything it could give me, in order to see the Iron Legion dead. We had both been wronged by Loran Orran. Ssserakis had been dragged from its own world, kidnapped and enslaved for a time. Even once released, my horror had matched power with the Iron Legion, and had barely escaped. I felt its wounded pride in that. A lord of Sevoari, a being as ancient as its world, enslaved and studied, then beaten and sent scurrying away into the darkness. It did not like to admit it, but I could feel my horror's fear over the coming conflict. Ssserakis had barely escaped with its life the last time it had matched power against the Iron Legion. I could also feel its hope, that things would be different this time, that I would make the difference. At my strongest, I might have believed it too, but there was no doubt I was diminished. Sources, I had, and the will to use them, but my body did not move like I needed it to. It went beyond my missing arm, though that was still something I struggled with at times. The Emperor had given me new scars, poorly healed, injuries that niggled and made certain movements agony. My body was a broken thing, struggling to remember how it once worked, and lacking the muscle and power it once had. Age had not brought me low, rather, the torturer's knife had.

When Picarr finally appeared on the horizon, the ruins of my former home again brought pangs of melancholy. The time Josef and I had spent up on Braggart's Tower, watching the city live out its day beneath us. Trading a show of magic, little more than tricks for Sourcerers of our power, for sweet rolls or coffee. We didn't need to, of course, the academy provided us with as much food as we wanted, but it felt good to trade our skills for something tangible. The time I showed off to all the apprentice blacksmiths by stoking the fire far hotter than all of them working together

on the bellows could have. How was I to know the forge
fires needed to be kept at manageable temperatures? The
blacksmith chased me out with a hammer raised above his
head, all to the whistling approval of his apprentices. A deep
melancholy for things lost, better times gone by. People I
once knew, now nothing but bones and fading memories,
their faces already long forgotten by the world.

What is there in the past you long for really? Easy days?
You would be bored with ease. People long dead? You of all people
know that death is a cycle which can be interrupted given the
correct application of power. Anonymity? Fool others or yourself,
Eskara, but I know the truth. You bask in your reputation. The fear
and awe of your name give you a greater power than any Source.
It's good to rule.

We drew up to the ruins, close enough I could see
the ghosts milling about, indistinct blurs floating around,
doomed to repeat their final days in isolation until not even
the memories of them remained. I could have spent time
unravelling all those ghosts, but there were so many of them.
An entire city, thousands upon thousands upon thousands.
They floated toward me as I came close to the city limits,
drawn by the fear Sserakis held inside.

We dismounted and tied our birds to a nearby tree.
Hardt and Tamura would need theirs again soon. We sat by
a stream and ate a final meal, dried meats and stale bread,
washing it down with fresh water warmed through by the
afternoon sun. Silence reigned over us, even Tamura, and we
all knew what was to come.

"The world changed the day Lokar and Lursa finally
embraced," Tamura said, his voice having fallen into the
storyteller's tone he used in taverns. "For years beyond
counting, they had moved through the sky, watching

Ovaeris. People like to say Lokar chased his mistress, but it was always the other way around. Lursa, larger of the two and red as life's blood, chased while Lokar fled. They were never lovers. Lokar was prey and Lursa predator, locked in an endless chase.

"When Lursa caught her prey, the embrace was both catastrophic and wonderful. From Ovaeris, the people, garn and mur alike, looked up at the sky and saw the surface of both moons cracking as they twisted and crushed into one another. Even Lursa, with her greater bulk, could not come out of such conflict unscathed. The surface of both our moons cracked and pieces were thrown out into the space between our world and the moons. Rocks the size of cities fell to the ground and catastrophe struck. So much was the violence, that the dust flung into the sky blotted out the sun, stars, and moons. A permanent night fell upon Ovaeris."

That sounds preferable to your sun's light.

"But things cannot grow without the sun. Life here cannot exist without the light. Creatures came up from the depths, venturing into a world they seldom tread. Grey monsters with cracked skin that oozed yellow, and teeth sharpened to points. Others, little beasts with mangy fur and no eyes, crawled from cracks in the earth to inflict their savage presence on the world they had so long hidden underneath. The collision of the moons had put into motion a cataclysm that none would survive. Seas boiled and mur died in the thousands. Jungles burned, and for the first time in existence the garn ceased their endless warring to die together."

"There a point to this, old man?" Hardt asked, a grin betraying his feigned annoyance.

Tamura sighed and rolled his eyes. "The tahren have

no eyes, yet they are not blind. Why?" He cupped a hand over his ear.

With light this bright, it's a surprise you aren't all blind. There was camaraderie in Ssserakis' mocking. I realised then that my horror wished to join in, to be a part of the group. It had been with me for so long, had spent almost as much time with Hardt and Tamura as I had. As much as any embodiment of fear could, Ssserakis regarded them as friends. Only they had no idea it even existed, let alone counted them as such. Well, maybe they knew but they would never admit it. I wondered then, on the loneliness that Ssserakis felt, trapped inside with only me for company. And I was not always the best of company.

Don't pity me. Camaraderie quickly replaced by indignation. *I am a lord of Sevoari. Friends are a concept of Ovaeris. Your world of light and bonds.*

"Who are you trying to convince?" Ssserakis had no answer for me, but I found Hardt and Tamura both watching me. "You were telling a story, Tamura."

The old Aspect grinned and slipped back into the story as though the interruption had never happened. "The end of days had come. Garn Astromancers had predicted it. The mur Hydrobinders, even with their combined might, had been powerless to stop it. Ovaeris was dying, and the creatures of the dark had risen to claim its corpse.

"But in the darkest hour of our world came a new light; one that had been freed by the same cataclysm that wrought the end of the world. Only it was not one, but two lights. Two that had ever been at odds with the other, linked in both life and hatred. Two that had been separated and imprisoned for the chaos they might cause if left unchecked. Power came to Ovaeris, the likes of which both garn and

mur had never seen before, had never dreamed possible.
Their power left the Astromancers and Hydrobinders in
awe. And then these now powers worked together to put the
world right."

The Rand and Djinn do not work together.

"I thought Sevoari was the first time the two had
worked together?" My words were almost an echo of my
horror's.

Tamura shook his head in that way he had. His
matted grey locks tumbled against each other and he let
loose a wide smile, his eyes seemed to look through me and I
had the suspicion then that he saw exactly what I harboured
inside. "Sevoari was a failure because they worked apart,
each trying to out manoeuvre the other to create something
new. Ovaeris already existed, in peril. And the only way to
save it? Unity of purpose. Working together to a common
goal."

Unity of purpose.

"The final augury."

Tamura grinned. "The most important one. The one
the Rand and Djinn never learned, refused to learn. In saving
Ovaeris they combined their powers. The Djinn scoured the
dust from the air and calmed the earth and seas. The Rand
took the monsters rampaging across the surface, made bold
by the failing light, and changed them into creatures of
thought and peace. They saved the world by changing the
world. Together."

"But it didn't last. Even with that success they
couldn't abide one another."

Tamura looked at me and nodded. "Consider the
coin." With a flick of his wrist, a gold coin appeared in
Tamura's fingers. An old Terrelan mint, some long dead

emperor's name on one side, a depiction of the moons on the other. "One thing, but two sides, always opposed and never able to meet."

"What about the edge?" Hardt asked.

Tamura snorted and sent a sidelong glance at Hardt. "We are the edge."

"I'm still not seeing the point of this story, old man."

Tamura sighed and pulled his gaze from Hardt, instead directing it toward me. "All things have value, but all value is subjective. One woman's pit, is another man's kingdom." He grinned.

"What about the thing on the other side of portals?" I asked. "Aerolis was terrified of it. Of it finding him."

"Ahhh." Tamura nodded. "The maker, the eyes, the nexus, the jailer. The parent. The god of gods. The Second Cataclysm."

It is cold. Power on a level even the Rand and Djinn cannot fathom. When the embodiment of fear, a creature of shadow and ice, tells you something is cold... it is worth listening.

"The Rand and Djinn did not end up trapped in our moons by accident. They were placed there. Rowdy children unwilling to work together, separated in their rooms." Tamura stopped and giggled. "But of course, they snuck out. Slipped away. Thought themselves safe."

Tamura's mind was ever a wonder to me. He struggled to remember yesterday, could not tell me of his past, and I'm not even sure he remembered the Pit, despite spending more years down there than I had seen. Yet he had all the memories of a Rand locked away inside, accessed easily when the contours of a story took him. Or when the correct questions were asked.

"But they aren't safe?"

"Making mistakes is easy…" Tamura paused.

"Correcting them is hard," I said.

"Impossible. One cannot unspeak a word, erase a footstep. What's done is done. During the War Eternal, at its height, there was a battle. Out in the Polasian desert, many Rand and many Djinn, tired with the stalemate of their war, collided. Power like that used to save Ovaeris, and create Sevoari, clashed." Tamura clapped his hands together, staring at me over the violence of it. "They tore a hole in the world. They brought themselves to the attention of their maker. And now it knows they have escaped. It watches, through the great hole above the desert, through the small tears that Sourcerers create. It watches, always looking for its unruly children."

Or those of us who carry their mark.

"A hole in the world over the Polasian desert?" Hardt asked. "I didn't see it."

Tamura pointed south. "What do your eyes see?"

Hardt squinted for a time and then shrugged. "The horizon."

"Past that?"

I laughed. "The desert is a big place, then. But this hole in the world. This thing watches through it?"

Tamura nodded. "Watches. Waits. Picks. Enlarges. One day the hole will be big enough to let it through, and Ovaeris will burn once more. The Second Cataclysm. Inevitable."

"It won't just take them and leave us be? There's only two of them left." Hardt didn't understand, he was thinking too rationally about creatures that defied rational thought.

"Look at the bottom of your foot," Tamura said. "What do you see." Hardt let out a growl of frustration.

"It won't care, Hardt." I decided to interject some clarity before the two started arguing. "It won't even see us. People, cities they mean nothing to a creature like that. We mean nothing to it."

Hardt grumbled. "I still don't see the point of the story."

I did. I understood it all too well. The third Augury, a unity of purpose. It made sense now. The Rand and Djinn were never meant to use their powers apart. They were linked intrinsically, to be unified. And every time they defied that purpose, disaster followed. I understood the point of the story, but not the timing.

"It's time," I said as I stood, staring into the ruins of Picarr, my eyes locked on the rubble, all that was left of the Orran Academy of Magic. Hardt stood too, yet Tamura remained seated.

He is a weakness that will get you killed.

"You can't come with me, Hardt."

He shook his head and fixed me with his dark eyes. "We've already been through this. I'm coming with you, Eska. You might think you're all powerful, but you're going to need me in there."

My turn to shake my head. "I won't. You'll only get in the way."

I saw his pride take the hit. He knew it was true yet refused to accept it. "Don't count me out just yet. I've still got a few tricks up my sleeve."

So have we.

A sad smile snuck its way out of me, and I lurched forward, wrapping my arm around Hardt and giving him one last embrace. I breathed in deep and he smelled of comfort. I do not deserve Hardt, I never have. Not the trust he places in me, nor the strength he lends me. I have never deserved him, but I will always be glad he stayed with me, no matter what came of us. When I stepped back, I tore open a portal with a wave of my hand. He looked over his shoulder, confusion plain for all to see. The portal showed a small river, a wooden bridge crossing it, and green grass on either side. We had passed the place earlier that day, no more than a couple of hours travel by trei bird. But Hardt would not have a bird, and I could only hope that slowed him long enough.

"Eska…" I interrupted Hardt with a kinetic push that sent him tumbling through the portal backwards. He tripped on his feet and collapsed, and for a moment we stared at each other through that portal, a gulf of many miles between us. I saw the hurt on his face; his pride crushed along with the pain of my betrayal. A betrayal I would make time and time again, as many times as it took, to keep Hardt safe.

I snapped the portal shut before I could change my mind, and before Hardt could change it for me. Tamura waited, not moving, eyes on me. "I couldn't send him far." I had never been a good Portamancer, my range and accuracy too limited. "Don't let him come for me. Stop him." I glanced at the birds. "Use the spare bird to help carry him away if need be. I won't need it."

Tamura stood then, stepped toward me and wrapped me up in a crushing embrace, strong despite his appearance. "Good luck," he whispered in my ear. I saw tears in his eyes as he pulled away, and I knew he understood. He alone understood.

Stop delaying.

I made my way into the ruins of Picarr alone save for my horror.

CHAPTER
THIRTY THREE

I PICKED MY WAY THROUGH THE RUINS OF
Picarr and ghosts swarmed around me. Hundreds of them
all drawn by the fear Ssserakis fed upon and held inside.
Ethereal blurs betraying my passage. The traps in the city
took on a new meaning now. Before, I had believed them
nothing more than the remnants of a magical battle, a by-
product of so much power clashing in a confined space.
Now, I thought them something else entirely. The Iron
Legion had seeded the ruined city with traps to keep the
people of Isha at bay. He wanted no intrepid explorers
accidentally discovering his lair. It was the perfect hiding
place. I moved past the traps with ease, my odd sense of
magic warning me whenever I drew close to one.

Braggarts Tower, or at least the crumbling ruin of it
frozen in time, passed by on my left. I glanced toward it to
see the two men trapped inside the bubble of timelessness.

A poor unfortunate Chronomancer, locked in the moment before his own death, and Prena's comrade. On his shield, I could still see an image of Ssserakis and I fighting against Vainfold. I could remember nothing of the time during which Vainfold held my body, used it to unleash his fire upon the city, but I could still remember the threat in his parting words. He would remember my name. I hoped he remembered it for all eternity.

Ghouls flanked me, watching from shadows, not daring to come too close. *Weaklings. Too young to even know their own names. We could use them. Throw them at our enemy and strike in his distraction.* It wouldn't work. Caught between myself and the Iron Legion, the Ghouls would likely fall upon each other rather than aid either of us. They are neither the smartest nor the most courageous of monsters. At least, not at that young age.

The Arcstorm still raged in front of the academy grounds, right where I had left it. Lightning sparked between rocks and rubble, and I could see the charred remains of the Ghouls that had died there. I did not bother to skirt the storm, but walked straight through the centre of it, letting it vent its fury upon me. A rush of energy filled me with every strike, making me stronger and more certain of my course. That storm had nearly killed me once. Now it was a part of me, and each bit of it I absorbed just felt like the power of the Arcmancy Source returning home. It belonged within me. It belonged to me.

The academy grounds were silent. The Arcstorm was outside, and the single tree no longer burned without Vainfold's crown to sustain it. The wreckage of crumbling buildings spread out all around me. The academy grounds were huge, where I stood was only the welcoming courtyard where I had first met the Iron Legion many years ago. I knew where I would find the entrance, over by the old archives building, or what was left of it, but I hadn't expected to find the entrance so welcoming. An archway forged out of the earth by way of Geomancy, precise steps leading down into the darkness below the surface.

He's expecting us. I only nodded by way of reply and took the first step towards the trap.

I didn't even notice the slight figure following along behind me at a distance, tracing my steps.

There was no light, but then, I didn't need any. I could have used fire, called upon my Pyromancy to create a flame that would light my way, but the Iron Legion already knew I was coming, and I had no desire to give him any more advantages. Instead, I let Ssserakis give me its darksight. The stairwell stretched downward, its wall and steps clear to me in shades of light and dark, no colour. It is difficult to see depth properly in that form of sight and the stairwell seemed to stretch on forever, no passageways left or right.

Sometimes it seems as though all the major events in my life have occurred underground. The Pit, the Red Cells, the Iron Legion's laboratory. I cannot complain, I felt oddly more at home in the dark confines with stone all around me. Though a part of me still looked favourably on the sky, I had spent my time among the clouds, and I had suffered for it.

My footsteps rang loud on the stone, echoing down empty passages. Even once I found the bottom of the stairs, all that greeted me was an empty, undecorated room with a corridor beyond it. But as I walked that first level, my memory put things into their place. I had been there before, long ago before the Iron Legion had changed me. Josef and

I had explored this cellar, looking for doors that I had been told never to open. So, I followed my memory and it led me to where it had once before. A wooden door set into stone, faint yellow light spilling out beneath it, and noises beyond I couldn't quite place it.

"We may only get one chance at this."

I am ready. Are you?

"No."

I heard Ssserakis laugh. It was a nervous laugh.

The best traps are the ones people see coming. There is an artistry in a trap that the victim has no choice but to step into. The Iron Legion had built his trap well. I say I followed my memory, but the truth is, I had nowhere else to go. All paths led to that door; all other ways sealed off with Geomancy. One way in and no way out, and bait I could never refuse. A trap tailor made for me. My only hope was to surprise the Iron Legion, move slowly enough and silently enough that he didn't see me coming.

I edged open the door and slipped inside on rustling feet, leaving the door ajar behind me. The room beyond was large and open with a low roof, just two of me high. Flames danced on torches on either side of the room, and the walls were lined with bookshelves and cupboards. A small, round depression lay in the centre of the room, a pedestal its only occupant. To my left I saw closed doorways, to my right I saw chains and cages, stacked up close together and on top of each other. Dozens of bodies littered the cages, and from my position I could not see if they were moving, but they were still alive. One thing I had discovered recently was my ability to sense the nearby dead. It was a disconcerting feeling when it struck. There was no one else in the room.

What did you expect? In truth, I had half expected the

Iron Legion to be sat waiting for me like an omnipotent villain from a bard's tale. The fucker always seemed to be a hundred steps ahead of me. *This is to our advantage. Catch him while he sleeps and end him.* I had never heard Ssserakis advocate for assassination before, always my horror had been adamant that we allow ourselves to be seen so our enemies, and all others, would know and fear us. I couldn't say I disagreed with the idea though. But there was something else that I needed to do, something even more important than my confrontation with Loran Orran.

I clung to what little shadows I could, letting Ssserakis blend us in against the walls, and crept closer to the rows of cages. The occupants were mostly terran, a few pahht but not many. Most looked malnourished and exhausted, some even showed signs of struggle. I passed each cage with a glance, searching for Josef. I could have freed them then, opened the cages and ushered them to the exit. Perhaps I should have, but a fleeing crowd makes noise, and I needed to find Josef before I gave away my presence. Some of the prisoners took notice as I passed, whispering for help and stretching out hands through their bars, as if grabbing hold of me would free them or ease their pain. I checked every cage, hundreds of prisoners. None of them were Josef.

He's already…

"Don't," I hissed the word. Useless, I could feel the sentiment even without my horror finishing it. Josef was already dead, and this was never anything but a trap. He couldn't be dead. He couldn't be. After everything we had both been through. Everything we had done and suffered. Everything we had survived, together and apart. How could it be over? I staggered, clutching hold of a nearby cage, my knuckles white from the strength of my grip. I was caught in a howling tornado of grief and anger and sheer fucking hate!

A door on the other side of the room opened and from the recess strode the Iron Legion. He looked older than the last time I had seen him, ancient even. His flesh loose and liver spotted, hung from his bones. His hair was gone, leaving nothing but a bald pate wrinkled with too much skin. His nose and ears seemed too large, and his lips were pinched and cracked. But his eyes… his eyes were still as sharp and piercing as ever. Robes swished as he walked, but where before they seemed well fitted and regal, they now hung on his diminished form. He paced towards the pedestal in the centre of the room, eyes down on the book in his hands. I froze, like a wild animal caught in sudden light. Even Ssserakis was silent.

The Iron Legion stopped at the pedestal in the centre of the room, placing his little book upon it, then looked up straight toward me. "Helsene?"

Attack! There was panic in my horror's voice, but I needed no prompting. When an animal is surprised by a predator it has two options. It can either flee or fight. I was never one to flee.

I stretched out my hand and unleashed the fury of the storm.

Lightning ripped from my chest, raced along my arm, and crackled from my fingertips. Five brilliant blue-white bolts of searing energy arced outward, crossing the distance between us in a moment. They struck as one hammer blow. The pedestal shattered, blown apart by the force, and the Iron Legion's body was thrown backwards to crash against the far wall. A smoking, charred ruin.

Again, I froze, not believing my eyes. I had done it. It was over.

Shouts from the cages behind me brought me out of my frozen confusion. The prisoners had been watching, of course. They saw their captor dead and wanted their freedom. For once I could be a hero instead of a monster. I could save them all. I turned towards them, staring down at the locks and wondered how best to go about opening them without a key.

Your Necromancy, Eskara. You can sense the dead.

"How does that help me open cages?"

We fool ourselves with hope. We do it time and time again, no matter how wise we may become to its insidious whispers. No matter how cynical life teaches us to be, hope will always blind us just when we need to see clearly.

As I reached out for the door on the nearest cage, the bars warped, wrapping around my arm and setting back into place, holding me tight. An instant of panic gripped me, my heart racing, thundering in my ears. A glance over my shoulder confirmed that hope had blinded me once again. The Iron Legion stirred amid his smouldering robes. It seemed to take forever for him to regain his feet, his old bones struggling to move. I tried to free myself, tugging my arm and bringing only pain. Another of the bars warped, wrapping itself around my right leg.

The Iron Legion pushed himself to unsteady feet. A jagged line of blackened flesh oozed on his face, evidence that my lightning had struck true. Already, I could see his skin knitting itself back together, Biomancy at work at a speed I had only seen once before when Prena had run Josef through.

Shadow pooled beneath me, inky and black, and raced up along my arm and leg, then ballooned outward. I slipped free of the metal bars and erected a shield around me, drawing on Arcmancy and Kinemancy and mixing them inside to increase the power of both.

Attack. Don't let him recover. We will strike as one.

My wings blossomed from my back and I charged, forming a slender Sourceblade in my hand and flicking it through the air, releasing lighting and fire toward the Iron Legion with each slash. He batted the flames away, redirecting them to scorch the wall behind him. The lightning struck, rippling harmlessly along a shield of his own. The roof was too low to use my wings to speed my sprint, but they had other uses.

When we clashed, I put everything I had into my first strike, momentum lending it extra power. But even wracked with age, the Iron Legion was not weak. He had been trained by the same school I had, only better. I flicked my Sourceblade at him time and time again, and he knocked each strike aside with metal coated open hands. All the while, I could see his flesh healing the wounds I had given him. How could I have thought him dead? How could I hope to kill him? He was stronger than I, stronger than Ssserakis and I together, and even when I did land a blow, the damage healed within moments. Doubt crept inside. He knew my measure and matched my skill, bolstered by having two arms to my one, but my wings were something he did not expect.

We were cold fury, fuelled by fear. I pushed fire and lightning into my Sourceblade, and each strike unleashed the magic, battering down the Iron Legion's shield. My wings struck over my shoulders, darting in between sword strikes. Razor sharp talons pierced his shield, tearing shreds from his robes and scoring strikes across his skin. Under the torrent of attacks we levelled at him, the Iron Legion struggled to mount any offence of his own. He backed up, step after step after step, always on the defence, his face a grimacing mask of pain as his Biomancy struggled to keep up with the wounds we dealt him. What little magic he mustered on the attack brushed harmlessly off my shield. I could see him weakening even as I grew stronger. Doubt crushed as Ssserakis fed me power through the fear of the hundreds of prisoners behind us.

Even with one arm, I am a capable swords-woman. Even with one arm, I am one of the most powerful Sourcerers alive. What I have never been is a tactician. I have always relied too much on raw power, on battering my way through any situation. The Iron Legion realised this long before I did and manoeuvred me, giving ground again and again, turning in a feigned retreat and coaxing me on with openings I rushed to take.

A construct thrust its way out of the nearby wall, a creature of rock and the Iron Legion's will. The first one fell to shadowy wing, cutting it in half. I didn't see the second one coming until it barrelled into me from behind, carrying me down to the ground. Solid rock weighs a great deal, but my Kinetic shield held, and I scrambled back to my feet. The Iron Legion had retreated only a few paces, but it was all the distance he needed.

The metal coating the Iron Legion's left hand turned liquid, flowing from his fingers into the shape of a small metal disk hanging from his grip. A gong. He struck it quickly with his other hand and the room turned into a deafening cacophony of noise.

Vibromancy is a hateful school of magic with very little in the way of counters. Sound is a weapon unlike any other I have encountered, and a Vibromancer can use it

to devastating effect. The ringing of that gong echoed off
the walls and the Iron Legion amplified it, catching the
noise and turning it back upon itself, forcing it to build and
build and build. The pain in my head was too great to fight
through, too great to do anything. But Ssserakis cared not
for the noise. My horror could feel my pain, but the sound
was an external pressure. My shadow snaked out, shooting
across the ground beneath us, dark spikes forming along its
sinuous length. And again, the Iron Legion was a step ahead.

The light in the room flared. It came from the torches
and the cupboards and books my Pyromancy had set alight.
It came from the Iron Legion himself, glowing bright like a
hearth fire. I heard Ssserakis scream even over the noise of
the Vibromancy as the light burned my shadow away.

I collapsed to my knees; hand pressed against
my right ear to no use. Caught in the maelstrom of such
madness, I could do nothing. Even had I the strength to
resist it I could not think over the noise and the pain it
caused. Distantly I felt a hand grab hold of my wrist and
yank my arm away from my ear. I think I was screaming,
but I can't be sure. It is odd, but when we are assaulted with
such a level of noise, we can no longer tell where it is coming
from or even if we are adding ourselves to it. Such thought
was blasted away in the cacophony. Something cool flowed
around my wrist and then went hard, locked tight against
my skin, cutting into the flesh of my hand. And the noise
and light both stopped.

As did my connection to the Sources I carried inside
my stomach. I reached for them, and could feel their weight,
but their power was locked from me. The Arcstorm was
silent also, like a distant rumble and flash I couldn't see or
hear. My wrist felt heavy and as the Iron Legion withdrew

his hand, I looked down to see a large band of metal wrapped around it. It was sharp on the inside, cutting into my skin and drawing blood, and there was a depression on the top of it, deep enough to fit a marble inside.

"That's better." The Iron Legion sounded weary, his voice lethargic. He took a single step back from me and panted, trying to catch his breath. "But I have the measure of you now. And I see my old friend didn't perish after all. How long have you carried Ssserakis?"

I paused, waiting for Ssserakis to scream inside. To rage and strike out with my shadow, but there was nothing. Not even a whimper from my horror.

The Iron Legion waited for an answer, hands on his hips, breathing heavy. He thought he had me beat. Taken away my magic and my horror, and he thought I had nothing left. What a fucking fool. I launched myself at him and saw the surprise on his face, his hands coming up to protect him. But I was not some untrained brawler, I had studied with Hardt and Tamura, and I knew how to fight. I leapt to the side, pushing his hands away with my right hand and then swung at his face with my left. With his shield down, his overconfidence would be his downfall.

Muscle memory is what makes a great fighter. Instinct and the ability for the muscles to act upon that instinct without the mind getting too involved. I had fought with Hardt and Tamura, been put through some of the harshest of training. My body knew how to fight, how to move. But I had let that training go, and since losing my arm, I had only trained with a blade. My body forgot that I only had one arm, and all I swung at the Iron Legion was a stump of fused flesh and rock. It passed between us harmlessly and for just a moment, the Iron Legion and I stared at each other.

It's hard to say which of us was the more surprised in that moment. But he recovered far faster than I.

A kinetic force slammed into me from above and forced me onto my knees. The stone beneath me seemed to melt and flow over my ankles before hardening once more, locking me in place.

"Enough, Helsene." The Iron Legion stumbled back a couple of steps, again breathing hard, wary eyes staring at me in case I had any more tricks. He needn't have bothered. I was done. Held fast to the floor, barely able to move, and whatever he had fixed to my wrist was keeping my magic and horror both unreachable. Still, I did my absolute best to glare the Iron Legion to death. It didn't fucking work.

"I didn't invite you here to fight you. I need your help." He said it with such sincerity I couldn't help but laugh, a harsh cackling thing.

"You want my help? My entire life you have done nothing but cause me pain and then thrown me to the wolves. You gave me to the Emperor."

Loran Orran sighed. "That was a necessary sacrifice. You were causing too much trouble, and Aras is… was not one to stand for it. I—"

"He took my arm!" I screamed the words at him, my voice breaking on them. Listening to him trying to rationalise the decision sickened me.

"I had no choice."

I screamed at him again. No words. Sometimes words cannot do justice to our feelings. Sometimes we have nothing but the anger, fury, sadness, and pain, and no way to express them save the violence of a scream.

The Iron Legion frowned, his ancient face growing even more lined. The man had been alive for only a decade longer than I, but his body had seen more than three times that many years. He was frail and slow and weak, but still strong enough to beat me. Seething is a good way to describe how I felt. Seething, and powerless to act upon it. It reminded me of Do'shan, after Silva and after Prena. The Iron Legion had me beaten then as well, held against my will.

"You were wrong." I forced out a bitter laugh. No humour to it, only hatred. "Josef wasn't the chosen one, was he?"

"I was not wrong. And yet also, I was." The Iron Legion waved a hand and a portal tore open. Through it I could see a dark cell, a body in the ragged remains of a robe lying against the wall. Josef. He was still alive!

My friend stirred, eyes squinting against the light coming through the portal. I saw recognition dawn on him, but he seemed different somehow.

"Come on, Yenhelm." The Iron Legion held the portal open while Josef stood and walked through it. He blinked rapidly, his face gaunt and his skin greasy. He looked like a scab, matted hair on his head and face. Malnourished and parched. "I finally have both of you. It's time."

Josef tore his weary eyes from me and glanced toward the cages stacked in rows. "Two hundred and sixteen. Please don't make me do it. Not again." He sounded weary, beaten. Numb.

The Iron Legion shook his head, his eyes hard. "No. Four hundred and thirty-two."

Panic gripped Josef and he shook his head wildly. "Not her. Leave Eska alone." Still trying to protect me. Still looking out for me. Still my brother. I loved him for that. That, and everything else.

"Yes, her. Both of you. You know what happens if you refuse." At the Iron Legion's words, Josef cowered, seeming to collapse in on himself. He slumped over and sobbed.

"What is going on?" Again, I tried to reach for my magic. To strike the Iron Legion down and save Josef. "Why do you need both of us?"

"Because I made a mistake," the Iron Legion snarled the words, as though they tasted foul. "The Auguries were instructions, yes. But not to create a chosen one. There has to be two of you."

"Unity of purpose," I said, and all the pieces fell into place. Finally.

"Indeed." The Iron Legion waved a hand my way. "One is the fusion of both life and death. A coin flipped and landing on both sides at once. Well, you certainly are that, Helsene. In more than just name."

He waved his other hand toward where Josef waited meekly. "Two is the renewal. A re-forging into something the same, yet different. Yenhelm was so very close to death. So close it changed something in him. Triggered the Biomancy Source I put inside. He can heal almost any wound within moments, and I have a feeling I have finally discovered the secret to immortality." He laughed then, an old man's cackle. "A shame it comes too late in my life. I will fix that."

The Iron Legion took a step back and gestured to us both. "Three is the unity of purpose. Two forces acting together for an uncommon goal. Not a chosen one at all, but a chose two. You are linked, just as the Rand and Djinn are linked. They cannot escape that one law that has bound them together for eternity. They've tried, I know all about it. The Djinn and their pocket realms, the Rand and their Aspects." The Iron Legion scoffed. "Vainfold and his brothers are not trapped inside their realms because they no longer have the power to escape. They're trapped there because it's the only thing keeping them alive. If such a thing can be called life. Their Rand counterparts are long dead, and if they re-entered Ovaeris, the laws of the world would affect them once more. They would die. They might as well be dead for the use they serve."

I barely heard his tirade. A question was rattling around in my head, so urgent I had to ask it. So important I dreaded the answer. "What about the Aspects?"

Again, the Iron Legion scoffed. "A nice attempt, but ultimately fruitless. The Rand and Djinn are linked. The Rand think that separating a part of themselves off would be enough to trick the laws of the world." He shook his head. "There are no loopholes for the laws of the world. If Aerolis dies, so too does Mezula. I suppose I shouldn't be too harsh on the Rand; it was a nice attempt and the Aspects did give rise to Sourcery."

I stopped listening as the full impact of his words hit me. *There are no loopholes for the laws of the world.* Silva didn't have to die. If I had only listened to her. If I had only trusted her. We could have pitted our combined power against Aerolis. We could have won. We could have rid the world of both the Rand and the Djinn right then and lived our lives together. She was gone because neither of us understood the rules of the world. Gone because I had killed her thinking I had no other choice. Gone and she didn't have to be. I killed the woman I loved for no reason. I hated myself. I hated the Rand and the Djinn. I hated the Iron Legion. I hated the whole fucking world! And as I realised the full consequences of my mistake, I became convinced... The world hates me back.

"Eska?" I felt grimy arms wrap around my shoulders and pull me into an embrace. I was keening, unable to stop myself. I wiped tears on Josef's rags. I felt like I had just murdered Silva all over again, only this time it was worse because it didn't have to happen.

The Iron Legion continued, oblivious to my pain. "With you I'm going to right the greatest wrong of this world. I'm going to correct it." He grinned and reached into the folds of his robe. Josef pulled away from me and Loran handed a small metal sceptre to him, a dark Source held at its head. Then he advanced on me and slotted another Source into the small depression on my single manacle. "I'm going to bring the Rand and Djinn back to life. All of them."

CHAPTER THIRTY FOUR

"START AT THE OTHER END, YENHELM. TWO hundred and sixteen." The Iron Legion released me from the rock holding me in place just long enough to drag me towards the cages. He was surprisingly strong for such an old man. I flailed a bit, even landed a punch on his chin with my arm, but I was struggling to find any real fight and he barely felt it. He pushed me against the bars of the first cell and the metal warped, winding around my arm and legs to hold me in place. I spat at him then. Anything I could do, any resistance I could put up no matter how fruitless. The bastard might have won, but I would be damned before I went down quietly. He gave me a reproachful glare and wiped the spittle away.

"I can't do this," Josef said from the other end of the cells.

"You know what happens if you defy me, Yenhelm."

Two men loitered nearby, not caged. They wore the remnants of Terrelan military uniforms, though the emblems had been cut away and the clothes had seen better days. The Iron Legion glanced their way. "Start bringing me the prisoners, one at a time."

I tried to pull against the metal holding me in place, but I was held tight. I even swung my stump at the Iron Legion, but it brushed against his robes harmlessly and the man shot me a pitying look. I hated him. I just wanted him to die. I heard Josef sobbing, but couldn't see through the gloom to where he stood. Whatever was happening, it was causing my friend, my brother, my other half pain and I couldn't do anything to stop it.

The first of the prisoners was brought forward, a thin woman who couldn't even stand without the soldier holding her up. Her hair was grey and matted, and her eyes dull brown, barely a spark of life within them. The Iron Legion gripped her around the neck with one hand and put his other on my chest. "This might feel a little unpleasant." Even as he said the words, I realised the truth of them. He dragged the woman's spirit from her body. I didn't even think such a thing was possible. But of course, it was. I could use my Necromancy to force a person's soul, their spirit back into their body. Necromancy and Biomancy were always two sides of a coin, it made sense that Biomancy could be used in such a hateful way.

I had a flash of memory as the soul was channelled through me. A brief flicker of another life. A grandmother sitting by a low fire, a daughter beside her and a granddaughter on her knee. Three generations of a family all huddled close near a fire. A house full of love and comfort. The memory was gone as quickly as it had appeared, like a dream leaving only fleeting emotion behind. Forgotten. Gone. I felt the spirit travel through me, had no say in where it went or what it left behind. Through my chest, down my arm, and into the manacle. Into the Source embedded in the metal.

I gasped, still trying to grasp what had just happened. My eyes met the Iron Legion's. "What…"

"Next." He reached for the next prisoner.

He was relentless. Prisoner after prisoner. Life after life. I found myself swamped in fragments of memories, subjected to a hundred different lives. I nearly lost myself in that maelstrom. Here, a young man proud to be a soldier in service of his emperor. There, another man with eyes for a woman who would never love him back. A woman searching for a lost shoe, her favourite pair forever split in two. A young boy stubbing his toe and crying for his mother. A wizened old crone tricking villagers into believing her a witch. A man with lands and title counting his money. A young girl playing with a dog down by a frozen river. Each one fleeting, a shard of memory and emotion, and then gone, replaced by another. And another. And another. I struggled to know where I ended, and the memories of others began.

If the Iron Legion felt the same torment of memories, he did not show it. I think neither he nor Josef felt them. It was unique to me. Two hundred and sixteen people were killed before me that day, and another equal number at Josef's hands. Two hundred and sixteen lives passed through me, channelled into the Source. Two hundred and sixteen souls to measure up to just one Djinn life.

I could not stop what happened next. As the last of the souls passed through me and into the Source, the same process was completed with Josef. The Source attached to my manacle began to glow, softly at first but brighter and brighter and brighter still. A blue glow. Time. Chronomancy. It popped free of the manacle and dropped to the ground. I sagged against my restraints, unable to do anything but watch. Near Josef, the Source was glowing a brilliant yellow and he dropped the sceptre. The Iron Legion rushed forward and collected both Sources, carrying them to the centre of the room where two new pedestals waited, risen from the very rock around us. Josef drifted closer to me, and we could only watch the atrocity we had just committed.

"I'm sorry." Josef said, though he looked more numb than apologetic. I never considered how the taken lives and channelled souls affected him. For me, each one left something with me, a fragment of a memory, the feeling of having lived others' lives. For him, each one took a little something from him on its way, something he could never get back. His sanity washed away in a flood of souls. "Your arm."

"Is gone." The words hissed from me. "Get me out of here."

The lights in the centre of the room were pulsing brighter and brighter, yellow and blue alternating their pulses, casting the laboratory in dizzying hues. Josef moved closer and pulled on the twisted metal of the bars that held me. They didn't budge. He shook his head at me. One of the soldiers chuckled.

"What about this manacle?" I asked.

Josef poked at the metal secured around my wrist and I winced at the pain as it dug deeper into my flesh. Blood welled up fresh and ran along my hand, dripping from my fingers. Again, Josef shook his head.

I sighed. Trapped. Beaten. We had lost. I wished

Ssserakis would speak, reassure me we could still fight, even if it was a lie. "What happens next?"

"I don't know." Josef turned his attention to where the Iron Legion waited in the centre of the room, between the two pedestals and their pulsing Sources. "It's never got this far before. They've always cracked and shattered."

The pulsing of the two Sources was changing, slowing, synchronising. A gradual process of the two forces being brought into tune with one another. A third soldier slipped into the room and paused, staring towards the Sources for a moment, before turning towards us. She wore the same faded uniform as the others but had a beautiful face and glossy raven-dark hair. I thought nothing of it and turned my attention back to the Iron Legion.

"Stop this!" I screamed the words so loud the Iron Legion had to look over. "You don't know what you're doing."

The Iron Legion took two steps toward me. "I am righting a wrong, Helsene. Ending the War Eternal. Fixing the world." He pitched his voice to carry and I realised there was noise escaping the Sources; two vibrating hums slowly merging into one. "Only the Rand and Djinn working together can undo what they did. It requires the union of their powers to close the hole in the world. And it requires them both to undo what their magic has done to me."

"How can you end a war that was dead before any of us were even born? Aerolis and Mezula ended the war, Loran. They conspired together to kill the last of their brothers and sisters because they knew there could never be any other end to the war. Even then, they can't stop trying to kill each other. The Rand and the Djinn may be one, two sides of the same coin, but they are opposite. They will never allow the other to live. You aren't ending the war, you're reigniting it!" My words fell on deaf ears, it seemed, and the Iron Legion turned back to the pulsing Sources. "You're perpetuating it! Giving them a way to kill each other endlessly and bring themselves back using our lives!"

Of course, he didn't care. Lives no longer meant anything to the Iron Legion, perhaps they never had. All he truly cared about was his own vapid life. His declaration of trying to save the world was never anything but justification for the murder of innocents.

Speaking of murder, the third soldier reached us, a grin on her flawless face. I might have realised had my attention not been rooted on the Iron Legion. Though, in truth it wouldn't have mattered, there was nothing I could have done. A knife flicked out, burying itself deep in the first soldier's heart. Before the second could react, the woman stepped close and dragged him down, kicking his legs from beneath him and snapping his neck. Recognition dawned on me far too late.

"Coby."

The Aspect grinned, savage and victorious. "Did you think I'd forgotten about you?" She glanced over her shoulder, but it was clear the Iron Legion was paying them no attention as the glow and hum of the Sources were almost synchronised. Coby turned back to me and leaned in close, hands going to my neck. I knew just how strong she was and even Hardt would look weak in comparison.

"Stop!" Josef, still trying to protect me, but Coby just shoved him away and he sprawled on the floor.

Coby's hands closed around my neck and I smiled at her. Death would be a victory of sorts. Without me the Iron Legion could bring no other Rand or Djinn back from the dead.

It would be a hollow victory I would not get to enjoy.

CHAPTER THIRTY FIVE

DEATH DID NOT COME. COBY PAUSED, HER hands around my neck, fingers pressing lightly into my flesh. "Why are you smiling, you mad bitch?" She could change her appearance at will, but her voice never changed. And it always dripped with scorn when she spoke to me.

"You're as responsible for Silva's death as I am. You and your mother both." Hands tightened around my throat and to say it was uncomfortable would be an understatement, but I ploughed on, desperate to get my own hatred out before I died. "You knew. You fucking knew and you let her go to Do'shan anyway. Mezula sent her to her death." I leaned forward into Coby's grip even though it strangled me, and glared at her, tears in my eyes. "You blame me because you're too much of a fucking coward to blame your mother, and you were too much of a coward to take Silva's place!"

Coby leaned in, thumbs pressed into flesh. I couldn't breathe. "She was supposed to die for something." Her breath was hot and warm and smelled of death. "Because of you she died for nothing!"

"She'd still be dead," I spat the words through the choking hands around my throat. And then they vanished, leaving me dangling in the metal bars, desperately trying to suck in air.

I had to blink away tears and when I looked up, I found Coby had changed. Gone was the tattered soldier's uniform and the cocky gait. Now she stood before me in a flowing red dress. She looked so much like Silva it hurt, her face almost an exact mimicry except her skin was dark instead of light and her hair as black as my own instead of shining with light. So similar, yet completely different. I wondered if this appearance was as close to the real Coby as anyone ever got. Only Silva had ever really known what her sister looked like under the constant shifting glamours, and it was a secret she took to her grave.

A thought struck me, a moment of clarity. Something Josef had once said to me after an Empamancy lesson back at the academy. *Anger is often misplaced. When it is not allowed one avenue, it will invariably seek another.* "You wish it had been you?" I asked.

Coby nodded slowly. "Me. Gol. Mercury. I wish it had been anyone but Silva."

"Me too."

The wrong thing to say. A snarl passed across Coby's face. It seemed so right there, where on Silva it would have seemed so wrong. "You killed her!"

"Not by choice." A traitorous thought that. I had stopped myself at the last moment, only to have Ssserakis turn my mercy into death. "Silva knew she went to Do'shan to die. Your mother sent her to die in her place."

Coby's hand shot out again, closing around my neck and for a moment I thought she was going to end it. I could feel the pressure, and her grip tightened. If I was going to die, it felt somehow right that it was in vengeance for my murder of Silva. I welcomed it. But it was fleeting. Coby let go and turned away, shaking her head. We both grieved, but we could never grieve together.

The pulsing synchronised and the laboratory was engulfed in a flash of light so bright it left me blind even through closed eyes. It took a few moments and lots of blinking to clear myself of glowing spots in my vision.

"What is this?" Coby asked, as though noticing the Iron Legion and his experiment for the first time.

"He's done it." Josef was back on his feet and at my side. "He's brought a Rand and Djinn back to life."

The yellow Source was oozing, a pallid flesh growing out of the cracks that had formed along its surface. As I watched, the flesh expanded and grew, reminding me of the Abomination I had once brought across from the Other World. It glowed with life and pulsed like a beating heart, growing larger with each pulse. The blue Source shook and sparked and smoke escaped its cracks, whirling as though caught in a vortex, collecting above the crystal coffin. And between them both stood the Iron Legion, an enraptured smile on his face.

"Well, this is bad," Coby said. "There was a reason my mother killed off the last of her sisters."

"Yes!" I hissed. "And Mezula won't want them coming back. The Iron Legion intends to bring them all back."

Coby sighed. "Idiot fucking terrans. My mother should never have raised you from the beasts."

"Coby!" I waited for her to look to me. "Get this thing off my wrist. You might hate me, and I might hate you," I had not forgiven her for killing Horralain, "but we have to stop the Iron Legion. He's too strong for me to fight alone."

"That's because you're weak." She grinned, but it was all insult and no humour.

The Sources were gone now. The pulsing mass of flesh was taking form; legs and arms stretching out, a great eye in the centre of the mass, blinking, its attention darting everywhere. The smoke had coalesced into a miniature storm, the heart of it growing more violent by the second, a heart of lightning.

"He's too strong for you as well," I said. "Even Aerolis fears the Iron Legion. The Djinn are scared of him. We need to work together, all three of us."

"I can't fight him," Josef said, his eyes fearful. "I have no Sources. No magic. And… and he kills people whenever I fight back."

My patience was wearing thin. "He's already killing people, Josef. I don't know what he's done to you, and I'm sorry I didn't come sooner. But we have to stop him somehow. You might not have any Sources, but you do have magic. You absorb it, the same as I do. At the very least, you have your Biomancy, even the Iron Legion admits you're damned near unkillable. So, stop acting like a fucking coward and fight him!" I think I shamed them into action. A one-armed woman bound and stripped of her magic, and I was the only one with enough fire still inside to take the fight to the Iron Legion.

Of course, we were too late.

A silence fell over the laboratory, broken only by the ambient noise of the Djinn. It swirled there, a vortex of smoke with a core of flashing energy. Time seemed fractured in its mass. Through its distorted form I saw the Iron Legion move, step forward, but it took seconds for him to actually make the move. On the other side of him stood a towering golden giant, all but terran in appearance yet she would have loomed over even Hardt. Her skin shone with a golden light and her form was so perfect to look at it hurt. She looked like a template from which all other terrans had been made unequal. And perhaps she was, it made sense that the Rand had altered us in their own image.

"Terthis?" When the Rand spoke, it was like a chorus of bells all chiming in perfect rhythm. A heart-breaking melody so perfect I could see why entire civilisations would bow before her. "What is this?"

The Djinn twisted, its form distorting for a moment. "You died, Elorame. I felt you drag me with you."

"You did die," the Iron Legion said, his voice booming throughout the laboratory. "My name is Loran Orran. And I have brought you back."

For a moment there was silence. Both Rand and Djinn were timeless, immortal. If there was one thing I realised from my conversations with Aerolis, was that the Djinn did not act rashly. It took its time to consider words and actions. It had the time to do so.

"Coby," I hissed, my voice a whisper. "Get this manacle off me." She didn't. Her attention was fixed on the meeting before her. I shouldn't blame her. Coby had never known another Rand, only her mother. This was almost a family reunion for her.

"This is one of yours, Elorame. Silence it." The Djinn

twisted again. "Time is different. Things have moved."

The Rand turned her head, her gaze sweeping over the room and coming to rest upon us. Upon Coby. "I must find my sisters. Where is Mezula? Is the war still on, child?"

Coby froze and I could feel the fear on her even without Ssserakis. It is never an easy thing to become the sole attention of a god.

The Iron Legion stepped into the silence. "The war is over. It has been for a thousand years. Only Mezula and Aerolis remain of you. I have brought you back. I will bring back all the others who have died. I…"

"Quiet child," Elorame said. "Aspect, where I can I find your mother?"

"ENOUGH!" The Iron Legion let loose a kinetic blast that knocked everyone from their feet. It was a humbling experience watching a Rand knocked down like that. Even the Djinn, without a solid form, sputtered as though its vortex had been interrupted. "I will not be ignored, nor talked down to. I have given my life to the study of resurrecting your people. Of bringing both Rand and Djinn back so that you might fix the damage you wrought upon our world. And I will bring back the rest of you, but not before you grant me a boon!"

The Rand slowly regained her feet with more eloquence than any terran could ever muster. She closed on the Iron Legion, and from the other side so, too, did the Djinn. There was menace and intent in those steps. These creatures considered themselves gods. They had designed our people to believe it too, yet the Iron Legion stood between them, unafraid and with the power to back up his demands.

"Only I know how to bring you back," the Iron

Legion said, a smile on his face. "Kill me, and your brothers and sisters will remain dead for eternity. How much is your immortality worth?"

That made both Rand and Djinn pause. They regarded the Iron Legion, and each other, and in that moment, I knew he had them.

"Coby!" I hissed.

The Aspect nodded, tearing her eyes from the meeting in the centre of the laboratory. "You might be right." She stepped closer to me, staring at the manacle around my wrist. "Just know that things aren't done between us, terran. You killed my sister."

"Name your boon, child," Elorame said. It seemed time was up, and they had come to a decision.

"Undo what the Chronomancy has done to me." And there it was. For all the Iron Legion's grandstanding about wanting to fix the world, it all boiled down to his own mortality. Magic comes with a price. Sources were never meant to be used in the way that Sourcerers do. I had lost ten years to a Chronomancy Source, but Loran Orran had lost decades. More of his life taken by magic, than by the natural process of time.

Unity of purpose. It takes the combined powers of both Rand and Djinn to undo what has been done. The Djinn to wind back time, and the Rand to repair the damage to the body. They did it then, Elorame and Terthis, came together in a flash of light that left the Iron Legion staggering. He collapsed to the stone floor, clutching at his chest, his body wracked with spasms. And again, the Rand turned her attention our way.

"Once more, Aspect. Where is your mother?"

Coby turned on the spot, like a child caught doing

something she shouldn't. "Ro'shan. And Aerolis is on Do'shan."

The Djinn and Rand turned to regard each other once more. A crackling power building between them, the Iron Legion forgotten in his agony behind them. Then Terthis shot upward, disappearing into the stone above. Elorame's golden form seemed to collapse in on itself, shrinking down until nothing was left but a thin golden line like a snake. It shot away into the darkness. They were gone.

"What have we done?" Josef's voice cracked on the words. He may not have had my dealings with the Rand and Djinn, but stories of their power were littered throughout our history. And through us, the Iron Legion had just released two more into the world.

The Iron Legion surged to his feet, a scream tearing from his mouth. He tore at his robes with hands that looked as though they were broken. Once he stood there, naked from the waist up, we could all see what the magic was doing to him. His skin was tightening, the wrinkles and blemishes vanishing. His bones seemed to crack and then mend themselves. Where before there had been sagging flesh, tight muscle bulged. The years fell from the Iron Legion in a chaotic spasm of pain, and I could see him growing more youthful before my eyes. Coby saw it too.

"What is this metal?" She poked at the manacle on my wrist. It was a finger width of solid metal, no lock or join.

"It fell from the moons," Josef said. "When it pierces the skin, it inhibits magic. He made the manacle and sceptre from Prena's sword."

"That's because it was made to contain the Rand and Djinn. The bars of their prison." Both Coby and Josef looked at me as though I had gone mad. "Josef, that sceptre, go and get it. Coby…"

Coby snorted. She was busy unwinding the metal bar that had twisted around my arm, her strength more than equal to the task. "I'm working on it."

"Forget the bars. Get this thing off my wrist."

The Aspect shook her head. "You terrans are so weak." She dug slight fingers into the flesh on my wrist and I grimaced against the pain, then she pulled. Even with Coby's strength, the manacle resisted. She growled, bending her full power to the task. Still, it did not budge.

Josef arrived at my side once more, the metal sceptre in one hand. "Maybe I *can* help," he said. He pushed Coby's hand away and lay his own over the manacle. Then he closed his eyes and drew on the innate Ingomancy he had absorbed from Neverthere. The manacle snapped open with a squeal and fell from my wrist.

Finally!

Everything returned to me in a rush. My eyes flashed as the Arcstorm burst to life around me once more, lightning sparking of the nearby bars. I could feel my Sources inside, the access to my magic returned. And Ssserakis. My horror came back to me with a shout of exaltation. My shadow wrapped around my legs and arm and tore the last of the bars away. I stepped free of the binding and spent a moment revelling in my returned power.

"Are you alright?"

Yes. I couldn't reach you. I was trapped inside again, but not by you.

"I'm fine." Coby shook her head at me. "Stupid terran. Do you have a plan?"

What did I miss?

I sighed. "He did it. He brought back a Rand and

Djinn."

Coby looked like she wanted to slap me. "I know. I was there."

"And I wasn't talking to you."

He looks different.

I nodded. "They restored his youth before fleeing. We need to stop him. If he gets hold of us again, he can bring more back."

Coby glanced toward Josef. "I think she's gone mad."

I snatched the sceptre from Josef and handed it to Coby. "You're the strongest of us, Coby. We'll distract him. You need to stab him with this, it needs to pierce his skin to cut him off from his magic."

Coby turned the sceptre over in her hands. "It has no edge."

I let out a growl of frustration. "Then stab him really hard."

The Iron Legion laughed. It was done, his unnatural ageing reversed. He looked no older than I, maybe even a few years younger. There was no hair on his head or body, but here was the man I remembered from my youth. Strong, straight backed, regal, powerful. The Rand and Djinn had granted him his wish, and I could already tell he was more powerful than ever.

"Josef…" I said.

My friend shook his head and I realised then he was younger than I. Barely in his twentieth year, shaped by the hardships of half a decade of pain and fear. For the first time in our lives, I realised I wasn't looking up to Josef. He was small and skinny, a broken young man. Our lives had changed so much since the fall of Orran. Once we had spent every moment of every day together, as inseparable as water from the sea. Yet we had grown apart, circumstance and betrayal forcing us down different paths. But he was still my friend. I put a hand on his shoulder, the same way Hardt had done with me a hundred times, and smiled.

"We can do this," I said. "Chosen two and all that. All the tutors always said we were so much stronger together than apart."

Josef nodded, though I could feel the fear in him. A terror that spoke of deep conditioning. The Iron Legion had held Josef for over a year, and whatever he had done had left scars that would mark Josef for the rest of his life.

"Ssserakis?"

I have dreamt of this moment ever since he pulled me from my home. My wings will be useless to you in such a confined space, but I have had another thought.

My shadow turned oily, viscous. It pooled beneath me and then raced up my legs and chest, gathering at my left arm before travelling down to the stone that capped the stump there. Shadowy bones grew through the cap, winding and twisting together as they formed into the shape of a clawed hand. I raised it to my face and stared at the thing. It was skeletal, no flesh to speak of, and dark as the night. I could both feel it and not. No pain or sensation there, but it was a part of me and mine to control. I had two arms again, one mine and one Ssserakis'. I drew on the Sources in my stomach and brought lightning rippling along the clawed digits.

No fire. Remember, it is still a part of me.

Coby watched me, an odd look on her face that I think was disgust. Josef drew in a deep breath and wiped his eyes. I realised they were waiting for me to make the first move. It was probably best to strike before the Iron Legion realised I was free.

CHAPTER THIRTY SIX

THERE IS A JOYFUL POETRY TO A FIGHT. TO throw yourself so completely into the tempo of it. It is not easy, nor calm yet there is an exaltation to it that cannot be denied. To lose yourself in the rhythm of combat is the truest form of the fight. Ishtar tried to teach me that. She tried to explain that the mind may win a battle, but a fight is won by the countless hours of training rarely seen by anyone watching. Muscles remember how to move, the body knows how to flow, and tactics are a thing better left fluid. I never understood it before, and perhaps that is why she had always beaten me. But in that laboratory, matching myself against the Iron Legion I threw away all inhibition. It was a losing fight, one we had so little hope of winning, but I set my will upon the path to that little glimmer of hope and I ran toward it with everything I could.

I crossed the distance between us in a handful of

loping strides, a thin double-edged Sourceblade forming in
my right hand, lightning rippling along it. The Iron Legion
noticed me at the last moment and a wall of rock shot up
between us. I threw myself into a pirouette, spinning around
the edge of the wall and into a two-handed strike that would
have cut the man in two. Of course, the Iron Legion was
not so easily beaten. Decades of training in both magic and
battle, a lifetime lived at speed and then a new infusion of
youth. He blocked me with hands coated in a thin layer
of rock, and lightning sparked off every blow I aimed at
him, scoring his skin in a dozen different places. He was an
Arcmancer too, but he could not absorb magic like me, he
did not have an Arcstorm inside. But his Biomancy seemed
as strong as Josef's and every wound I dealt him healed
within moments.

　　　The wall of stone exploded towards us and in the
centre of the flying rock was Coby, a vicious snarl on her
face, still a dark mimicry of Silva's. I saw a moment of panic
in the Iron Legion's eyes, his face so much younger than
before. Then a shockwave of kinetic energy erupted from
the Iron Legion and sent Coby crashing backwards with the
remnants of the rock wall. I weathered the wave of force
with a shadowy hand digging into the stone floor, steadying
me.

　　　Up close, the fight savage and quick, any sort of
shield would be useless, but if the Iron Legion managed to
erect a bubble around him, we might never get through.
I had to keep him distracted, give him no time to form a
proper defence, and hope Coby could get in close enough to
put an end to it.

　　　I clawed up a handful of stone and launched it at the
Iron Legion, following it in with a new Sourceblade in hand.

The rocks I threw at him struck his hands and stuck there, reinforcing his armour and shoring up the holes my blade had struck loose. I aimed high, bringing my Sourceblade down in a one-handed slash towards his head and letting the blade vanish in a puff of kinetic energy at the last moment. A new Sourceblade, no longer than a dagger, formed in my shadowy hand and I plunged it into the Iron Legion's side. He screamed in pain and I caught a rocky fist to the face that shook loose a tooth and sent me sprawling. The Sourceblade I left in his side exploded as I let it go, widening the wound.

It should have killed him, would have killed anyone else, but the Iron Legion staggered back onto one knee and clutched at the gaping wound in his side. Strain showed on his face, sweat pouring down his skin, and his eyes furious with the pain. Coby leapt at him, sceptre in hand. Too slow. Even with him injured she was too slow. The Iron Legion raised one hand and released a gout of flame into Coby's face. The Aspect staggered away, screaming amidst a searing blaze. I struggled back to my feet and a kinetic waved knocked me right back down again. Already I could see the wound in the Iron Legion's side closing, flesh knitting itself back together at an impossible rate.

Before I could recover, I found a boulder hurtling my way. No chance to raise a shield and even my shadow was too slow to stop it. Then Josef was there, throwing himself in front of me and taking the blow meant for me. The rock crashed against his back and I heard bones snap. I rolled away as the boulder crashed down upon my shadowy hand. There was no pain and my shadow slithered free before reforming. I ran to Josef to find him trembling, in so much pain he could not even scream. His back was broken, but the spasms running through him did not seem natural.

404   ROB J. HAYES

Josef's eyes darted to mine and I saw something there. Determination. Pride. "This…" He coughed and blood spattered his lips. "Is what… I can do." I realised then that he was healing. Broken bones snapping back into place, mending. Torn flesh renewing itself. His innate Biomancy was healing him through wounds that should have killed him.

You have never been good at being the shield, Eskara. Let others carry that burden. Be the weapon.

I saw another kinetic wave coming and met it with my own. The two forces crashed together in an explosion of purple energy that shook the laboratory around us. The Iron Legion was on his feet again, the wound in his side all but gone and the stone covering his fists replaced by metal, solid but moulding to his movements. Several little golems started tearing their way free of the stone floor behind him, each one like a spider the size of a dog, small bodies and barbed legs.

"Why are you fighting me, Helsene?" the Iron Legion's voice rang out loud, echoing in the confines of the laboratory. "Can't you see what we have done? They can be brought back. Together we can resurrect them all and save this world."

In my darksight, I saw Coby creeping around behind the Iron Legion. The flames were gone, extinguished when she changed her form. Now, she was a small girl, half my size and wearing nothing but a loose shift as dark as her skin. In her hand she still held the sceptre, our only chance of stopping the Iron Legion. It dawned on me that not all fights could be won with brute force; some were won with guile and misdirection. I had to distract him.

"You really don't understand the Rand and Djinn do you, Loran?" I pitched my voice to carry, all but shouted the words to cover any sound Coby might make. "They hate each other in a way we can't even fathom. It's written into their very being. You could bring them all back, and they might even work together for a time, but it will not last. It cannot last. In time, they will go back to warring with each other, and it is always those caught in the middle who suffer most. How many terrans died last time during the War Eternal? How many pahht? Tahren, garn, even the mur. Countless deaths." It was an argument he had heard before, I had made before. It wouldn't sway him, but then that wasn't the point. The Iron Legion was beyond swaying with words, beyond reason or doubt. A fanatic beyond anything but the argument of the blade. "There is always another way, Loran. A way that doesn't involve sacrificing tens of thousands of lives to bring back a war that will cost ten times that many."

The spidery golems flanked the Iron Legion, more and more of them tearing their way free from the stone floor around him. He stood amid them all, his hairless face making him seem surprised. "I do not need your cooperation, Helsene. Like Yenhelm, you can be forced or coerced. The portal must be closed. I will see it done."

He's lying. A justification he once told himself and now fears to let go.

I took a step forward. There were nearly a dozen golems between us now, waiting on a multitude of legs. "The portal has stood that way for a thousand years and will stand for another thousand." The truth seemed so obvious to me. "I have seen the creature beyond that hole in our world, Loran. It has no interest in us or Ovaeris. It made the Rand and the Djinn. It separated them, jailed them inside our moons. A monster that powerful… if it wanted to come through, it would do so." Coby was close now, picking her way through the golems behind him.

The Iron Legion shook his head. "There is no reasoning with you." It is the last recourse of those with no reason to accuse others of being beyond it.

It took no gesture or signal from the Iron Legion to command his golems. In a moment, they were crowded around him and the next they surged toward me. One of them bumped into Coby, only a few paces from the Iron Legion and he turned just as she leapt at him. They clashed then, but I lost sight of them as I backed away, sending out kinetic wave after wave to knock the skittering golems back. My Arcmancy did nothing against the constructs. Fire, too, did little against their stone carapace. I could knock them away, even separate limbs, but they only reformed and came at me again. And over the swarming horde I could see Coby struggling against the Iron Legion. She had both the speed and the strength to swat him, but it seemed she had no magic save her ability to change form. Silva had been a Sourcerer and a powerful one, but either Coby carried no Sources or could not.

Josef barrelled into the golems; his broken back already healed. He used no magic and each of the little constructs attached itself to him, tearing into his flesh. He took the wounds with screams of pain and staggered on through them. It opened a small hole in the swarm, and I ran for it.

The Iron Legion had the measure of Coby now and caught her hand around the sceptre, plucking it from her grip. Before the Aspect could recover, the Iron Legion whisked his hand upward and two pillars of rock, one from above and one from below, snapped together, crushing Coby between them. I could not even see her childlike form anymore, only cracked stone where the two pillars had crushed together. Before I could reach him, the Iron Legion whisked his other hand upward and the sceptre disappeared into the rock above, lost. He had seen through the ruse and taken away our only weapon. He turned to me and released a plume of flames so large it required both hands. I skidded to a halt and caught the fire on my right hand, drawing on my own Pyromancy Source to shield myself from the heat.

Ssserakis hissed out its displeasure. My horror was not a fan of fire or heat. Given the ferocity of the flames, neither was I. I could feel the skin on my right hand growing uncomfortably hot. But the Iron Legion had made a mistake by releasing such a plume of fire. He had blinded himself. I formed a Sourceblade in my shadowy hand, a spear at least twice of me long, and thrust it forward into the heart of the flames.

The Iron Legion shouted in pain and the flames gutted out. I leapt forward, not willing to give him even a moment of respite, and slammed my shadowy talons into his mid-section. I would have managed even more, but one of the stone golems tackled me to the ground, slashing at me with sharpened limbs. I wrestled the thing for a moment, tearing it apart with my shadowy hand. Only to find the Iron Legion staring at me, rage in his eyes. He had a hand clutched to his chest, but I could see the wounds I had dealt him sowing themselves shut already.

The rock beneath me went fluid, only for a moment, just enough that I sank an inch into it, and then solidified again, holding me in place. The Iron Legion took a staggering step forward, blood leaking out between his fingers and from his nose. He was wincing from the pain.

"I am done playing with you, Helsene!" the Iron

Legion roared, blood spitting out with each word.

I have never been one to let another's anger outdo my own. "You think rock will hold me?" I had no idea how to use Geomancy, but I knew I had absorbed some before the Source rejection almost killed me. I had been using it without realising, bit by bit, to move the fingers of my stone arm. Now I used it to loosen the rock around me just enough to pull free.

The pillar of rock nearby exploded outward and Coby stood there in the form of a hulking pahht, as big as Hardt and thick with muscle and fur. She roared and leapt forward, tackling the Iron Legion to the ground and savaging him with claws and teeth before he could raise a new defence. It should have been enough. But I'm not sure the Iron Legion still counted as terran. His Biomancy had always been strong, but it had been bolstered by the souls he had stolen from others. All his magic was made stronger by the strength of others. But his Biomancy was not like Josef's, it was not innate. I realised then what I was seeing. Magic mixing together. Biomancy and Chronomancy drawn together to heal wounds that should be fatal.

The Iron Legion's screams of pain grew louder as he took hold of them with Vibromancy. I clutched at my ears to no avail. Coby's assault slowed and then stopped, the pain of the noise driving her back and then to the ground, her whimpers lost amid the cacophony.

Ssserakis saved us all then. All sound stopped save for the rushing of my own heartbeat as Ssserakis formed shadowy plugs over my ears.

I cannot help the others. We must end this, Eskara. How?

The Iron Legion's wounds were almost completely healed, but I could see fresh blood leaking from his nose and ears, and panic on his face. He was overtaxed. Holding too many Sources, using too much magic, mixing Chronomancy with Biomancy had only sped the process. He was in mid stage Source rejection. The Iron Legion's abilities were legendary, even back at the academy, his strength to hold off rejection something even the most powerful of Sourcerers could only wish for, but even he had limits. Even he was subject to the laws of our world. And he was nearing his limit now.

Ssserakis didn't need to hear my words to understand. My horror already knew my plan. I reached out with my right hand and unleashed the Arcstorm upon the Iron Legion. Lightning burst from my fingers and wreathed the Iron Legion. His constructs leapt into the way, piling stone on top of stone to block the attack, but Ssserakis reached out with my shadow and swept them aside. Caught in my storm, the Iron Legion could no longer keep his Vibromancy going and the sound of his amplified scream died away to leave only the new screams echoing around the laboratory.

Coby had changed again, assumed the form a young terran woman with flame red hair, but she struggled to find balance, the effects of the Vibromancy persisting even once the noise was gone. Josef, finally free of the constructs, struggled to my side. We both knew he couldn't help now, only watch.

"Run!" I hissed the word. Lightning still arced between my outstretched hand and the Iron Legion, spasming in pain as his magic mixed inside to heal the damage I was doing him.

Josef shook his head. "I'm not leaving you."

I managed to glance his way. "He's suffering from

rejection. Get away while you can." We both knew what final stage Source rejection did to a person. It was bad enough with only one Source inside, but the Iron Legion could apparently carry ten and the mixture of such magics breaking down within the body was likely to be… explosive.

I felt frustration. It wasn't mine. *That's enough, Eskara. Get us out of here.*

I shook my head. Lightning still arced from my fingers, striking the Iron Legion and causing him to spasm in pain. "I can't give him the opportunity to find Spiceweed."

You'll die this close.

I had no reply to that.

Fire, sound, rock, metal, lightning, kinetic force, portals, constructs, emotion, the Other World, life, time. Rumour had it the Iron Legion could carry ten Sources inside. For once, the rumours were not equal to the truth. Twelve types of magic, the Iron Legion carried, and when final stage Source rejection took him, they all broke down at once. It was an explosion of magic unlike anything the world had seen since the War Eternal. Forces that had no business mixing. Wild energies that could not be contained. Magic in its rawest form, that even the Rand and Djinn do not fully understand. And at the last moment, before the Iron Legion died and took me with him, Josef threw himself in front of the blast.

CHAPTER
THIRTY SEVEN

HOW TO EXPLAIN THAT DETONATION OF magic? It was chaos. It was light and noise, heat and cold, joy and sadness. It fragmented time and happened across all realms at once. Both the roof and the floor caved in, and there is seemingly no end to that hole. Perhaps it goes all the way through, a bottomless pit ten of me across leading to the other side of the world. The storm that rages in that hole is as much mine as the Iron Legion's, I think. I put everything I had into it, the full force of the Arcstorm inside of me. I all but emptied myself of that fury, but I couldn't help but keep the smallest part back. My eyes no longer flashed like a raging storm, but like distant lightning caught behind a blanket of clouds. The detonation was madness in its rawest form. It should have killed everything within that ruined city. It would have, if not for Josef.

Like me, Josef had been changed by the Iron Legion's

experiment. On some level I could never understand, and by a process that will always be a mystery to me, we could absorb magic. By throwing himself in front of me, Josef took the brunt of that magical discharge and absorbed it into himself. The forces must have been terrible, tearing him apart inside, but his innate Biomancy sustained him through it, kept him alive. Sometimes I think it would have been kinder if he had died. Some fates are worse than death.

Is he dead?

I was staring at Josef, slumped over and not moving, but I knew who Ssserakis meant. "Yes." The hole in front of us, sparking with a storm was proof enough of that. Never before had any Sourcerer broken down so violently. It left a strangeness to the place. The walls between realms were thinner there, and I could feel things pressing in on our world. I turned from that feeling and knelt over my friend.

Josef was slumped over on hands and knees, his face hidden and pressed to the ground. The clothing on his back had been burnt away and his skin seemed wrong. It was like something in a constant state of flux, unable to decide what form it should take. One moment it appeared flesh, and the next it was rough stone, then translucent so I could see blood pumping beneath the surface and bones and organs. I will admit, I was afraid to touch him, of what it might do to him and to me. I took solace in the fact that he was alive. I could see that when his skin went clear, his heart was pumping. He was alive. Yet he did not respond to his name. When I finally gathered the courage to touch him, I shook him a little and his skin was like ice, then a few moments later like fire. He was struggling for control of himself, locked in a battle with his own flesh. An eternal war he is ever on both the winning and losing side of.

Where is the Aspect?

I found Coby in a similar state to Josef, though she was conscious. I could tell by the anger. A section of the roof had collapsed nearby, and she was pressed up against it, knees drawn up and arms hugging them. A young woman, willowy with skin as dark as any I had ever seen. She was entirely hairless and her face… It is difficult to describe, but she was featureless. It was not that she had no eyes or mouth, but that there was nothing to distinguish her at all. Just a moment after seeing her, I had already forgotten what she looked like. Fair to say it was disconcerting, perhaps more for her, than I. Silva once told me that Coby's curse was that she could be anyone she wished, but nobody could see her true face. Well, the Iron Legion's explosion of magic took that from her. With Silva dead, I think I was the only one who could claim to have seen the real Coby.

"Don't look at me!" Coby hissed. Even her voice seemed oddly indistinct. A monotone drawl, instantly forgettable. "I can't change with someone looking at me."

I looked away. Yet when I looked back, she still had not changed. Coby hugged her knees and rocked back and forth, and I'm certain I heard her sob. I can understand that. All her defences had been stripped away and for the first time in her life she was forced to be herself. It was, perhaps, made worse that she suffered that way in front of someone she hated.

Now would be a good time to rid yourself of another enemy.

I shook my head. "There's no sense in hating the dead."

I don't understand.

I crouched down near Coby, making certain not to look at her. "Will you be alright? Will it wear off?"

Coby drew a sharp intake of breath. "I don't know."

I pulled on the ties of my jacket and slipped my arms from its remains. It had suffered during the battle and was torn and singed and stained with blood and sweat, but it was all I had to give. I held it out to her, and Coby snatched it from me. She didn't thank me.

"I have a favour to ask you," I said.

Coby snorted. "You aren't forgiven. You killed my sister."

"So, did you." I couldn't keep the anger from my voice. Blame and hate we both shared and misdirected. A cycle neither of us could escape as long as we lived. "So did your mother. It doesn't matter anymore, Coby."

What are you planning, Eskara?

"When you recover. Take Josef with you, please. I don't know what's wrong with him, but maybe Mezula will."

"Why should I do anything you want?" Coby snarled the words.

"Don't do it for me. Do it for him. Josef had nothing to do with Silva's death, he never even met her." An odd thing to realise just then, but my best friend had never met the woman I loved. I wished they could have. I have a feeling they would have gotten on well. "And if it helps, I'm sorry, Coby." I've never been very good at apologising, but that one felt right. "I am truly sorry."

I moved closer to the hole and the storm that raged within it. So close, I could look down into the depths and feel the charge pulling at my hair. I closed my eyes and swayed there, feeling the call of the void. Maybe it was Lesray Alderson's lasting curse, or maybe I have always felt the desire to end it all. To take away the pain and the suffering. To just stop.

Step back.

My eyes snapped open and I realised I was leaning over the edge, nothing more than an errant breeze away from toppling. I lurched back a step and drew in a ragged breath. I was readying myself for what was to come. Building both my courage and my determination.

What is this, Eskara? I will not allow you to kill yourself.

"Can you feel it, Ssserakis?" I asked. "The world is thinner here. Closer to the other. Can you feel your home?"

I can always feel it. It pulls at me. Steals my thoughts. You cannot understand the constant pressure trying to tear me in two. I must cling to you to remain here or the pull of my world will destroy me.

"I feel it too. Is it because of you that Sevoari feels more like home than my own world?" I was stalling, afraid to take the next step. Scared of saying goodbye.

Are you saying you can take us there? Can we return home?

Us. When had Ssserakis stopped thinking of itself as separate? When had I? The ancient horror had been with me for so long now I sometimes struggled to tell our thoughts apart. We had escaped the Pit and made our way to Ro'shan. We had brought Kento into the world and grieved at her loss. For a time, I thought Ssserakis had no connection to my children, but the lie of that was obvious. Ssserakis had grieved for Kento even when I refused to. Together, we fought against Silva and then threw every last bit of ourselves at Aerolis. It had not been Ssserakis' grief that had driven it into a frenzy in our struggle against the Djinn, but the horror had reacted to my pain. We raised an army together, and my horror had suffered for my time down in the Red Cells as surely as I had. It was not physical torture that pained it, but the agony of separation. I had tried to spare Ssserakis my torment, but only provided it with its own by keeping us apart. My second child, Sirileth... I sometimes think she is as much Ssserakis' daughter as my own, she certainly shares many of the horror's traits. And finally, our struggle against the Iron Legion. I could not have managed without Ssserakis. In all the events great and small, ever since the Pit, Ssserakis had been there with me. Support, advice, strength. The horror had given me all three in surplus.

The embodiment of fear, anxiety. Mine. And now I feared to let it go.

There is no need to fear, Eskara. Ssserakis did not understand. *Sevoari is not like this world. It is simpler. Here we are strong, but there we will be unmatched! We will retake our rightful place as lord of Sevoari, and teach the others for ever doubting our return.*

I raised my left hand, a shadowy mimic of bone, each talon dripping with darkness. I drew on the Portamancy Source and the Impomancy Source at once, mixing the magic inside and directing the power through that arm. It was Ssserakis' connection to Sevoari that allowed me to find the realm, and my power that tore open a new hole in the world. Something that had never been done before. A portal to Sevoari.

Through that portal I could see the Other World. A lightless grey expanse. Everything in that place seemed to have softer edges than our world. There was a city in the far distance, lifeless and dull. It was Ssserakis' home, the place it had once ruled from. Where the light from our world spilled through the portal, the life in the Other World shied away. Blades of grass leaned from the portal and I saw small insects scurrying away, fleeing. The edges of the portal seemed to burn as though the contact of the two worlds was causing a violent combustion, and the sound was like a river made of roaring flame.

We will be a dark queen. Even Hyrenaak will bow before us. I could feel the truth of those words. Ssserakis' power was limited by the laws of Ovaeris, but in Sevoari, who knew what we could become.

"You'll need to be quick," I said. "The portal will not stay open for long." I drew on the Arcmancy Source in my stomach and set lightning crackling around my right hand. I could feel it tingling across my skin, the charge would be deadly.

What do you mean? Step through, Eskara. We will take our rightful place at the pinnacle of Sevoari.

"I'm not going, Ssserakis." I could feel fresh tears welling in my eyes. "I don't belong there any more than you belong here. I fear what we might become if we went there together."

But I cannot leave you, Eskara. I am bound to you as long as you live.

I smiled. "I know." I tried to move my arm, to slap it against my chest and let the lightning stop my heart, only to find my shadowy hand locked around my wrist, holding it still.

I will not let you die, Eska. There was real emotion in Ssserakis' voice. Not just fear or pride, but sorrow and determination. *Why sacrifice yourself? We can go together. We belong together.*

"Let go, Ssserakis."

Fine. Close the portal. I'll stay here.

"Let go."

I don't want to leave you!

"I swore to send you home."

I've changed my mind. I don't want to go.

Still Ssserakis held my death back from me, the strength in my shadowy arm irresistible. "What about saving your world? The monster eating away at the heart of it."

Let it die. I would rather stay here with you.

A horror so ancient it could almost remember the birth of its world, yet in many ways Ssserakis was so childish. It meant what it said, it would let Sevoari die to stay with me. But that was not a decision I could live with. I stopped my resistance, stopped trying to fight the strength of my shadow, and instead tried reason.

"Ssserakis. You have to go. You said yourself none of the others have the strength or the will to resist Norvet Meruun. If you stay with me, that monster will destroy an entire world. Your world. Your home. You have to go. Resist it. Kill it."

Come with me! Please. A last-ditch effort on my horror's part. My decision was made, and I would not unmake it. I felt the shadowy talons uncurl from around my wrist, and a sullen silence settled between us.

"Be quick, Ssserakis." I smiled. "Save your world."

Eska…

I slammed my lightning wreathed hand against my chest and for a brief moment felt the pain of it as the lightning surged inside and shocked my heart into stillness. Then I was toppling backward, my vision already fading.

You won, Lesray. That insidious call you put in me so long ago, I finally gave in. But fuck you if I didn't make it mean something in the end.

CHAPTER THIRTY EIGHT

I WOKE WITH A GASP TO CONFUSION AND pain. It took a while for things to make sense and most of that time was spent dealing with a body that had almost forgotten how to live. Slowly, my vision cleared, and my mind made sense of the things I saw.

A dark, swollen face hovered above my own. One eye was shut, a cut above it leaving a line of dried blood. The nose was bent and bulging at the bridge and there were red grazes across the cheeks and chin. So badly battered was it, that it took a moment for me to recognise it as Hardt. A smile split the face and my heart surged with joy to see such a thing.

A deep breath led to agony and convinced me I had at least one broken rib. There have been many times in my life I have envied Josef's innate Biomancy. His ability to heal from any wound within minutes far outstrips my own ability to raise ghosts.

"Can you hear me, Eska?" Hardt's voice sounded a little slurred, as though spoken through swollen lips.

I nodded, still trying to draw in enough breath without my chest feeling as though it were imploding. Still trying to understand why. Why was I alive? Why had they brought me back to this life of pain? I was lying on my back and everything hurt. My chest, my head, my arms. No. My shadowy arm was gone. I had only the one arm again.

"Ssserakis?" My first word was part question, part plea. I felt the emptiness inside and knew the truth of it. My horror was gone. Back to its own world, back to being a lord of Sevoari. I could not contain my grief at the knowledge, nor the despair that rose up in me. I was alone again. I didn't want to be alone. It hurt to cry. With broken ribs and a body bruised from the fight, it hurt so much. Yet I couldn't stop the tears. It is so strange that we can force a loved one to go, and yet feel so abandoned when they do. Of course, Hardt did not understand, but he did what has always come most natural to him. Hardt held me and provided safety and comfort and assured me everything would be alright. He couldn't know the lie of his words. Things could not be alright, could never be alright. A part of me was gone. I kept waiting for Ssserakis' voice inside my head, the mocking whisper of my horror's words. But there was nothing. Only the question rolling around in mind over and over again. Why did Hardt have to bring me back? It was over. All the pain and effort and grief. I had finally worked up the courage to end it, and I had made my death mean something. Hadn't I earned oblivion? And yet he dragged me back to this world of agony and noise and... I hated him a little for that. Even as I loved him for the same thing.

After a time, I realised I could see stars. Up past Hardt's shoulder where the roof had caved in, the sky waited. Night had settled upon us and it was a clear sky. Stars twinkled and at the edge of the hole, I could just about see Lursa in dominance over Lokar, her red bulk stark against the black of the void. Something about the sight of the sky settled me. It was a feeling I had thought lost. The sky no longer seemed like something oppressive to fear, but an open expanse of endless possibility. Freedom.

"What happened to your face?" I asked from the floor. I didn't try to move. The mere idea of it seemed an impossibility.

Hardt smiled again and winced at the same time. "You told Tamura to stop me. We had a disagreement."

"Is he…"

"Fine, fine, fine." Tamura said with a giggle. I turned my head to see the crazy old Aspect perched on top of a fallen rock, cradling an arm in a sling, and sporting a face as bruised as Hardt's. "Like a house without foundation." And I saw the stress hidden behind his madness. Both my friends were in bad shape, beaten and injured, and it was me who had set them against one another. I have since gleaned the details of that fight from both of them and I must say I am sad I missed it. And even more sad I caused it.

"I'm alive?" It was half a question. I had died, I was certain of it. I felt myself die.

Hardt nodded. "Brought you back myself, the same way you did me up on Do'shan."

"Why?" I asked, tears in my eyes. "Why couldn't you just let me die?" The crushing loneliness inside made me choke on the words.

Hardt rocked back and sat on his arse. He seemed to

deflate, the strength fleeing him. "I couldn't. You've got too much to live for. No, don't argue with me. Just listen, Eska. For once in your life, just listen." He paused and grimaced. I said nothing. For once in my life, I said nothing.

"I know it's hard," Hardt continued. "You feel like everything is your fault. You try to take all the pain and guilt and grief, and make it your own. Ever since I met you down in the Pit, you've tried to protect us. You made yourself a target to take the heat from Isen, you stood up to Yorin when no one else would. You convinced us to try to escape, even when we called you crazy for it. And any time it didn't go well, you always blamed yourself. For your actions, for others', for things beyond anyone's control.

"I know how it makes you feel. Alone. Alone against the world. You feel like you have to take everyone else's burdens on your shoulders and yours alone. But you can't. Because you're not alone. You never have been. You have me, you have Tamura, you have Imiko. You have a daughter. You have Sirileth! We might not be perfect… We're not perfect. But we're here. We've always been here, right beside you. You're not alone, Eska!"

He was crying. I was crying. How did he know? How had he seen past all my defences right to my greatest fear? How did he know how to blot out that fear and make me feel… loved.

I cried then, really cried. I had no guard left, I had nothing to restrain me. I bawled out my pain and loss, and I cried in love and joy. I did it without reserve because I simply couldn't hold it in anymore. And all the while, Tamura held my hand, and Hardt gripped my shoulder. He was right. They had all been there with me, for me, every step of the way. Even when I tried to push them away, they had stayed with me. I might not deserve it. I didn't deserve it, didn't deserve them. But they were mine, all the same, and I was their's. And for all the pain of the life Hardt had brought me back to, he had also given me a second chance. A second chance to be a mother to my daughter. To be the mother for Sirileth that I should have been for Kento.

Hardt was right. About everything. One day, I imagine they'll write that on my tombstone.

"Josef…" The thought struck me so suddenly I tried to lurch upright. That was a bad idea. There is no relief from the pain of a broken rib, only the knowledge that it will get better with time. Time that never seems to move fast enough.

Hardt put two big hands on my shoulders and held me down. "We'll deal with moving you soon enough. Josef is alive. We think. It's really not that clear." Coby was gone, and she had ignored the one thing I asked of her. She left Josef here to die with me. But then, she owed me nothing.

"Can you help him?" A hard question to ask, especially of Hardt. The man who had killed his brother was in bad shape, and I was asking Hardt to help. I wonder if it crossed his mind that he could use the opportunity to kill Josef instead? Probably not. Hardt has always been better than I.

Hardt turned his head and I saw his jaw clench. "I don't know what's wrong with him. He's… beyond any healing I know of. I'm sorry, Eska."

"Help me up." I started to move, but Hardt kept his hands on my shoulders.

"You shouldn't move."

"Noted. Help me up." It took quite a struggle and even more pain before I was on my feet. I say on my feet, but I think more of my weight was supported by Hardt than myself. He limped over toward Josef and lowered me down by my friend's side.

Tamura crouched on the other side of Josef and met my eyes. "You cannot unmake grey."

I nodded at that. Life is an ever-changing thing. Our experiences, our actions, interactions, the people around us and the environments we inhabit. They all change us in ways that cannot be undone. I was not the young girl who had once made mischief in these halls, exploring where I shouldn't and dragging others into my trouble. I was not the girl who had sat upon the tallest tower of Fort Vernan, kicking her feet over a fatal drop and waiting for a battle with callous disregard for the lives she was about to take. I was no longer the young woman who had been sentenced to a life of digging down in the Pit, willing to manipulate anyone to reach my own goals. Nor was I the woman who had fallen in love up on a flying city, and given away a child because she did not feel ready to be a mother. I had been all those things, but they were not who I was, only part of what made me. I could not undo the things that made me, and nor could I undo what made Josef who he was now.

I reached out with my hand and paused before touching Josef. Tamura caught my eye and gave me a reassuring nod. I gripped hold of Josef's hand, feeling the icy chill of his skin, and squeezed. There was something there. I can't explain it. An awareness that went beyond touch or sight or sound. Josef opened his eyes and uncurled from his foetal position, his hand gripping mine tight. He straightened up until he was kneeling, and warmth returned to his flesh, though it felt hard and took on a metallic sheen. When finally he met my eyes, I felt my heart quicken and had to stifle a sob. People say in my eyes they can see a brooding storm beyond the horizon, but in Josef's eyes I saw everywhere he had ever been and every time he had ever lived. Yet at that moment, and for that time, he was lucid.

There were no words that could bridge the gap that had grown between Josef and I. No apologies could ever make up for the hurts we had dealt each other since the fall of Orran. But sometimes, when words cannot suffice, they are better left unsaid. With a lurch we were in each other's arm, and all the hurt and betrayal and time apart seemed petty things.

CHAPTER THIRTY NINE

LIFE IS PAIN. OR SO PEOPLE SAY. THEY'LL tell you that life is pain and suffering and misery and heartache. It's all true. Life is all those things. It is also joy and happiness and love and hope. And it's one more thing besides. No matter what you've been through, no matter what you're going through, no matter what will happen. Life is worth living, because the truth is, you only get one go round. There is no life after death, no rebirth, no glorious eternity in the realm of the gods. Life is life, and after it is death. You get just the one shot, a brief flicker of a moment in the grand scheme of things. So, you might as well live it. Make your brief flicker mean something, not to anyone else, but to yourself.

We stayed in the laboratory for a few days while Josef and I recovered well enough to travel. The little tahren steward seemed happy to show us around once he realised

the Iron Legion was dead and not coming back. We freed
the last of the prisoners down in the cells, over a hundred
terrans huddled in the dark. They were fed from the
laboratory stores and I led them out of Picarr, keeping them
safe from both traps and Ghouls. A few of them thanked me
and none of them met my gaze for long. I heard whispers
though, they talked of the brooding storm behind my eyes
and my missing arm, and I heard the name of Corpse Queen
thrown around more than once. It seemed my reputation
spread even to the darkest, most remote corners of Isha.

    We found children locked away, not in cells, but
in a room designed for two. They were Sourcerers and
the steward claimed each was attuned to four different
Sources. A boy and a girl, each no older than I had been
when the Orran recruiters took me. The Iron Legion had
changed them, his experiment on Josef and I repeated upon
them, a forced bond of captivity cultivated between them.
Apparently, when he thought I was dead, Loran tried to
create more chosen ones. He might even have succeeded;
it was impossible to tell. It took some coaxing to find their
names, Tris and Vi, and even more to get them to trust me
enough to come with us. Neither had been trained with
their magic, and neither knew the fate of their parents. But
the steward knew. I would not let them return to their old
homes to find their parents gone and no welcome for them,
so I took them in.

    Josef improved, and deteriorated. Ever since
absorbing so much magic he has his good and his bad
days. Some days he is lucid and can remember everything
with such detail it is as though he is living it again in the
moment. Other days he cannot remember his own name
or how he got where he is. Some days he cannot even look

after himself. Those are the hardest days, for him even more than me. It is more than a case of his mind though, the magic acts upon his body in ways beyond strange. I have found him made of stone before, his skin all over like rock, and he is unable to even more. The next day, his skin has returned to normal and it is like it never happened. Some days he awakes to find himself an old man, ancient beyond anything natural age could do to a person, and then other days he is a child again. Josef exists within a state of constant flux, of both his physical body and his mind, and there is nothing I can do to help him other than be there when he needs me.

I have sent messages to Ro'shan, requests for aid from the Rand for Josef. No response ever comes, and I do not think Mezula would allow me to leave if I went there in person. I admit freely that I hate both the Rand and Djinn, for their idiotic war and making me a pawn in their games. The feeling is apparently mutual, and I have no doubt both Mezula and Aerolis would jump at the chance to teach me a lesson for my defiance of them both. Then again, it undoubtedly has not escaped their notice that Josef and I are the only ones left who know how to bring the Rand and Djinn back. It's a secret I will happily take to my grave.

Our journey home took time. We had just three trei birds and on those we mounted Josef and the two children. I walked with Hardt and Tamura, and we did not walk fast. A part of that was the pain of my injuries, and a part of it was dread anticipation. I feared what waited for us back at my city, and I feared even more facing it without Ssserakis. Yet my fears were unfounded. Imiko had held the city together well in my absence, had even expanded its influence, bringing new villages under my banner. Did I forget to mention? They made me a banner, a symbol the people could wear proudly. A hanging corpse. Fitting, it might be, but I would have preferred something a little less morbid. Unfortunately, it was decided in my absence and the people were not mutable to change on the subject. My throne had been sculpted by the best masons the survivors of the Pit had to offer and had been fashioned to look like bones and screaming skulls. The Corpse Queen sitting upon the Corpse Throne. Is there any wonder my reputation has spread so far and wide?

Despite her competency, Imiko was glad to see us, and even more glad to hand off her many duties. Chief among them had been looking after Sirileth, and I could see my daughter had grown a little in my absence. Her skin was fair and soft, her hair almost as dark as my own, and her eyes were still the darklight of an eclipse. She was a noisy child even then, always screaming, always demanding, and my heart soared to hold her in my arm again. I think she missed the presence of Ssserakis within me almost as much as I did. I like to believe that Ssserakis missed us both also.

I have been to the Other World many times in the ethereal form of an Impomancer. I study the world and its inhabitants, make notes in my copy of the Encyclopaedia Otheria. I think my personal copy is the only one with details on all the lords of Sevoari. It is information I do not let others see for good reason, but I gather what I can from their world and their minions. You never know when some fool Sourcerer might manage to bring a true monster across. I look for Ssserakis, always, I look for my horror, but without its guidance, I struggle to find its territory. Sevoari is a big place, after all, an entire world, and I am just one woman. There is only so much I can explore. I'll keep looking. Trying to find the other part of myself in a world that is both alien and familiar all at once.

We have, in all of us, the potential for greatness. To reach higher and achieve more than those who came before. I was born to a basket weaver and an herb gatherer, yet I have worn the mantle of a queen. I have fought against gods, and also by their side. I even killed a god once... or at least a fragment of one. I gave birth to a monster. I taught terror itself to fear me, and to love me. I changed the world, perhaps not for the better, but I changed it by my will.

It is my hope that my children, both those I brought into the world and those I raised, will take my life by example. Do not repeat my mistakes but make your own and learn from them. See the world for what it is, but also for what it can be. Work hard to change what you can, and perhaps even harder to change what you can't. Don't walk into Arcstorms or wear any crowns of fire. Find love. Find hate. Find the balance between them.

I have gone on too long, rambling when I should be succinct. Know this: This is not where my story ends, but only where I choose to end the telling of it. For now.

I have heard it said that I was at my most dangerous when I had something to die for.
But I've always been stronger when I have something to live for.

Books by Rob J. Hayes

The War Eternal
Along the Razor's Edge
The Lessons Never Learned
From Cold Ashes Risen
Sins of the Mother
Death's Beating Heart

The Mortal Techniques novels
Never Die
Pawn's Gambit
Spirits of Vengeance

The First Earth Saga
The Heresy Within (The Ties that Bind #1)
The Colour of Vengeance (The Ties that Bind #2)
The Price of Faith (The Ties that Bind #3)
Where Loyalties Lie (Best Laid Plans #1)
The Fifth Empire of Man (Best Laid Plans #2)
City of Kings

It Takes a Thief...
It Takes a Thief to Catch a Sunrise
It Takes a Thief to Start a Fire

Science Fiction
Drones

.

Lightning Source UK Ltd.
Milton Keynes UK
UKHW010629240622
404878UK00005B/100/J